COLLECTOR

C800369149

Also by Ted Dekker

Adam
Bone Man's Daughters

TED DEKKER

THE BRIDE COLLECTOR

HODDER &
STOUGHTON

First published in Great Britain in 2010 by Hodder & Stoughton
an Hachette UK company

I

Copyright © Ted Dekker 2009

A CIP catalogue record of this title is available from the British Library

ISBN 978 0 340 96498 9

Typeset in Plantin by Palimpsest Book Production Limited,
Grangemouth, Stirlingshire

Printed and bound by Clays Ltd, St Ives plc

Hodder & Stoughton policy is to use papers that are natural, renewable
and recyclable products and made from wood grown in sustainable
forests. The logging and manufacturing processes are expected to
conform to the environmental regulations of the country of origin.

Hodder & Stoughton Ltd
338 Euston Road
London NW1 3BH

www.hodder.co.uk

CHAPTER ONE

'Thank you, detective. We'll take it from here.'

FBI Special Agent Brad Raines stood in the small barn's wide doorway and scanned the dimly lit interior. Dusk fell on an ancient wood floor covered in dust and disturbed by numerous footprints. Shafts of light streamed from cracks in a sagging roof.

Long abandoned. A natural choice.

'With all due respect, Agent Raines, my team is here,' the detective replied. 'They can work the scene.'

'But they won't, Detective Lambert.'

Raines turned his head slowly, taking it all in.

One rectangular room roughly fifteen by forty, covered by a tin roof. Interior walls formed by six-inch greying wooden planks. Ten, twenty, thirty, thirty-two on the narrow side. Fifteen feet, as estimated. Two shovels and a pitchfork on the floor to his right. A single window with dirty, tinted panes, crowded by empty cobwebs.

A dust-covered wooden bucket rested in the corner, its rusted handle covered with filth. Several old rusted tin cans – Giant-brand peas with the label mostly missing, Heinz canned hotdogs – were scattered on the floor, left by a camper long gone. An old plough blade lay against the near wall. An even older work table sat to the left, near the far wall.

All unsurprising. All except what had brought Brad.

The woman's body was glued to the wall to his left, arms wide, wrists limp. Like the other three.

'. . . Chief Lorenzo for clearance.' The detective's voice edged in on his thoughts. Lambert was still there.

Brad looked over his left shoulder, where Nikki Holden, a

leading forensic psychologist, stood staring at the woman's body with those wide blue eyes of hers. She caught his get-rid-of-the-cop glance and turned to face Detective Lambert. Brad returned his gaze to the shed's interior as she spoke.

'I'm sorry, Detective,' she said, in her most reasonable tone of voice, 'but I'm sure you can appreciate our position here. Give my team a few hours. If this isn't our guy, you'll be the first to know. The police department's been more than helpful.'

Brad looked upwards to mask his knowing grin. One of the rafters was cracked, and its grey husk revealed a lighter, tan core. Freshly broken.

'I don't like it,' Lambert said. 'For the record.'

Brad pulled his eyes away from the crime scene and smiled at the detective. 'Thank you, Detective. Noted. There's quite a bit about this job not to like. If your men could secure the perimeter, that would be helpful. Our forensic team will be here any minute.'

Lambert held his gaze for a moment, then turned away and addressed a man behind him. 'Okay, Larry, cancel the forensics, this is now an FBI investigation. Tell Bill to secure and hold the perimeter.'

Larry muttered a curse and flicked away a bit of straw he'd taken from a pile of old bales. A white unmarked van rolled over the yellow perimeter tape and slowly crunched over the gravel driveway. It had taken the forensics team an hour to reach the scene, just south of West Dillon Road, from the Stout Street field office in downtown Denver. A farm had evidently once occupied this empty field in Louisville, twenty-plus miles northwest from Denver up the Denver Boulder Turnpike.

Brad glanced at Nikki. 'Tell them to start on the outside,' he said flatly. 'Give us a minute. Bring Kim in when she arrives.'

Kim Peterson, the forensic pathologist, would determine what the body could tell them post-mortem. Nikki headed for the van without comment.

Brad turned his attention back to the small barn. The shack. The farm shed. The killer's nest. The rest of the story was here, in the dark corners. The walls had watched the killer as he'd methodically ended a woman's life. The work table had heard his words as he confessed his passions and fears in a world turned inside out by his compulsions. It had witnessed her pleas for mercy. Her dying moans.

Careful not to step on the exposed markings in the dust, Brad entered the room and approached the wall on which the woman was affixed. He stood still, filtering out the sounds of voices from a dozen law-enforcement personnel outside. The hum of rubber on asphalt from the main road two hundred yards down the driveway settled in with the sound of his breathing. Both faded entirely as he brought his senses in line with the scene before him.

Her nude torso rose pale in the glow of a single light shaft. As though by magic, her body seemed perched on the wooden wall behind her, both arms stretched out on either side. Two round dowels that supported much of her weight protruded from the wall under her armpits. Her heels were together, each foot angled away from the other to form an upside-down V.

A white veil of translucent lace had been carefully arranged to cover her face, like a bride.

The out-thrust posture sent a collage of art-history remnants cascading through his mind – the Venus de Milo; a thousand renditions of the Crucifixion; the Louvre's Winged Victory statue, her marble bosom jutting forwards as if it belonged on the prow of an ancient ship ploughing through a Mediterranean surf.

But this was no museum. It was a crime scene, and the mixture of cruelty and ostentation pouring from the garish exhibit filled him with a sudden wave of nausea.

Slowly, his analytical faculties began to reassert themselves.

She was naked except for thin cotton panties and the veil. Blonde. White. Everything about the placement was symmetrical. Each hand was set in identical form, with thumb and forefinger touching; each shoulder, each hip had been carefully manipulated into perfect balance. All but her head.

Her head slumped gently to the left so that her long blonde hair cascaded over her left shoulder before curling under her armpits. Through the veil he could see that her eyes were closed. No blemish, no sign of pain or suffering, no blood.

Only blessed peace and beauty. She could as easily be an angel painted by DaVinci or Michelangelo. The perfect bride.

Brian Jacobs, seventeen, had brought his girlfriend here after school for reasons unrevealed and found the Bride Collector's fourth victim. Brad preferred to think of them as angels.

He peered closer and felt strange words of empathy well up inside of him.

I cry with you, Angel. I weep for you. For every strand of hair that will never again blow in the wind, for every smile that will never brighten someone else's day, for every look of desire that will never quicken another man's pulse. I am so sorry.

'She's beautiful,' Nikki said behind him.

He felt a momentary stab of regret for having been pulled away from his connection with the woman on the wall. Nikki walked past him, eyes fixed on the woman, touching his arm gently with her fingers as she passed. Her breathing was steady, slightly thicker than usual. He knew the cause: the dark waters of the killer's mind, which she now probed by staring at his handiwork.

Like an avalanche, the poignancy of his relationship with Nikki crashed through his mind . . . and then was gone, replaced by the image of her standing next to the woman. A blonde angel hovering over a brunette. One with arms stretched wide in complete resignation, the other with arms folded. One nearly naked, the other dressed in a blue silk blouse with a black jacket and skirt.

She's beautiful, he thought.

'What a shame.' Kim Peterson's voice cut softly through the room, grasping what the other two were too proud to verbalize. The forensic pathologist stepped up next to Brad, withdrew a pair of white gloves from her bag and then set it down. 'What do we know?'

Brad would have preferred to spend more time alone with the victim, but the opportunity had passed. 'No ID. Discovered an hour ago by two teenagers.'

They stared for a moment in silence.

'She's beautiful,' Kim said.

'Yes.'

'This makes four.'

'Looks like it, doesn't it?'

The pathologist approached, opposite Nikki, who remained quiet, lost in thought as she studied the body with searching eyes.

Kim sank to one heel and gently lifted the woman's toes for a better view under the foot. 'Care to tell us how you think it happened before I begin my preliminary examination?'

He wasn't ready, of course, not yet, not without a complete analysis of evidence yet to be gathered. But he'd been credited with an uncanny ability to accurately judge events from the thinnest of evidentiary threads. And he'd cracked three major cases in the Four Corners region since leaving Miami and joining the Denver field office a year ago. At thirty-two years of age, he was on the fast track for high ground – much higher ground, according to his superiors.

But, unlike them, his motivation had nothing to do with climbing an organizational ladder.

'Male, size eleven by the shoe prints. They were here for a while, maybe a day . . .'

'How so?' Nikki asked.

A distant murmur carried over to him: an officer speaking to the curious driver of an approaching car outside, instructing him to head back to the main road. The roof over their heads ticked as it began to cool in the late afternoon.

'That smell. It's baked beans. He was hungry, so he ate. You won't find the can. He wouldn't leave any DNA evidence in here.'

'She was alive when he brought her here?'

'Yes. And he killed her like the others, by draining her blood from her heels. No struggle. A tarp under the table caught most of the trace evidence – bodily fluids, skin cells, hair. He was careful not to use too much force, keeping her on the edge of control and submission. She was lying prone, sedated, conscious and fully aware when he numbed her heels and drilled up into them. He was forced to clean up the blood on the table and floor where it ran off the tarp. Then he sealed the wounds, lifted her into position, held her long enough for the glue on her shoulder blades to cure on the wall, reopened the wound on each heel, and watched her blood drain into a three-gallon bucket.'

All of this Brad had guessed from the markings on the table and floor, the ring from the bucket beneath the woman's heels and the lack of bruising. The physical evidence had painted a picture in his mind as clearly as if he were staring at a Rembrandt.

'He did it out of respect, not rage,' Brad added.

'Love,' Nikki said.

He nodded, even willing to go that far. 'Love.'

'Both heel wounds are plugged with the same fleshy putty we found on the other three,' Kim commented, standing. 'And what kind of love is this?'

'The groom's love,' Brad said, savouring his response.

Special Agent Frank Closkey spoke from the door. 'Sir?'

Brad held up his hand without looking back. 'Give us a few more minutes, Frank.'

The agent retreated.

Kim continued her initial examination, gently prodding the woman's flesh, checking her eyes, lifting her hair, inspecting the back of her shoulders. But Brad already knew what she would find.

The question was *why*? What motivated the Bride Collector? How did he make his selections? What good or evil did he think he was doing? What had been done to him to motivate his taking of life in such a manner? Who had he decided to kill next? When would he take her?

Where was he now?

The questions spun through Brad's mind as one, yet distinguishable from each other. Some were clearer than others, but all whispered from beyond, tempting him to listen, because each question already contained an answer. He simply had to find it and unpack it.

Nikki paced with one arm pressed against her belly, the other propping up her chin. It struck him that, like her, two of the first four victims had been blondes. Like her, all four had a beautiful complexion.

What would enter the killer's mind if he were staring at Nikki through a hole in the wall at this moment? Brad pushed back a fleeting impulse to check the wall behind them to see if there might indeed be a hole, filled with a single eye peering in at them.

Instead, he let his eyes wander over Nikki – her calves well defined beneath the hem of the black skirt, her wavy long hair cascading over her shoulders, her eyes bright with question. Her forefinger absently brushing full lips. A perfectly symmetrical face.

Would the killer feel any desire?

No. No, it wasn't desire, was it? She was beautiful, but beautiful women filled the world. Something else drew the Bride Collector, in the same way that something else was drawing Brad now, though he had a difficult time putting a finger on it.

Of the numerous women he'd dated over the past ten years, only four relationships had lasted two months or more, each ending sooner than the previous one. Nikki had once accused him of playing the role of 'bad boy'. He thought *picky* was a better label. He had taste, after all.

After what he'd been through, he needed to be picky.

Nikki was thirty-one, married once at age nineteen, divorced six months later. She held her doctorate in psychology from CSU. Highly intelligent, witty, reduced to deep introspection by scenes that left most people heaving.

This would excite the killer, wouldn't it? And if Nikki came on to the killer, would that excite him?

No, Brad thought.

'He would like you,' Brad said.

Nikki glanced back at him, arm still folded around her waist. 'Excuse me?'

He caught himself. This was one of those frequent times when honesty might not be so wise.

'I was just thinking that he liked her. You. That is, speaking to the victim. He. *He* would like *you*, meaning he would like *her*.'

Kim saved him. 'Speaking to cadavers now, Brad? Don't worry, I do it all the time.'

'You were looking at me when you said it,' Nikki said.

'So I was. I tend to do that.'

'What, stare at women? Or specifically at me?'

'Both, on occasion.'

A faint smile turned the corners of her mouth up. She winked. Not a full wink, but the movement in her right eyelid was unmistakable. Or was it?

Nikki turned to face the wall, leaving Brad feeling somewhat dirty. In an attempt to help the woman on the wall, he'd somehow violated her privacy. Yet the woman's story was still unknown and demanded respect.

Silence. Remorse. Shame.

'Sir?' Frank's voice intruded again.

Brad turned from the wall and walked to the door. 'Bring the team in. Photograph every inch, dust every exposed surface. Blood, sweat, spittle, hair; bag and tag the air if you have to. I want preliminaries from the lab this evening.'

'Um . . . It's getting late. I don't—'

'He's staring through a peephole at another woman already, Frank. We have less than a week to stop him from showing that woman his love. Preliminaries tonight.'

Brad, however, left the shack thinking he might have chosen better words to express the urgency burning across his nervous system.

CHAPTER TWO

FBI field office, Stout Street, Denver. Nine p.m.

Nikki Holden stood next to Brad beside the stainless-steel examination table in the basement morgue. Watching Kim gingerly turn the body onto its back, she noted the pathologist's care not to disturb the shoulder-blade skin, which they'd cut to release it from the wall.

The victim was a twenty-one-year-old named Caroline Redik. The name had surfaced when the lab ran her prints through the Automated Fingerprint Identification System, better known by its acronym, AFIS. The ever-expanding database now included anyone who applied for a passport, which is what Caroline had done before taking a trip to Paris one year earlier, for reasons yet unknown.

Calm and delicate, Kim laboured with a plastic face shield in place. Not much could ruffle the forty-three-year-old. She was as comfortable dipping her hand into a bloody gunshot wound as she was, when it mattered, peeling back the layers of society's skin with a well-placed question. She kept her blonde hair short. Easier to keep out of the way. If there was a mother in the office, it was Kim. Her manner created an interesting but somehow fitting contrast to her well-known love for a smorgasbord of men.

Nikki turned her attention back to the body. The skin was very pale, translucent, showing the blue veins beneath. She lay prone, looking like a dressmaker's dummy, displaying perfectly formed breasts, a flat belly and well-defined hips. Nikki found her rather bony, actually. While affixed to the wall, her flesh had settled over her bones and given her a less emaciated appearance. On her back, however, she looked quite gaunt.

Her makeup was far more obvious under the bright halogen lights than it had been before the evidence team had illuminated the shack. The eyeliner and eyeshadow had been carefully applied, evidence of a steady, experienced hand. Was the killer a cosmetologist? Or a drag queen, even? Nikki could just see vertical streaks running down from the corners of her eyes and ruining the perfect surface, as if poor Caroline had cried before the final application.

Nikki recalled a memory of her father holding her shoulders when she was twelve. He'd knelt and brushed a tear from her right cheek, where a dime-sized birthmark darkened her skin. 'You are beautiful, Nikki, and your birthmark makes you even more beautiful. You don't need to cover it up. And if the boys don't see that, it's only because they're foolish, prepubescent puppets of the system.' Then he'd kissed her on the cheek.

The memory still brought a tightness to her throat; maybe because his noble ideals hadn't really survived him. She'd had the brown mark surgically removed when she was eighteen.

If she had it to do over again, would she remove it today?

'. . . drugs in her system,' Kim was saying. 'Benzodiazepine, the same psychoactive sedative he's used on all four. More than enough to make her susceptible to suggestion.'

'No sign of sexual contact?' Brad asked.

'None.'

Nikki caught Brad's sharp look. 'That doesn't mean this wasn't a sexual act,' she interjected.

He offered her a slight nod. Just that, a simple gesture of acknowledgement and appreciation for her input. Funny how he could lighten her mood without the slightest knowledge of his overall effect on her.

The other women in the office insisted he was a dead ringer for a blond-headed George Clooney, but ten years younger, perhaps. She could see the similarities. The dark, perpetually smiling eyes, probing deep. The short hair, the soft boyish face, slightly elongated. The quintessential look of a perfect gentleman reinforced by his often thoughtful and polite demeanour.

But her closer working relationship had taught her that those qualities didn't make Brad a soft or pliable man. If anything, his edges were rougher than they first appeared. Clean on the outside, giving great attention to detail, but confident enough to say what was on his mind whenever he saw fit.

His unapologetic talent for drawing women with his boyish good looks and strong conviction was tempered only by his notorious refusal to commit. Which, in turn, made him a considerable mystery.

To Nikki's way of thinking, he carried all the markings of a man with a past so deeply scarred that he was compelled to build walls of self-preservation. Which is why she had resisted her own attraction to him for so long. Even if he was interested in her, as she suspected, she wasn't sure *she* was interested in a man she couldn't quite peg. As a psychologist, it was her job to analyse people down to their uttermost depths. The fact that she could not do so with Brad nagged her with an unshakable sense of wariness.

His eyes were soft and kind, but what lay hidden behind those eyes gave her pause. The unknown. She'd misjudged a man once before and wasn't eager to do it again. Her training in behavioural science hadn't made her any more trusting.

'He wouldn't grow impatient,' she said. 'He would relish his time with her.'

Another nod, this time looking at the cadaver. 'He would.'

Kim looked up, then turned to the victim's other side and dramatically ran her index finger over the foot, tracing each toe. Always one for theatrics when the opportunity presented itself.

'She took care of her feet. The toenail polish is fresh, applied in the last twenty-four hours. But she's taken care of her feet, her whole body for that matter, for a long time.'

'He likes to apply makeup and give pedicures,' Nikki said.

A half-inch hole, now bloodless and black, ran up into the heel. 'He used the same half-inch bit size, maybe the same bit. Ran it directly through the skin, the calcaneus bone, severing the *peroneus longus* tendon, and into the anterior tibial artery.

Everything's as it was with the other three, except for this.' Kim traced her finger down to the victim's right heel. 'This is what's new.'

She picked up a small roll of bloody paper, maybe two inches long, and held it up between her thumb and forefinger. 'This time he left this in the right heel.'

Brad stepped forwards. 'Writing?'

'I can see some markings, yes. But I haven't unrolled it yet. I thought you would want a look before I sent it up to the lab.'

Brad's face lightened a shade.

The killer had left them a message.

Special Agent in Charge James Temple sat against the edge of the secretary desk on the conference room's north end and gazed at them with brown, glassy eyes, hands folded up by his chin. Nikki leaned against the wall, arms crossed, fixated on the enlarged photograph of the Bride Collector's note on the screen. Two other agents, Miguel Ruffino and Barth Kramer, lounged in chairs, their focus divided between the note, the SAC, Nikki and Brad, who paced at the head of the conference table.

There was a reason these two would always be good, but not great, at their jobs, Brad thought. They lacked the obsessive personality required to bring inordinate focus to any single task.

'So this is it,' Temple said to Brad's left. 'We have us a certified wacko. A freaking lunatic from some funny barn who's out there drilling holes in women to make a point.' He looked around with a bemused look. 'No pun intended, of course.'

Ruffino and Kramer guffawed, just as Nikki shot the SAC a sharp look. 'I wouldn't put it like—'

'Spare me the psychobabble.' Temple stood and shoved his hands into his pockets. 'If this isn't certified crazy, I don't know what is.'

The man stood maybe three or four inches shy of six feet, wiry as a bull snake. He shaved his head and took pride in his body, which he regularly and rigorously brought into submission at the gym. The man was a misfit in Denver, Brad thought. In the southeast, from where he'd been transferred a month earlier, his attitude would have been less of a problem. But up here, gunslingers were frowned upon, and James Temple was most definitely a gunslinger – hotheaded, quick to conclusions and choleric to the bone.

'On balance, most pattern killers are mentally stable,' Nikki said. 'They are well-educated, financially stable, often good-looking, seemingly well-adjusted people. Unlike mass murderers, whose delusions feed beliefs of supremacy, serial killers act for personal gain or revenge. They do so in a calculated, thoughtful way. Hardly your freaking lunatic.'

'Read it.' Temple frowned and jabbed his sharp, dimpled chin in the direction of the screen. 'Any idiot can see that this religious nutcase slobbers on himself. You're saying you see something different?'

Nikki's face reddened, but she didn't point out the man's blunder in essentially calling himself an idiot. She looked at the screen.

The note was written in black lettering, with a fine ballpoint pen. The two-by-three-inch piece of white paper had been cut using a straight edge, then folded several times before being rolled and inserted into the hole in Caroline's heel, at least several days after it had been written.

Brad read through the poem again.

The Beauty Eden id Lost
Where intelligence does centered
I came do her and she smashed da Serpent head
I searched and find the seventh and beautiful
She will rest in my Serpent's hole
And I will live again

'He can hardly spell.'

Brad regarded the man. 'I'm sorry, James, but I don't see an imbecile.'

The SAC raised a brow and pulled out a chair to sit in. At times like this, Brad's reputation proved useful. And he'd hailed from Miami before dazzling the Four Corners. That made James Temple basically kin, at least in Temple's mind. He would think twice before dismissing anything Brad had to say.

'Is that right? Well, please . . .' He opened a palm of invitation. 'Fill us in.'

Nikki shifted her gaze to the dark window, struggling to hide her frustration.

'I think Nikki's assessment is right,' Brad explained. 'We're dealing with a highly intelligent individual who knows exactly what he's doing within the context of his own world.'

'Just because he knows how to drill holes and clean up after himself doesn't mean he's not barking mad.'

'No,' Nikki interjected, 'but even if he is suffering from psychosis, it doesn't mean he's an animal.'

'I see motivation and intention,' Brad continued, nodding at the note on the screen. 'But it would be a significant mistake not to assume the author knew exactly what he was writing and why he was writing it.'

'You're saying he's broadcasting his next move,' Temple said, glancing back at the note. 'How so?'

'Assume with me that this was written by a scholar, a poet with the intelligence of Hemingway. And written for our benefit, with some bad grammar thrown in to make himself look less intelligent.'

'Grammar has little to do with intelligence,' Nikki said.

'I realize that. But go with me. What's he really saying?'

'The beauty *of* Eden *is* lost,' Nikki read. 'The fall of innocence.'

Temple closed his eyes momentarily in a show of impatience. 'Fine. Something less obvious.'

Brad nodded at Nikki. She exchanged an inquisitive look with him, nodded her appreciation and looked up at the screen.

'He's saying that where once beauty, innocence and intelligence were found, this Eden, it's now lost. The serpent – read evil or the devil – is responsible. Not sure about the third line – I came to her and she smashed the Serpent's head – doesn't make sense to me.'

She glanced at Brad.

'Motivation,' he said. 'He, the serpent, destroyed beauty but was wounded in the process. He's upset. Go on.'

Nikki nodded. 'I can go with that. The last three lines seem straightforward. He's after a replacement for the beautiful one who fell, so he can live again.'

'He's looking for a wife,' Brad said. 'A new Eve.'

'And this helps us how?' Barth Kramer asked.

The SAC ignored him entirely, having stood again to pace. 'Okay, I'm with you. Tell me more.'

Brad walked behind the conference table, keeping his eyes fixed on the words, written in the killer's own hand. He could see it all. The desk. Neatly arranged. Perfectly ordered. A pen poised over the paper just so, while the words he had recited to himself a thousand times flowed through his mind, sung by a choir, a chorus in a symphony. A requiem that thundered the truth, demanding to be heard.

Now such truth was reduced to mere words on a simple piece of white paper, for his greatest enemies to see. It was like being stripped naked, both terrifying and thrilling at once. The killer was coming out. His whole life was here, on this piece of paper.

Brad cleared his throat. 'His killings are ritualistic, leading him to life. He's not doing it out of anger. None of the crime scenes have shown signs of rage.'

Local authorities had found the first victim three weeks ago in a barn just south of Grand Junction, in the arid Grand Valley near the border of Utah and Colorado. Serena Barker had been twenty-three and the police had assumed her to be a victim of satanic ritual. She'd been dead for three days, and a coyote had got to her left foot.

The Denver FBI office hadn't been engaged until the second body was found sixty miles northeast of Denver, in an apartment near the plains cattle town of Greeley. Karen Neely, twenty-four. Again carefully preserved, nearly flawless in her final presentation. Brad had been assigned the case and immediately requested copies of the file from Grand Junction. A studious detective, Braden Hall, had meticulously documented the case. There was little doubt that they had a serial killer on their hands.

The Bride Collector killed his third woman a week later in Parker, south of Denver. Julia Paxton was twenty and had been found less than eight hours after her death, a vision of twisted beauty glued to the wall of her own house.

All women under the age of twenty-five. All exceptionally beautiful. As of yet, only one murder had been published – that of Julia Paxton, who was a well-known model for Victoria's Secret. Other than the distinctive circumstances of death, they could determine no other connection between the women.

As for the killer, recovered evidence from the previous scenes put him at 180 to 200 pounds, based on the depth of his shoe indentations in soil. No DNA to run through Combined DNA Index System (CODIS). No hair or cell samples. No saliva, blood, semen or latent prints tied to the killer.

He was essentially a ghost.

'His motivation is in finding life,' Brad continued, 'not in delivering death. He believes he's leading the women into life.'

Temple stared at him. 'You see, now there's where my psycho-nutcase warning bells start going crazy. Forgive me if I don't see torturing and killing someone "into life" as nothing less than barking mad.'

'Psychotic, maybe,' Nikki said. 'Mentally ill, maybe. But not necessarily less intelligent than any of us. The direct link between psychosis and intelligence is well documented in some subjects. We should assume that the Bride Collector is more intelligent than anyone in this room. If we don't, we risk seriously underestimating him.'

'That's your profile? Our man's a genius?'

She hesitated. 'Yes.'

Temple crossed his arms and settled back against the desk. 'Okay, I'll let you go with that.'

'There's more,' Brad said. 'He wants us to know he's going after beautiful women, that much is unmistakable in his writing. I would say he knows we'll see through his attempt to look unintelligent. He wants us to look for a supremely intelligent person who has a penchant for killing beautiful women because he's been jilted by one. In reality, that's not the case. Sound right to you, Nikki?'

Her blue eyes widened. She nodded, lost in thought. 'Eerily right.'

Temple drummed his fingers on the desk. 'Okay, so we play his game his way. We look for the most beautiful women in and around Denver.'

'That's what he wants us to do,' Frank said.

'I'm open to suggestions. In the absence of any, we keep him engaged, even if it means playing things his way. Keep it under wraps. We don't need everyone who thinks they're decent-looking in a panic. Any tyre tracks lifted at the shack scene?'

'None.'

'Other evidence processed?'

'So far he's clean. The fresh hair, bodily fluids and fingerprints match the victim. Three other hair samples we're running now. Could be from anyone messing around in there.'

Temple nodded at Frank and glanced at the others. 'Any other ideas?'

Nikki shifted off the wall and paced. 'You want to play his way? Start with all known cases of mental illness in Colorado.'

'So now he's a wacko again?'

'You're not listening. Again, being a genius and mentally ill are not mutually exclusive.'

'But you're willing to concede that he could be nuts.'

She breathed out slowly. 'I think our guy could be deeply disturbed, just not nuts. Maybe psychotic and delusional, maybe suffering from acute schizophrenia, but he doesn't slobber.'

'Then until we learn differently, we assume he's both mentally ill and a genius. Fair enough?'

She nodded. 'The ones that aren't complete loners tend to congregate on the internet, in psychiatrists' offices, psychiatric wards. It's a starting point.'

'As of now we start looking for records of any anomalies or patterns in mental health facilities, residential care homes, whatever.' Temple turned quickly to Brad. 'Pull whatever resources you need, cross-check what we know of the Bride Collector against the files of every known psycho released from any facility in the last' – he looked at Nikki – 'ten years?'

'Too many cases. Mental illness is more widespread than you think. Nearly 700,000 mentally ill are jailed each year in this country. Start with a year.'

Temple looked stunned. Brad found it odd that the man wasn't already familiar with this statistic.

'God help us all.' Temple glanced up at the wall clock, which was closing in on ten. 'A year then. I have to go.'

Brad spoke before the man could move. 'We should also assume he intends to kill seven women. The seventh and most beautiful may refer to his final target.'

That brought a pause.

'Unless he's killed three others without anyone's knowledge,' Frank said.

'As long as we're assuming the worst, he has three more to go.' Eyes on Nikki. 'And being the smartest mind in the room, he knows that *we* know that. He wants us to know that he's going to kill three more women.'

'It fits.'

Brad pushed on quickly. 'He's going to go again in a few days. If it takes him a few days to kill, then he's likely already engaged. It's a short cycle for a pattern killer who kills to satisfy compulsion. But our guy's method is based on reason, not raw compulsion.'

They stared at him, arms crossed.

'Okay. I gotta go.' Temple grabbed his cell phone and walked towards the door. 'We assume our guy's out there now, outwitting us morons, stalking a beautiful woman he intends to kill in the next few days.' He turned back at the door. 'For the love of all that is holy, stop him.'

CHAPTER THREE

Quinton Gauld was his name, and at the moment he was preparing to enjoy a thick, juicy, prime-cut rib eye at Elway's Steakhouse at the corner of 19th and Curtis, just one block from the FBI building on Stout Street, downtown Denver, Colorado, USA, North America, World, Universe, Infinity.

The thought of being so close to the only humans capable of ruining things put him in a calculating mood. It was a time for reflection and self-examination, soaking in the fluids of truth.

And upon such introspection, Quinton was feeling abundantly satisfied.

The waiter, a tall blond man with a slightly protruding belly and sharp elbows, set a ceramic plate down using a cream-coloured hot pad folded over the dish's rim to protect his palm and fingers from being seared like the steak. His name was Anthony.

'Be careful, it's hot.'

'Thank you, Anthony.'

'Is everything to your satisfaction?'

'I'll let you know in a moment.'

'Are you sure I can't get you anything else? Vegetables? Bread?'

'I am all set, Anthony.'

'No drink?'

'I have water, Anthony. Water washes steak down quite nicely after so much bloodletting.'

The waiter offered a coy smile, signifying his appreciation for Quinton's choice of words to describe a cow being slaughtered. But Quinton was speaking of Caroline, not the cow. Caroline wasn't a cow, and she hadn't been slaughtered.

She was one of God's favourites, and she'd been drilled. And then bled.

Bless me, Father, for I have sinned.

Quinton picked up his fork and held it in his large, bony hand. He paused for a moment, staring at the gold cuff link that buttoned the sleeve of his shirt. An inch of white, and then the blue Armani suit reserved for special occasions.

He never worked in a suit and tie because he found them too constraining, preferring instead nakedness encumbered only by black briefs.

He was momentarily fascinated by the chrome fork in his fingers. Larger than many forks. A real man's fork. His own fingers were larger than most by as much as an inch in length. By his hands alone, one might guess him to be nearly seven feet tall. In reality, he stood only six foot four.

He twisted his wrist, caught up in the sight of flesh against metal, such a harsh surface in the embrace of soft flesh. He'd once considered his hands too large and gangly, alien appendages on the end of long bones. So he'd decided to take special care of his hands and in the process had come to truly appreciate them. They had a unique beauty, a subject about which he knew far more than most. He'd allowed various women from Asia to give him manicures and pedicures twice a week for nearly a year now, and the results were impressive.

Quinton moved his forefinger. Then he did it again, trying to trace the messages that spread across neurons in his brain at a rate of six hundred per second before being shot down his nerves to the muscles in his hand. Little bundles of energy were racing from his brain to his hand with clear, precise directions at this very moment, yet he was completely unaware of how or when his brain began or ended the cycle. How decision became instruction. How instruction became movement.

The brain was a mystery for most humans, and as of yet for Quinton Gauld.

It occurred to him that his moment of exploration into the finer things of life had stretched on for a full minute or more.

Not a bad thing, for, after all, he was here to enjoy himself. No enjoyment could exceed the power of the mind to amuse itself.

And the whole time he had been contemplating his hand and the utensil in that hand, he was in perfect tune with all else in Elway's place of feeding.

The bartender with silver earrings who had apologized after spilling beer on a customer's hands. He offered the woman a free drink. She declined, but she despised him for his carelessness. She was a real cow who'd been convinced by inner delusional voices that her black polyester slacks were not too tight despite the fact that she had gained ten pounds in the last three months, thanks to her meds. He would say depression was her demon.

The two new customers, one with bratty kids, who'd entered the premises since he'd picked up his fork.

The husband and wife two booths over, arguing over the price of a new minivan and whether the van should be blue or grey. Black got too dirty. No, white got too dirty. Quinton briefly entertained the thought of helping them gain a more expansive understanding of the word *dirty*.

The pretty waitress wearing a white halter top who smiled as she passed his table. She found him interesting. Handsome. A real gentleman, judging by his appearance and his posture. He knew this not only by her look, but because women always commented on these admirable traits. This particular woman, whose nametag identified her as Karen with a *C*, or Caren, was also likely attracted to his tall frame. They said size didn't matter, but most women had preferences when it came to size. Caren liked large men.

There was a single fly caught in the window to his right.

A hundred other stimuli had been trapped by his brain as he contemplated the fork. Not the least of which was the aromatic steam rising off his charbroiled steak.

Quinton held his fork in his left hand with one finger on the bridge to steady it. He sliced through the tender meat with a serrated blade, one provided by Jonathan Elway, the famed Denver Bronco quarterback, who, based on Quinton's research three days earlier when he'd carefully selected the restaurant for this occasion, had indeed been a favourite among all of God's children.

Bless me, Father, for I have sinned.

A man with enviable strength and intelligence, able to hurl an inflated leather sack through the air with such accuracy and power that few defenders could see it coming, much less stop it from reaching its intended receiver.

On his God-given field, Jonathan Elway, known to the rest of the world as John Elway, had been a god. He didn't mistakenly think of himself as a god, like most humans desperate to live out their pathetic fantasies did. He actually *was* a god, something he himself likely didn't know.

Quinton placed the first bite of meat into his mouth, pulled the tender morsel off using his teeth, and closed his eyes. The taste was heavenly. The seared crust gave way with a faint crack to the moist fibres beneath. Juice flooded his mouth and pooled under his tongue as he sunk his molars deep into the flesh.

So delectable and satisfying, he allowed himself a soft moan. Two more chews with his eyes still closed to shut out all other visual stimuli. The pleasure demanded more vocalized appreciation. Whispering this time.

'Mmmm . . . Mmmm . . . Delicious.'

It was important not to be plastic. Pretending to himself only minimized who he was. Most humans wore a public façade, an attempt to compensate for their own flaws and weaknesses. The whole world was plastic, populated by people playing roles, fooling only the foolish. Sadly, they'd worn the façades for so long that they had lost even their awareness of the habit.

I am an important executive who has made money – the Rolex label on my wrist should make that clear.

I am a powerful lover and provider, signified by the way I've engineered my body to appear strong and symmetrically lumpy.

I am comfortable with myself, signified by the way I walk so nonchalantly wearing only sweats and a T-shirt.

I am nobody. But please, please don't tell anyone.

The voice of the bratty boy, who was now seated across the

room in a booth, scraped at Quinton's mind. He fought back a grimace of frustration. It was important not to be plastic, but it was also important not to step on the sanctity of others' space. The boy was upsetting the balance of peace and tranquillity in the room. No doubt, every last patron would readily shove a sock or boot down the boy's throat if they were not so afraid of being found out for who they really were.

He shut the boy out and focused on the cavalcade of flavours dancing around in his mouth. He began to chew with powerful strokes of his jaw, drawing the juices into his mouth and throat. Swallowing deep.

The details of his earlier activity, which he was now celebrating by breaking an otherwise strict vegetarian diet, slipped through his mind. His special time with Caroline had been satisfying in the same way all great accomplishments were rewarding. But he'd drawn no physical pleasure from the bloodletting.

Eating the steak, however . . . This was indeed like sex. And because Quinton had not known any sexual gratification since that terrible night three years earlier, he relished every other physical pleasure that reminded him that physical pleasure was indeed an immeasurable gift.

News of Caroline's death would soon fill the world with a single question: Who is it? Who is it? Is it my neighbour, is it the grocery clerk, is it the high school principal?

Humans were predictable. Like animated carbon units. Cardboard cut-outs with fancy trim, far too much of it. There was only one human who really mattered, and at the moment that was him. Everything around him was stage dressing. He was the only real player on this stage.

The audience was watching him only; the rest were only extras. It was the same for all of them, but few were courageous enough to understand or confess this single beautiful, bitter truth: Deep down inside, each of them believed they were at the centre of the universe.

But at the moment, it was Quinton, and he was wise enough to embrace it.

God had chosen Quinton Gauld. Simple. Indisputable. Final.

Which brought Quinton to the task set before him. Three more, as he saw fit. Ending with the most beautiful.

The boy in the booth was whining his dislike for peas. A perfectly good vegetable, but this dark-headed boy who looked to be about ten or eleven was refusing to consider reason, in part because the father wasn't delivering reason, but distraction. 'How about ice cream, Joshie? How about lobster, Joshie?'

Quinton cut off more meat and savoured the bite. So delicious. Rarely had he drawn such pleasure from meat. But the boy was undermining the experience and Quinton felt regression pressing in on his psyche. *Joshie* was mad as hell and there seemed no good reason for it. The boy was simply misfiring. Going kaput. Rotting before his time in the grave.

Few things distracted Quinton any longer. He'd long ago conquered his mind. A doctor had once diagnosed him with schizoaffective disorder, a condition that supposedly involved the complications of thought disorder and a bipolar mood disorder. Five years of his life had vanished in a fog of heavy medication, until he silently protested the oppression.

The condition was his greatest gift, not a disease. He still took a very low dosage of medication to control the tics – a natural by-product of a supercharged mind – but otherwise he relied on his own substantial focus and enlightenment.

At the moment, it took every fibre of his formidable intellect to remain calm. The square of seared cow flesh in his mouth was tasting more like cardboard than meat. After his significant accomplishment earlier today, the heavens were cheering, but the rats on earth were totally oblivious. There was no respect left in the world.

The father suggested that Joshie take a 'time out' to think about it, and the boy raced screaming to the restroom. None of the others seemed too put out by the scene.

The whole mini-drama was more than Quinton was willing to bear. He calmly set down his knife and dabbed his lips with his serviette seven times, alternating corners, a habit that helped to bring order to his mind. He took one more deep draft of the purified water, slipped a hundred dollar bill onto the table, and stood.

With a nod and smile at the waitress who wanted him, he walked towards the restroom.

It was important not to stand out in a crowd while simultaneously living a non-plastic life. An authentic life. Authentic, but not proud and obnoxious either. That was the boy's problem: he was standing out in the crowd, acting as if he were a coddled king who eats ice cream while the rest of the kingdom is subjected to peas.

Quinton's problem, on the other hand, was how to enlighten the boy without making the same mistake and drawing attention. He neither wanted nor needed the spotlight, particularly not now.

He walked into the bathroom with a backward glance, noting that no one else was hurrying to relieve themselves of dinner or drink. The door closed with a soft clunk. The boy faced the urinal, uttering a long, mournful wail that might be expected at a funeral procession, but not here after being offered ice cream.

Eager to deliver his message quickly, Quinton walked to the stalls, checked both to be sure they were alone, then approached the boy.

He tapped Joshie on the shoulder. The boy was zipping up, and he spun with a short gasp, swallowing his annoying cry.

'Why are you crying, lad?' Quinton asked.

Joshie got over his initial shock and flattened his mouth. 'Mind your own business,' he said. Then he made to walk past Quinton.

Quinton knew it now: the boy was deeply disturbed. Perhaps mentally ill, though more likely just rotten to the core. An intervention was both reasonable and necessary if the boy were to have any hope of entering adulthood well adjusted.

Quinton stuck his hand out and prevented his escape. 'Not so fast, young lad. I asked you a question and I do expect an answer.'

He shoved the boy back, gripping his shoulder.

'Ow! Let go!'

'Don't be a baby,' Quinton said calmly. Then he added 'lad', because the English word gave the whole sentence a proper ring. And this was a very proper occasion. 'Tell me why you thought you had the right to cry. If you give me the right answer, I might let you off with a warning.'

The boy struggled against Quinton's grip. 'Let me go, you freak!' The boy's mouth twisted. Did he have no sense at all? Did he possess even the faintest awareness of whom he was dealing with?

Quinton squeezed hard and leaned forwards so that he wouldn't have to yell. He spoke in a stern whisper. 'Someone's going to put a bullet in your head one of these days. I would, under different circumstances. You're not the only snot in the world, and the truth is, most people would rather kill you than listen to your whining little hole.'

The boy stared up at him in shock. A dark circle spread over his groin. Apparently, he hadn't drained his bladder quite so completely after all.

'Be very careful what you tell them. They won't believe I hit you anyway; your face is already beet-red from acting like a baby. But if you do go out there and tell them I hit you, I might sneak into your room when you're asleep and pull your tongue out.'

But the boy did what most humans do in times of crisis. He became himself. He started to scream bloody murder.

Quinton's hand moved with calculated strength, slamming open-palmed against the noisy brat's jaw. Had he not been gripping the boy's shoulder, it would have been enough force to send Joshie across the room, but not enough to break his jaw or neck.

Crack!

'Bless you, boy, for you are a sinner.'

It was enough to shut the boy up. And shut him down. He shoved the boy's limp body into the corner, wedged between the wall and the urinal.

Satisfied that he'd got through, Quinton crossed to the mirror, adjusted his collar, tugged each sleeve so that his shirt showed just the right measure of white at the cuffs, smoothed his left eyebrow, which had somehow ruffled during the commotion, and left the bathroom.

No one in the noisy restaurant gave him a second glance. The whole room might have stood and cheered to learn that Joshie had fallen asleep at the urinal, had they known. If they all kept their fingers crossed long enough, though, the boy would one day fall asleep at the wheel, crash through a bridge railing, and plummet into a river to meet an icy death.

Quinton felt doubly good with his accomplishment. Although he hadn't been able to eat every bite of his steak, he had been able to help both Joshie and the rest of the rats in this establishment without so much as raising an eyebrow from one of them. Except Josh, of course. And he'd raised more than an eyebrow on the lad.

Quinton walked between the tables, gathering only the casual looks of appreciation offered to the best looking. So few realized just how many psychotic members of society walked past them at the grocery store or through a restaurant each and every day. What would frighten them even more was how many ordinary people were mentally sick and didn't know it.

Quinton winked at the waitress on his way out, then thanked Anthony for the wonderful meal. The hostess greeted him kindly at the front door.

'Was everything to your satisfaction?'

'Yes. Yes, Cynthia, it was. Do you happen to have any sanitized toothpicks?'

She glanced at the clear dispenser full of toothpicks, then reached under the counter and pulled out a box in which each toothpick was individually wrapped. She smiled knowingly.

'Thank you.' He counted out seven, then nodded. 'For my friends.'

'No problem. Take the whole box if you want.'

'No, I couldn't do that. I doubt John would appreciate being robbed.'

She laughed. 'Oh, I doubt that. Mr Elway is very generous.'

'Well, judging by his choice of steaks, he doesn't skimp, so I can agree to that. Have a great evening, Cynthia.'

'Thank you. Drive safe.'

He stopped at the outer door and looked back. 'Oh, I almost forgot, I think a boy fell asleep in the restroom.'

'Really?'

'I don't know, but he looked asleep to me.' He flipped his hand in a casual salute. 'Anyway, thanks again.'

Then he was alone outside, surrounded by the night. He took a deep breath, appreciative of the rich scent of searing steak from the establishment's kitchen vents.

A man's choice of car was telling. He once heard that an extremely wealthy man, whose name he'd purposefully forgotten, chose to drive an old pick-up truck rather than a Mercedes. Quinton had known at once that the man was either hopelessly insecure, or completely mad. No one comfortable in their own skin would try to hide their wealth unless they supposed that others didn't approve of wealthy people or of people who wanted to be wealthy, thereby necessitating a disguise.

Quinton appreciated the need for subtlety, something Josh hadn't understood until just a few minutes ago, but driving a pick-up truck when you're worth a hundred billion was the furthest thing from subtlety. If the man wasn't insecure, he was deeply deluded into thinking that pretending to be a common man would make him so. If anything, such eccentric behaviour drew more attention than it would had the man been honest with himself. Perhaps he longed for the extra attention, not willing to be just another rich man in a rich car, and it was insecurity, not madness, that compelled the man?

The circular logic of it all came slamming home with a nauseating *thunk*. Quinton had spent considerable time mulling over the question and never landed on a definitive answer.

He rounded the restaurant, walked up to his Chrysler M 300 and noted that a BMW M6 had parked next to his ride. At well over a hundred thousand dollars, the M6 was BMW's most expensive vehicle, an overstatement of any owner's testosterone. The small 'M6' symbol was all that told a passerby that this car was far more expensive than its lesser, otherwise identical sibling.

Nevertheless, the styling was subtle. A reasonable choice in extravagance. He briefly courted the notion of slashing the tyres on the M6, then dismissed the idea as a lesser man's fantasy.

Quinton found pleasure in the knowledge that he directed no resentment or jealousy towards those who pretended to be more important than he was. Though he felt no compulsion to do so, he could this very moment walk into any bank or down Wall Street and be greeted with the same warmth and respect saved for any successful business executive. Yet he derived no undue pleasure or derision from that fact.

Or he could dress in one of his many identical pairs of grey slacks, don one of his blue short-sleeved shirts, put on a wedding band, take out his older green Chevy pick-up, which he preferred to the M 300, and be accepted in any bar or any grocery store checkout line as the respectable guy next door.

Quinton slipped out of his jacket and settled into his car. Before going home, he would drive to Melissa Langdon's house. She would be arriving in the next half hour. If he hurried, he could arrive before she did.

It took him a full twenty-five minutes to navigate his way south on I 25 to C 470, then north on Santa Fe Drive to Miss Langdon's neighbourhood. He eased the car to a stop on the street adjacent to Peakview, far enough away to avoid suspicion from the blue house, but close enough for him to view her coming and going.

The night was still, and no streetlights compromised the darkness. Most of the homes in this track had two-car garages that could only effectively house one car, forcing many residents to park their second cars either in their driveways or on the street. His black M 300 rested among a dozen similar vehicles bedded down for the night.

He checked his mirrors, first the right, then the left, then the right again and the left again. Each time his vision acquired more information, scanning further down the street, taking in the white Mustang, the fire hydrant, the intersection, the row of junipers two houses back, the cat that scampered across past the stop sign a block behind.

But no people. No threats.

After searching his mirrors seven times, Quinton turned off the ignition and let silence filter into the cockpit. He withdrew one of the toothpicks and stripped off the plastic wrapping, careful not to touch the sharp wood tip he would insert into his mouth, and began to methodically clean the spaces between his teeth.

Ahead, Melissa Langdon's blue home waited quietly, lit only by a single porch light. A ranch house, roughly sixteen hundred square feet. Seven windows facing the street, including the bathroom off the master bedroom. The backyard was large, but she was too busy right now, serving drinks and crackers thirty thousand feet above sea level, to care about lot dimensions.

The last time Quinton had walked behind the house, the weeds had been calf-high. A cat had rushed from the brush and caused him to fall backward. He'd strangled the cat that very night, suffering several nasty cuts in the process. Funny how dispatching a witless animal had proven more perilous than bleeding several grown human beings. After the act, he had laid it under his front tyre to make it look like the cat had been accidentally run over on the street. He didn't need the pet's owner finding and reporting their strangled cat at the back of Melissa Langdon's house.

Some might wonder why God had chosen Melissa. She was beautiful, any man could see that, but not even Quinton had recognized the flight attendant the first time she'd walked down the aisle and asked him if he would like something to drink. But by the end of that flight, he knew. God had made his choice through Quinton.

Melissa was sweet and her smile was genuine, unlike most of the whores who flew the friendly skies. She had a round, kind face framed by straight blonde hair that hung to her shoulders. Her blue skirt draped seamlessly over her narrow hips. She kept her ruby fingernails short but carefully manicured, and her fingers moved with grace, caressing every object she touched. She used disinfecting towelettes frequently during the flight.

But the ultimate truth shone in her green eyes. Unblemished innocence. Deep, like a jungle pool. Melissa was one of the favourites.

Unable to keep his own eyes off of her, he'd finally had to slip on his sunglasses. By the time the plane landed, his shirt was soaked in sweat and his left hand was trembling. He'd received a nod and a friendly smile from her as he deplaned, and he'd offered his hand in a gesture of appreciation.

She'd taken it. Her cool dry skin had sent shivers of pleasure down his spine. He'd been so distracted by that single contact that he took a wrong turn and exited the security area before remembering that he had a connecting flight. Forced to go back through security, he missed the connection.

Quinton knew from the schedule he'd taken from her dresser last week that, barring any delays, her plane from New York had landed at DIA roughly one hour ago. Hopefully, she wouldn't make any diversions before coming home.

He could smell the meat on his breath as it deflected off his hand. When he'd asked the last one, Caroline, if she liked the way his breath smelled, she had given him a tearful nod. He'd switched to Crest three days ago after using Colgate for as long as he could remember and . . .

Lights brightened the street. Melissa's blue Civic rolled past his M 300.

Quinton felt himself weaken, something inside him quailing before the prospect of an impending thrill. 'Bless me, Father. Bless me.' He swallowed deep and sat perfectly still, watching her pull into the driveway. The garage door opened, then closed behind her car.

His bride was home.

CHAPTER FOUR

October in Denver. It could be cold one day and hot the next. Like working a case, Brad thought. The trail could turn at any moment. Usually due to fairly basic investigative work, collecting mounds of evidence and carefully sifting through them.

Someone once told him that good doctoring was a process of eliminating potential diseases until a physician was left with the most likely ailment to explain the symptoms. Detective work was the same.

As long as you were eliminating suspects in the investigative process, you were moving forwards. It was sometimes Brad's only consolation in the face of relentless pressure.

In the case of a serial killer like the Bride Collector, knowing that the suspect would continue turned the work from a simple elimination process into a chess match. Success wasn't just a matter of sifting through the evidence from the past, but of trying to anticipate the future.

Anticipating a killer's next move meant climbing into his mind. Not out of desire, of course. No one with any skill or a sane mind would ever relish that journey. It was only ever launched out of necessity.

Brad had settled himself with a late-night drink at McKenzie's Pub, a block from his downtown condo, then spent the balance of the night alone, tossing and turning, climbing inside the Bride Collector's mind.

He'd woken early and headed to the bathroom to shower, eager to return to the crime scene, before seeing that it was only three in the morning. He slipped back under the covers, pulled his second pillow tight, and thought about madness.

Insanity. The mentally ill.

The Bride Collector.

It was seven now – he'd slept in after missing sleep in the wee hours. Showered, shaved and dressed in blue slacks and white shirt, he poured his half-finished cup of coffee down the drain, chased it with a squirt of lemon fresh and rinsed it away.

Buttoning his shirt, he wandered over to the window and gazed out at the city.

His condo was on the fifth floor of a ten-storey building off Colfax, a two-bedroom affair with floor-to-ceiling one-way glass for walls. Even with the lights on at night, there was no way to see inside, but from where Brad stood at the sink, he could look past the breakfast bar over an expansive view of downtown Denver.

Against the horizon, a row of Rocky Mountain summits wove in and out of view, knitted between the outlines of a crowded, gleaming skyline. To the south, he could imagine the summit of Pikes Peak in the distance. Turning right towards the north, he could also glimpse the massive slopes of Longs Peak, crown of Rocky Mountain National Park and rough northernmost boundary of the massive mountain chain.

He sighed. Somewhere between the two boundaries and within the urban sprawl before him, the killer was probably waking up as well.

Tragically, so was his next victim.

I see you, but you can't see me. Fitting for an investigator. Fitting for a killer. How many hours, days, had the killer hid behind the darkened glass of his car or van, watching others, potential victims, women who warranted his attention because they fit a certain profile? Beautiful, weak, trusting, innocent.

Who are you watching now? Whose peaceful world of hope will you soon crush?

He turned the water off and quickly scanned the kitchen. Spotless. As was the entire condo. The living room furniture was built around chrome frames with clean lines and black velvet coverings. Glass tables, but not the cheap kind available at any

Rooms to Go. Brad's tastes ran rich. A generous inheritance allowed him the opportunity to satisfy those tastes.

Two large urns sat against the far wall, filled with coloured reeds. Nothing extravagant, but well made, well placed and well kept. It was the way he liked his life. In order, so that he could maintain perspective in a disorganized and chaotic world.

He checked the tap, making sure it was firmly off. Glanced at the Movado watch on his wrist, saw that he had time, and called Nikki's cell. He left a message asking her to meet him at the crime scene at nine, then strode to his bedroom for shoes. A spot of orange cloth caught his attention as he bent for the third pair of black leather loafers.

A woman's top. He recognized it immediately. This was Lauren's orange tankini, left from her visit three weeks ago. How it had found its way behind his hanging slacks and remained there without attracting his attention sooner was a mystery.

He picked up the top, recalling the specifics of that night. He'd known Lauren, a stunning woman who lived on the floor beneath him, for nearly a year. She worked as a fashion consultant at Nordstrom downtown. Light-hearted, carefree and smothered in sensuality. Their relationship was casual, not intimate, and he had no ambition to ruin a strong friendship.

That night, however . . . Things got interesting that night. He had managed to avoid calling her since the following morning.

He checked his watch again. Still plenty of time. He folded the article of clothing, placed it into a manila envelope, and wrote a note to Lauren with a Sharpie. *Let's talk soon.*

Retrieving the soft leather briefcase he'd packed last night, he took the stairs to Lauren's condo, wedged the package under her door, then rode the elevator to the ground floor.

The killer more than likely lived in an apartment or house out of the way, where his comings and goings at odd hours would be undetected. Or was he the kind that turned heads, a Ted Bundy of sorts, adapting to a suburban or city environment where he was greeted warmly by unsuspecting neighbours and clerks?

'Morning, Mr Raines.' Mason, one of half a dozen guards who rotated duty from the counter, nodded.

Brad glanced out at the blue sky. 'Looks like a nice one.'

'That it is. Sure's got Miami beat. But come January you'll be wishing you were back in Florida.'

'You forget I've already lived through winter here.'

'True. Beats Minneapolis.' Mason grinned.

Brad left the parking garage beneath the building and wound his way to Maci's, a breakfast-and-lunch café. He glanced at his watch again: seven twenty-three. In no hurry to battle traffic, he grabbed a paper at the front door and let Becky, the proprietor, seat him at a street window near the back. 'Amanda will be right with you, Brad.'

'Thanks, Becky.'

Amanda approached wearing the same yellow dress and white apron all the waitresses wore, a cute cut that was supposed to convey a faint country motif but looked a little more candy striper on Amanda, twenty-eight and divorced.

'Coffee with Stevia,' she said, setting down a cup and bowl of the sweetener.

'Thanks for remembering.'

'You may be good-looking, sweetie, but that doesn't mean I swoon at first sight like the rest of the ladies you string along.'

She grinned and he laughed to cover his blush. 'I'm not sure whether to take that as a compliment or a slap on the wrist.'

'Uh-huh. I don't see a ring on your finger yet.'

'I guess I'm not one to rush into a relationship.'

'I don't blame you for a second.' Her flirting came from a place of familiarity. The safety she offered him was one reason he was attracted to Maci's Café. But she'd never been quite this flirtatious.

'I'll have your eggs right out. Over easy with two pieces of whole-grain toast, half an orange, peeled. Like clockwork.'

He offered her a smile and thanked her. She strode away, wearing an amused grin. This was home. Although he'd only been in Denver one year, his living habits had returned him to the same restaurants, stores and gas stations so often that he'd become a fixture in their worlds.

If the Bride Collector was psychotic, truly mentally ill, he would have a harder time fitting into normal social contexts. Unless his intelligence compensated for the instability of his mind.

Brad left Maci's at seven forty-four, headed north on the Denver-Boulder Turnpike, and arrived at the scene off of 96th at eight twenty-nine. He parked his BMW next to a patrol car, gathered his briefcase and approached the officer on duty beside a yellow-tape perimeter.

'Morning, Officer.' He flashed his identification. 'Brad Raines, FBI.'

'Morning, sir.'

'All quiet?'

'Since I took over at six. We're a ways out.'

'I want some time. No one comes in but Nikki, okay?'

'You got it.'

He stepped over the yellow tape and walked up to the shed, thinking the sound of his feet on the gravel would have been similar to the sound the killer had heard on his approach. But he'd had Caroline with him. Had she walked willingly? Had he carried her? There were no fibres on her person to indicate she'd been wrapped. No bruises on her wrists to suggest she'd struggled against restraints. Drugged, but enough for such complete compliance?

What do you tell them? How do you win their submission?

The room was as he'd last seen it, minus the body, the rough shape of which was now outlined in chalk.

He scooted the single chair to the table, withdrew several books on mental illness, his laptop, a drill. On the wall next to the outline, he posted eight-by-ten photographs of each victim, placing the image of Caroline where her body had been. Surrounding each photograph, he pinned a dozen more, detailing their angelic forms and drilled feet.

The drill went on the table.

He wrote the Bride Collector's confession on the adjacent wall using a fresh piece of chalk.

The Beauty Eden id Lost
Where intelligence does centered
I came do her and she smashed da Serpent head
I searched and find the seventh and beautiful
She will rest in my Serpent's hole
And I will live again

Brad set the chalk on the table, stepped back, gently pressed his palms together in front of his chin, and stared at his approximation of the Bride Collector's work. The shed, the women, the drill. The confession.

What had crossed through his mind, taking the drill for the first time, pressing the bit against flesh, feeling it hit bone? Like a dentist drilling for his goal.

In this case, blood. He took a deep breath and settled. The roof creaked as it expanded under the sun's heat. He let himself sink into the scene, in no rush to coax truth from what could not yet be seen.

From his own mind.

For a few moments, Brad felt himself become, however faintly, the Bride Collector. Or, at the very least, he felt himself stepping, first one foot, then another foot, into the Bride Collector's shoes.

'I'm psychotic,' he whispered aloud. 'No one knows I'm psychotic – why?'

'Because you appear normal,' Nikki's voice said softly behind him.

She was early.

He spoke without turning. 'Good morning, Nikki.'

'Morning. Sleep well?'

'Not really, no.'

'Me neither.'

He'd wanted to be alone, but he felt comforted by her response.

'I choose beautiful women,' Brad said, staying in the killer's role. 'Tell me why without thinking too much.'

She stepped up beside him. 'Because you're jealous.'

'I kill out of jealousy, why?'

'Because you were made to feel ugly.'

'If killing beautiful women makes me feel better about myself, why don't I abuse the bodies?'

Nikki hesitated. She had been the first to employ this form of rapid response, plumbing the mind for thoughts that sometimes only surfaced in a form of pressured speech.

'You let them have their beauty but take their soul.'

'Why do I take their soul?'

'You need it to make you beautiful on the inside.'

'Why do I drain their blood?'

'Because the blood is their life force. Their soul.'

'No, I take their blood to make them beautiful,' he said.

Another hesitation. Brad felt a trickle of sweat break from his hairline. It was all conjecture at this point. Nikki stepped into the role of interrogator.

'Why do you drill their heels?'

'Because it's the lowest point in the body, largely unseen, so it doesn't spoil their beauty.'

'Why do you need to kill seven beautiful women?'

'Because seven is the number of perfection. The number for God.'

'Do you fear God?'

'Yes.'

'Are you religious?'

'Deeply.'

'Are you a Christian?' she asked.

'Yes.'

'Are you Catholic?'

'No.'

'Protestant?'

'No.'

'Why not?'

'They're all liars. Unable to live the life they suggest others live.'

'But you, on the other hand, live the truth?'

'All of it. That's what makes me special. That's why I kill, to be true to myself.'

'Why seven women?'

'I told you, because seven is a perfect number.'

Cycling back provided a thread of intellectual honesty that mirrored normal interrogation techniques. A simple aid to both of them.

'Okay, let's talk about how you choose your victims. Why—'

'They're not victims.'

'What are they?'

'I'm not hurting them.'

She paused, probably because he hadn't answered her questions.

'Why is Eden lost?' she asked.

'The *beauty* of Eden is lost. Innocence was corrupted.'

'Where is intelligence centred?'

'In the mind. Innocence was lost in the mind.'

'Are you the serpent?'

'No.'

'Who smashed the serpent's head?'

'She did.' Brad nodded at the wall of crime scene photographs.

'She hurt you?'

'Yes.'

'But you're not the serpent. Are you the serpent?'

'No. Not always.'

'Why do you kill her?'

'So that I can kill again.'

Only that's not what Brad meant to say. He lifted his hand, considering the response.

'*Kill* again, or *live* again?' Nikki asked. '*She will rest in my Serpent's hole And I will live again.* His poem seems to indicate that he's doing this so that he can live again.'

'I meant to say *live again.*'

They both stared at the confession posted on the wall.

'But if he's playing the role of the serpent in this self-fulfilling tale of his, it does stand to reason that he kills so that he can live *as the serpent* and kill again,' Nikki said.

'It does.'

She looked at him. 'So, then, Temple could be right. We're looking for a delusional schizophrenic who's suffered a psychotic break.' She swept a long strand of dark hair from her cheek and absently touched her neck where it met her jaw. Long, delicate fingers, French manicure.

He had always found Nikki's attention to seemingly insignificant detail appealing. She lived her life with passion; truth be told, with far more energy than he could usually muster. Running an hour every day to bring stability, she said. Putting in long, twelve-hour days. She also seemed to have energy left over to keep up an active nightlife, if all the stories were true, and he had no reason to think they weren't.

Their relationship had always remained purely platonic. There were times when Brad regretted his avoidance.

'Maybe,' Brad said. 'We established last night that he was probably psychotic.'

'*You* might have, but I'm not convinced. A mentally ill serial killer is atypical, short of mental illness caused by severe trauma to the frontal lobe through a head injury. Otherwise, nearly all pattern killers are middle- to high-income earners, are good looking in general and usually articulate. Nearly all kill out of either a sexual compulsion or a need for revenge. In both cases, most have been severely abused by their mothers and are reacting to that abuse through some ritualistic act, which relieves their compulsion for gratification or revenge. Environment, not psychosis, forms most serial killers. This is not the profile of the mentally ill.'

He knew all of this, naturally, but investigative work was an exercise in rehearsing details, coaxing new truth from them.

'And yet the note indicates delusions of grandeur, which is a form of psychosis.'

'Yes,' she said.

He looked at the drill, pacing. 'His killing doesn't appear to be sexually motivated. It's ritualistic. He's courting delusions of grandeur. He's intelligent. He's killing so that he can kill again, because, in his mind, unless he carries out his role, he can no longer play that role and live.'

'Right,' she said. 'And whatever that role is, it's not the role of executioner or punisher. He thinks he's serving his victims well. He's loving them.'

They stood in silence for a full minute.

'So. We take an exhaustive look at the mental health facilities in the Four Corners state hospitals,' Nikki said. 'Residential care facilities, nursing homes, state prisons, convictions involving the mentally ill . . . That's a ton of data.'

'Frank's got six agents buried in the data already. We've put in a request for additional assistance from the field offices in Cheyenne, Colorado Springs and Albuquerque. I've asked him to cross-reference the confession with all related databases. He left the note because he wants us to find something.'

'Agreed.'

He put his hands on his hips and studied the walls. 'Meanwhile, we have the mysteries hidden here, in his place of work.'

Nikki nodded. 'You ever get tired of it?'

'Field work?'

'Trying to see past what a person allows you to see.'

An odd choice of words. 'Can't say that I do.'

'I mean, think about it, we all have our mysteries, right? We live our lives letting people see only what we want them to see. It takes years, even in a marriage, to know someone. Not that you'd know that, Brad.'

She'd said the last part with a good-natured smirk.

'Even then,' she continued, 'how many spouses are eventually blindsided by some deep, dark revelation about the person they thought they knew?'

'No argument here,' he said, hoping he'd avoided the whole morass. 'Everyone hides something.'

She nodded. 'Classic existentialism. In the end the human being is alone. We are all confronted by our own complexity, which we try to unravel, but all the while we're confronted by our own isolation. This is what we eventually learn. It's why so many lean on faith, a relationship that isn't dependent on another human being.' She crossed her arms and studied him. 'So how about it, Brad? What mysteries are you hiding?'

At first he wasn't sure he'd heard her right. They'd always been candid with each other, but never probing. He wasn't quite sure how he felt about it.

'I don't mean to pry,' she said. 'Not too deep, anyway.'

A smile softened her face, and looking into her soft blue eyes, he suddenly wanted to tell her everything. About how he'd fallen in love with a young tennis player named Ruby while attending UT in Austin in the wild carefree days when the world was at both of their fingertips and everyone who saw them together knew it. About the way her eyes twinkled and her laugh echoed on the tennis court, about how completely he'd given himself to Ruby.

About her suicide.

The thought of it brought a familiar lump to his throat. It had taken Brad three years to uncover the secrets that had led to Ruby's decision to take her life.

'Think about it, Brad. The killer's playing us. Probing us. Tempting us, egging us on, daring us to stop him. My job is to take his challenge and beat him at his own game. Uncover his true self. So how do you get someone to reveal their secrets?'

She was talking about the killer, but as much about Brad.

He motioned at the wall with a nod. 'They do what they do out of pain, and a small part of me can understand that. Not the way they react to it, of course, but the pain itself. Let's just say I've loved and I've felt the pain of a terrible loss. A woman I once knew. It's why I can identify.'

He stopped, not knowing where he was heading. Suddenly uncomfortable.

After a pause, Nikki stepped up to him and touched his shoulder in a show of empathy. But she seemed awkward, and he felt the same. She removed her hand and faced the wall.

'You've never mentioned that before. I never knew.'

'I know. We were talking about long-harboured secrets, remember?'

She nodded. A long pause flowed between them, one Brad made no effort to end.

'I'm sorry you had to go through that,' she finally said.

'It's okay. We all do at some point.'

But he wasn't sure about that. The pain he'd felt had left him wishing for death. In a way, he was waging his own personal campaign against death even now. It was why he'd joined the FBI, now that he thought about it.

'But you're right,' he said, resuming an earlier thread, 'part of understanding someone else comes from exposing yourself.'

She looked at him, then grinned at his choice of words.

'So to speak . . .' *There*, he thought with a surge of relief. Back on familiar ground – the tinged banter. Their usual territory.

His cell rang and he picked it up, thankful for the interruption.

It was Frank. The staff had registered an interesting hit while cross-referencing the killer's note with the mental health facilities database.

'You ever hear of a place called the Center for Wellness and Intelligence?'

'No, I don't think so. Hold on.' Brad asked Nikki if she'd heard of the facility. She stared upward for a moment, then shook her head.

'It's a private residential facility in the hills south of Boulder that only takes mentally ill patients with high IQs,' Frank said. 'As far as we can gather.'

Brad glanced at the wall. The confession. A single line expanded in his field of view. Where intelligence does centered. The *Center* for Wellness and *Intelligence*. Nikki followed his eyes and saw what he saw.

'The program picked up on the words *center*—'

'I got it, Frank. Text me the address and advise the administrator that we're on our way.'

'Yes, sir.'

He snapped the phone shut.

'You think it's something?'

'It's a lead,' he said. 'He's playing us, right? So let's play.'

CHAPTER FIVE

According to Colorado's Department of Mental Health, the state's organization had certified and currently regulated fifty-three facilities that cared for the mentally ill, ranging from state hospitals to residential care facilities and nursing homes.

The Center for Wellness and Intelligence was listed as a referral facility, privately run and uncertified.

State by state closure of state asylums and hospitals between 1960 and 1990 had flooded the streets with mentally ill patients who had no provider to take up their care or cause. Many, as much as half, by some estimates, wound up incarcerated.

Over time, a range of facilities began to take up the slack, but no national care system had yet replaced the atrociously run asylums that once blanketed the country. There was more to the story, though. Much more, according to what Brad had learned while in Miami. Some said that mistreatment of the mentally ill was one of the country's few remaining dark secrets. No one wanted to lock them up in expensive institutions. Yet no one knew how to treat them effectively through any other means. Better to sweep them all under a rug, otherwise known as the streets and alleyways of the modern city.

They left Nikki's car at the crime scene and headed east towards Eldorado Springs. The small town was nestled at the base of the Rocky Mountains, roughly six miles southwest of Boulder.

Eldorado Springs Drive wound through the foothills, populated by scrub oak and smaller pines. 'Never been out here,' Nikki said.

'I haven't either.'

The wheels hummed on two-lane blacktop.

'Beautiful,' she said.

'Peaceful.'

'Hmmm.'

Mental illness. Brad mulled over the words. The mystery of the mind, hidden in the folds of hills beyond the tangles of life in the city. Nothing of the placid landscape spoke to him of the killer. Less than half an hour before, they'd stood before a wall on which a madman had glued a woman whose heels he'd drilled and drained. Now they rode through God's country. The incongruity of the two images brought a faint buzz to Brad's mind.

While Brad drove, Nikki glanced at the notebook where she'd jotted down notes from a conversation she'd had with the director of CWI, Allison Johnson.

'Something strange about her.'

'The director?'

Nikki stared ahead. 'There's our road. Before the village,' she said. 'South on a dirt road two miles.'

Brad slowed, turned, and headed the BMW down a winding gravel road. 'Isolated.'

'I think that's the idea. It's a privately run facility for families or patients who can afford a hefty room and board fee. Used to be a convent run by nuns. There's a place like this in Colorado Springs, something about the healthy air that once attracted caregivers and patients.'

'It's religious?'

'Actually, I'm not sure. Wouldn't surprise me; health care administered by the Catholic church has a strong history.'

'You said she was strange.'

Nikki nodded. 'Maybe *strange* is the wrong word. Don't get me wrong, she was delighted to have us. She just sounded rather eccentric.'

'Maybe she has a little of what they have,' Brad said, then added, so that he didn't sound demeaning, 'Maybe we all do?'

'She said they only accept patients who display exceptional intelligence.'

Brad wasn't sure what to make of that.

They rounded a bend and saw the large gated entrance immediately. A white sign above the heavy metal gates left no doubt: *The Center for Wellness and Intelligence.* And under it a motto of sorts: *Life Never Shortchanges.*

A high fence ran in both directions away from the gate; the kind of fence that brought images of concentration camps to mind, complete with barbed wire and charged lines. Beyond lay a long paved driveway bordered by manicured lawns and tall pine trees. Brad chuckled appreciatively. The Center for Wellness and Intelligence might be mistaken for an upscale resort.

He rolled up to the guardhouse and presented his identification. 'Brad Raines and Nikki Holden here to see Allison Johnson.'

The uniformed man, with a badge that said he was 'Bob', nodded and checked his log sheet.

Brad indicated the barbed wire. 'Nice fence.'

'It's not as threatening as it looks.' The guard handed the IDs back. 'They installed the barbed wire and monitors last year after someone broke in and raped two of the residents.' He hit a switch and the gates rolled back. 'Head up the driveway, visitor parking to the left. You'll find Allison in the reception room.'

'Thank you, Bob.'

'No problem.' He sat down and picked up his phone, probably to report their arrival. A Brad Meltzer novel lay open at his fingertips. Plenty of time to read out here.

They rolled past the trees towards a circular driveway that rounded a white stone fountain. To their right, a woman wearing a yellow flowered dress and a large sun hat was trimming bushes that had been sculpted into perfectly formed poodles, a larger one trailed by three smaller puppies. She waved as they passed, then stopped to watch them.

'Nice,' Brad said.

'Very nice,' Nikki replied.

'Is she . . .'

'Clearly.'

He pulled into a parking spot reserved for visitors and stepped out into clean, cool mountain air. Birds chirped above them.

Shadowed by a cheerful sun, mountain ramparts towered against the near distance. A loud, distant voice carried to them from deeper inside the compound. With a glance back, Brad met the eyes of the woman in yellow, who was still staring at him with fixed interest.

She must have mistaken his glance as an invitation, because the moment she saw his look, she started to walk towards them. Nikki stood from her side and the woman pulled up, looking from one to the other. Cheerful and harmless looking, the woman was maybe in her sixties, with grey hair and bright eyes.

Her eyes settled on Brad. 'You are very wonderfully built. I could do you, right here in the bushes. Would you pose for me? You like my poodles? I started on them this morning, because Sami said he hated dogs. I love dogs and I love pigeons, but it takes twenty-seven pigeons to fill one poodle. Poodles aren't like rats, because rats breed quickly and eat crackers. My favourite crackers are sodium-free.'

She said it all with a warm smile.

'Thank you, Flower.' Another grey-haired woman, probably in her early fifties, had appeared from the administration building. She possessed the lean, compact features of so many foothills residents. Piercing green eyes, with slim wrists sporting a dozen silver bangles and bracelets of the most intricate design. She was dressed in jeans and a white blouse. Three silver chains, one supporting a rhinestone-studded cross, hung from her neck. She looked like someone who fully intended to take what life owed her, but she managed to pull it off without appearing gaudy.

'I think this kind gentleman would look wonderful on our front lawn. What a nice offer.' She looked at Brad with knowing light blue eyes and winked. 'What do you say, Mr Raines? It would only take her half an hour; she's quite skilled.'

He was caught flat-footed. This must be Allison Johnson. Was she serious?

'No?' she asked. 'We're in a bit of a rush, are we?'

'Actually, yes, we are a bit pressed for time.'

The director addressed Flower, who stared motionless,

awaiting a verdict. 'I'm sorry, Flower, he's in a hurry. Can you do him from memory?'

A grin flashed on Flower's face and she spun away without another word. She marched towards the hedges, stopped after ten paces and measured him up using her hands to approximate his height and dimensions, then continued in a brisk stride.

'Welcome to CWI,' Allison said. 'Please come with me.'

Allison Johnson struck Brad as the kind of woman who'd seen it all and remained both uncompromised and unflappable, a wise woman who wore her experience with beauty and grace. He found himself immediately drawn in with an ease that unnerved him a little.

She led them into what looked more like a living room than a reception area. Two high-back chairs in plaid and a gold sofa surrounded an oval coffee table made of wood. An unlit fireplace beneath a large painting of a seaside Mediterranean village filled the brick wall adjacent to the couch. Large windows looked out to the inner courtyard, and, beyond that, to a large lawn with another fountain, several wrought-iron benches and two sprawling maples. A few residents loitered about the grounds, some dressed in jeans, others in slacks, one in what appeared to be nightclothes or a smock.

Allison faced them. 'Would you like to sit inside, or would you rather wander the grounds with me?'

'Well . . .' Brad still felt oddly off balance.

'They won't bite, Special Agent Raines. My children are rarely violent.'

'Rarely?'

'Well, come on – we all like to throw a tantrum now and then.'

Brad nodded at the lawn. 'After you, then.'

'A good choice.' She turned and walked through a glass door. 'We are very proud of our home.' A light breeze rustled through the massive maples' leaves above them. The setting was entirely serene. Calming.

'So, Mr Raines, tell me how I can help you.'

'This is Nikki—'

'A forensic psychologist who works with you. Yes, she told me. I suspect she knows more than most about what goes on here.' She paused. 'You're looking for a killer?'

He felt an oddly unsettling sensation. Being stared at. He glanced around and saw that, indeed, all eyes from the residents standing or sitting about the grounds were now fixed on them. It struck Brad that he and Nikki were the spectacle in the zoo at the moment, not the other way around. To the residents' way of thinking, *he* was the intrusion into a perfectly normal world.

'Yes. A pattern killer we've dubbed the Bride Collector. He's taken four women in the last month. We have reason to believe he intends to take three more. Our team cross-referenced a note he left with mental health care providers in the state and found a connection to your facility.'

'Residence,' she said. 'And please don't use the terms *patient* or *mentally ill* around them. It doesn't sit well with them.' She smiled and winked. 'May I see it?'

'See what?'

'The note.'

Brad caught Nikki's inquisitive eye. She seemed fascinated. Perhaps amused. He withdrew a copy from his pocket and handed it to the director. She read it as she strolled, then handed it back. Her smile softened, but he noted that her eyes had brightened.

'How does he kill them?' she asked.

'We haven't shared any of this with—'

'Mum's the word, FBI.'

'Alright. It seems that he takes women he considers beautiful, fixes them up to appear without blemish, and then drills into their heels. He glues them to the wall and lets them bleed to death.'

'Dear me. That's a ghastly image, isn't it? The note would suggest classic schizophrenia. What makes you think he's highly intelligent?'

Nikki responded. 'Despite apparent delusions of grandeur indicated by his note, he's clearly capable of avoiding the typical mistakes in cases like this. If not for the note, we wouldn't at first focus on anyone with a history of mental illness. As you probably know, most pattern killers aren't mentally ill.'

'Then, apart from his use of the words *center* and *intelligence*, you have no reason to suspect any connection to the Center,' Allison said. She pointed to a round building across the lawn. 'That's our hub. Games room, gathering room, television, the cafeteria, it's all centrally located. On either side are two wings, one reserved for men, one for women. We run a structured schedule and environment to help our residents avoid any confusion. Our primary objective is to facilitate their reintegration by helping them learn to live *with* their gifts and challenges. The world's a hostile environment. We hope to give them the skills they need to navigate it using all the brilliance God has gifted them with.'

'Gifted?' Nikki said. 'Forgive my boldness, but isn't that just a little naïve? Most of humanity sees mental illness as a curse.'

'Exactly. That's the whole point, now, isn't it? We cater to no more than thirty-six residents at any given time, and we are very careful about who joins us. No criminal records. They or their loved ones must be able to afford our room and board as well as the nurturing and medical care we give them. They must exhibit a high level of intelligence, indicated by a string of basic tests we administer ourselves. Currently, over half have tested with IQs that classify them as geniuses. Most are extraordinarily creative. To the world, they are crazy. In our minds, they are truly gifted individuals. Wouldn't you agree?'

Nikki raised her brow. 'Put like that . . . I see your point. Why only the intelligent?'

'Ah, why? Yes, of course, why.'

Allison stepped off the walkway and headed towards the trunk of the large maple, nodding at a young man who stared at them from a park bench. His plaid shirt was buttoned all the way up. 'Hello, Sam. How are you this morning?'

'Two hundred seventy-three thousand,' he said. 'Plus or minus three hundred.'

'Wonderful.'

'Fewer leaves today. The wind. Yes, good, I'm good, Allison Johnson.'

Allison sighed. 'Not that I didn't wish we could take them all. Those considered mentally ill have been treated like refuse for far too long. First incarcerated in asylums, then in prisons. Reduced to shells of humanity through Thorazine in the fifties, now refused medication and left to fend for themselves until they prove a danger to others. In which case, they're thrown behind bars. They say at least one third of all people in prison today are so-called mentally ill. I'm not talking about early onset disorders like autism or retardation. Strictly psychosis, which presents itself later. It's quite widespread. Do you know what percentage of the world's population suffers from some form of schizophrenia?'

'Nearly one out of a hundred,' Nikki said.

'Point seven percent, to be precise. In our country, nearly three million people suffer from chronic mental illness of some kind. In Colorado alone, we estimate seventy thousand untreated cases at any given time. Caring for the mentally ill is far too expensive and, in the opinion of most, the illness is untreatable anyway. You can load them up with dopamine suppressors and send them away in fog, but you can't treat the illness. It's like blinding the person who sees too much, or putting the person with a broken leg to sleep so they don't stumble and fall. To date, only the mind itself can treat the mind. And that, FBI, is where we come in.'

'Their intelligence offsets their illness,' Nikki offered.

'Close, but not quite. Take Flower, whom you met earlier. She has been diagnosed with schizoaffective disorder – both bipolar and psychotic, a thought disorder that sometimes presents in the flight of ideas you heard. Sometimes amusing, always fascinating. If Flower had typical intelligence, her gifting, as we like to call it, would make life very difficult for her. Without drugs and a caring family she might end up on the street, homeless like so many others in similar straits. But she is extremely intelligent and her mind has the capacity to deal with her unusual skills. We coach her, help her deal with her gifting so that she not only copes, but can share her gift with the world.'

'Sculpting hedges.'

'Oh, that's the least of Flower's many talents. Many of the world's greatest contributors find themselves in this group. John Nash, the schizophrenic professor from the movie *A Beautiful Mind,* is well known. But many have had mental illnesses. Abraham Lincoln, Virginia Woolf, Beethoven, Leo Tolstoy, Isaac Newton, Ernest Hemingway, Charles Dickens . . . you get the idea. At the Center for Wellness and Intelligence, we provide an environment that allows the John Nashes of the world to be themselves. Acceptance, facilitation and very carefully regulated medication on a case-by-case basis.'

Brad took another appraising glance about him. The whole thing seemed too good to be true.

'I understand this used to be a convent,' Nikki said. 'Are you still religious?'

'Religious? We do receive some supplemental funding from the Catholic church, if that's what you mean. But we're not officially tied to any organization. The Center is privately owned and run. The brainchild of Morton Anderson, a wealthy businessman. His son, Ethan, was thrown in prison at age twenty-one after a psychotic break compelled him to enter a home of a congressman and dress up in his wife's clothes. They found him eating a candlelight dinner by himself, dressed as a woman. Before the episode, he was preparing to graduate summa cum laude from the University of Colorado. As they say, there is a fine line between insanity and genius.'

'And you're suggesting that in some cases, no line,' Brad said.

'Of course. Unfortunately, the world has taken some of the greatest minds God has given us and locked them up in cages. Most very brilliant or creative people seem strange to ordinary people. Geniuses are almost always outcasts. The intelligent are bullied in the playground. They see the world differently and are shunned for it. They nearly all turn out to be lonely at the least, locked up at the worst. It's human nature to encourage the status quo and shun those who see life differently.'

Allison sat on a bench and folded her hands in her lap. 'That being said, several of our staff, including myself, were once nuns. So, back to your killer. How can I be of assistance?'

Brad eased down beside her, leaving Nikki to study the residents, who'd become bored with them and resumed their prior activities. A man in a blue striped bathrobe was playing some sort of Hop Scotch game, enunciating each hop with a 'Hup'. Hop. 'Hup.' Hop. 'Hup.'

The man stopped and pointed at the sky. 'And that's what I'm saying, you bunkered, commonwealth moron! I know when the sky is falling and I know how high I can jump!' Then a hop and a 'Hup'. This was the man they'd heard from the parking lot.

'Assuming we're dealing with an intelligent serial killer who is mentally ill,' Brad said, 'and considering his choice of wording, we need to look at the possibility that he is somehow connected to the Center.'

'You're looking for a resident who may have left us and gone off to commit these brutal acts.'

'Something like that.'

'A psychotic male who suffers from delusions of grandeur. Someone with a propensity for violence, is that it?'

'Yes.'

Allison frowned, thinking. Brad noticed that, even with a frown, she seemed to be smiling. 'Hundreds have come and gone in our seven years here. Most residents leave within six months. Some have stayed longer. A handful have been here since the beginning. I can think of only seven or eight who ever showed any violent tendencies.'

'What about those who might have demonstrated a tendency for regression?' Nikki said.

'Well, that's just it. Follow-up is voluntary, naturally, and the illness can grow over time. It's difficult to predict without . . .'

She blinked and faced Brad, eyes bright.

'Detective work, huh? I think you might like to meet Roudy.'

'I'm sorry. Roudy?'

Allison stood, delighted by her own idea. 'Of course! Roudy is one of our residents. He is quite the detective. And he's been here since the beginning. He remembers everything about every resident who's entered our gates.'

Nikki caught his eye and nodded. 'Okay. Sounds promising.'

Brad wasn't sure just *how* promising, for Allison seemed more fascinated with subjects in her field of study than in cracking the case. But he could see no harm in the notion.

'Or even better, Paradise,' Allison said, now fully engaged in the notion.

'Paradise?'

'Paradise. If you're fortunate, she might even talk to you. Now there's a special one, my friends. She can see what many can't.' Allison started for the round community building between both wings, glancing back as she walked. 'You're going to love them, I can promise you that. But don't say I didn't warn you.'

CHAPTER SIX

The hub, as Allison had referred to the central gathering place, was an atrium with couches, stuffed chairs, snack machines, floral paintings on the wall and two flat plasma televisions glowing manically on opposite walls. Round tables with wooden chairs sat in groupings about the large room. A central gas fireplace that, according to Allison, never really got hot, and two snack stands completed the area.

At one end, a sign over an arched door indicated that a cafeteria lay beyond. A wide hallway ran into the other end of the building. Out back in the sunlight, a gleaming fishpond was sealed off for the residents' safety.

A dozen residents hung around the main room at the round tables, near the televisions (which were both playing *I Love Lucy* reruns), and at a long snack bar. Half turned and stared at Brad and Nikki as they entered. The rest were too engrossed to pay attention.

'People, say hello to our guests,' Allison called out.

As one, clearly rehearsed, they all spoke in unison. 'Hello, guests.'

A black man larger than most football players looked up from where he sat hunched over a chess match at one of the round tables. 'Hello, guests.' His voice rumbled like a base guitar. Several snickered.

'Way to go, Goliath,' a thin man called out from the group collected around the television. 'Way to greet the guests three and a half seconds after they wanted to be greeted.'

'That'll do, Nick,' Allison said. 'You don't think Goliath is stupid, do you?'

'I didn't say he was stupid.'

'You looking for a rematch?'

Silence.

'He's not so bad himself,' Goliath said. He faced Nick and broke out into a wide grin. 'But I got you right, Nick. You was the best and I beat you ten straight games.'

A woman howled with laughter at the television, provoking Nick to whirl around to see what he'd missed. Goliath hunched back over his chess game; moved a pawn.

'Anyone see Roudy or Paradise?' Allison asked.

'Roudy is in his office,' someone said.

Allison led them across the room towards the hallway. An older woman, whose dark hair looked as if it doubled for a rat's nest at night, followed Brad with her eyes.

Brad searched within himself and finally realized what about the place unnerved him the most. Somehow, the Center's oddity didn't arise from the residents' strangeness, but from the lack of it. Each person's behaviour plucked at a well-worn string in his own mind and resonated in countless familiar strains. He could call them childish or loud or quirky or obnoxious or a hundred other things, but these were all tendencies he recognized in himself.

'He's good?' Brad asked.

'Goliath? World class. He plays chess ten hours a day on a slow day. Our challenge is helping him apply his skill to other pursuits.'

'And how's that going?'

She chuckled. 'He's been communicating with a lab doing cancer research. Turns out some parts of medicine aren't unlike a chess game. Go figure.'

'Where are all the staff?' Nikki asked.

'Everywhere. They fit in. Here we are.'

They entered a small classroom with a white board and ten desks. A couch sat beneath a window that looked out to the fountain on the lawn. Three people sat in the room: a middle-aged man lounging on the couch, dressed in a black silk bathrobe and fluffy white slippers; a young blonde woman, hardly twenty, pacing by the white board and picking her nails; and a goateed man dressed in corduroy pants and a bow tie, sitting back against the teacher's desk.

The three clearly had not expected to be interrupted. For a moment, the trio stared at Allison and her two guests as though they were spotting aliens who'd landed the mother ship. The two men slowly straightened. The girl grinned.

'Hello, friends,' Allison said. 'I'd like you to meet our guests.'

'Hello, guests.'

'Any concern of ours?' The one with the goatee stroked his beard.

'Why, yes, Roudy. They would like to speak to you.'

'They would? But of course they would. Did you hear that, Cass? They've come to speak to me.'

Cass, the man in the silk bathrobe, stood and smoothed his robe, eyes on Nikki. 'She's more interested in what I have to say.' He stepped forwards, eyeing Nikki with a raised brow and crooked grin.

'This isn't about you, Cass,' Roudy chided. 'Step back, man. Show some respect. About what? Speak to me about what? Are you saying this fine gentleman and woman are with the Federal Bureau of Investigation?'

The girl by the white board giggled, then lifted a hand to her mouth to cover the sound. 'I'm Andrea,' she said sweetly.

'We call her Brains,' Roudy said. 'But I don't suppose that plays any factor in your judgment, now does it? You've come to speak to me and I will decide if you interest me enough to offer my assistance.'

'What's the matter, Sherlock?' Allison asked, entering their flow of speech as if it were wholly to her liking. 'You no longer trust me? I wouldn't have brought them if I didn't think they would interest you.'

'True. I do trust you, Madam. And they do interest me.' He toyed with his bow tie. 'It was merely a figure of speech, a delaying tactic to put them on guard while I sought to ascertain whether my deduction was correct. So, was it?'

Brad found it difficult to suppress a grin, but he managed. 'How did you know?'

'Aha!' Roudy snapped his fingers. 'I knew it! The FBI has come calling yet again. And how could I not guess? You come every day, begging for my opinion. Are we British really so clever? Is there something missing from the American mind that compels you to look across the pond?'

The man in the silk robe was interested only in Nikki, and he'd approached her while Roudy said his piece. He now took her hand, lifted it while his eyes remained fixed on hers, and kissed it.

'My name is Enrique Bartholomew. They call me Casanova. Have you heard of Casanova?'

'Cass is a ladies' man,' Andrea said, in a voice dripping with irony. She was jittery, twisting slightly like a valley girl who needed to use the bathroom. Brains, they called her. A savante?

Still holding Nikki's hand, Enrique faced Andrea. 'Please, Brains, don't pretend I haven't made you the woman you are.' He turned back to Nikki with an even more lascivious glance. 'You are very lovely.'

A beat of silence.

Brad smiled and inwardly gave Nikki her due; she knew how to stare down an impertinent speaker, or an awkward pause, when the occasion warranted.

'They came to speak to me, Enrique,' Roudy snapped.

'And I'm the one who told you that if you dressed the part they would believe you. Now look who's come to dinner.'

He touched his lips to Nikki's hand again, then stepped back and winked at her. Brad was surprised that she didn't object. Her fear of germs couldn't compete with her interest in a new subject.

'Look who's come to dinner?' Roudy said, disgusted. 'They come every week, you idiot.'

'They call me Brains,' Andrea said, in her own world, eyes still on Brad, still playing the part of a shy girl. 'I think I need a shower.'

The exchange had all come in a flurry of words. Then it seemed they ran out of steam.

'First our questions,' Brad said, holding up his hand. 'Fair enough?'

Andrea's eyes darted over his shoulder. Brad glanced back, provoked as much by the sense of an incoming presence as the other woman's look.

A young, slight woman who looked to be in her mid-twenties stood in the doorway. Her stringy brown hair, parted down the middle, framed petite features – a small nose and delicate, pouting lips and light brown eyes that sparkled with life.

Brad glanced down her body. She was short, hardly taller than five feet, dressed in a well-worn blue T-shirt with a Nike logo on her chest. The hem on her jeans hung an inch too short above old white canvas tennis shoes.

She stood with both arms by her sides, unflappable but light, as if a strong gust would blow her away. The skin on her arms was pale and he couldn't see her fingernails, but her bare thumbnails were chewed short. Unlike Andrea, she wore no makeup at all, not even a dab to cover the few red spots of acne on her forehead.

The newcomer's probing eyes seemed to peer through Brad. Her expression was flat, as if she was undecided about whether she approved of their presence.

'That's Paradise,' Roudy said.

'Does this mean we have to split the fee four ways?' Andrea asked, with a perturbed expression. 'That's only eight point three cents per second.'

'We're going to help the FBI crack a case,' Roudy said. 'And Paradise is good with dead people.'

Brad wasn't sure if it was Allison's earlier comments about Paradise or the way the young woman looked at him now that piqued his pulse, but he found he couldn't remove his eyes from hers. Paradise.

She broke off her stare, walked around to Andrea's side and faced Brad again, eyes still undecided.

Once more, Brad couldn't help but think he'd fallen down the rabbit hole and landed in Alice's Wonderland. The director's assurance that these were all highly intelligent individuals had twisted his thinking. Hearing this bizarre exchange, anyone on the street might think these four had misplaced their minds.

And so they had, he reminded himself, with a now-fraying sense of certainty. The classic symptoms of schizophrenia were all here: the paranoia, the hearing and seeing things that did not exist, the voices and threats. The compulsion to shower expressed by Andrea, the delusions of grandeur demonstrated by both Roudy and Casanova.

'I don't think Allison would mind one more joining us,' Nikki said. 'Thanks for coming, Paradise. That's a beautiful name. Please call me Nikki.'

She didn't respond.

It was immediately apparent to Brad that this homely counterpart to Andrea might be comfortable in her own skin but uneasy with anyone else's assessment of her. Despite her calm, vulnerability seemed to glimmer off the young woman in waves, like heat rising from a desert road.

He nodded at her. 'Hello, Paradise.' Then to them all: 'Let's start over, okay? Tell us who you are. What your . . . gifts are.'

'Oh that, oh that!' Roudy blurted. 'You want to know what makes us all bonkers, is that it?'

'No,' Nikki corrected, stepping forwards. She looked completely at ease in their environment. 'We know that you're each highly intelligent. And that each of you has rare gifts. Or was the director wrong about that?'

They all stared, as if judging how serious she was. Evidently deciding that she was, all but Paradise spoke at once.

Nikki smiled and crossed her arms. 'Let's start with you, Roudy.'

'Of course.' He glanced at the new girl. 'The director put me in charge, Paradise.' She said nothing, so he ploughed ahead.

'I stand five foot eleven inches, am forty years old and have been stationed here, at this secret installation, for seven years. Some would call me choleric in personality, and it's true that I am a natural leader, but my primary skills are those of perception and deduction. Most common cases, the kind the FBI regularly seeks

my advice on, are easily decoded using an algorithm that assists
me in isolating key evidence. I'm involved in several longer-term
operations, which I'm not at liberty to discuss.'

He paused, adjusting his bow tie. His trousers hung an inch
too high, revealing black leather shoes with one shoelace missing.
As part of his delusion of grandeur, he'd evidently chosen Sherlock
Holmes as his fashion influence. Still, he didn't strike Brad as
the kind who would wander around with a magnifying glass and
a pipe.

'Thank you, Roudy.' Nikki glanced at Casanova, who spoke
with no further encouragement.

'My name is Enrique Bartholomew, thirty-two—'

'Eight,' Roudy interrupted.

Without a break, he continued: 'Or thirty-eight, I forget. They
say I'm schizophrenic, but I tell the ladies that all fighters and
lovers are schizophrenic. Allison tells me that not all women can
appreciate' – he used large hands to draw out his full meaning
– 'an experienced, fearless lover. But I think she's wrong. Don't
you, Nikki?' A coy smile.

Brad wondered how many women had slapped Casanova over
the years.

'I don't know, Enrique. But the man I'm interested in is both
strong and gentle.'

'Cass tried to date the president's wife when she was visiting
Denver,' Andrea said, with a sly grin. 'They put him in jail.'

Enrique only smiled back at her. 'She wasn't too bright,' he
said. 'Hardly a woman at all. I can't recall what I saw in her. Are
you busy this evening?'

'I am. But thank you for asking. What about you, Andrea?'

'Nineteen. I've been here a year. Manic depressive. Bipolar.
OCD. Prodigious savante, but that part's wrong.'

'Nonsense,' Roudy said. 'She's the brightest of the batch. Just
because you pay attention to your body doesn't make you their
idiot.'

Andrea grinned apologetically. She wiggled her manicured
nails, polished in green. 'I like to . . . take care of myself.'

'You like taking showers.'

'Sometimes.'

'How many times?'

'Today?'

'Sure,' Nikki said.

'Two.'

It was ten o'clock in the morning.

'You do your nails and hair each time?'

'Yes.'

'She's clean and she's smart as a whip,' Roudy said. 'Smartest informant I've ever come across.'

Brad looked at Paradise, who seemed content to let them speak without offering an opinion. 'How about you, Paradise?'

She glanced at the others, then eyed Brad. He couldn't tell if she felt awkward or put off. 'Um . . . What's happening?'

'I'm sorry, I'm Brad Raines, with the FBI. This is Nikki Holden, a forensic psychologist. We're here to see if you can help us uncover information about a killer called the Bride Collector.'

'I've never heard of a killer named the Bride Collector,' she said. 'I don't know anyone by that name.'

'That's the name we've given him.'

'More details,' Roudy said, pacing again. 'I need to know all that you know if I'm to help you. Shoe size?'

Brad decided to run with him. 'Eleven.'

'Uh-huh. Estimated weight based on impressions?'

'One ninety, two hundred.'

'Secretor?'

'No. No bodily fluids found at any of the scenes. No hair, no skin cells, no prints, nothing.'

'You have the file on you?' He held out his hand.

'No.'

'Paradise didn't tell you about herself,' Andrea inserted.

'No file? How do you expect me to be of any use?' Roudy demanded.

'What does he do to the women?' Enrique asked.

Brad glanced between them. 'He kills them. He makes them

up to look beautiful, and then he kills them and leaves their bodies glued to the wall.'

Silence engulfed them.

Andrea's face twisted up and she started to cry into her hand. 'Sorry. Sorry, sorry.'

'It's disturbing, I know. Have any of you known any resident, present or past, who might fit this profile? Roudy, the director told us you remember everyone who's come through here.'

'I think I should take a shower,' Andrea said. 'My skin is itching, you know. Size eleven, he's six foot one. Big hands, could break their necks pretty easy. We don't allow anyone like that here. He uses makeup on them?'

Brad hesitated. 'Yes.'

Andrea started to cry again, this time accompanied by a gentle pawing at the makeup on her face.

'It's okay, Dre,' Paradise said, speaking for the first time. Her voice was light and sweet, but sure and authoritative. 'We're safe here. This is home. We have guards and Miss Allison. And Roudy and Enrique would never let anything happen to us, would you?'

'Never,' Roudy said. Enrique frowned.

Andrea stepped over to Paradise and offered the girl her hand. Paradise took it and rubbed her shoulder. 'Don't let them scare you. Pretend it's just a story.'

'Paradise writes novels,' Roudy said. 'But I have to say, I honestly can't recall any resident whom I would judge as matching your description – assuming you mean a person who demonstrated a tendency towards this kind of violence. However, if you could get me the file, I could almost certainly shed some light on the case for you.'

'You're sure you're busy tonight?' Enrique asked. He was looking at Nikki.

'I am. But thanks again.' She smiled.

Brad took a deep breath, suddenly afflicted with an overpowering sensation of time's passage. A serial killer was inexorably cycling through to his next murder, yet here Brad sat, whiling away the hours in the company of several mental health patients. It became abundantly clear that, however fascinating and gifted they might be, Roudy and friends weren't going to help stop the killer.

'Paradise didn't say what she did,' Andrea said.

Brad nodded, thinking they should leave soon. But Andrea seemed determined. 'She's right. Why don't you tell us about yourself, Paradise,' he said.

She blushed. 'I don't think I can help you.'

'She sees dead people,' Roudy said.

Psychotic hallucinations, Brad thought. Paradise didn't attempt any denial.

'And spirits,' Andrea added.

'You mean ghosts?'

She shrugged. 'Something like that.'

'If she touched the woman's body, she would see who killed her,' Andrea said. 'Isn't that right, Paradise?'

'I doubt it. Please, Dre, you're just talking now.'

'It's true.'

'How long have you been here, Paradise?'

'Seven years. I arrived when I was nineteen.'

There was something different about the girl. The woman. Unlike the others, she held her secrets close.

'And nothing comes to mind when I describe what we know of this killer? Any men you might have gotten to know?'

She thought a second. 'No.'

Andrea clearly wasn't satisfied. 'Paradise doesn't trust men. She was hurt.' She began to cry again and Paradise comforted her.

Brad wondered what it would be like to be either of these women. What it would be like to live with them. He'd spent the last dozen years of his life mourning the loss of Ruby, an angel from heaven. She'd been ripped from him and he'd crumbled. He'd been searching for Ruby's replacement ever since, but his memory of her spoiled him for anything less.

But his pain surely couldn't compare to whatever secret pain Paradise was hiding. What circumstances had brought her here, to this facility for the forgotten? Who loved this lost woman? What hopes steered her journey through life?

Empathy washed over him, joined by a stab of shame. Compared to this one woman, his own life was like a king's. Yet he spent his life alone in regret. Sorry for himself.

His emotion was so strong that for a moment he thought the others might be picking up on it, despite his best attempts to remain detached. He glanced away.

Nikki took up the slack. 'Some say it's possible to sense things about people, pick up on their . . . energy, even after they're dead. Maybe that's what you mean, Paradise.'

'I don't know how I see it, I just do. My doctors say they're visual hallucinations. That I'm psychotic, suffering from schizophrenia. I see an image and I can't tell whether it's a memory or an imagination.'

'That's right, that's what they would say. But you disagree?'

'Like I said, I don't know. I only know what I see.'

'Are you on medication?'

'No.'

'I am,' Andrea said. Her pretty face twisted up again, once more threatening to burst into tears.

'She's just come off a short manic cycle,' Paradise said, without a trace of weariness or disdain. Turning to Andrea, she asked, with a note of real concern, 'Do you want to take a shower now?'

'I have to, Paradise. I should go now. Sorry. Sorry, sorry.'

She hurried from the room, finally allowing herself to sob.

'Does this mean we aren't getting the one thousand two hundred dollars?' Roudy asked. 'Bring me the file and lay out all the evidence. Trust me, it will be the cheapest one thousand two hundred dollars the FBI ever spent.'

'You, my lady,' Enrique said, taking Nikki's hand, 'are welcome back at any time. I will wait for you and show you heaven.'

This time, Nikki hooked her hand in Brad's elbow. 'But I have a lover, Enrique. Still, it's a nice gesture.'

His grin did not falter. Undeterred. Brad wanted to slip the unflappable resident a hidden high-five.

He looked at Paradise and saw that she was staring at him. Eyes bright and brown. Mystery caressed her face, as if she was one of those ghosts she supposedly saw. The ambiguity instantly haunted him.

What was she thinking?

Nikki excused them and they made their way back to the reception area, where they found Allison. She had already prepared a list of all CWI's residents dating back seven years, complete with diagnosis, medication, prognosis at time of departure and all follow-up.

'So. Did our investigative team offer any help?'

'It was enlightening,' Brad said. 'But no. No breakthrough, I'm afraid. Paradise is an interesting one. She claims to see ghosts?'

Allison lit up. 'You met Paradise? Delightful! One touch of your victims and she might tell you how they died.' She looked away, catching herself. 'But then that would be impossible. She could never work up the courage.'

'I doubt the FBI would agree to that.'

'To what? To such foolishness? That's not the point, FBI. The point is, she suffers from two severe phobias, agoraphobia being one of them. Her fear of leaving her home here has confined her behind our gates for seven years.'

He was familiar with the debilitating fear. In fact, it was surprisingly common – he recalled a case in Miami involving a woman who had starved to death in her apartment for fear of going out for any reason, even to buy food. He'd experienced patches of it himself, immediately following Ruby's death. The mere thought of dealing with the outside world, even the onslaught of sunshine, became oppressive. The fear dissipated after a few weeks, but it had left him with a healthy sympathy for those it afflicted.

'It's not unheard of among our residents. They've been banished by the world, ostracized and made to feel so odd that they're only comfortable alone or in a community of their own. Not unlike the devout in any religion. They stick to their churches for fear of being chastised.'

'What's her story?'

Allison looked at him with a raised brow. 'You should ask her.'

'She's schizophrenic?'

'Truthfully, I'm still not sure. Before we got temporary custody, the psychiatrist in the state hospital diagnosed her with schizo-phrenia and bipolar disorder. Besides the agoraphobia, she also suffers from a deeply rooted distrust of men – those are her primary challenges.'

'And her delusions? These ghosts she sees?'

'Delusions?' Allison turned and led them to the door. 'That's the question, isn't it, Mr Raines?' She tapped her head. 'Whether or not it's just up in here.'

Flower was too engrossed in her unfinished sculpture of Brad to notice when they drove past her.

CHAPTER SEVEN

Quinton Gauld had come to accept the four fundamental rules of life only recently. In the last year to be exact. And being only forty-one years of age, he still had time to perfect his enforcement of those rules.

This soothing realization had brought him more happiness and relief than he'd felt for seven years, ever since he'd been so soundly rejected by the first woman he'd chosen and loved. He still couldn't comprehend her failure of reasoning.

Did a bird reject its own fluffy feathers?

Did a car throw away its growling engine?

Did a woman cut off her own beautiful head?

And yet, despite those unshakable truths, she had rejected Quinton. Thrown him off. Cut off her own head when he'd actually offered to be her head. His only consolation had come from his conclusion that she must be mentally ill. Worse, her soul was sick, for she'd rejected God's choice.

Which brought his mind to the first of the four rules. He turned to face the mirrored wall in his bedroom and said it aloud, so the three wigless mannequins to his right could hear it clearly.

'Beauty is not defined by man, but by God, who determines the most beautiful.'

He glanced at the seven ceramic dolls on his dresser, each watching him with rapt interest, dressed in the pink dress, the blue dress, the green, the black (which was his favourite), the lavender, the yellow and the white. Seeing their vacant stares, he expounded on the rule lest they not comprehend its full meaning.

'Not dirty politicians. Not slimy preachers. Not stupid with a capital S neighbours. Not Holly-weird. Not me. Not you. Not mother. Not sister. Not brother. Not teacher, student, pimp or rock star. God and God alone, who forgives all who have sinned if they follow his rules, defines beauty.'

A pause for effect.

'Even the most beautiful, that one called Lucifer. He forgives him as well.'

Quinton walked into his closet, slipped out of the black bathrobe and hung it on the hook behind his door. His preparations for the work ahead of him had proven both refreshing and encouraging. As always, he'd fasted during the day and given himself a colonic. It was important that his body be clean, inside and out.

Though he could taste the steak he would consume in a few days, he would hold off until then, feeding only on the milk and beans he found so adequate and nutritious for his needs. Afterwards, he might go back to John Elway's place again – on balance, the experience had been satisfying.

He stepped into a pair of black Armani Exchange underwear, the only kind he owned. The brand cradled him firmly, but didn't cut off his circulation like the Tabitha brand, which he'd burned in disgust after a single hour. It was no wonder he hadn't been sexually satisfied for so long. Society was conspiring to strip him of his huMANity.

He slipped into white socks, his customary grey slacks and light blue button-down shirt. At times like this, it was important to look respectable without attracting attention. Brown Sketchers shoes. Though the clothes made him feel at ease with himself, he felt at ease with himself wherever he went. It was undoubtedly one of the chief reasons why God favoured him. He could adapt and feel at home anywhere.

Unless, of course, there were bratty kids about. Or when his nails were dirty. Or when it was too hot or too cold, or when the carpet wasn't clean, or, for that matter, when a hundred other imperfections disturbed his satisfaction. In fact, to be perfectly honest (something he insisted on being at all times), he was only at ease with himself when all rested in the perfect order God had originally intended.

Which was okay, because Quinton Gauld's purpose was to put things back in order. Even his own inconsistencies, some of which had betrayed themselves just now, were on the mend with this work. He was a work of progress in perfection.

Bless me, Father, bless me, Father, for I have sinned.

He walked from his bedroom, scanning his apartment with a studied eye. Rules and order brought a symmetry to life that allowed for balance and joy. This is why he'd given himself a manicure an hour earlier. This is why each red throw pillow on his peach velvet-covered sofa wasn't thrown at all, but carefully placed with attention to balance and beauty.

Not a spot on the walls – he painted each every three months with the non-odorous paint now available at Home Depot. Each wall featured a large mirror, which allowed him to see himself from all highly trafficked regions.

He bent and picked up a piece of lint, a fluffy white feather that must have squeezed through one of the pillows' tiniest, fraying seams. Was it time to replace the pillows? The stuff that was made these days was cheap junk, mostly from China. Or Washington, D.C.

Quinton dropped the piece of lint into a large urn that he'd used as a depository for all such random offerings. The lunatics in the mental ward had suggested he suffered from an obsessive-compulsive disorder and schizophrenia. They were liars, and he'd taken their drugs only to outwit them. Truth was, he could outwit them with his mind tied behind his back.

He crossed into the kitchen, seven steps. He wondered how little Joshie from the restaurant was feeling, having learned such a valuable life lesson from Uncle Quinton. Fortunate little punk. Better now than on the streets, where it might be a sledgehammer to the head rather than the soft side of a hand doing the teaching.

But the real winner now would be Melissa, the flight attendant who would discover her true purpose in . . . he glanced at the clock on the wall . . . two hours and twenty-one minutes, when the clock struck two a.m.

His nerves sent a shiver of anticipation through his tailbone, up his spine. For a moment he felt as if he was standing on the edge of a bridge with a bungee cord strapped to his ankles, ready to launch himself fearlessly into the void. But he had found a better way to fly.

Bless me, Father, for I have sinned.

The rules. Always the rules. Beauty is defined by God, who determines the most beautiful. True, so true.

But there was more. There was another rule; rule two. Because what Quinton had learned only recently was that God had favourites. God loved some more than others. He was passionate about his creation and would bend over backwards to impress those that he favoured.

Even more than that, there was *a* favourite. A single human who was so favoured, in fact, that by comparison the rest didn't even rate on God's list of things worthy of his attention.

The Creator was fixated on one.

Quinton opened the door to a pantry lined with precise rows of canned baked beans made by Hornish, his favourite because of all the sugary syrup. Brain food.

He withdrew the Hitachi electric drill case, then closed the door. He'd boiled the half-inch bit in water to sanitize it for Melissa. Not a germ to be found around its twisting edges.

Yes, God was obsessed with one, like he'd once been fixated on Lucifer. All of heaven and hell had peered down from their lofty, unobstructed view and watched the one courted by God. The rest of creation had existed only as a stage for his courtship. All other humans were extras.

Heaven and hell wanted to know: would the chosen one love God in return?

He placed the drill in a black suitcase, next to the sedative. The rest of what he would need was already neatly packed. He clasped it shut and looked around the room. How long before he returned depended on how cooperative Melissa was. A day, maybe three days.

Satisfied that all was in order, Quinton turned off the lights and headed down to the garage where the green Chevy pick-up waited.

He slid onto the seat and grinned at the inaudible debate raging inside him, between himself and an unseen adversary.

Imagine that, you insane freak. Imagine for a second (and I know this is difficult because your intelligence is less than mine), imagine for even a few moments that it's all about you.

You're at the centre of it all. Your choices are the only ones that count. Like Neo from The Matrix, *Quinton's favourite movie, you wake up one day and learn that YOU are the chosen one.*

Insane, but so true. You are his bride. God's favourite.

But here's what'll really tweak your gourd, Neo, you blithering idiot. This is Rule Two: in God's infinite character, he can have more than one favourite without any of the others losing their status.

That's right, Neo. You are the favourite one, the chosen one. But so am I.

And so is every living soul to walk this cursed earth.

And the rules are the same for all of them. Unfortunately, most are too insane to realize just how critical they are in the game called life.

Until recently, Quinton had hated all humans because of their utter worthlessness. Then he'd learned that the exact opposite was true. That, to a man, woman and child, they were all infinitely valuable. This had caused him to immediately hate them for being as important as him.

But now he no longer had to dwell on such mysteries. He had a role to play. He was God's angel. A messiah sent to help those whom God loved the most join him in eternal bliss.

Because every human was the most beautiful in God's infinite capacity for affection, Quinton was allowed to select seven, God's holy number. He would deliver seven to God, a symbolic gesture of service for which he would be richly rewarded. At the end of it all, he would be given the capacity to procreate again. His body, now at rest like a bear in hibernation, would rise from a deep slumber and join with his own bride.

He'd lost one bride when she rejected him. He would right that wrong, and never allow it to happen again.

Quinton whistled as he drove the green Chevy out of the parking lot. His sense of sheer purpose and self-worth at that moment was almost overwhelming. He was soaring. He waved at Mary, a single mother who lived two apartment buildings from his. He'd helped her with her groceries once, wondering if she might be a suitable bride.

In the end, it all came down to the seventh one, the most beautiful of them all, and he knew her like he knew how to breathe. But the first six, being the number of man, were his to choose at random. His to drain of all humanity so that God could accept them as his brides.

Melissa, a beautiful young woman, was about to become a bride, the fifth choice. If she knew what Quinton knew, she might also be giddy with joy and anticipation.

A part of Quinton knew that most flawed humans would find his reasoning slightly off. They might even think he was insane, and he was okay with that. Humans had an extraordinary capacity for stupidity. They had once sworn that the earth was flat, that the polar ice caps would soon be gone, that Quinton was ill in the head.

All were equally fallacious. Ignorant, childish, gullible, manipulated, foolish, STUPID, all caps.

Sometimes Quinton wondered at God's capacity to love them all. His heart was indeed as big as the ocean. Were it left up to Quinton, he would have taken a handgun with six billion rounds, neatly laid in the world's largest clip, and laid them all to rest, one by one.

The thought made his hands tremble on the steering wheel. He struggled to focus past a momentary blurring of his sight and bring himself into submission.

It took him an hour to reach the blue house. He parked the pickup in a vacant lot at the end of a greenbelt behind the structure and turned off the engine. Seven checks of his mirror assured him that he was alone, and, at one a.m., he expected no less. He'd spent a total of six hours behind the house, stepping behind each tree, around each bush, lying and scooting on his belly, feeling the terrain, relishing the anticipation of this night.

No street lights back here. No moon tonight.

Tempted to whistle but refraining from the indulgence, he placed the shower cap firmly over his head, pulled on the same boots he'd worn during each taking, and slipped on fresh rubber gloves.

He stepped out of the truck and pressed the door closed with hardly more than a click. Locked it with his key. An overgrown walking path wound between scattered trees, thin paltry apparitions that looked like they'd been planted by the developer when the subdivision first opened. Houses hid behind the trees on either side; he could see their fences and darkened rear porches.

He felt as one with all of nature at moments like this, as invisible as a midnight breeze and just as perfectly matched to his mission. No mere mortal could see him there, floating through the darkness, and no insane human could possibly stop him.

Quinton stepped up the path quietly, keeping his senses finely tuned to his environment. Did any of the residents suspect that a man had been walking behind their house for several weeks now, watching from the dark?

Likely not. They were favourites, yet they were stupid and entirely too trusting of their own flesh. Melissa's house came into view ahead, on his right, and a vast surge of satisfaction rose within him. He peered, exulting. Dark windows. She was sleeping already.

An image of her heel with his bit pressed lightly into her calloused skin spread goose bumps over neck and shoulders. The base of his spine tingled and his breathing quickened.

Bless me, bless me, bless me, bless me, bless me, bless me, bless me, Father.

He approached the edge of Melissa's blue house, hardly more than a shadow on a moonless night. From the Google satellite, the house was indiscernible. From God's vantage point, it was nothing more than a speck, then a flake among a million flakes, hardly distinguishable from a tree. Then – zooming in – a computer chip, then a postage stamp, and only finally a house. A black car was driving past when the satellite had taken its last image.

No one peering down, no one except God, could possibly know what slept in the bed inside the tiny house. Just one in six billion, but tonight the only one.

Selected by none other than himself, Quinton Gauld.

He stood still, like a small tree in the dark, and watched for a moment so long that any other person would have found the stillness impossible to maintain. Finally, he unzipped his pants and urinated into a small plastic jar, which he then returned to his pocket.

For a long time he stood and stared, rehearsing details, resuming his inward deliberations.

Brad Raines. Nikki. Nikki, Nikki, Nikki.

His mind shifted to the seventh. You know, don't you, Brad? That I'm going to take her because she belongs to me, not to you? That she will come to me because she is the seventh?

What the FBI agent couldn't possibly know was that he was nothing more than a puppet on a string. He'd reacted to the note precisely as intended. Smart, Quinton would give him that. Even brilliant. But Quinton depended on exactly that level of intelligence.

Brad would likely have to die to make eight, but this was a small sacrifice. One even the agent would willingly make, once he understood just how beautiful she was.

Quinton set the thoughts aside and let his mind walk around the bed inside the house. He mentally placed himself mere inches from his choice, so close now that his presence would be deemed by the world as an illegal intrusion, a trespass. A violation brash enough to earn a scream from her, should she awaken early. Yet he belonged there, waiting in the dark, savouring the bittersweet pause before her taking.

No longer willing to wait, Quinton decided that he would fetch the bride half an hour early. He retraced his steps to the truck, set his plastic bottle of urine under the seat for disposal later, and withdrew the chloroform. Before she understood what was at stake, she might be frightened by his appearance. He had to transport her safely to the place he'd chosen near Elizabeth, where he could begin his work.

Ten minutes later, he stood at the edge of her back lawn. Not a sound of objection. No new pet, no sleepwalker or insomniac, no neighbour's barking dog. Perfect. He walked up to her bedroom window and peered in past the slats. Did Melissa realize there was a thin gap between her mini-blinds and the window frame that allowed anyone to see a sliver of the room, including part of her bed? Perhaps she had known and dismissed the concern, confident that she was special, immune to the outside world.

He made out long lumps in the half-light. It took a full minute for him to understand that he was seeing her legs under the floral bedspread. She was home, as he knew she would be, but seeing her helped him relax.

Though Melissa used deadbolts and had an alarm system with adequate contacts on all windows and doors, cutting the glass on the closet window, though time consuming, raised no alarm. He climbed in, careful not to dislodge the frame and activate one of the contacts.

Using a small penlight to give him enough light to work by, he applied a few tacks of super glue to the edges of the cut glass and replaced the pane. From the outside, no passersby would ever see it had been cut.

Now safely inside the favourite's house, Quinton took a few minutes to calm himself. He breathed in the warmer air, redolent with the unique smells of the fifth one's daily existence. He smelled a savoury fragrance wafting from the kitchen; some sort of late-night takeout dinner. He smelled dust stirred up by a hidden ceiling fan, whirring in the dark. He even caught a whiff of her perfume, its profile unforgotten since that first encounter weeks before.

At last, he stood, careful not to let his knees crack. He'd studied the house from every window and knew the layout well. He was in the spare bedroom's walk-in closet on the north side. A hall ran past the living room to the master bedroom, where Melissa now dreamed of anything except the wondrous fate poised to engulf her.

He pulled the small bottle of chloroform and rag from his

pocket, cracked the door and then eased into the spare bedroom. He'd measured the spaces and walked them on the bare ground a dozen times, so even now, encased in pitch darkness, he knew how many steps to the door, how many down the hall, how many to her bed.

Quinton took them all on slow, padded feet. He waited a moment outside her bedroom door, then turned the knob.

No lock. Of course not. Melissa might be favoured and stunning, but she was still quite stupid. Still, he loved her the way God loved her.

Easing the door wide enough to accept his body, he slipped inside. A slight grey glow from the city outside worked past the mini-blinds and offered a hint of light. Enough for Quinton to see her form, slowly rising and falling in peaceful slumber.

He was there now, in the place he'd obsessively fantasized about for the past several days. He let the vast smile within him swallow up the infinite details of his success: the delicious proximity, the sense of power, the barely tolerated anticipation.

It always amazed him how unsuspecting they were. Asleep in their own dull comforts, unaware that there was a higher calling to life. Like sheep wedged together in the pen. Six billion of them.

But he would go after the one.

Quinton doused the rag, returned the bottle to his pocket, and took two steps when the room erupted with light.

He pulled up sharply, stinky rag in his right hand. Melissa stared at him with round green eyes, hair tangled and flung over her left cheek. Her hand was still on the lamp switch.

She wore a white mask of horror that seemed to have muted any scream. But Quinton knew her silence wouldn't last. Now what? He'd never found himself in this situation. She must have been awake all along.

'Sorry,' he said. 'I think I'm in the wrong house.'

That gave her just enough pause to keep from crying out.

'Sorry. I must have stumbled into the wrong . . . Is this 2413?'

She swallowed and closed her mouth. But she was still too terrified to respond. Her eyes dropped to the rag in his hand.

'Okay, I'll leave now,' he said, his voice suddenly weak and lame sounding. 'I'm terribly sorry for barging in like this. Talk about embarrassing. Though you are really quite a pretty woman.'

He chided himself for sneaking in the last comment.

'Wow, now I'm really embarrassed. If you can show me how to get out.' He looked over his shoulder at the door. Meanwhile, the scent of chloroform wafted through the air. 'Do you mind showing me how to get out of here?'

'Get out!' she cried.

He held up his hand. 'No, no don't do that... I'm sorry, I just . . .' Quinton pointed at her window. 'Look!'

She looked. Childish, but it worked.

He dived then, while her eyes were momentarily averted. Coiled and then unleashed, every muscle in his body, unswervingly aimed at her. He latched onto her knee and threw his whole two hundred and ten pounds on her frail form, hand with rag extended.

But Melissa wasn't a favourite for her looks alone. She rolled quick, squealing.

He rolled with her but she beat him to the far side of the bed and sprang to her feet. Her flannel pyjamas were yellow with small white butterflies. How cute was that?

Quinton threw up both hands. 'No, don't run. You're the bride. He wants you, you have to . . .' But she was already running around the bed, headed towards the open bedroom door.

He launched himself for her just as she bolted past the end of the bed. His hand caught a handful of her soft flannel pyjama bottoms and pulled her to a ripping stop as the seam split.

She pulled away, grunting, panicked. But now Quinton was on his feet, looming over her. He brought the rag down again and stuffed it over her mouth, to help her calm down and sleep so this wouldn't be such a difficult adventure.

Melissa twisted away to her right and let a scream rip from her throat. But as soon as the cry began, it was abruptly cut short by a loud *thunk*. Her attempt at escape had caused her to slam her head into the corner of her dresser.

The woman dropped like a dead deer. Immediately, blood sprang from a wound at her temple.

'No . . .' The sight of the blemish made his stomach swim. 'What . . . What did you do?' He felt fury well up and flush his face with heat. 'What do you think you're doing?'

Nausea swept over him as he stared down at the blemish on her otherwise spotless face. She'd ruined it! She'd slammed herself into the dresser and marked her flawless visage. What was he to do now? For a moment, he thought he might actually throw up on her. He pushed back the nausea only to struggle with a very strong urge to punch her in the face.

Slowly, he brought himself back under control. It was a setback, but nothing was lost. With any luck, no one had heard her short scream. Even if they had, more than likely they were already rolling over and going back to sleep once again, confident that nothing threatened their sanctity. Melissa was certainly back asleep. To be sure, he pressed the rag over her mouth and counted to ten.

Then he shoved the rag in his pocket, threw the girl over his shoulder, and left through the back door, being sure to lock it behind him.

CHAPTER EIGHT

The hours ticked relentlessly by and one day stretched into two.

Brad Raines hovered over the case like a mother hen, knowing that, for all he could not see, something was indeed happening. The killer wasn't curled up in bed, sleeping. His evil harvest was proceeding apace.

The FBI team had scoured the evidence, searching for the elusive lead that would close the gap between hunter and hunted, but nothing new of significance had presented itself.

Brad stood in his office alone, staring out of the window at the cars passing by three storeys below. He and his team had all they needed, a mantra that Brad lived by. Somewhere in the pages of evidence on his desk hid a key that could unlock the case: a dot, an Easter egg, a word that said more than had been spoken.

Brad had returned from the Center for Wellness and Intelligence haunted by an uneasiness that lodged on the edge of his mind. Associating pattern killing with the likes of a Roudy Sparks or an Andrea Mertz – or any of the residents he'd met at CWI – was like pinning a bank robbery on a ten-year-old child. They were capable of outbursts related to delusions, but their cruel illness just wasn't consistent with calculated patterns of harm.

He'd met *victims* at the CWI, not perpetrators capable of heinous murder. But there had been more, this haunting that was slowly creeping into his mind.

In their eyes, he'd seen a small part of himself.

The revelation came back to what Nikki had said just before they got the call to check out CWI. This notion that each human was truly alone in the world, confronted by the complexity of life. And finding themselves alone, they felt insecure. Not loved the way they should be. Not really wanted. Outcasts. Pretenders on some subtle but profound level.

Whether or not they were willing to admit it, all humans were self-contained and alone. The wisest and hardiest among them managed to acknowledge that fact and surpass it. More experienced adults had found ways to cope, but many if not most felt it still. Younger adults suspected it deep in their bones and cried out for significance. Some retreated from that insecurity as a matter of survival.

Sadly, supportive examples flitted through his mind.

A wife who'd been abused as a child, unable to engage her husband in a mutually gratifying sexual relationship because she couldn't lower the walls of protection she'd built around herself. A man told all his life he didn't measure up, now safely encased in his own shell, afraid that even those closest to him might learn he really didn't.

Some covered their insecurity by overcompensating with talk, talk, talk. Or food. Or athletics. Or addictions. Or ridiculous behaviour to garner attention.

In the last three days, Brad's world had become a wasteland of victims on all sides. Everyone – and not just Nikki and Frank and Kim, and Mason in the lobby and Amanda at Maci's Café but everyone – was a lonely victim of life's complexity; Brad wondered what mysteries they hid behind. What secrets and fears secured their loneliness?

You're a pretty girl, Amanda. Thin and fit. Do you constantly diet to fix yourself? Do you hate yourself? Or do you love yourself and regret that others don't appreciate you more?

Who was the skateboarder practising on the rails by his condo, really? A young man who wasn't ready to begin *really* living because he wasn't yet satisfied with who he was? Life for him was still practice for some real test, which lay a month or a year or maybe five years away. When he passed it, his peers would truly appreciate him. Cherish him, even. He would find his significance.

Problem was, that day would never arrive. Everyone was still either telling themselves it was all just around the corner, or they were living with the haunting suspicion that the pot at the end of the rainbow was all a fantasy. That, in reality, they were alone in a jungle and the rainbows were just illusions.

So then, life was really just a mind game, wasn't it? And most people really were handicapped. Mentally.

Ill.

Brad tapped the windowsill with his forefinger. Nonsense, of course. This was simply his way of dealing with his *own* insecurities. Unlike most, he was at least able to see the truth. Still, he was fated to face the same monsters of inadequacies, insignificance and isolation everyone faced.

If Nikki knew the full story, the psychologist in her would say that he was a man trapped by the profound despair of never finding a woman who measured up to the one soulmate he'd loved and then lost.

A slap behind him jerked him from his thoughts. Frank stood over a manila folder he dropped on Brad's desk.

'The rest all check out. We have three more leads we're chasing down, but, of this bunch, nine are now dead; ten are in jail, mostly on misdemeanours that have them cycling in and out of the system like yoyos; five are in other assisted-living facilities; and twelve are in the mainstream, living normal lives with family or friends. Not a hint of the killer.'

At his instruction, Nikki had studied the residents on Allison Johnson's list of discharged cases and identified forty-three that she deemed capable of violent behaviour. The team had tracked down thirty-six of them, eliminating each as suspects.

He frowned and nodded. 'Okay. Chase the other seven down.'

'Already have. Just waiting for the final report.'

Brad nodded and Frank left.

He pressed the intercom button on his phone. 'Nikki, can you come to my office for a minute?'

He settled into his chair, closed two open files on his desk and set them neatly on top of the others. Six books he'd pored over stood side by side at his elbow. *The Center Cannot Hold*, an autobiography of a schizophrenic. A couple of harrowing books on the deinstitutionalization of the mentally ill. A book that shredded the controversial atypical psychotropic drugs, another that supported them. *Mad in America*, a history of the treatment of mental illness in the US.

Three mechanical pencils lay in a wooden tray next to the Bride Collector files. Other than these items, his desk was clear. The rest of his office was as carefully arranged.

He picked up one of the pencils, crossed his legs and tapped the plastic casing on the desk's Formica top.

Nikki tapped his open door. 'You called?'

'Have a seat.'

She walked in and slipped into one of two chairs facing his desk. Jeans today. White sandals that nicely complemented her red toenail polish. She'd had a pedicure last night or this morning. Her foot started to swivel slowly.

He lifted his eyes and saw that she was watching him. Dressed in jeans and a white short-sleeved blouse, with her dark wavy hair, she looked a bit like Ruby, he thought. For an extended moment he forgot to remove his eyes from hers, and, by the time he realized that he was staring, he'd betrayed himself.

Life is a mind game, he thought. *And what mysteries are you hiding, my dear?*

He shifted his gaze to the stack of files. 'We're running out of time.'

'If you mean he's going to go again, you're probably right. I don't know what else we can do.'

'We can expand the search beyond the forty-three people you pulled out of CWI's files.'

She nodded. 'I'll pull more, but it's highly unlikely—'

'I realize that. But we're missing something.'

'From CWI?'

'Maybe. I don't know.'

She nodded. 'The place got under your skin, didn't it?'

'The Center for Wellness and Intelligence.' He set the pencil back down. 'It doesn't appear there's any connection to the case.'

'But you saw something else,' she said. 'You've been to mental health wards before. Correctional facilities for the insane. The banging of heads on toilets, the twenty-four-hour suicide watches, the cries of prophets telling the ward that Jesus is coming back at the turn of the century. But this was different.'

'They were . . . I don't know . . .'

'Human,' she said.

It sounded so cruel.

'No, more than that.' What could he say? *I felt like I was looking in a mirror?* That wasn't entirely true, but he couldn't deny that he'd seen something oddly familiar.

Nikki stood, crossed to the door and shut it. 'The thing of it is, Brad, I get you. I know you're good at what you do because of the pain that's driving you. I know they got under your skin, because you connected with them on a level that confuses you.' She crossed to his desk, placed her palms on the surface and leaned over. 'How am I doing?'

He suddenly wanted her to know it all. So he told her.

'She killed herself, Nikki.'

'Who did?'

'Ruby. She committed suicide. Everything was perfect. We were going to get married when we graduated. She loved me, and I was head over heels. One night, she took some pills and killed herself.' His voice was strained by emotion. 'She didn't think she was pretty enough.'

Nikki sat. 'I'm sorry.'

'It took me a while to figure it out – the details aren't important now. She didn't think she was pretty enough, but she was beautiful. Not just in my eyes.' He pulled open his top right drawer and withdrew a five-by-seven photograph of Ruby tossing her dark hair, holding a tennis racket on the court. He slid it over to Nikki.

She picked up the picture. 'You're right, she was beautiful. I'm so sorry, I had no idea.'

'It's taken a while, but I think I'm finally understanding that her death was debilitating for me. Incapacitating.'

She pushed the picture across and leaned back in her chair.

'And you see the same in the residents at CWI. It got under my skin too.'

Her eyes lingered on his, studying him. But not the way a psychoanalyst might. Unless she was falling in love with her patient. She was the only woman he'd ever told.

'What does your gut tell you?' she asked.

'About what?'

'Me.' Her lips curved gently. 'About Roudy and his group, naturally.'

'Naturally. My gut? It tells me to talk to them again.'

'Then follow it. Talk to them.'

'To what end? There's no connection to the case.'

'Use them.'

'Use them how?'

'Use Roudy. Use them all.'

'On the case?'

'The director seemed to think they might be useful. It takes one to know one, right? So recruit some schizophrenics to help us find a schizophrenic.'

'Assuming he really is schizophrenic.' The idea seemed a bit far-fetched, even to him. 'Sounds more like a case study than an investigation.'

'Maybe. You have any other strong leads? Use Paradise. Who knows? Maybe she's onto something.'

'Ghosts.'

Nikki shrugged. 'I'm just saying, Brad, trust your instincts. They told you that the killer would leave a clue in his confession. The first place the note led us to was CWI. So run with it. I'm a psychologist, but I've seen some anomalies in my day that would make your hair stand on end. Seeing ghosts isn't the worst of it by a long shot.'

'You're suggesting I resort to a psychic?'

'Why not? You have a better path? Various law-enforcement agencies have utilized psychics on countless cases with some fascinating results.'

He cocked his head, intrigued. 'I wouldn't have pegged you as the psychic type.'

'I'm not, trust me. But there's a lot I don't understand about life. The only suggestion I'm making is that you trust your instincts. They led you to CWI. Roudy. Paradise. Follow your gut.'

'My gut tells me to forget psychics.'

'But not to forget CWI. And by extension the residents at CWI.'

Her suggestion felt more like permission to him. She wasn't his superior, but having that permission, he felt strangely compelled to seize it.

Nikki offered him a coy smile. 'We all have our hang-ups, Brad. We all see our inadequacies in others. For the record, I like you, hang-ups and all.'

The air felt heavy.

'You busy tonight?' he asked.

'Actually, yes,' she said. 'But I'm free tomorrow night.'

He'd sworn never to follow this path with her, but that was before. Just dinner, nothing more.

'You like seafood?'

The phone rang and he grabbed it.

'Raines,' he said.

'We have another body.'

The abandoned barn sat among trees at the end of a dirt road, west of Elizabeth, Colorado, and, if not for a realtor, who'd taken a prospective client out to view the property that morning, the body might have gone unnoticed for a week or more.

Or so it appeared. Brad doubted that the killer would have allowed his work to go unnoticed so long.

Melissa Langdon's licence lay on the grey floorboards inside the ring of broken dust where a bucket had collected her blood. The crime scene read like a book.

Melissa had been abducted, presumably from the address on her licence, to which Brad dispatched a team. She'd then likely been taken to a separate location, subdued and prepped, then brought here for the final act. As in the other locations, there was no sign of struggle.

Melissa was affixed to the wall, white and naked, except for the same brand of panties found on Caroline, and an identical veil fixed neatly over her face. She was supported by a wooden peg under each armpit and glued in place.

Then drained.

Same careful arrangements, same angelic lilt of her head, same makeup application. The lipstick was likely the same brand they'd isolated – a red colour called Calypso manufactured by Paula Dorf. Having drained their colour, the killer was insistent about putting some back on them.

Nikki had remained at the field office with Frank and most of the team, sifting through lists that extended beyond CWI to other mental healthcare facilities that had discharged violent offenders in the last three years.

Kim Peterson, forensic pathologist, had joined him at the scene and was on one knee, peering under the victim's right heel, where a plug of putty sealed the hole.

'Now?' she asked. 'Or in the—'

'Now,' Brad said.

She placed a large plastic bag on the floor and prised the plug free. It dropped onto the plastic, trailed by a thin string of blood. The killer had likely waited fifteen or twenty minutes as gravity pulled most of the blood down, but pooling remained in the fleshy sections of the body. Horizontal veins and capillaries would not drain easily, even if massaged or milked.

'Anything?'

In answer, Kim used her tweezers to withdraw a two-inch rolled tube of paper, covered in blood.

'Can you open it here?'

She delicately peeled open the note, careful not to disturb any latent prints on the paper, though they both knew none would be found.

Kim read the message stoically. 'Be careful who you love. I just might kill all the beautiful ones. I am more intelligent than you. Bless me, Father, for I will sin. Oh yes, yes I will.'

'That's it?'

'That's it.' Kim looked up at him. 'This is personal?'

'No. Not that I know of, no, it couldn't . . .'

Surely the killer wasn't someone from his own past come back to haunt him. The killer had simply learned who was working the case and was messing with him. Egging him on.

Be careful who you love. I just might kill all the beautiful ones.

'What else are you seeing?'

'The same as before.' She placed the note in an evidence bag and stood, motioning at the body. 'Lactic acid is building, rigor mortis is setting in, but not more than, oh, I'd say ten hours. She's still pretty flexible. I'd say she died sometime last night.'

'Four days since the last one.'

'Four days. There's a nasty cut on her temple that he went to considerable lengths to cover up. Looks like she either hit her head or he delivered a blow.'

'No, he wouldn't risk wounding her. He wanted her clean. Okay, process the body and the scene. Let me know if you come up with anything else. I'll be on my phone.'

'Will do.'

Brad stepped out of the barn and flipped open his phone. It took him two minutes to get Allison Johnson at the Center for Wellness and Intelligence on the line. She was evidently with a resident and required some urging to break away.

'Hello, FBI. Did you find your man yet?'

'No. He took another girl. She's on the wall in the barn behind me.'

The line was silent for a moment. She sighed heavily.

'I would like to speak to one of your residents again, Miss Johnson. If you don't mind.'

'No, of course not. I don't mind at all. Like I said, Roudy is much better than his antics might suggest.'

'Actually, I would like to meet with Paradise.'

'Oh? Not Roudy?'

'No. Paradise, if you don't mind.'

'Chasing ghosts now?'

'No. Chasing my gut. Is she available?'

'I'm sure she could be.'

'Good. I can be there in an hour. And Miss Johnson?'

'Yes?'

'I would like to speak to Paradise alone this time.'

'That could be a problem. She's nervous about being alone with men, as I said.'

'I realize that. You could be nearby, but I really would like to talk to her without any . . . interference. If that's not possible, I'll understand, of course.'

Allison hesitated.

'I'll see what I can arrange.'

CHAPTER NINE

The tall shrub that Flower had sculpted into a statue resembling Brad was completed, but there was no sign of the artist. The surprisingly realistic likeness brought him to a stop for a second look on the driveway. He imagined what she could do with clay or stone. Flower was truly talented.

A man dressed in plaid slacks met him in the reception area. 'You're with the FBI?' he asked, sticking his hand out. He had a beak for a nose, but his eyes twinkled, which made him appear fun rather than snooty.

'Yes.' Brad took the hand.

'Jonathan Bryce. Allison's waiting, follow me.'

He led Brad out to the back, where the massive maples spread their branches over the tranquil lawn, now nearly empty. They walked towards the towering wing south of the main hub in which they'd met Roudy and company three days earlier.

What stories, what mysteries, what hauntings hid behind the brick walls ahead? So quiet and peaceful, yet so far removed from normalcy. The world of the mentally ill. The gifted. A chill tickled his spine.

'You're staff?'

'I'm one of the nurses,' the man said. 'Medications mainly.'

'I thought CWI wasn't big on medications.'

'We're not. But sometimes it's our best option.'

'Just not as often here as in other facilities,' Brad said.

'This way.' Jonathan turned on the sidewalk and waved at two women on a bench who were watching them with keen interest. They both waved back and flashed big smiles. 'The Pointer twins. There's a story.'

'I'll bet. Why not medicate the way most facilities do?'

'Think about it in terms of a broken leg. Someone breaks their leg and we know how to set it so the body can heal itself. But mental illness is still a mystery.' He used his hand to form a ball, eyes bright. 'First, we don't necessarily know where gifting leaves off and illness begins, so there's that confusion. Even when we can make a diagnosis, say severe bipolar disorder, no one knows how to set the bones, so to speak. We have no idea how to put the mind back in order. We can't fix it, all we can do is take away some of the pain, follow?'

'So you treat the symptoms, not the illness.'

'Exactly. Relatively speaking, at CWI we give aspirin where many psychiatrists might prescribe tranquillizers.'

'And that's better for the patient?'

'Please. You know how these drugs work?'

'Not really, no.'

'There are no drugs that specifically treat mental illness, as it was once believed. The so-called miracle anti-psychotic drugs like Abilify inhibit serotonin and dopamine in the brain, which can alleviate symptoms like delusions and hallucinations. Fine. But the new drugs also come with a long list of adverse side effects that many patients – not all mind you – find intolerable.'

'But at least they're stable, right? Better.'

'Depends what you mean by stable. Depends on the person. For some, the meds are lifesavers. For others, their overall health is worse off. A recent major study found that out of fifteen hundred schizophrenic patients, only about twenty-five percent found the side effects tolerable over the long haul.'

'What kind of side effects?'

'You name it. Seizures, severe weight gain, cardiac problems, gastrointestinal complications, paralysis of the bowels, sexual dysfunction, facial hair, skin rashes, eye disorders, etcetera, etcetera, etcetera.' He sounded like a medical dictionary. Then again, despite the odd clothing, he was a nurse. Or at least claimed to be.

And he wasn't finished. 'But the worst may actually be the

emotional problems that often present. Toxic psychosis. Delirium, confusion, disorientation, hallucinations, depression, delusions. Point is, neuroleptic drugs inhibit the neural processes like sleep inhibits activity. But a person's gotta live. They can't sleep away their lives.' He pointed to a glass door. 'In here.'

'Thank you.'

'So we use drugs, but we do so with a watchful eye, pray for better options to emerge quickly, and provide an environment that helps each feel wanted and special.'

Jonathan stopped at the door. 'Interesting fact that no one seems to know what to do with: in less industrialized countries, like Columbia and India, for example, over sixty percent of schizophrenic patients recover fully within two years. They depend on family nurturing, religion and other non-medical treatment. No drugs. In America, the recovery rate is much less than a third, and that's using anti-psychotic drugs. What does that tell you?'

'Hmmm.'

'She'll meet you inside. Have a great day, sir.'

Brad thanked him again and walked into a small lobby, now vacant.

Allison walked out of a side door. 'Hello, FBI.' She wore a blue dress today. Silver jewellery and cork wedges. She'd fixed her hair differently. It was tied back in a ponytail, but not haphazardly. Same contagious smile. An angel in her own right, in the service of wounded souls.

'Well, well, well, isn't this your lucky day?' she asked.

'Is it? I wish the same could be said for Melissa.'

Allison's brow arched in question. 'Oh?'

'The girl we found this morning.'

'Oh. Terrible. Awful. I suggest you say nothing of it to Paradise.'

'So she's agreed?'

'She has. But it took some coaxing on my part. You have as much time as she will give you. Unfortunately, I'm a bit shorter on time and I'll have to wait here while you talk to her. So why don't we say fifteen minutes?'

'Half an hour.'

'What exactly do you plan on asking her?'

'You said she had a gift.'

Allison thought about that.

'Let's just say I'm running out of options and time.'

She nodded. 'Okay, FBI. Half an hour.'

Brad stepped through the door and entered a room with a large window, Coca-Cola and snack machines, and a sofa grouping that faced a wall-mounted flat-screen television.

Paradise stood by a counter with a sink, watching him as he shut the door behind him. She wore the same too-short jeans and canvas tennis shoes she'd worn the last time he'd seen her. A grey sweatshirt hung on her slight, five-foot frame. Her dark hair still looked stringy – he suspected she looked the same every day of the week. Not unclean, but certainly not very attentive to appearance.

'Hello, Paradise. Good to see you again.'

'Hello.' Her voice was tight. Nervous.

He stood still for a moment, caught up in the little he knew about her history. Something in her childhood had broken her. She was bipolar, but Allison had said that her initial diagnosis of schizophrenia could be wrong. That she might not suffer from hallucinations but actually saw these ghosts. The notion seemed ridiculous now. Paradise didn't look like anything more than a damaged young woman who needed to be told when to shower.

'Thank you for agreeing to talk to me,' he said. 'Do you mind if we sit?'

'Sure. Have a seat.'

He walked around the couch and sat down. She made no sign of joining him.

'Would you like to sit?'

'Not really,' she said.

'Okay. So you're probably wondering why I want to talk to you.' The moment the words came out, he wanted to pull them back. 'Not that people wouldn't want to talk to you, of course. It's just that I'm an FBI agent and I've come back here asking specifically to speak to you. I'm sure that's a bit unnerving.'

'It's okay, sir. I—'

'Call me Brad. My name is Brad Raines.'

She hesitated. 'Well, then, Mr Raines, it's understandable why you think I'd be uncomfortable with your request to speak with me. Or with any of us. Most people would rather we didn't exist. It's hard for us to trust people who don't like us – I'm sure you can understand that.'

He was surprised by how well spoken she was. Sounded a bit like Allison, who was clearly her mentor.

'I can understand that. Are you uncomfortable?'

'Yes. But I wouldn't go as far as Andrea or Roudy.'

'Really? What did they say?'

'Roudy thinks you're a conniving weasel who's trying to cut him out. After all, he offered to help first, and everyone knows he's pretty good at what he does.'

'What does he do?'

'Connect dots that most people miss.'

Astute. Maybe he *should* talk to Roudy again.

'And what did Andrea say?'

Paradise crossed her arms. 'She said you're a handsome devil and that your only interest for wanting to see me alone is to get into my pants.'

Brad failed to suppress a sharp chuckle. 'Well, you can tell Andrea that I appreciate her flattery, but it won't help her get into mine.'

Again he wanted to take the words back. But a hint of a smile registered on her face, so rather than pull back, he pushed forwards.

'On the other hand, if I wasn't sworn off women, I might find either of you—'

'Don't say it,' she snapped.

He blinked.

'The comment about Andrea was funny. Leave it at that. Now, please tell me what I can do for you. I'll be as helpful as I can be.'

'Well, whatever you think I meant, you were likely wrong.

I'm not here to take advantage of anybody, mind, body or spirit. I'm just trying to break the ice.'

She looked at him for a long while, and for a brief moment he wondered if she was seeing one of her hallucinations.

He let her stare. She finally lowered her arms and eased herself down onto the arm of a stuffed chair opposite him. 'Sorry for that. I'm not normally so' – she waved a limp hand – 'edgy. Whatever you might think, Mr Raines, I'm not like some of the others here. Not that I'm proud of that. I wouldn't mind having some of their gifts, schizophrenic or not. But the fact of the matter is, I'm not schizophrenic. I do, however, struggle with bipolar disorder. I assume you know the difference.'

'I do. For the most part.'

'Bipolar disorder, once called manic-depressive illness, is a mood disorder that presents with quick onsets of manic highs that yield to usually longer lasting depressive lows. It's inherited. Medication helps, but I hate the way the stuff messes with me, so I avoid it and work through the cycles. Some people can't cope. Fortunately, I can.'

'That's good.'

'Clearly. Schizophrenia, on the other hand, is a thought disorder. A form of psychosis that typically presents itself in the late teens and early twenties. It's thought to be linked to the way dopamine and serotonin work in the brain, but no one really knows whether it's more about chemical imbalance or the receptors in the brain.'

'You seem well studied.'

'I read the medical journals. They're all working in a fog, trust me. Most psychotic illnesses like schizophrenia present with delusions – either paranoid or grandiose; hallucinations – visual, auditory, and so on; or other thought disorders that mess with the processing of ideas in the mind. Pressured speech, flight of ideas, word salad, that kind of thing. Does that all make sense?'

'Yes.' Brad had a new respect for Paradise already.

'Schizoaffective disorder is essentially a combination of a mood disorder like bipolar and schizophrenia. Just to clarify a few terms. I do have a mood disorder – bipolar – but I am *not* crazy.'

She slipped from the chair's stuffed arm down onto the seat cushion. 'So, what can I do for you?'

Sitting here looking into her brown eyes, listening to such succinct articulation, Brad saw an entirely different person from the one he'd seen a few days earlier.

'We found another victim this morning. A girl named Melissa, just a couple of years younger than you, in her early twenties.'

Paradise just stared.

'She was dead. The killer drained her blood and left her for us to find.'

'That's pretty sick.'

'I agree.'

She leaned back in the chair and crossed her legs. 'Who could do such a thing?' Her eyes misted and she averted them.

His own throat tightened.

'We thought the killer might have a history with the Center for Wellness and Intelligence, but nothing's panning out.'

'Then why are you talking to me?'

'Honestly? I'm not entirely sure. I'm following my gut. Something Allison said the other day.' He crossed his legs, matching her. 'Can you tell me about your gift?'

Her eyes stared into his. 'My hallucinations, you mean.'

'Allison insists they aren't just hallucinations.'

'But this isn't Allison,' she said. 'This is you and me. Don't tell me you believe in ghosts.'

'No. I don't. But I do know how powerful perceptions and instincts can be. In my line of work, a computer would do a better job investigating and deciphering evidence if the human equation wasn't more important. Instinct, gut feelings. I don't believe in ghosts, but I do believe that some people have an extraordinary ability to perceive what others do not.'

She nodded. 'Latent inhibition.'

'Which is?'

'Why are you so afraid of women?'

'Excuse me?'

'You don't have a ring on.'

'I'm not married, but that—'

'You take meticulous care of your hair and nails.'

He glanced at his fingers, thrown off by her line.

'You're dressed in the same slacks you wore on Tuesday, and your apartment is spotless. If you could bring yourself to trust a woman, you might let her in, but there's too much in your world that you need to protect. Too much order and comfort. Your sofa is purple, the window behind you is open to another world, and if you hit it at ninety-four miles an hour, you're there and flying through space with the angels, who ask you if you would like some tea before meeting with the Roush.'

'Roush?'

'Yes.'

They faced off in silence. He had no clue what kind of mythical creature a Roush might be, and it didn't matter.

'Black,' he said. 'My sofa is black velvet.'

'Sorry about that,' she said, blushing. 'The window stuff was just a slip of the tongue. I didn't mean to say it aloud.'

But she was right about the rest, he thought, and now she picked up on his hesitation to correct the rest of what she'd said.

'But I was pretty close on the rest,' she said. 'You want to know how I know?'

'Something like that.'

'Ghosts,' she said.

'You . . .' He glanced to his left where her gaze had shifted earlier. 'You're seeing ghosts?'

'No, not now. Although one did walk past the window three minutes ago. But that was just my imagination.'

'So . . . I'm lost. Catch me up here.'

'My imagination sees "ghosts" now and then' – she made quotes with her fingers – 'because of my low latent inhibition. Most people's minds inhibit the streams of stimuli that their senses are exposed to – sight, sound, feel, smell, ideas – and focus only on what the mind determines to be critical at any given moment. Like a filter. Latent inhibition is the mind's perception filter.'

'And low inhibition, or this latent inhibition, is a breakdown in that filter,' he guessed.

'Extremely creative people – artists, writers, etcetera – often see more than others. Not all of it is real. I look at you and I see a flood of details that most would miss at first glance. I look at the window and see another universe. Some of what I see is imagined, some real. According to Allison, a high intelligence allows a person with low latent inhibition to process the extra stimulation effectively. But without high intelligence, the flood of ideas and senses can be debilitating.'

'Like the bit about the window opening to another universe . . .'

'Yeah, like that.'

'And the ghost you saw a few minutes ago?'

She shrugged. 'But I have seen them a few times, for real, as far as I can tell.'

'But you wouldn't know,' he pointed out. 'To the observer, a true hallucination is impossible to differentiate from the real thing.'

'No, these are different,' she said in a soft voice, as if afraid to disturb some unknown balance in the room. 'I don't hallucinate.'

Regardless of her true state of mind, Paradise was plainly brilliant. Into this small package, God had seen fit to deposit a mind that made Brad's own spin with awe. He couldn't help but feel just a little intimidated.

'Well, you're not what I expected,' Brad said.

'Hmmm. What did you expect, a raving lunatic?'

'No.' He covered his embarrassment with a short laugh. 'And what did you expect, a monster?'

Now she smiled in earnest, revealing perfect white teeth. Like her bipolar disorder, likely inherited.

'So tell me, Mr Raines, what *did* you expect?'

'I don't know. Not someone who is so well spoken, for starters. I understand you write novels?'

'A few. But they're useless.'

'How do you know?'

'Even if they aren't, they're just my world. They'll never leave this place. I can't write when I'm on the meds.'

'Allison told me that you have agoraphobia?'

Her mouth fell flat and she fiddled with her fingers, absently picking at one of her fingernails, which was chewed to the nub. 'That's right.'

'You never leave the compound?'

'No.'

She didn't seem to want to talk about her fear. That certainly presented a problem, considering the idea he was toying with.

'Anything else? Other fears or special challenges?'

'Now you're starting to sound like a shrink.'

'No, that's not what—'

'Can I trust you?' she asked, interrupting.

'Of course you can trust me.'

'Because the last time someone told me to trust them, I unlocked the door and they shoved a shotgun barrel into my mouth.'

She said it without batting an eye.

'Then don't trust me.'

Her eyes misted and she looked back at the window over his shoulder. 'I can't remember anything else about what happened except the gun. My father was a strict disciplinarian. Eccentric, wealthy. He was convinced we were all conspiring to steal his money and turn it over to the devil. He suffered from paranoid schizophrenia.' Her fingers trembled in her lap.

'I . . . I'm sorry.'

'He tried to shoot me after keeping me locked up for a month. He killed my mother and my brother and thought he'd killed me before he shot himself.' Her glassy eyes turned back to him. 'But my older sister, Angie, had already moved out, so she was okay. She lives in Boulder and visits me when she can. But she knows that I have to stay here.'

The story overwhelmed him, and he couldn't think of an appropriate response. 'I'm sorry,' he offered again, weakly.

'It's okay. I lived, obviously. I'm here, right? I just remember the darkness and the knocking on the door, begging me to open up.

Pleading for me to open up because he loved me. Then the gun and that's it. The rest I know because they told me.'

'I'm so sorry, Paradise.'

'You asked if I have any other fears. Well, yes, I do. Mnemophobia. The fear of memories. I can't seem to remember the really bad things that happen.' Tears pooled in her soft brown eyes, but they didn't run down her cheeks. 'I feel the feelings, so I know something terrible happened, but I can't remember what exactly.'

'Maybe that's a good thing.'

'Yes. Maybe.'

'What about things that have happened since coming here? Do you remember those?'

'Yes.'

What could he say to her? He hadn't come here expecting his heart to be broken, but seeing Paradise swallowed by such a cruel past, like the stuffed chair that enveloped her now . . . A part of him wanted to rush over and give her a hug and insist that she would be safe with him.

If not for her twin phobias, Paradise probably could have left the Center long ago. Who knew what she would be today except for them? Married with children or working on Wall Street. Serving with the FBI? – she certainly had the aptitude. In fact, Paradise's unique perception of the world might be invaluable to any investigative body.

Yet her illness compromised her acceptance of him. As long as there was a possibility that he held the proverbial shotgun behind the door, she couldn't trust him.

Unless he disarmed himself and gave her the shotgun.

'I was once in love with a woman named Ruby. She was beautiful. Dark hair, like yours, about the same length. Quite short, a real bundle of energy, you know. We played on the tennis team together at UT. But she didn't think she was beautiful, so she killed herself. I don't think I've ever recovered. I've only told this to one other person.'

He let the confession stand and watched her face.

'Do you think I'm beautiful?' Paradise asked.

Brad had expected any reaction but this, but he immediately saw the connections she was making. Suicides, death, heartache – these were all things she was overly familiar with and shut out as a matter of survival, like she shut out terrible memories. Instead, she focused on the fact that he'd lost a beautiful woman.

When he didn't respond immediately, she spoke.

'No,' she said, 'but that's okay. I don't have the faintest clue about beauty. All I know is that I don't fit in anywhere but here. This is my home. My own father rejected me, and the world rejects people like me. I don't know how to be beautiful or what clothes to buy or how not to stink.'

Her words crushed him, but he didn't know how much of what he felt was empathy and how much was respect.

'I don't think you realize what women on the outside are like because you've been trapped in here for so long,' he finally said. 'It's not all that it's cracked up to be.'

She looked at him with those haunting brown eyes. 'It must have hurt,' she said quietly.

His breath suddenly came hard. She had that knowing tone and it made the hair on his neck bristle.

'You still wonder how she could have killed herself if you made her life worth living.'

The words felt like a gut punch. Emotion swelled in his throat and he turned, fighting off a wave of sorrow cresting under the force of her words.

'It's okay,' she said. 'I struggle with self-worth too.'

And then she was quiet. But in that moment, whether or not she'd meant to, Brad felt as though she'd made them equals. Bearers of the same awful secret. Soul mates of a kind, however absurd that might sound.

And then he pushed the feeling aside, cleared his mind, and offered her a polite grin. 'Don't we all,' he said. 'Life can be hell.'

She didn't respond, but her eyes refused to move from his.

Brad brought his thoughts back to his purpose for coming.

The killer was out there, and Brad was here to stop him, not wallow in his own past.

He cleared his throat. 'You might be able to help me out. To be honest, I wasn't sure what I expected coming here. We're running out of options and, if we don't find a way to stop the killer, he's going to kill more women. But now that I've met you I think maybe you can help us save an innocent girl's life.'

'You're trying to manipulate me. But put that way, how can I refuse?'

'I'm not . . . *Manipulate* is too strong a word. What would you do in my situation? A girl's life is at stake.'

'I doubt I can help. You seem intelligent enough – why do you need me?'

'Because you might be more intelligent than you think. Because we're here. Because I feel like I'm chasing a ghost and you see ghosts.'

She nodded. 'Okay. What can I do?'

'Allison said you see things about the dead. We have a dead body.'

She looked at her fingers in her lap, swallowing. 'Sometimes people die here, the older ones. A couple of times I saw some things. I think I saw the last things they saw.'

Crazy as it sounded, Brad had come across another report of a similar psychic phenomenon, a person's ability to somehow connect with the freshest memories stored in a deceased person's brain. He'd dismissed the report as rubbish.

'Ghosts,' he said.

She looked up, concerned. 'I would have to be with them. In the same room. I have to touch them.'

Brad nodded. 'I can assure you I would personally accompany you and . . .'

She stood to her feet, face white. 'No. No, I can't leave.'

He instinctively stood and stepped closer, reaching for her. But she slipped to his left and hurried around the chair like a scared rabbit.

'We could keep the shades drawn, you wouldn't even know—'

'No. Absolutely not.' Her eyes darted towards the window. 'You don't understand, I can't leave.'

The colour had vanished from her face – now she really did look as if she'd seen a ghost. She bolted towards the door and slammed it shut behind her.

Brad jerked himself from a moment of immobility, leaped over the chair and threw the door wide just in time to see her fleeting form disappear into the hall.

Then she was gone.

Allison stood from her seat across the room, smiling.

Always smiling.

'That evidently went well,' she said. 'Maybe she'll change her mind?'

'Do you think?'

'No.'

CHAPTER TEN

'What do you mean you said no?' Roudy demanded, marching across the lawn. He frantically pulled at his goatee with both hands. 'This is an outrage, my dear. They ask you for our help and you turn them down?' He spun back and glared at Paradise. 'Your selfishness and insensitivity will ruin my reputation!'

I see you and your ghosts, Sherlock, and at the moment your ghosts are shouting at me, so I will ignore them. Be gone, ghosts, or I'll dispatch you all with a word of power that lives deeper in me than in you. It sits on your shoulder like a butterfly, so watch out, Sherlock . . .

She thought the words as if they were water flowing through her mind. Fuel for her soul. Imagination was her lifeblood. She'd long ago exchanged hopeless attempts to stem her imagination for the challenge of focusing it.

. . . because that butterfly is truly a dragon!

'Your reputation doesn't extend beyond this place, Roudy,' Paradise said quietly. 'They want me to leave here.' Her throat felt as though it had been tied in a knot and, if she wasn't careful, she would burst out in tears right there. 'You know I can't do that.'

Andrea flung her arm out, flushing red. 'Yeah, you insensitive lobster! How dare you try to convince Paradise to leave us!' Her face twisted, pained. 'That's what's selfish. All you can think about is your . . .'

She whirled to her right and yelled at empty space. 'Shut up, shut up, shut up!'

Paradise didn't pay any attention to the imagined voice that was upsetting Andrea. Likely a voice telling her something about how stupid she was, the most common of her auditory hallucinations. But there was nothing there.

I can't, I won't, it would kill me. I am dirt out there. I am cow dung on the outside. The thoughts crowded Paradise's head.

The difference between Andrea's hallucinations and the ghosts that Paradise 'saw' was that Andrea's mind couldn't distinguish between real and imagined. Paradise could. Most of her ghosts were simply the product of an overripe imagination. Like the 'ghost' she'd seen in the window while talking to the FBI agent. And the thoughts entering her mind now were not audible voices.

But on some occasions she had actually seen, not imagined, the so-called ghosts. Six times to be precise. Two of those times had been when she'd touched the dead.

They stood under one of the aspens on the south side of the compound, where Paradise had agreed to meet them when her meeting was finished. The space offered some privacy and a wrought-iron bench, which was now empty. Enrique wasn't here yet – probably trying to coax a vixen into his bed, though they all knew that any hanky-panky had to be approved by Allison.

Roudy pushed a pair of round, lensless spectacles up the bridge of his nose. 'I may do my work here, but don't think for a moment that the entire investigative community doesn't benefit from my methods. They likely study my cases in every university and FBI field office in the country. Not to mention the English, the French, the Israelis . . . all of them! They need me. Don't try to steal that from them.'

Andrea was in a tizzy. 'You can't leave me, Paradise!'

'I'm not leaving. And I'm not saying that your work isn't appreciated on the outside, Roudy. But are you willing to go out there yourself? Would you leave this place and start lecturing in the universities?'

'If I were called upon, of course! Each of us must rise to the challenge. I have no doubt that the day will come when they ask me to travel to Moscow or London to put a halt to the dastardly deeds of some impervious rogue who's eluded the best of the best.' He was breathing heavily, agitated. 'This is your call to greatness,

Paradise. Rise!' He made a fist and shook it as if he were a general trying to rouse the troops.

I can't, I'm a bug out there. I'm dead. I died out there! Panic crowded her mind. 'You rise. You're so smart, you go out there and solve this case for them, why not?'

'Because you stole my thunder! Now they want *you*. It's a betrayal at the highest level. Treachery! Maybe treason; even!'

'Don't be stupid.'

Roudy looked hurt. 'You're accusing me of being stupid?'

'No. I said *don't* be stupid. Don't accuse me of treason; this has nothing to do with treason. I have agoraphobia. I would fall apart if I set a foot out of the place, you know that. Why are you demanding I do something that I can't do? Does Allison encourage you to quit being Sherlock? No. So stop demanding that I do something I can't do.'

Roudy stared back at Paradise for a moment, then humphed and turned his back on both of them, crossing his arms. The argument stalled.

She was only like this when fear pushed her to the edge. She hated confrontation, hated that she felt like she had to yell at Roudy, hated that Andrea was crying. Hated that she'd come over so strong with Brad Raines.

Her mind was back in the room with him.

You're a handsome man, Brad, too good looking for your own good or my good, because it means I'll never measure up in your eyes, which in turn means you're here for you, not for me. You want to use me, then dismiss me. I'm just a monkey in your zoo to do some tricks. Toss me a banana and I'll jump up and down. Do you want to kiss the monkey, Mr Raines?

The last thought made her blink.

'I don't like it,' Roudy said. 'You should have insisted that I go to the meeting with you. This would have all turned out differently if I'd been there to protect you.'

Andrea jumped to her feet. 'He made a pass at you, didn't he, Paradise?'

You're the beauty queen, Andrea. You're the one they all want.

They all mistake your smooth skin and long blonde hair and blue eyes and full lips and painted nails and slim figure for beauty, and they all want to kiss you. You're their monkey, you rather than I.

'I knew it!' Andrea cried, tensing as if to spring into the air. 'What did I tell you?'

'Don't be ridiculous. He did nothing remotely similar.'

'Because he knows he's outclassed,' Enrique announced, walking up from behind. He stopped next to Roudy and winked at Paradise. 'But, if you like, I could give you a few pointers, teach you how to help the man feel more at ease with your femininity.'

'She doesn't need your nonsense,' Andrea snapped. 'She needs to push that man as far away as possible before he has his way. I told you all this would happen; don't say that I didn't warn you.'

'Mr Raines didn't do anything of the sort,' Paradise said. 'He was a perfect gentleman.'

Andrea wagged a manicured, red-nailed finger at her. 'Never trust a perfect gentleman.'

'Nonsense,' Enrique objected. 'You're suggesting no one trust *me?*'

'You're all driving me crazy!' Roudy said, turning around from his pouting. 'This isn't about men and women and all that rubbish, so will you all please try to control yourselves? The point is quite simple. We have to make a decision quickly, before it's too late.'

Enrique's brow arched. 'Before what's too late?'

'The FBI, Mr Brad Raines, approached us this morning and mistakenly asked the wrong person's assistance in tackling a case. They asked Paradise to go with them to examine the body of a victim, the Bride Collector's fifth victim. But' – he politely motioned to Paradise – 'our friendly ghost-buster, who insists she's not in any way mentally unstable, by the way, panicked. Evidently she's too mentally stable to overcome her agoraphobia for the sake of the Bride Collector's next victim. So now the FBI has left and another girl will be dead shortly. Did I miss anything, Paradise?'

You missed the window that leads to the perfectly peaceful space full of angels escorting me to my rightful place at the feet of the king

*who has called to his princess in white. Yes, Roudy, I am a princess,
no matter what I look like here.*

'You missed that the FBI fellow is not to be trusted,' Andrea
said.

Paradise pulled herself from her imaginations. 'No, that's not
true, Andrea.' Why the poor girl was so fixated on this point was
a bit of a mystery. Did she know something the rest of them
didn't? 'Why do you keep saying that when I told you he was a
gentleman? In fact, he seemed to genuinely care.'

'Because he will hurt you, Paradise. Trust me, men always end
up hurting you. Do you know how many men have come on to
me over the years?'

*No, I don't know, but I can imagine, because you're pretty and you
are capable of letting them get close to you. Because when you opened
the closet door, your father didn't put a shotgun in your mouth. You're
a flower in the trees, a rose for the bees, a star in the sky. And I'm
the dried mud on the side of a cow's rump, as far as men are concerned.*

'No,' Paradise said.

'They've come on to me a lot. They always get pissed when I
break up with them.'

Silence. *And?*

But there was no *and*.

Roudy grabbed his hair with both hands. 'Focus, people! Time's
ticking. Another dead girl.'

'So why don't they just bring the body here?' Enrique asked.
'Never hurts to have another woman's naked body hanging
around.'

Roudy slapped his shoulder. 'Not appropriate.'

'You're sick,' Andrea said. 'Sick in the head. What did I say
about men?'

It struck Paradise that Andrea was being overly obstinate on
this issue of men. Either she really did know something about
Brad Raines that the rest of them didn't, or she felt somehow
threatened by his request to see Paradise. Could it be that jealousy was subconsciously motivating her antagonism? Imagine
that, Andrea jealous of Paradise!

She'd always felt completely out of her league next to Andrea, and no wonder: the girl was beautiful. Her antics actually drew men rather than repelled them. She was a safe toy in most men's eyes – beautiful and alluring, yet too strange to consider for marriage. And she knew how to flirt.

Paradise, on the other hand, had never even thought about flirting. Yet Andrea was jealous?

'I think he can be trusted,' Paradise said.

They all looked at her, clearly not expecting an opinion.

'And I think that Enrique might be onto something,' she continued.

Enrique smiled. 'That's the spirit, my dear.'

Andrea shook her head. 'I'm telling you, Paradise. And it's not because I'm jealous. That's not it. Guys like this steal hearts and you will be a heap of dog dirt when this is all over.'

'I appreciate the concern, Andrea. But Roudy made a good point. I have to help them if I can. And Enrique's right; if they agree to bring the body, I'll try to help.'

'That hocus-pocus is worthless,' Roudy snapped. 'We need solid investigation, not ghost hunting. Tell him to bring the body to me, with the file.'

'You get the file, I get the body,' Enrique said.

Paradise turned away and started to walk towards the centre of the compound.

'Where are you going?' Roudy demanded. 'We have a girl to save.'

Paradise turned back. 'No, Roudy. *I* have a girl to save. And no, Casanova, you can't have the body; that is really sick. And, yes, Andrea, I will be careful. Don't worry, my heart isn't going to be broken. He thinks I stink. Literally. And I probably do. The whole idea of it is insane. No pun intended.'

That settled them.

Paradise left them standing.

CHAPTER ELEVEN

Brad spent the afternoon at the FBI office downtown, hovering over Kim Peterson's autopsy and grilling the forensics lab on the evidence that had been collected at the barn near Elizabeth. Correction: he spent the afternoon *attempting* to get Kim to hurry her autopsy (which they agreed would consist of a careful examination of Melissa's head wound and her heels – no need for an examination of her internal organs) and crowding Bill, the lab tech scouring the samples from the scene. In both cases he was hardly welcomed.

The visit to CWI had been a bust. What had he been thinking? His strange discussion with Paradise seemed as if it had occurred in a different universe. And somehow that bothered him. The fact that he'd taken three hours of his day to drive out there and sit down with a deranged girl who saw ghosts tugged at him like a sharp hook. The trip had left him irritable, and he wasn't entirely sure why.

To complicate matters, the Bride Collector's note made it clear that he'd been watching Brad. Was watching him. He found himself second guessing every glance, every car he passed on the road, every agent. He paced the field office racking his brain for images of a watcher out of place, on the street, in the diner, his building, anywhere.

Be careful who you love.

How did the Bride Collector know him? Or did he? Maybe he'd somehow learned that Brad was taking the lead on the case and was trying to preoccupy the FBI. Throw a monkey wrench into the investigative gears.

'Please, Brad, she's only been on the table for half an hour,' Kim said.

'He's out there, Kim. Right now the killer's stalking the sixth girl and I need to know if he's given us more.'

'He has. The note.'

Yes, the note. Nikki was with it.

Brad nodded at the white body lying face up on the examination table. 'The cut on her forehead.'

'It'll be the first thing I examine, but I won't be able to tell you much beyond the likelihood that she hit her head on a counter or dresser.'

'You know that?'

'No, it's conjecture, like much of my work, Brad. What's eating you?'

'Show me.' He walked over to the woman's head, illuminated by a five-hundred-watt bulb. Her hair lay back off her forehead, and he could see the faint break in the makeup along her hairline. Kim had cleaned the area above her temple, exposing a bruise and a sharp gash.

'You can see that the bruise is essentially rectangular, meeting the cut line here.' Kim's gloved finger delicately traced the wound. 'Whatever she hit, or whatever hit her, was squared and flat, with an edge sharp enough to split the skin. A countertop or the edge of a desk.'

'An escape attempt. She hit her head on her bed or her dresser.'

The phone on the wall chirped and Kim picked it up, spoke into it. She nodded, thanked a lab tech, and faced Brad.

'Dresser,' she said. 'They found her hair and blood on the edge of the dresser at the foot of her bed. This one almost got away.'

'Maybe.' The makeup, all of it, had been applied with a careful, experienced hand. The killer wasn't just caking on foundation to cover imperfections. He was accentuating his victim's own beauty with a nearly flawless application. A makeup artist.

He dabbed her white cheek with a light touch. Cold. Like putty.

Kim spoke quietly. 'He uses a Maybelline mineral foundation, nearly white, anticipating their skin tone at time of death so that they look nearly perfect dead. Alive she probably looked like she was wearing a mask of white.'

'Same makeup?'

'My guess is yes, but no confirmation from the lab yet.'

Brad traced her skin. A hint of blush, but only enough to make her face appear . . . human. The eyeliner looked as if it had been applied by a laser tool rather than a human hand. A hint of grey eyeshadow. Red lipstick . . .

His mind drifted to an image of Paradise swallowed by the huge chair like a rag doll with stringy hair. Her brown eyes seemed to climb inside his head. They haunted him still. She'd told him as much about himself in the space of thirty seconds as he'd learned in five years. Perhaps more.

'She's stunning.'

Brad twisted back. Nikki had walked in on them. She held a photocopy of the killer's latest note in her hands. Her eyes lifted from the body on the table and met his.

'Be careful who you love,' Nikki said, handing him the note. She continued to recite the Bride Collector's words from memory. 'I just might kill all the beautiful ones.'

'He's doing that already.'

She didn't appear satisfied by Brad's attempt to dismiss the threat. 'I am more intelligent than you. Bless me, Father, for I will sin.'

Brad glanced at the note and saw that she'd repeated it to the word, except for the end. *Be careful who you love. I just might kill all the beautiful ones. I am more intelligent than you. Bless me, Father, for I will sin. Oh yes, yes I will.*

'And we're here to stop him.'

'This doesn't bother you?' she demanded.

'The whole case bothers me.'

'And this note elevates the case to an entirely new level. He's making your involvement personal and has issued a direct threat against those you love.'

'Then we shouldn't have to worry. I'm not married and I'm not dating anyone.'

For a long moment they held the gaze, lost in the mysteries behind the case. Behind the Bride Collector. Behind the killer's note. Behind this silent exchange between them.

Nikki spoke without breaking eye contact. 'Can I talk to you for a minute? Outside?'

He glanced at Kim, who dismissed them with an arched brow. 'Don't let me stop you. I've got plenty to do.'

Nikki took his arm and led him into the basement hallway. She turned towards the stairs leading up to the offices and lab, then stepped into a supply room across the hall. The door swung closed behind them.

'So then, who is it?' she asked, facing him.

'I'm not . . . what do you mean "Who is it?"? Who's the killer?'

But she had that look in her eye that could make a grown man confess his deepest fear, and Brad knew she was talking about the two of them, not the killer.

Worse, she knew that he knew. 'You know what I'm talking about. Would you agree that this means the Bride Collector is watching you?'

'I've already taken steps to set up surveillance in high-probability locations.'

'He's not that dumb,' she said. 'We have to assume that he's watching you and we have to assume that he knows some things about your personal life.'

'Such as?'

'Such as who you love.'

So . . . He was right. She was afraid the note was directed at her. That the threat had been made against her.

And truthfully, Brad couldn't be sure that she was wrong. For starters, he wasn't sure what his feelings towards Nikki really were, and, either way, he wasn't sure how someone else might interpret his behaviour towards her. Clearly Kim, at least, suspected he and Nikki shared more than casual interest in each other.

'You're saying you want to cancel our dinner plans for tomorrow night,' he said. 'You don't want anyone watching to get the wrong idea and think you—'

Nikki stepped forwards and smothered his words with a kiss. Her lips were warm and soft and she wasn't being delicate. He was so surprised that he didn't have the presence of mind to return the kiss before she pulled back.

'No, you lummox, I don't want to cancel anything.' Her face was flushed with embarrassment. 'Sorry. Sorry, that wasn't appropriate.'

'No, it's okay. You're right.'

'Right about what?'

He wasn't sure.

'We have to assume that he sees you as a potential target. I've already made a call to the Denver police. They're putting a squad car outside your apartment tonight. The officer will follow you to and from work. I'm putting you under protective surveillance.'

She stepped back. 'When were you going to fill me in?'

'Now. As soon as I was done with Kim. Sorry, I hope you don't—'

'No, it's fine. Overkill, maybe, but . . . I appreciate the thought.'

His cell phone rang. Frank. He flipped it open. 'Hello, Frank.'

'I have the director from the Center for Wellness and Intelligence on the other line. She says that a resident named Paradise has agreed to see the body. On one condition: that you bring the body to her. She insists that you'll know what she's talking about and wants your answer.'

'That's impossible.' His head swam. It was outlandish, really, taking a body to a woman who claimed to see ghosts when she touched dead bodies. There were a dozen reasons not to even consider it, beginning with the fact that Melissa's distraught mother was coming to the morgue in a few hours to identify her daughter's body.

But there was another reason that now flooded Brad's mind. Paradise.

There was something about Paradise that he couldn't shake. And in the absence of any other reasonable paths that might lead to the killer . . . why not? Yes, well there were plenty of reasons why not, but next to the slightest chance of breaking the case, they suddenly felt trivial.

'I'll tell her,' Frank said.

'No.' Brad held Nikki's stare. 'No, tell her we agree. Tell her we'll be there in two hours with the body.'

The night was cooling, hastened by mountain shadows that crept towards the city. Quinton Gauld stood between two boulders on the ridge overlooking the compound below, peering through binoculars. The Center for Wellness and Intelligence.

This was Brad Raines' third trip to the isolated centre for nutcases in as many days, and Quinton had watched him from this very vantage point on two of those occasions.

He knew some things about the Center for Wellness and Intelligence. The fact, for example, that the facility was made for people like him. Intelligent and gifted. But watching the nutcases wandering around the grounds, he found himself disgusted that anyone would mislead these fools into thinking they were even remotely like him.

There was God, there were the angels, there were humans, there were dogs, there were bugs. A man had to know where he fit in. To compare those jerking about below to him was like trying compare a child tooting a plastic horn to a maestro conducting Beethoven's fifth symphony. It was, in fact, people like these who gave people like him a bad name.

Still, there was something fascinating happening with the FBI agent. He'd picked up on the clues Quinton had planted and thrown himself into an exhaustive search of mental health facilities, which had led Raines to this small compound nestled away in the foothills.

And while they were buried in their 'investigation', he'd taken the fifth favourite right out from under their investigative noses. Which was important to him, doing it under their noses, so to speak. God moved about under the collective nose of most ignorant humans, as did angels and demons.

As did Quinton Gauld. He'd seen the red and white ambulance pull out of the city morgue, and immediately a dozen questions flooded his mind. Were they taking a body or going to get a body? Or was the ambulance for a body at all?

Surely they weren't transporting Melissa so soon.

Careful not to be spotted, he'd followed the ambulance in his Chevy pick-up. The moment he identified their destination, he frantically raced along a shorter route and put himself in a position to watch them arrive. The ambulance came to a stop in the circular drive. A driver and one other person Quinton quickly identified as Agent Raines exited the front doors and the back of the van.

The very idea of his perfect maiden delivered to this den of idiots, whatever the reason, revolted him. There was no reason for it, and his fears were therefore unfounded. He was seeing ghosts where none existed. He was imagining the horrors of a lesser beast. He was being a demon rather than an angel. He wasn't giving the FBI agent enough credit, because not even the FBI would haul his beautiful, nearly matchless bride here as if she were a side of beef.

If they've dragged my bride out into the night like this, I swear I will sin. Forgive me, Father, but I swear on your holy name that I will sin.

Raines and the paramedic pulled out a gurney. Quinton felt his chest seize. A body was strapped to the thin mattress and, although a white sheet was pulled over her face, Quinton could make out the nose and, even from this distance, he knew, without the slightest doubt, that he was staring through the binoculars at the fifth favourite.

A buzz ignited at the base of his head and gripped his mind as though a hand had reached up into his skull and latched its fingers into his brain. A hand with an electrical current. God's hand.

It had been many months since Quinton had felt such hot, swimming rage. He was so focused on their wheeling the gurney over the sidewalk – the jerking of her body, the flow of germs over her form, the door of the centre opening to accept her – that he was only dimly aware that his body was shaking. An incoherent mumble spilled from his mouth, a word salad about God and death and beauty and favourites that was far too advanced to be understood by anyone but himself.

The body disappeared inside. Quinton quieted and stared for

another ten minutes, begging God to grace him with another sighting; just one more glimpse of her body. But none came.

He lowered the glasses, squatted on his heels and began to rock. He knew it was behaviour favoured by unstable nutcases seeking cadence for their offbeat thoughts, but no one could see him, so he gave in to the comforting motion.

This changed everything. No, it didn't. But it did. Everything. Nothing, in the task at hand. But everything in terms of how that task might be fulfilled. As with any great objective, there were major forces in opposition, and for the first time, Quinton had seen them face-to-face. Having been drawn out in the open, the murderous enemy would now undoubtedly play a role.

He'd tested Raines, tempted him with a simple note. *Be careful who you love, because I will sin.* The FBI agent had latched on like a snake. Why? Why had Quinton felt so compelled to draw the man in? Because the snake needed a garden; even God needed an audience.

He closed his eyes and tried to calm himself. After a few minutes, his heart rate started to decrease.

Okay then, Mr Raines, I accept your challenge. Okay, Rain Man. I take up your gauntlet. Stop me if you can, you heathen witch doctor. Because I fully intend on stopping you.

CHAPTER TWELVE

Roudy sat in the corner of his room, hugging his knees close to his chest. His hair looked as if a twister had passed through it overnight, his face was as blank as a bleached sheet, his lips moving in a rapid but inaudible whisper. Paradise stood at his doorway, doorknob in hand, momentarily frozen by the change in him. It wasn't often that this kind of depression overtook Roudy, but when it did he spiralled to the lowest of lows.

'Oh, no.' Andrea stared at the tossed room from behind Paradise. Roudy's white bed sheets lay in a heap next to three books spread open where they'd been dumped. A bowl of uneaten Cheerios sat on the desk, surrounded by spilled cereal from a tipped yellow box.

'Oh, no, oh no . . .' Andrea had woken in a state of terrible anxiety herself, and seeing Roudy in this state would likely push her even deeper into her own fear and misery.

'It's okay, Andrea,' Paradise said softly, stepping into the room.

'No, no, no.' She rushed past Paradise and flew to the corner, where she dropped to her knees and threw her arms around Roudy, weeping. 'I'm sorry, I'm sorry.'

Roudy mumbled softly, but otherwise gave no indication he was even aware they'd entered his room.

Paradise walked halfway to them and stopped. She'd come to inform Roudy that the FBI needed her. That she, Paradise Founder, the simple twenty-four-year-old girl who'd supposedly suffered a psychotic break at age seventeen, was finally valued by someone on the outside. The world needed *her*.

The FBI had brought a body for her.

It was exhilarating! And downright terrifying. They were

looking to her, Paradise. Special Agent Brad Raines, a real man who pressed his clothes and wore cologne and who was a star in the real world, needed her.

She'd come for Roudy's enthusiastic support or maybe a bit of his jealousy; honestly she didn't know which. Instead, she'd found this – a shell of a man stripped of his sense of worth. He would have nothing for her, and for a moment she resented him, sitting there so helpless and feeble, whimpering with grief.

To make matters worse, Andrea would join him, leaving Paradise to glory in her small spotlight alone, which made it no spotlight at all.

When Roudy didn't respond to Andrea's weeping, the girl sank to the floor, curled up in a ball and continued crying softly.

'The FBI are bringing me a body, Roudy,' Paradise said. 'They want my help. Maybe you could help too?'

At any other time, Sherlock would be consumed by his own delusions of grandeur, pacing, jabbing the air, insisting that he join her; that without his help all would be lost; that not to include him would be criminal, prosecutable.

Andrea would be snapping at him, telling him to mind his own business. That this was Paradise's time for a little attention, although they all knew that Mr Raines only had one thing on his mind. Still, it was something.

Instead they were both ravaged by the monsters inside of them.

Paradise's empathy for Roudy washed away her own need for attention. Dark depression was a beast that visited many here, a debilitating illness that could be managed by drugs at times, but never at the expense of human touch and love.

The FBI could wait.

Paradise walked up to Roudy, settled to her knees and gently rubbed his back. The only time she could hold a man was when he was broken and in need of comfort.

'It's okay, Roudy. It's going to be okay. This will pass.'

In response he just moaned.

'You have to get better quickly, Sherlock. They're going to need you. They're at their wits' end and they're going to need the best.'

He began to relax, then slowly he turned his wide eyes to look at her. She believed his mind was working, screaming for him to acknowledge her wisdom, but his emotions had shut him down for now.

She kissed him on the forehead and gently placed both arms around his shoulders. 'This is the price we pay for being so good at what we do, right? But it's okay, because you help so many people, Roudy. I'm very proud of you. We all are.'

He went limp, and she let him lean into her. Andrea was looking up from the floor like a puppy who wanted some attention as well. Paradise stroked her hair. 'We're so proud of both of you.'

They remained on the floor for several long minutes, letting the pain work its course, and for a while Paradise forgot that she had been on her way to the front office. Her ability to bring comfort to a few here at CWI had become the greater part of her identity. The attention from the FBI, however flattering, was only a recent and likely passing distraction in her world.

But they were waiting. Brad was waiting.

'I have to go, but I'll be back,' she finally said. 'This will pass, Roudy. And when it does, we're going to need you.'

Andrea pushed herself to her knees, then stood and walked out of the room like a zombie. Headed to her own room for a shower, undoubtedly.

'I'm the best,' Roudy mumbled.

Paradise returned her attention to the man who was staring at the wall. 'Yes, you are. You always have been.'

He looked at her, lips quivering. 'Tell them I'm sorry. I'm not so good right now. I'm very sorry, maybe later.'

'I will.'

She stood, patted him twice on his shoulder, and left. She closed his door behind her, slipped down the hall and hurried through the hub. Becky Horner stood in the middle of the floor with her hair teased up into an afro, staring. Flower sat next to the wall tracing something on the window, watching Paradise, along with half a dozen other residents. Was her reputation getting out?

For a moment she was tempted to run back to the room and stay with Roudy where she belonged. What did she think she was going to do anyway? Touch the dead and give them the name of the killer? She was almost certain she couldn't help them. Truth be told, she'd gone along with all of this because of him.

Because of Brad Raines. The first man in her memory who had shown the remotest interest in her beyond the kind Casanova routinely offered.

But they were waiting for her. She'd put herself in a predicament, and now she had to finish what she had started.

She walked down the path and entered the front reception area. The nurse, Jonathan, was waiting for her. 'Hey, Paradise. They went to the kitchen.'

'Behind the hub?'

'Something about refrigeration. Allison said she'd meet you there.'

'They have the body in the kitchen?' She was dumbfounded. It would mean going back through the hub! Jonathan must have seen the look of concern on her face.

'Come on, I'll take you around through the delivery entrance.'

'It goes by the fence,' she said.

'It's either around the wing or through the hub. Your call.'

'Fine, around the wing.' But she never liked being so close to the fence, the only thing between her and the outside world.

Jonathan led her back across the lawn, around the building, and unlocked the entrance used for deliveries. 'You know where you're going from here?'

'Yeah.'

'Okay, see you around.'

'Yeah. See you.'

At the moment she felt like anything but a ghost reader. She was sure to make a complete fool of herself.

Paradise walked down a hall littered with boxes of olive oil and soups, a few crates of onions and potatoes. She stepped through the kitchen's back door and studied the scene before her.

The kitchen had a large centre island covered in stainless steel, which was used for food preparation. Utensils and pans hung from a rack overhead. The stoves lined the far right wall; a large walk-in fridge opened on the left. There was no sign of a body anywhere, so Paradise assumed they had put it in the refrigerator to keep it cool.

Brad Raines was talking quietly to Allison, both of them with their backs towards her. Something about the funding behind the centre and cost of operations. He stood a full head taller than Allison, blond hair neatly trimmed around his ears, above his collar in the back. He wore a white shirt with sleeves rolled up. Black slacks and shoes. A belt. Very neat, very ordered.

Paradise stood still, aware that they hadn't expected her to come through the back. She could still turn and sneak out, avoiding the embarrassment of talking to him again after running away. Did he think she was crazy? Surely he did. She'd lectured him and then fled at his mere mention of her leaving her safe haven.

Maybe she really was crazy? But she wasn't, she knew that. She was, however, intimidated by the man who stood across the room. He completely outclassed her. He, the specimen of perfection, standing head and shoulders above her.

He had watched her with sincere interest. And honestly, that was the real irony, wasn't it? He had no business looking at her with any kind of interest, because she neither deserved nor wanted it. She was dirt in his world.

Paradise had no adult experience in that world, and looking at Brad now, it occurred to her that the only way to cope with him was to bring him down to her level, even if just a little. Not by being mean to him, but by pretending to be his equal, maybe even his superior in some respects.

Isn't that what she'd done during most of their first meeting? She'd protected herself by coming over distant and in command of the situation. She had to do that again or risk falling apart in front of him.

She couldn't let him know how much she liked him.

Paradise gasped and jerked back into the hall. How could she think such a thing? It wasn't true, of course, not in the faintest. She liked him, but not in that way.

Allison called out. 'Paradise?'

The thought that she might actually be attracted to this man terrified her. It made her feel like a worm, knowing that he couldn't ever, under any circumstances, bring himself to return any affection for a piece of waste like her.

'Are you there?'

She had to control herself!

Paradise took a deep, calming breath, absently smoothed her hair and stepped out. They were both looking in her direction. She thought she should say something that demonstrated anything but the fear she felt, but instead she stopped and stared at them.

Mr Raines (she couldn't call him Brad any longer) smiled. 'Hello, Paradise.'

'Hello.'

'Thank you for coming.'

The way he was looking at her . . . She knew it was just normal and friendly. After all, he needed her help, so he was being nice. But it was so easy to misinterpret his look as something more. As interest. She had to gain control!

'Well, I doubt I can be of any help,' she said, walking forwards, hoping that he didn't see the slight shake in her hands. 'But so that you can get this off your mind and move on, I'll do my trick for you.'

'Trick?'

'Trick, show, whatever. I'll be your monkey in this little zoo you've set up so you can get down to real work.'

'Paradise . . .' Allison warned her.

'Sorry, but it's true, isn't it?'

Mr Raines looked tongue-tied, and that gave Paradise a moment's encouragement. She might be nothing in his world, but here she could still be somebody. And was. Roudy and Andrea might even be proud of her.

'So where's the body?'

The walk-in refrigeration unit was around the wall to the right, and Mr Raines called to someone. 'Bob?'

A few moments later, a paramedic wearing a stethoscope wheeled a gurney around the corner. The body was covered in a white sheet, but the woman's form was unmistakable.

Paradise stared at the body and let her mind go where it wanted to go, into the hidden folds of the story behind what her eyes saw.

I see the woman rising from the sheet, swinging off the gurney, stepping backwards towards the door. The sheet becomes a dress on her fair frame. Back through the door, then fast through the city to her own house and inside, where a man is waiting for her. She is kissing the man, turning in circles as if they are lovers dancing. But then he comes around again, and I see that he isn't a man at all. The woman is kissing a gorilla that suddenly bares its fangs and . . .

'Paradise?'

She looked at Allison. 'What?'

They just looked at her. She had to get back on track. She felt panic crowding her mind, but managed to push it back.

'There's too many people here.'

The paramedic glanced at Mr Raines, who nodded. 'I'll just step outside,' the medic said, then left the three of them with the body.

'Is that better?' Allison asked.

Mr Raines – Brad to those closer to him, to his friends, his peers and his lovers – was watching her. She had to stay strong.

'Yes, that's better,' she said, moving forwards. 'So what exactly do you want me to do, Mr Raines? Fondle a dead body in front of you?'

'Paradise!'

'You're right, that wasn't called for,' she said, horrified at her choice of words. 'Sorry, that's not what I meant.'

'No need to apologize,' Mr Raines said. 'Trust me, I'm grateful that you've agreed to try to help us out. I realize that this is unprecedented. I feel a bit awkward myself.'

'Why, because you're not used to working with monkeys?'

'Well, no, that's not what I was thinking.'

'But it's at least partly true. You could never feel comfortable in the company of people like us. We're all just too weird for you.'

Allison tried to steer her right again. 'Please, Paradise, this isn't the time for—'

'For transparency?' she interrupted. 'No, not in front of real people.'

Even as she spoke, Paradise heard the unkindness of her own words and wanted to take them back. They seemed to jolt even Allison. For a long time she stared at Paradise, while Brad shifted his eyes between them.

'You're right,' Allison said. Then turning to Mr Raines, 'She's right. This whole thing is absurd. You're using her for your own selfish purposes without rightly respecting her own needs. I think this is all a mistake. Maybe you should just leave.'

What? No! Not yet.

'I'm sorry.' Brad – Mr Raines – looked dumfounded. The poor man must be thinking he'd entered the twilight zone. 'I thought we had an understanding. We went to considerable trouble bringing the body here.'

'But, you see, that's the problem,' Allison said. 'To you this is all considerable trouble. Where does that leave Paradise? I think we need to consider her needs in this exchange. Don't you?'

'Yes. Of course, but I wasn't aware that we'd failed to do that.'

It occurred to her that they were both treating her like a child. She wasn't a child. 'I don't have any needs you can take care of, Mr Raines. And the last thing I need is for you to play matchmaker, Allison.' Too much information. She couldn't seem to stop putting her foot in her mouth! 'I don't have the slightest interest in that aspect of this encounter. But you've come all this way, so let's finish.'

Before I ask you to hold me, Brad, because the truth is I would dream about a man like you every waking moment if I allowed myself to. I would lay myself on a sacrificial altar to float through space with you. But I can't, so I won't, not ever.

Nonsense! It just wasn't true!

She stepped around the stainless-steel island and approached the gurney.

'I'm sorry, Paradise. Really, we don't have to do this if you feel uncomfortable.' Brad, yes Brad, because his name was Brad, stepped to the other side of the body. Allison seemed content to remain where she stood.

'It's fine, Mr Raines. I just don't know exactly what you expect me to do.'

'You said you saw these . . . ghosts . . . a couple of times before. Twice when you came in contact with deceased bodies.'

'Yes. But I have to tell you that most of the "ghosts" I see are just figments of my imagination.' Blue butterflies flying through the window behind you, sailing into space, singing wonderfully. 'I can't explain what I saw or why I saw it.'

'What did you see?'

She hesitated, reaching back for the memory. 'I saw the ghost of the paramedic leaning over one, telling her that everything was going to be okay. I saw his ghost.'

'Or the dead person's last memory of him,' he said gently, with true interest.

She nodded. 'Or her memory of him.'

The exchange bolstered her, all of a sudden. And Brad Raines was a beautiful man. She couldn't pretend that he wasn't. It was no wonder that Andrea was so suspicious of him. His face was smooth, like a boy's, even though his jaw was strong and he was maybe thirty. His brown eyes looked like dark amber crystals, his lips were smooth and his hair looked soft. She would like to touch it, in her dreams of him.

She was ashamed that she was still looking at him. Why didn't he look away? Was he so amazed at her courage, staring back at him even though she couldn't measure up? Was he surprised that she didn't understand her place as the rag he might use to shine his shoes? How dare she stare into his eyes!

The moment of silence stretched and Paradise fought an urge to run away.

'Thank you for doing this, Paradise,' Brad said. 'I realize how awkward this is for you, and I want you to know that I don't expect anything. It doesn't matter if you don't see anything.'

It was kind of him, and she thought he meant what he said.
'But since we're here, why don't we give it a try?'
She nodded.
Brad reached down, took the hem of the sheet in his fingers
and pulled it down. Her eyes were on his fingernails, how clean
they were. Being clean and tidy must be important to him. She
didn't know how to be like that, and she hated herself for it.
'Her name is Melissa,' Brad said.
Paradise blinked and looked at the dead woman's pretty, pasty-
white face. There was a cut above her right temple. Perfect lips,
perfect skin.
She hated Melissa.
But that was ridiculous. She hated no one, not even her own
father. What was getting into her? 'She died last night,' Brad said.
Her mind began to fill with the circumstances surrounding the
woman's death, abstract images that came from her own imagination. The dancing lover and the ape biting off her face.
Paradise was suddenly unsure she could go through with this.
Mnemophobia offered only a fine line between the fear of bad
memories and the fear of creating new bad memories, and though
she'd worked through it all with Allison, she now felt those old
fingers of fear reaching up inside of her.
It should be me, she thought. *I should be dead instead of this
beautiful woman. I'm not even a woman, not really.*
But she was here and he was waiting and the fear of disap-
pointing him was as great as her fear of creating a bad memory
by touching such a beautiful dead body. So she stretched out her
hand, tried and failed to still her quivering fingers, and gently
touched Melissa's white cheek.
She felt only the bloodless skin, chilled by the refrigerator's
cool air. She saw no ghosts. No visions. Not even an image
spawned by her own overactive imagination. Just a dead girl on
a gurney, cold to the touch.
Paradise left her fingers on the face and glanced up at Brad,
whose eyes rose to meet hers, searching.
What did you expect? A butterfly to fly out of her mouth when I

touched her? A frog to leap out of my shirt? A ghost to pop out of her? I never did deserve to be in here with you, so may I crawl back into my corner now? I'll just rock and moan for a while like a good monkey.

'I'm sorry,' she said.

'Nothing, huh?'

'I told you.'

'Nothing at all? Not even a . . . thought?'

'Nothing.' She removed her hand. 'I'm s . . .'

But she didn't get to say *sorry*, because in that moment her vision suddenly went black. A voice echoed in the darkness, speaking to her. 'I'm going to drill some small holes in your heels, about half an inch wide, but don't worry, as soon as your blood drains out, I'll plug them back up. You'll still be beautiful. Perfect. Okay?'

A woman's voice: 'Okay.' Melissa's voice, only it felt as if it was coming from Paradise, because in this moment, Paradise was Melissa.

Her mind reeled with objection and she reached for something to steady herself. Flesh filled her hand. Melissa's flesh. But Paradise was in a full panic and felt as if she was going to fall, so she held tight.

'Melissa?' A man's voice filled her head. *His* voice. Did she know this voice? Had she heard this voice, felt this hot breath on her cheek?

A face filled her vision. *His* face. A handsome clean-cut face with strong cheekbones and dark hair. Genuine, smiling eyes as he reached a gloved hand for her cheek and stroked her skin with his thumb.

'So beautiful, my dear. You are his favourite, remember that. And that makes you my favourite, because you were lost but now you are found. I found you. Think of me as God; it will help you.'

Horror at the sound of that familiar voice slammed into Paradise and robbed her of breath. She tried to pull her hand away, but her fingers were latched onto the body's cold flesh as if they wanted more. A part of her needed to know more.

Paradise screamed and jerked back with all her strength. Her hand slipped free and the blackness cleared, but now she was reeling backwards, tripping. She crashed into the stove behind her and fell to the ground, hard.

The landing knocked the wind from her, silencing her scream. She lay on the smooth concrete floor, shivering. Allison's calm voice reached out, but Paradise was already clawing on her belly for the safe place. For the white fog, where all that was bad would not find her.

Slowly, she inched towards it, desperate to reach the safety before the monsters grabbed her legs and pulled her back into the darkness.

Dear God, save me. Don't let them get me. Take me in your arms, hold me, don't let evil eat me. Please, don't reject me!

She struggled to all fours and crawled forwards as the first wisps of white fog drifted past her. She was shaking on the kitchen floor, and two voices, a man's and a woman's, were trying to calm her, but in her mind she was entering the fog.

The monsters nipped at her heels, ripped off one of her shoes. She crawled faster, on bloody knees now. And then she was in the fog and she zigzagged to her left and right to shake any final pursuit.

Bloodied, winded and too weak to crawl another foot, she collapsed in a heap and hugged the earth, relieved, so terribly relieved. She'd made it. The blackness was gone. She was safely in the fog that had protected her for so long. And Paradise began to cry with gratitude.

Gradually, calm settled over her, like the loving breath of God. The monsters were gone. She couldn't even remember what they'd looked like.

Thank you. Thank you, my saviour. Thank you for taking my pain.

Brad stood back from Allison, who sat on the floor with her legs folded underneath her, comforting Paradise, rubbing her back. 'It's okay, honey. Take your time, it's all going to be okay.' Paradise lay on the ground, crying softly.

He wanted to do something, help in some way, but he was at a loss. Whatever had just happened, he was neither trained nor prepared to process it. His professional boundaries felt confining. They were silly borders meant to help ignorant people cope with complicated life.

Paradise had either had a psychotic episode that resulted in a powerful hallucination, or she'd actually connected with some *thing* that had caused her to react immediately and violently to its threat.

Ghosts did not exist. But the idea that she'd suffered nothing more than a hallucination made a foolishness out of his bringing the body here in the first place. The fact that he had brought the body meant he was willing to consider that Paradise could connect with these so-called ghosts, however impossible it seemed.

A dozen times on the ride here, he'd asked himself why he was so willing. It certainly wasn't because he'd suddenly developed a belief in the supernatural. Nor because they just might get lucky.

Really, he'd come because of her. Because of Paradise. Because of the way she'd looked out of the window earlier today and told him about another world. Because her eyes had scanned him once and told him who he was with unnerving calm and precision.

There was mystery in her eyes. It was as if her mind really did open to another world, and he'd been given just one glance into that world. Into Paradise.

He'd brought the body to Paradise for *her* sake. Because she deserved the chance to complete what he'd asked her to do. Having asked once, he could not turn his back on her decision to help him. Whatever else he did, he could not hurt Paradise. She'd suffered too much.

So he'd brought the body. And despite her insistence that she would not see anything, Paradise had seen something.

Now what? He wanted to reach out to her and reassure her the way Allison was, but that would be inappropriate. He was a special agent, not her psychoanalyst.

Allison looked back at him. 'It's okay. Just a simple defence mechanism. It's the way she's learned to cope.'

'She'll be okay?'

'Of course she will.' Allison lovingly drew a strand of hair off Paradise's cheek and tucked it behind her ear as she might her own daughter's. Paradise calmed. 'Every mind has its fuse. Every circuit has a reset. The more powerful the computer, the better the firewall must be. One of our residents taught me that.' She smiled and looked at Paradise with gentle eyes. 'Paradise has a powerful mind. She's just protecting it.'

For the first time since coming here, Brad considered the possibility that he had entered a world where the minds were not sick when compared to his; simply greater – and learning to cope. Like Paradise's, they were so powerful they required special systems that lesser minds, like his, did not.

'What happened?' he asked.

'Well, like I told you, she sees ghosts. Don't tell me you don't believe in ghosts, Mr Raines.'

He didn't know what to say.

'Not to worry. Learning to love is more important than learning about ghosts.'

'Whatever she saw—'

'Is probably gone by now,' Allison said. 'Unfortunately, her experience appears to have been a bad one, which means it probably involved a man. The killer perhaps. Her mind's probably erasing it now, as we speak. Her defence mechanism isn't always useful, but until she can learn to cope . . .'

Paradise's eyes suddenly opened and she sat up, looking like a small child who'd woken from a long afternoon nap. She stared at them, then at the floor, confused.

'What happened?' Her eyes settled on the gurney and recognition filled them. 'It happened, didn't it? I saw something.'

'Yes, I think you did.' Allison smoothed her hair.

Paradise brushed Allison's hand away and pushed herself to her feet. 'Now that I'm totally mortified . . .'

'There's nothing to be embarrassed about,' Brad said. 'This is why we brought the body.'

'Then I guess it was a waste of time. Even if I did see something, I can't remember what it was.'

'You remember touching her?'

'Yes. And I remember standing here making a fool of myself before I touched the body, but that's all I remember. I'm sorry to say that I can't help you, Mr Raines. This has all been a mistake.' Strong emotion was creeping into her voice. 'Maybe Roudy can help you?'

Brad felt his heart tighten with empathy. Paradise walked towards the door, trying to hold her shoulders square, but she walked as if she herself were a ghost.

'Paradise, please . . .'

She left without looking back.

CHAPTER THIRTEEN

'So. This is it, huh?' Nikki sauntered across the living room, carrying a glass of pinot grigio, perusing Brad's choice of décor. Women were always interested in his tastes, in part because his choices were so well defined. Most men, it seemed to Brad, didn't have refined preferences. They had tastes, sure, particularly when it came to cars and women. But ask them about fabrics and colours, about women's clothes, paint colours and accessories, and they would usually just shrug their shoulders.

'I didn't realize you were so metrosexual.' She took a sip of her wine. They'd spent two hours sharing crab legs and two lobster tails at Trulucks on their so-called date. A second long day after the fiasco at CWI had produced only more dead ends, and a quiet dinner with Nikki had been a welcome break.

Brad set the bottle back in the built-in wine cooler under the kitchen counter and picked up his own glass. 'Black velvet and chrome isn't exactly feminine,' he said.

'Did I say feminine? But you're right, *metro* is the wrong word.' She looked at the five-foot-high Tuscan floral painting over two chairs between the urns.

'Yeah, not exactly contemporary, I know,' he said, crossing to her. 'I like to' – he motioned at the room with his glass – 'blend styles a bit. I know . . . contemporary with a rich Tuscan décor would have most decorators rolling their eyes. But every piece in here is deliberate. The couch is from France, a designer named Trudeau, whose chrome work is sought after. The urns were once museum pieces in Mexico, not terribly valuable but originals nevertheless.'

'And the painting?'

'José Rodriguez. An original. The other paintings are also originals, nothing too fancy. Just carefully selected.' He winked and lifted his glass to her.

'So you like originals?' she asked.

'I guess you could say that.'

'And does this taste extend to women?'

She was referring to herself. But the first image that filled Brad's mind was of a shorter woman, frail, with long dark hair and pale skin. She chewed her fingernails and bathed maybe twice a week if encouraged. Her mind was an ocean of mystery and, although she didn't know it, she had pulled him in with a single look.

Nikki took another sip and set her glass down on the etched-glass coffee table. 'Because I would have pegged you more as the kind who went after perfection. I mean, look at this place.'

'Well, yes, I like to keep things clean.'

'Clean? Okay, this is not clean.' She made a dismissive gesture with one hand to accentuate *not*. 'This is immaculate.'

'I don't like dust.'

'And what about your closet? Don't tell me . . . All your socks are lined up. Sorted by colour.'

Brad felt himself blush. Thankfully only two lamps lit the living room, providing some cover. He managed an apologetic smile. 'It makes things easier to find.'

'It's more than that, though, isn't it? The way you keep your office so ordered, the way you wipe down the counter at work, the way you go over files again and again, reading and rereading. We have a term for people like you.'

'So I've been told.'

'Borderline obsessive-compulsive personality. Not OCD as in *disorder*, mind you, but personality. Big difference. Thankfully.'

He shrugged, feeling awkward.

'It's okay, Mr Brad Raines. I happen to find your attention to detail attractive and endearing.' She crossed to the drapes in bare feet, having left her black heels by the door. 'You like original.

But you also like perfect. So which is it? Or is that what the hold-up is, your search for that perfect original?'

She swept the drapes wide and two images struck Brad at once. Nikki's well-toned body, hugged by a short, sleeveless black dress, silhouetted by Denver's bright lights – a vision of its own kind of perfection.

And the piece of paper taped to the outside of the window.

Nikki gasped. Brad's attention shifted to the piece of paper and, in the space of a single breath, he knew what it was. The Bride Collector. The killer had found a way to tape a note to the outside of his window, three storeys above the street.

Outside of *his* window? Why? How?

The possibilities crowded Brad's mind. A ladder. A window washer on a ladder. He'd done it this way to avoid surveillance cameras. A window washer in the middle of the day, or a repairman of some kind. A city worker. However it was done, it required careful work.

This note, then, was important to the killer. Assuming it was from him.

'Brad?'

He broke from the thought gripping him, set his glass down, and stepped up behind Nikki. The white paper was dimmed by the tinted glass, but it had been taped flat at the top and bottom with Scotch tape, and the Bride Collector's handwriting was unmistakable.

They're trying to kill me, everyone is trying to kill me.

But the advantage of being God is that I get to change my mind. Why did you move my bride? My time. Have you killed Jack lately? The snake waits in the garden, seeking a new bride to join him in the hole. Perfect twice. Me.

Paradise lost. It takes one to know one. To know the insane. When the jack is in the whole. Does jack

want me to hide from you? No, I'm not sick, I'm just better than you.

I'm the sunshine and you're the Rain Man.

A chill bolted through Brad's body. He stared at the writing, then reread the note.

What could he say? It was suddenly all very . . . personal.

'Flight of ideas, but hemmed in to make an odd kind of sense,' Nikki said, her voice shaky. 'How did he get this note up here? Surely he was seen.'

'We'll canvas and take a look at any surveillance data in the area, but I'm sure he covered his tracks.'

'No one can see in here?'

'No.'

'But he obviously knows where you live. For all we know he watched us tonight. Or is watching us right now!' She sounded a bit frantic. Not surprising, all things considered, but not typical for her.

Brad scanned the office building across the street. Most windows were dark, only a few lighted. A parking structure four buildings to the right could make a decent perch for a man with strong binoculars. But none of that mattered. At night his apartment's glass would look black from the outside.

He snapped open his phone, called the agent on duty and requested that an evidence team join them as soon as possible.

Nikki paced in front of the window, hands on hips, rereading the note. 'This is getting crazy. What do you think?'

It wasn't like him to be easily disturbed, but this was significant. Brad set his phone on the sofa table, hands shaking, then stared back at the note, trying his best to ignore the pins pricking his skin at the back of his neck.

Paradise lost. The Bride Collector was referring to the Old Testament story of the snake in the garden. The fall of man, paradise lost. But the coincidence between his use of the word and Brad's connection with Paradise at the CWI was uncanny.

'Paradise,' Nikki said.

'Yeah. Paradise. Who's Jack?'

She faced him, face drawn. 'He knows you went to see her?'

'Not necessarily. But he clearly knows we moved the body.'

'Let's assume he is referencing her, Paradise.' She spoke quickly, tense. 'So first he makes some oblique reference to the women in your life, possibly me. Then you go to CWI with the body of his victim, and he goes to great lengths to leave a note, this time with a direct threat. So, what, his fixation is now *you*? Every woman you come in contact with?'

It wasn't uncommon for pattern criminals to develop unhealthy fixations with those they saw as adversaries. In psychopaths' minds, the blame for their ruined lives lay not with their behaviour but with whoever threatened their ability to engage in that behaviour.

'He knows I'm trying to stop him. He sees me as a competitive threat and, in his world, that means women.' Brad glanced at her. 'How does that sound?'

'It's tough to know how the insane think.' She faced him. 'Tell me more about Paradise.'

'What do you mean?'

'Humour me. I mean, you've seen her, what, three times now? You spent half our dinner talking abut her. If I didn't know who she was, I might be jealous.'

What? The revelation came out of the blue.

'She's part of the case. We only discussed her for a few minutes.'

'Whatever, I'm just saying. Not that I have the right to be jealous.' She forced a sharp chuckle. 'Listen to me, I'm pathetic. She's . . .'

'She's what? A mess? Is she? Unlike us?'

Nikki's right brow shot up. 'Come again?'

It was his tone. In one moment he had dismissed Paradise, and in the next he was sounding desperate to defend her. In some strange way he felt as if he *should* defend her. She was defenceless. Abandoned by a world that had brutalized her.

'Come on, of course I feel for her.' There, he'd said it. 'Who wouldn't? She's a victim of the monster in all of us.'

Nikki nodded. 'I feel sorry for them too. But there's a difference between empathy and affection. I hope you understand that.'

'Actually, I don't think it's either empathy *or* affection.' He studied the note again. 'I think it's more respect.'

'In what way?'

'She sees things I don't. She's the fastest study I've ever met. A natural.'

Nikki broke off her stare. 'I can see that.' But her tone wasn't reassuring. 'I can see that' rather indicated that she saw something totally different.

'I'm just a little unnerved by all of this.' She waved at the note. 'Point is, this guy isn't kidding around. He's pressing through with this, and he's not even thinking about quitting.'

'Unless . . .'

She walked up to him and read the note over his shoulder. The scent of her perfume was still pleasant, a hint of spice in flowers. Her breathing came soft near his ear. 'Unless what?' The sound of her voice, light and clear. He was a fool, wasn't he? In so many ways Nikki was the perfect woman for him. He should be pursuing her now, regardless of the case.

Brad cleared his throat. 'Do you know what's crazy?'

She took two breaths before answering. 'Us.'

'Here we are, facing the work of a psychopath who's killed five women, two of them in the last week. We're both staring at a note threatening me, and instead of breaking the note down, we're posturing.'

She sighed. 'You're right. Sorry, it's all the stress. I hardly slept a wink last night.'

'Well, you have the day off tomorrow. Take it. Go see your mother. Meanwhile, there's a squad car outside your apartment.'

'This guy doesn't strike me as the kind who would let that stop him.' She waved it off. 'Don't worry, I can take care of myself. So, back to the original question: unless what?'

'I was thinking, unless he's changed his mind. Instead of another woman . . .'

'He's got you in his sights,' she finished. 'He's turned this into a game with you.'

'*I'm not sick, I'm just better than you,*' he read. '*I'm the sunshine and you're the Rain Man.*'

Nikki picked up her glass and took a sip, lost in thought. Swirled the wine and took another. '*Takes one to know one.* Does she trust you?'

'Who?'

'Paradise. She's young and impressionable.'

'Only a few years younger than we are.'

'Not in experience. She's probably taken with you. Star struck even.'

True. Paradise's lack of subtlety in her dismissal of him had in fact signalled her affection for him. The thought had returned to him several times since.

'She's not that naïve,' he said.

'Oh, I wouldn't count on it. You're a good-looking, powerful man, and you needed her. That's pretty strong medicine.'

'So now we're back here again? What's the point of this?'

Nikki walked over to the note. 'Maybe she knows more than she's telling you?'

'Not consciously.'

'You can't know that, not yet.'

The thought was offensive, but he couldn't dismiss it entirely. He could, however, give Paradise the benefit of the doubt. 'I doubt it.'

She turned to him. 'Then show them the file. Let them read the notes. I said it before, and now he's said it: *It takes one to know one.* It may only be circumstantial, but CWI is now directly tied to this case, and for all we know the key is locked in Paradise's mind. Use them all.'

Brad had already considered the possibility, however thin the reasoning. Roudy would certainly agree to it. But Paradise was another issue.

'I doubt she'd agree to see me—'

'Oh, please. You have her wrapped around your finger! She's playing you.'

'I don't think you understand. She's not like that.'

'She's a woman. I get women. Turn on the charm, ask with a twinkle in your eye. She'll agree, trust me.'

'You're actually suggesting I lead her on?' He turned away from her and shook his head. 'I couldn't do that. She's . . . No.'

'I'm not suggesting you lie. One way or another you have to find out what she knows. What she saw when she touched the body. She's your only lead.'

'I can't just pry her open and read her mind!'

'Listen to you, Brad. Why so cautious suddenly? This isn't like you.'

She was right, of course. He didn't know why he was so annoyed by her suggestion, but the thought of disturbing Paradise, regardless of the reason, felt wrong. She'd suffered enough already.

He dropped down on the couch and stared at the note plastered on the outside of the window.

'Earn her trust. Get her to lower her guard,' Nikki said. 'She might know more than she realizes.'

CHAPTER FOURTEEN

Two full days had passed since Paradise had attempted and then utterly failed to encounter the dead. Roudy had emerged from his black fog that first afternoon, and by sundown he was back to his pestering self. She'd spent the night alone in her room, with the door locked, ignoring the *tap, tap, tap* of her friends, who kept stopping by and knocking. They weren't rude enough to pound, but the taps might as well have been screams of ridicule.

'Come on, Paradise, what did we tell you?'

'I could have helped them, Paradise! I am the one they really want.'

'He only wants to get in your pants, Paradise! What did I tell you?'

'Go away!' she finally cried.

Twenty minutes later they were back. *Tap, tap, tap.*

But Paradise wasn't insane. Nor was she mentally ill. She had some issues with phobias relating to her past, and she was bipolar, yes, there was that. But she wasn't psychotic and she wasn't crazy. Slowly, she managed to pull herself out of the deep hole into which she'd thrown herself after escaping the mortifying ordeal in the kitchen.

As the night quieted she grew annoyed with her pouting and forced herself out of bed. She took up her yellow notebook and pencil and continued her work on *Lost Highways*, the novel she'd begun to write two weeks earlier. It was mostly scratching at this stage, just ideas and sentences haphazardly written on the page, a guide for when she was ready to begin the actual story on the computer.

There was a significant difference between thinking and writing. Writing wasn't just the translation of interesting ideas to paper. It was its own kind of thinking, which seemed to kick in only when the pen made contact with the page, or her fingers touched the keyboard.

But tonight not even that faithful connection seemed to yield any useful thoughts or emotions. She gave up after an hour.

Hungry, she warmed a bowl of noodles in the microwave. She lived alone in a one-bedroom unit that was comfortably, if sparsely, furnished. A twin bed and a desk in the bedroom; a brown sofa in the living room; a small kitchen area without a stove, but it had both refrigerator and microwave, all she ever used.

She spent half an hour on the internet using the small grey Compaq computer the Center provided all residents who could conduct themselves appropriately in the virtual world. They didn't want someone who was deeply depressed posting suicide videos on YouTube, now did they? The computer was her gateway to the world, but she found little in the world that really interested her, so she used it primarily to research topics of interest, like mental illness and religion and nature.

Cats and dogs cheered her up. If there was one thing she longed for, it was a dog, a golden retriever or maybe a labrador. But pets were forbidden, so Paradise had to settle for pictures or videos that never failed to bring a smile to her face.

Warmed by Top Ramen and cheered by a web video of a cat trying to catch a butterfly on the other side of a window, Paradise slipped under her covers at one in the morning and fell asleep. A black day was behind her, but she'd survived many black days.

She woke in a grey mood, haunted once again by her failure. But she was determined not to let it keep her down, so she ventured out. Her friends gave her about an hour of space, during which they subjected her to overt glances, but the looks lengthened into unbroken stares of accusation until Roudy finally decided they'd waited long enough and approached.

Paradise didn't want to talk about it. She made her position clear: if they wanted to be with her, they must not say a single word about the FBI, Mr Raines, or the case involving the Bride Collector.

'Did he try any funny business?' Andrea immediately wanted to know.

'What did I just say? Nothing about Mr Raines.'

'I didn't say Mr Raines. I said he.'

'But you meant Mr Raines. Nothing about any of those things, no matter what words you use to describe them.'

Casanova lifted a finger. 'Did *anybody* try any funny business?'

'And nothing about my nonexistent love life. Period. No more questions, period.'

'What?' Roudy cried. 'I haven't even asked a single question. They both got one. I demand an opportunity to cross examine the witness!'

'No. Absolutely not.'

Paradise stuck to her decision for the rest of the day. When Roudy *tap, tap, tapped* on her door at ten that night, she buried her head under her pillow until he left.

But today was a new day, and she was finally feeling distant enough from her failure to open up. There was, after all, some benefit to being at the centre of attention, and her refusal to give them even a snippet of information the prior day had worked all three into quite a tizzy. She was practically a celebrity. They acted as if they'd won the lottery when she announced that she would meet them in Roudy's office at nine to break her silence.

Now, here they sat: Casanova, who was having a bad morning and hardly able to concentrate on their discussion; Andrea, who was sinking fast into a full-blown depressive cycle; Roudy, who sat against the desk like the lion king who had finally found his place, leading the hunt; and Paradise, who had just told them what she could remember and was suddenly wishing she'd kept her mouth shut about her suspicion, however remote, that Brad Raines found her interesting.

'What did I tell you?' Andrea said.

'How many times are you going to remind us what you told her?' Roudy demanded, glaring at Andrea. 'We're faced with the crime of the century here and all you can think about is whether some high and mighty FBI man likes Paradise more than he likes you.'

Andrea poked her head out of her depression and glared back

at him. 'That's not true. I'm just more interested in her than I am in some dead girl that none of us knows. Not that I don't care about the dead girl, but I care more about Paradise. Right, Paradise? That makes sense, right?'

Paradise sighed. 'See, this is why I didn't want to tell you anything. The truth is, Roudy, this isn't the crime of the century, at least not as far as we are concerned. The FBI came, they got what they could, which was nothing, and they left. We're still here. Our lives still go on, here behind these walls. There is no FBI man, not any more. It's all past. Gone. Finished.'

In his delusion as a world-renowned investigator, this was impossible for Roudy to comprehend. In his mind, he was all that stood between the killer and the next poor victim.

His face turned red and his jowls shook as he spoke. 'How dare you give up on innocent victims who've been thrown to the wolves?'

Paradise put her hand on his shoulder. 'Listen to me, Sherlock, you're being reassigned to a new case. A more important case that involves dozens of victims.'

'Don't try to tempt me.'

'I am temptation,' Cass mumbled, eyes tilted down, far off.

'I'm not. The choice is yours, but you're needed elsewhere. If the FBI decides you're not qualified to lead this other more important investigation, they will let you know. But I think you're up to it.'

He blinked. 'Not qualified? This is a blatant attempt at misdirection.'

'Is it? If the FBI wants you back on the Bride Collector case, they'll come begging, I can promise you that. But they won't, because he's gone. You're too important for Mr Raines.' Then she added, as much for herself as anything, 'We all are.' She believed that as much as she believed she really was a monkey in a zoo.

Roudy looked stunned. He settled back, forced to at least consider the possibility.

'Then at least answer my question,' Andrea insisted.

'I will. If we can all promise to move on.'

No one objected, which was a kind of confirmation in itself. 'What question?' Paradise asked.

Andrea glanced at Enrique. She seemed hesitant, which wasn't like her. 'I just want to know, would you have gone with him?'

Gone with him?

'I mean, you know, not like I was saying. But if he . . .' A tear spilled down her left cheek; she was fighting the downturn. 'If he really showed interest in you, I mean real affection, that might be nice, right? Because that's what she keeps saying.' She motioned at the wall. 'That's what Betty keeps saying.'

Paradise blinked. It was the first time Andrea had said anything positive about this whole thing. 'That's not the point, Andrea. It's stupid to even think along those lines. That's their world and this is ours.'

'But I know what it's like, Paradise. When I was on the outside, before I came here a year ago, I was, you know, quite popular with guys. It's not just my brains.' Her eyes darted to the wall. 'And, no, it's not just my body either. You're acting like a baby!' This was obviously said to Betty.

Paradise felt perturbed by this new direction in their conversation. She picked up a Webster's dictionary from the desk, snapped it open and showed the spread to Andrea. 'How many words are on these two pages?'

A glance told the girl what she needed to know. 'Three hundred ninety seven.'

Paradise closed the book. 'You see, normally the kind of people that can tell you that are savants, maybe autistic. They don't often look like Texas beauty queens who can flirt like cheerleaders. So the boys see you, and they trip.'

'What are you saying? That I'm just a monkey? You always say that they think we're all monkeys, monkeys, monkeys!' Andrea paced, agitated. 'Well maybe we are, Paradise, but I was trying to be nice. Maybe I was wrong, you know? Maybe the FBI man is really a nice guy and he really does like you. Maybe you deserve that. But now you've ruined it!'

Paradise was about to snap at the girl, to tell her that it was all a horrible fantasy. Her emotions boiled and she was reminded just why she hated men so much. In the end, they dashed hope. They were a curse.

'He likes you,' Casanova said, staring up at Paradise from the couch. 'All men want you.' They'd clearly given him more medication than usual, and his eyes looked only half lit.

'Maybe Mr Raines likes you?' Andrea said.

'You can have him, Andrea. I can't afford this. My mind can't take it. Neither, for that matter, can my heart.'

'So you like him too,' Cass said. 'I know what that's like. Having my heart broken. It happens quite a lot.' He stared at them for a moment, then went back to watching the floor.

'Nonsense. He's all yours, Andrea. But it won't matter; they're gone.'

That seemed to settle the issue, at least for the moment. Roudy, in the meantime, was still trying to comprehend the nature of her suggestion that he was needed for a much more important case.

'So, you really think this case is beneath me? Maybe you're right.'

'Of course I'm right. The FBI has moved on.'

A voice spoke softly from behind her. 'No, Paradise.' She turned to face Allison, who stood in the doorway. *No, Paradise?*

'I'm afraid the FBI hasn't moved on.' Allison walked in, watching Paradise with her ever-smiling eyes, and Paradise couldn't help but think the director was up to something.

'I just got off the phone with Special Agent Raines.'

Paradise found the air heavy to breathe.

'After your help the other day, Mr Raines and his partner have decided that you offer the Federal Bureau of Investigation their best chance of saving those young women. All four of you.' She looked at the others. 'And I think you should help them. It will be good for you, and it could be very good for those young women who will probably otherwise die.'

Roudy sprang forwards, fist raised. 'We can't let them down!

We must help them. Bring the body, bring the files, bring it all! We'll put that vermin back into the cage where he belongs!'

Brad Raines was coming back. Paradise stood immobilized.

'Do you all agree, then?' Allison asked.

'Of course!' Roudy shouted.

'Andrea?'

Her eyes were bright, and Paradise didn't want to guess what was going on inside her brain. 'Yes,' Andrea said. 'Absolutely.'

'You said the beautiful brunette would join us?' Casanova asked, rising unsteadily, dumb grin already plastered across his expression.

'Her name is Nikki. I'm sorry, Casanova, but I don't think so. Not today.'

His smile flattened. 'No?'

'No. But if she comes, you'll be the first to know.'

Casanova stared for a moment, then headed for the door in a drug-induced shuffle.

Allison looked at Paradise. 'Well?'

Her chest was still frozen and a chill shot through her, but Paradise recognized both as excitement as much as fear. The kind of excitement that a person must feel looking over a cliff with a parachute strapped to her back. And the thought that she might be excited terrified her even more. She wanted to run from the room.

A glance at Andrea chased away that desire. The girl had lit up like the stars. She was already smoothing her hair. And Paradise was already regretting her earlier words; she couldn't let Brad face this monster on his own.

She turned to Allison and shrugged. 'Sure.'

'Good. I assumed as much. They're already on their way.'

'Now?' Paradise asked, terrified again.

'Now.'

CHAPTER FIFTEEN

The method and execution of a taking were equal parts God and equal parts Quinton Gauld, Quinton being the messenger from God empowered to carry out his bidding on earth. What so few humans knew was just how thrilling being God's proxy could be. Some knew, in the haze of a trance brought on by some hallucinogenic tea in the Amazon, or swaying to heavy music at the altar in church, but even these poor souls could not travel fluidly from human to divine as Quinton could.

Indeed, his hallucinogenic capacity was built in. What the medical community erroneously called illness was actually a fantastic gifting. He could as easily drift into what they called delusion as they could breathe.

It wasn't really delusion, as he'd once been led to believe. When the doctors had captured him and shot him full of drugs, then, yes, he'd believed their lies. But now, having lived so long without the drugs, he'd learned to embrace his connection to God for the true gift it was.

And now there was a devil hunting the messenger, a witch doctor bent on stealing the bride of Christ before Quinton could take her and deliver her to God. It was eerily similar to the movie *Men in Black*, in which monsters were out to stop highly gifted agents working for truth. Only, in this case, the agent, Rain Man, was the monster, and he, Quinton Gauld, dressed in grey, was the gifted agent of God protecting his own.

His bride.

For his mission today, Quinton had taken the black Chrysler M 300. His abduction would occur during the day, and the FBI likely knew that he was driving a truck, based on the tyre marks left in the soil at the scene of each killing. The M 300 would glide along the highway without being noticed.

Quinton followed the police cruiser south on I 25, headed towards Castle Rock, careful to keep at least one, usually two cars between his own and the target. She wasn't alone, which added a complication, but this didn't mean he wasn't up to the task. God was testing him. Seeing just how good he was before he walked the true and most beautiful bride down the aisle. The rest were a kind of prenuptial ceremony, preparing the way. A bride price offered to the Father.

It was uncommon to find such a beautiful woman as this in law enforcement. He'd taken such a range of women, the last being a flight attendant, showing that he could snatch them from the sky as well as the ground. And now from the authorities, from right under their noses.

Quinton had long ago selected another woman who lived in Boulder, a college student in her twenties named Christine. But the Rain Man had inserted himself into the equation, and God had changed his mind. It was important that people learn their place in the pecking order. Rain Man was near the bottom of the pile, far below the favourites he was trying to save. Certainly far below the sunshine, being the rain.

A drizzly little pretty man.

Quinton whistled the old 'You Are My Sunshine' tune, but he only got seven or eight notes in when the police car's indicator began to blink, signalling their intention to turn off the highway into the rest stop ahead. He held the tune and spun through his options. All of them. So many he couldn't count them, but only a couple interested him much.

Of those that did, one rose as a solid possibility. They were making an unscheduled stop, likely to relieve a bladder or two. He needed only thirty seconds of quiet time with Theresa and her partner. Depending on how many other cars were in the rest stop, this might be the perfect thirty.

The cruiser broke right and angled up the ramp into the tall pine trees. Cover, plenty of it. Quinton's pulse built steadily. The two cars between his and the cop car drove on, and he clicked on his right indicator.

The silenced Browning nine-millimetre semi-automatic lay on the passenger seat, and he placed a gloved hand over the steel. He disliked guns because they were blunt, impersonal tools that were used to kill, and he wasn't a killer. But they were sometimes useful as tools of motivation.

The M 300's steel-belted radials glided over the asphalt up the ramp, like a blade on ice. Generally speaking, the Americans made junk vehicles, but the M 300 suited Quinton well. The tinted windows prevented passersby from seeing the occupant, and any person looking directly through the front windshield would see a dark-haired man wearing aviator sunglasses and black leather gloves, but beyond imagining Tommy Lee Jones from *Men in Black*, they would think nothing of it. Yet another common man trying to look suave was far less noticeable than a big farmer-boy type hauling around a meat cleaver.

The police cruiser pulled between two parking lines next to the restrooms. Quinton scanned the rest area and saw that they were two of only three cars and one eighteen-wheeler that looked bedded down. He let his pulse surge. He could not pass up this opportunity. God had sent him a gift.

Both doors on the cruiser opened. Quinton slowed his approach. Theresa got out first, a woman with a small bladder. Her dark hair was pulled back in a ponytail, easy to tuck up under her hat when she wore it. She looked stunning in her uniform. Casting a glance backwards, she headed to the rest-rooms, followed immediately by her uniformed partner, name yet unknown to Quinton.

He pulled the M 300 into a parking spot two down from the eighteen-wheeler and waited. His only prayer now was that their bladders would empty as quickly as they'd filled. The conditions were good at the moment, but that didn't mean they would remain optimal.

Theresa, being the first to head in, was the first to head out. Working as smoothly as Tommy Lee Jones now, Quinton slipped out, shoved the pistol behind his belt, retrieved his case from the back seat and locked the doors. *Bleep.*

After one last look up and down the driveway to be sure no one was pulling in, he headed towards the police cruiser. Theresa, being a cop, watched him. Watched her enemy approaching head on, powerless to stop him. She likely assumed he was a salesman headed into the facilities.

Her partner, a bullish looking man with red hair, came out, walking fast, eager to catch up with her. He probably had a thing for her and didn't want to miss an opportunity to offer a witty come-on. Perhaps he wanted to take her back for a quickie?

Both saw him. Both watched him. But he acted nothing like anyone who'd want to harm a flea, much less them. And he didn't have to act, because he really didn't want to harm them any more than he'd wanted to slap Joshie in the restroom at Elway's restaurant.

Quinton timed his approach, allowing them both to slide into their seats before he pulled the silenced weapon from behind his back and stepped up to the passenger's door.

He shoved the barrel in Theresa's face. 'Get out, please.'

Brad Raines stood back and watched Roudy make quick work of the photographs, pinning each on a large map of Colorado he'd insisted they hang against the wall. Each time he pushed in a pin, he uttered a soft 'There we go. There we go.' Each of the five victims was already affixed to the map, surrounded by a dozen photos from each crime scene. The pictures formed a large symmetrical shape, but Brad had no clue what that shape could mean.

Next to the files of each crime sat half a dozen artefacts from the scene. The group had already spent twenty minutes poking and prodding, asking endless questions. But, thus far, nothing of interest had presented itself to any of them. Getting all the photos up on the wall was Roudy's inspiration, and he'd tackled the task with an animal-like frenzy. 'There we go, there we go.'

Having satisfied some threshold in his mind, he sprang back. 'Tell me the first thing that comes to mind. What do you see?'

Andrea and Paradise looked at Brad. Neither had been too talkative, evidently preferring to give Roudy his time in the sun.

'A butterfly?' Brad offered.

'Uh-ha. And now?'

He hadn't changed a thing.

Brad humoured him. 'A . . . flower.'

'Interesting.'

'I don't see what the point is, Roudy,' Andrea said.

'Understanding Agent Raines' baseline helps me judge his methodology for perception,' Roudy said in a dismissive tone. 'Please, no comments that don't help the process.' He went back to studying the wall.

At the moment, Roudy's methodology struck Brad as absurd. Certainly neither brilliant nor particularly insightful. But then Brad didn't think the way Roudy did. Either way, he hadn't come for Sherlock's insight.

He was here for Paradise.

She'd greeted him cordially enough but remained distant, dressed in jeans and a black T-shirt. Brad smelled the scent of shampoo when she passed. For the most part she stood by the window, watching Roudy and Andrea.

Andrea seemed more interested in Brad than in the case. In fact, the only one really engaged in the case was Roudy, who leaped about the evidence like a tiger dressed in grey corduroy pants and black bow tie. His hair was a rat's nest and his goatee had been twisted and bent in all directions by nervous fingers.

Brad's conversation with Allison several hours earlier had come as a surprise to him. Rather than scold him for requesting a return to CWI, she paused only a second before agreeing. 'And Nikki just might be right,' she'd said. 'I say so for ulterior reasons, naturally. I care about your case, don't get me wrong. But I'm more interested in seeing Paradise break out of her shell. What you're suggesting will challenge her, but I think she could use a good head-to-head confrontation with a man.'

'I'm sorry, I think you're misunderstanding me,' he'd said. 'Nobody's suggesting a head-to-head confrontation. I would only try to encourage her to trust me so that—'

'Oh, I realize what you're doing, Mr Raines. And I'm saying it will lead to conflict with someone like Paradise. But that may be good for her.' Then, after a pause: 'Win her confidence, sir. Sweep her off her feet if you can. You have my full blessing.'

Brad had called Nikki at eight fifteen, right after he'd hung up with Allison, and informed her that the director had agreed. He was heading out to the Center with the files as soon as he could get it all together. Nikki was headed to her mother's for the day, but said she'd be available by phone and would check in the minute she got back in the afternoon. Maybe she could join them then?

Her reaction to finding the note on Brad's window the previous night had surprised him. He found it interesting that Nikki, whom he'd always considered such a secure woman, had expressed some jealousy over Paradise. How could she have interpreted his care for her as anything more than concern?

Was there something in his voice or eyes that had drawn a question mark in her mind? Had she picked up on something that not even he had consciously considered? Thinking about it now, in the same room as Paradise, made him feel self-conscious. The notion that Nikki had picked up on something distracted him from Roudy's antics. If he looked at Paradise, would she see what Nikki had seen in his eyes? Would she get the wrong impression?

Then again, wasn't he here to win her trust? He was, yes, but he felt awkward stepping in that direction. The whole idea of leading her on so that she might lower her guard and cough up the images trapped in her mind was offensive to him.

He glanced in her direction and saw that she was staring at him. To avoid any embarrassment, he shifted his eyes to Andrea. But she too was watching him. The blonde beauty smiled, then looked at Paradise, who still hadn't broken her stare.

Brad offered Paradise a gentle smile. 'So, you've been quiet.'

'She's had a couple of hard days,' Andrea said.

'I'm sorry to hear that. You okay?'

'Well, I'm not sure, Mr Raines,' Paradise said. 'They say I'm mentally ill, but even in my state of insanity, I can see that you're not getting what you came for.' Her arms were crossed and she held his gaze. From the corner of his eyes Brad could see that Andrea was glancing back and forth between them, surely picking up this strange chemistry. Is this what Nikki had sensed? But it wasn't anything to be jealous about. He and Paradise simply had an understanding. A connection that bypassed normal pretence. She was bone-deep honest, and he was attracted to people who exchanged society's shell of propriety for such stark truth telling.

Then again, she wasn't transparent, was she? Truth hid behind her eyes, in her mind. And if Nikki was right, she might be complicit in that hiding.

Paradise finally averted her eyes, lowered her arms and walked towards the evidence spread all over the desk and wall. 'So, let's see if we can't help him out a little. What do you say, Roudy? Right, Andrea?'

Roudy looked over his shoulder. 'What do you think we're doing? We've made tremendous headway already. I'm working as fast as humanly possible and then some.'

'Remember what you said,' Andrea said in a soft but firm tone. It sounded like a warning.

'I know what I said, Andrea, but I've changed my mind.'

Whatever had been said didn't sit right between these two.

Paradise faced him, eyes bright now. 'So, maybe it would be helpful if I summarized what we have here. Would that be helpful? Get us back on track?'

'Okay. Yes, that would be good.'

Roudy turned and lifted a finger. 'The first question I'm considering is *why?* The why before the who. And on that front, I do have some thoughts.'

'If you don't mind, Roudy,' Brad said, 'I would like to hear what Paradise has to say.' The man looked shocked. 'Before you offer your full analysis.' That calmed him.

Paradise caught his eyes and, for the first time, she hinted at a smile, as if to say, *That was nice of you, thinking of me without dismissing Roudy.*

'Should I give you thoughts on why, then?'

'Yes. Roudy?'

'Yes. Yes, by all means.'

'I have some thoughts too,' Andrea said, stepping closer to Brad. 'They don't call me Brains for nothing. But I'm good with more than just my mind, as you can probably see.'

Paradise shot her a stern warning. 'Andrea!'

'I have to take a shower, Paradise.' Andrea's face wrinkled in pain. 'I feel dirty.'

'Then you'll have to go on your own.' Her tone softened. 'Our guest is depending on us to help him.'

This was like playing a game with children. If he wasn't mistaken, there was some kind of rivalry brewing here. Surely not over him . . .

'Paradise?'

'Thank you.' She looked up at the three notes pinned to the right of the map. 'It's painfully clear that the Bride Collector is psychotic. He sees himself as God's messenger, thwarting a terrible evil. It's the most common kind of delusion suffered by even the most intelligent psychotics. Thoughts of grand plots to upset the war between good and evil invade his every waking moment.'

'This is more the who,' Roudy said.

'No, this is the why,' she returned. 'Let me finish.'

'Sorry.'

'Sorry,' Andrea said. 'Sorry, sorry.'

'As I was saying, the Bride Collector is doing the right thing, in his eyes. He knows he's evil, and he thinks of himself as a demon who is enslaved and tasked to find the bride of Christ. This is why, Roudy. He is taking these women because God has chosen them, through him. If he decides, it's God's decision.'

Her theory was similar to Nikki's, but somehow more complete and certain. And with only a few minutes' exposure to the evidence.

'What else?' Brad asked, fascinated by her insight.

Paradise stared at the victims spread like angels on the wall of each crime scene. A tear from her right eye ran down her cheek. She walked up to the wall and traced the picture of the latest victim, whom she'd seen in person two days earlier.

'In his mind, taking their lives is a necessary act. He does it for their sakes as much as for God's purpose. There's no anger. No revenge. He wouldn't take someone because he's angry with them.'

'So he wouldn't kill a victim out of, say, spite?'

'No,' Roudy said. 'If you don't mind me interjecting.'

'Go ahead, Roudy.' Brad walked up behind Paradise. The scent of her shampoo lingered in the air. She glanced up as he came close, then quickly looked at the wall again.

'The question is, who's next?' Roudy said. 'We must fixate on that question. Who, who, who, not just the why. And I do have a theory.'

The man seemed to be contradicting himself. 'Do you mind if Paradise finishes?' Brad said, looking down on her dark hair. It was parted in the middle and ran in long strands down either side of her head, recently combed but unevenly cut and with split ends.

'Don't delay me much longer, Agent Raines. I have some light to shed here!'

'Of course. But I think Paradise has hit on something crucial.' He was deferring to her in part to show her a preference that would earn her trust, but it wasn't all posturing on his part. Her analysis really was quite amazing.

'Don't forget about me,' Andrea said, stepping up on Brad's other side. He ignored her for the moment, at a loss.

'Please continue, Paradise.'

She looked up into his eyes and again they shared a moment of connection. 'Thank you,' she said.

Then, frowning at the wall of pictures: 'No, I don't think the Bride Collector would kill someone just to hurt that person. I don't think he's wired that way.'

'Be quiet!' Andrea whispered, looking at the corner. 'I will.' Beat. 'Sorry. Sorry, sorry.'

They ignored her.

'But he would see you differently, Mr Raines. You're not a woman. In his mind, you're the one trying to stop him from doing God's will. If he's evil, you are even worse. And he will try to stop you.'

'How?'

'He'll try to kill you.'

The room went silent. A hand gently touched his right palm. Andrea slipped her fingers into his hand. He felt frozen, standing with Paradise on his left, engrossed in the case, and Andrea on his right, obeying the voices that had told her to win his affection. It couldn't be . . .

But one glance into Andrea's big blue seductive eyes and he knew it was. He'd never been hit on so blatantly by such a stunning woman, by any woman, for that matter. She clearly didn't have the social sensitivities that kept most men and women at arm's length. Brad tried to pull his hand free and had to tug to accomplish separation. Her face fell, then twisted in pain. 'I need to take a shower, Paradise! I need to take a shower right now!'

'No, it's okay, Andrea,' Brad said. Then he said something he was sure he'd regret later, but saying it felt right. 'I need to . . . stay with Paradise, okay? Maybe Casanova can help you out.'

She stepped back, horrified. 'Cass? Cass is a dirty old man!' she cried. 'Is that what you have in mind? Are you going to rape Paradise? Is that it, FBI, are you going to take advantage of her when no one is looking?'

'That is totally inappropriate!' Paradise said, brushing past Brad. 'Totally. Stop listening to Betty or whoever is whispering that nonsense into your ear. I know you are used to being the centre of attention with all the men, but it's not always all about you. So stop this.' Then she added, as if to make sure she wasn't misunderstood, 'We have a woman to save here. And Brad's life might be in danger. He's the victim here, not the criminal.'

'My, my, my, this won't do,' Roudy said, massaging his scalp. 'They're waiting for my report!'

Paradise quickly pulled Andrea back in, speaking with the skill of a seasoned counsellor. 'We need you, Andrea. None of us can read the tea leaves the way you can. There's a pattern here. Roudy is right about that. There's a jack in the whole and you may be the one to help us find it, so please, please don't listen to Betty.'

A jack in the whole? 'What jack in the whole?'

'A pattern,' Roudy said. 'That's my point. He left us with a jack in the whole.'

CHAPTER SIXTEEN

Quinton Gauld loved the feeling of doing what was right, even if the potential cost was high. All of God's chosen paid a price at some point in their lives, and his day to burn at the stake would also come. But as long as he was playing the role he was destined to play, he could revel in his higher calling.

A buzz swept through his mind, and he shook it free with a grunt. Preachers were idiots. Churches were dens of thieves. They talked about love and forgiveness, then turned their backs on any who fell short of the glory of God. Didn't they realize that they were all snakes, all needing love and forgiveness? Were the preachers any different from the pew sitters?

Hypocrisy was a form of mental illness. And, like the mentally ill, hypocrites were unable to see their own illness. It was no wonder God had rejected them as the bride. *Depart from me for I knew you not, you snakes. I will spew you out of my mouth.*

He shook another buzz from his head and blew some air out to ease the tension. *Let not your heart be troubled. The bride is waiting and I will deliver her to her husband.*

Feeling once again uplifted, Quinton brought his mind back to the task. He'd left his M 300 back at the rest stop beside the eighteen-wheeler and now drove the police cruiser. It had taken a bit of doing to make his intention clear to Rodger, the policeman. The man didn't want to give up his uniform, and Quinton needed it. He'd shot the man in the head and stuffed him into the trunk.

On the bright side, the man's square sunglasses were stylish and his uniform fit Quinton well, except for the length of the inseam. Rodger had been a good-sized man with sawn-off legs, so Quinton had opted for his own slacks rather than look like an utter fool. Above the waist, he was practically Rodger's twin.

The blue Range Rover that he was following turned off at the first Castle Rock exit. Within half a mile the traffic on the narrow road had fallen behind. Tall pines reached for the sky on either side, providing all the cover he could hope for.

The SUV pulled onto a dirt road and headed up a long driveway that ended at a lone house built into the trees. One of those classy log homes with large windows. There was evidently some money in this family. He followed the Range Rover in, then parked twenty yards behind it.

He glanced at Theresa, who sat next to him, facing forwards. 'This is it, Theresa. I need your help now. No talking, not a word. You sit there and look like nothing in the world is wrong and maybe God will have mercy on you.'

The woman climbed out and waved. Quinton smiled and waved back.

'Everything is going to be just fine, Theresa. Not a word, not even a sharp breath. You know I have to do this, so that there will be no witnesses. I just can't afford to leave a woman who's seen me alive. It's only one more life, and it's distasteful, but what's a man going to do?'

Forgive me, Father, for I will sin. I will now sin.

Paradise couldn't remember ever feeling the kind of elation she'd experienced these past few minutes.

She'd started as the sceptic who felt tricked into meeting with Mr Raines yet one more time, as if the wound they'd opened now required some salt to aggravate the pain. But her feelings had changed slowly, starting early on with the way Brad had looked at her, as if he was the one who felt awkward for coming again. It had taken half an hour and a dozen stolen glances to convince herself that he really was uncomfortable.

Now, whenever she wrote a story, the character who averted his eyes and blushed, however faintly, was either guilty of some sin or felt he had been outdone. If her judgment was any good, and it was, Brad felt subservient to her. An irrational idea, but there it was, on his face, like a moustache of white betraying the person who'd been at the milk jug.

Roudy went on about the case, hopping around with the pictures, and all the while Paradise was lost in thought, trying to figure out what had gotten into Brad, this tall, exquisitely fashioned man who looked too good to be any good at all. Why did his eyes shift when she looked at him? Why did he offer shy, awkward smiles, as if they shared some deep secret?

Slowly she'd come to the only conclusion that made any sense to her. Brad liked her. Not in a romantic way. But enough to feel nervous around her. He might even be – and this was really absurd – he might even be awed by her.

Suddenly it occurred to her that maybe her mental illness was worse than first assumed. Had she finally suffered another psychotic break? Panicked by the idea, she determined to test her insecurities.

Her test had started with a long stare, right at him. He'd blushed. Disbelieving, she'd forgotten to break off her stare and he'd looked back. They were locked in a kind of embrace with their eyes.

Paradise thought about fleeing the room. Instead, like metal dust drawn to a magnet, she'd taken it further. And so had he, she thought. He was responding the way she thought someone who liked a girl might, and she didn't know what to do with the idea. But she did like it. Yes, she liked it more than she thought she should.

She felt a bit dizzy. Light, like a balloon.

And then Brad had dismissed Andrea and chosen Paradise, and her world was transformed.

He'd walked up behind her and her mind was spinning with the story – daring, forbidden tangles of love. He kept saying her name. Paradise. Paradise. And then she'd seen Andrea try to steal him away. Watched from the corner of her eye as she took his hand. Saw him pull away.

Heard him say those words. *I need to stay with Paradise.*

Paradise began to float. She could hardly contain her enthusiasm, however pathetic it was, however angry she tried to be at herself for feeling that way.

'Why don't you tell him, Andrea?' she said, trying to shake the feeling. 'Cards are really your field of expertise.' They weren't, but she didn't need Andrea to pop her balloon now.

'Jack in the whole?'

'I could explain,' Roudy said. And then did, before Andrea could. 'A jack in the whole is one card, a jack, as part of a whole deck of cards. It's a code-breaker's term used to mean the key that unlocks the puzzle.'

Brad had never heard such a thing. 'The killer's saying that he's left us a jack in the whole? A key to unlock his pattern?'

'That's right,' Paradise said. She nodded at the third note. '"Do you want me to hide from you?" he asks. He has a face card hidden somewhere in all of this evidence. A jack in the whole bunch of evidence.'

Brad spread his hands in amazement and the left one came close to her, at the level of her chin. She thought about backing up. Instead she stared at it, close enough to reach out and touch it, if she wanted to.

'. . . looked through all of this until I was blind!'

Strong hands. Clean. Nails cut short. No rings. Andrea had put her hand in his.

'You're sure that's what this means?'

Paradise glanced up, saw that he'd noticed her stare, and pushed forwards, refusing to blush. 'That's what it means to us. But then, we're all a bit strange.'

His eyes were bright. 'Strange, huh? Then tell me why I'm not seeing strange.'

'What are you seeing?' Andrea asked.

'I'm seeing pretty darn smart.'

'Smart but strange,' Paradise persisted.

'Smart. Very smart. Interesting. Beautiful. If that's strange, then I need some of what you've got.'

Andrea was staring at him as if he'd just ripped off his shirt and flexed. But Paradise was grappling with that word *beautiful*. Who had he been looking at when he said that? At Roudy, right? Not at Andrea. Definitely not at *her*.

But it took no brains to know that in Mr Raines' world, beyond the fence, Andrea was the beautiful one. Brad might be able to flatter them all with kind words in this zoo, but out there? Andrea got the boys, and Paradise was a joke who couldn't even make it past the gate.

'Well, that's nice of you, Mr Raines,' Paradise said. 'The monkeys in here appreciate such kind words.'

'Monkeys in here as opposed to the monkeys out there? I've been on both sides of the fence and I'm here to confirm the rumour: they are pretty much the same. Some a little smarter, some not nearly as smart, some with dark hair, some with jeans. Beauty is in the eye of the beholder.'

And this time he was looking directly at Paradise. She blushed.

'So,' he said, facing Andrea, 'what do you make of this jack in the whole?'

'You want me to find it?'

'Can you do that?'

She shrugged. 'Sure. It might take some time. I'd have to look at everything.'

Brad looked at Paradise and winked. 'I'm in no rush.'

It wasn't meant as anything more than a natural gesture to express friendship, but the wink proved too much for Paradise. She couldn't remember a guy winking at her. Ever.

Fighting waves of heat and dizziness, she turned and walked towards the couch. She was having a mild panic attack and she wasn't sure why. He was a man. She liked him.

But Paradise *couldn't* like men! This was a fact discussed at length during hundreds of therapy sessions.

'It's just a matter of finding the pattern,' Roudy was saying. 'No one is better at finding patterns than Andrea and me.'

Paradise eased to her seat, breathing deeply, trying not to appear unnerved. But Brad was suddenly there, sitting down on the couch next to her.

His knee touched hers. 'You okay?'

'Sure.' But she wasn't okay. And she wanted to cry.

CHAPTER SEVENTEEN

The day had started out well, a badly needed break after a week of mind bending. Nikki's mother, Michelle Holden, had suggested they get out of the city for a day. They could do lunch at Pepe's Grill in Castle Rock, maybe hit the outlet mall and have some ice cream. She needed a new pair of capris.

Why not? Nikki had thought. There was something therapeutic about sitting on the back porch with Mother, watching tall pines grow and listening to birds chirp. No phones, no orders, no deadlines.

No victims.

Brad insisted that her protective detail follow her down; Castle Rock was only half an hour south of Denver. They were being overly cautious, perhaps, but she couldn't escape the obvious message hidden in Brad's actions. If she were Frank, Brad wouldn't have insisted on the detail, would he? He was ordering the protection because Nikki was the one person he *did* have strong feelings for, and the killer's caution that he be careful who he loved might actually refer to her.

Brad loved her. He was too confused by his own feelings to know it yet, but she would swear it.

The cruiser had called her and suggested a break at the rest stop – too much morning coffee. But she was eager to get to Mother's and told them to catch up with her, which they'd done ten minutes later, flying up behind her like a kamikaze.

The minute she'd left the highway and headed down into the foothills of Castle Rock, she knew that coming had been the right decision. Amazing how a large forest could swallow life's most stressing challenges. The towering trees on either side were doing what they had done for centuries. Regardless of any turmoil that came and went, they slowly, majestically inched their way skyward. Now, in their shadow, Nikki felt safe.

She pulled into her mother's driveway and climbed out. The cruiser pulled up behind and looked settled in. The cops would whittle away the day making small talk, catching up on paperwork, drinking coffee and whatever else they did while keeping an eye out.

She waved at the driver, who acknowledged her. So, the detail was overly cautious, but she welcomed the added layer of security, especially at Mother's house.

Nikki headed up the steps to the front porch, rang the doorbell and tried the door. Open. She stepped in without waiting for an answer.

Her mother's sweet voice called out. 'Come in, honey. In the kitchen!' The familiar smell of freshly baked cinnamon rolls filled her nostrils. It was good to be home. She should bring Brad by one of these days.

'Hi, Mom.'

So good to be home.

Quinton Gauld waited five minutes, thinking about his good fortune. His decision to take Nikki Holden as the sixth favourite had come only two days ago, after Rain Man dragged his fifth favourite out to the loony barn. God could change his mind and so could his messenger, but it had meant cutting his planning short. He'd never have imagined the chips falling so quickly in his favour. Having pleased God, his master was obviously smiling on him.

Even with short preparation time, his plan was decidedly perfect. In fact, he now saw that his old one had been somewhat flawed. This latest change had been a providential correction that would result in a perfect union between the final bride and God.

God was good. All the time. So very good. All things worked together for the good of those who loved and served God. Even if they had to sin now and then to show their love. *Forgive me, Father.*

He checked the rear-view mirror and saw the empty driveway, then checked again. And again until he was sure, without doubt, that they were alone out here in God's country.

Satisfied, he looked at Theresa. 'Thank you for helping me out, Theresa.' The jacketed bullet he'd put into her forehead back at the rest stop had made a mess of the seat behind her, but from the front she appeared to be sleeping. Her hat covered the small entry wound nicely. 'Sorry about the mess.'

Three black garbage bags covered his own seat, a precaution that would allow him to clean up his own hair and sweat when he was finished with the car.

He retrieved his case from the back seat, closed the door, and walked up to the blue Range Rover. A quick check confirmed that she'd locked the doors, but this wouldn't be a problem. He intended to take the keys from her.

Leaving the case beside the driver's door, he headed up to the house. A bird cawed in the branches above him, then another replied, though the second was more of a chirp. He wasn't crisp on the knowledge of birds, but he could imagine a black bird and a blue bird, the former being larger. When all of this was over, before he was called upon to find another bride for Christ, perhaps in another city, he would spend some time in the forest and learn more about birds. Blue ones, black ones, red ones, all wonderful creatures in God's country.

Buzz, buzz, the bees were back in his head. The birds and the bees.

He pulled out his nine-millimetre, lighter by two bullets than it had been before he'd borrowed the cops' car. But it still had nine rounds, and he didn't think he would need any more.

The front door was unlocked. This was a nice surprise. He twisted the knob, pushed the door open and stuck his head inside. Just a friendly cop coming in to use the toilet.

A hall ran into the house, empty now. Soft voices floated to him from around the corner at the end. By the luscious scent of freshly baked pastries, he thought mother and daughter were probably enjoying breakfast. He himself hadn't yet eaten this morning and, although he typically ate only beans after cleansing himself for his task, Nikki was a change in protocol, a gift for a job well done. Everything about her taking would be different. Including what he ate. The pastries were another nice surprise.

Quinton slipped into the house and walked quietly down the hall, pistol by his side. An absurd thought that maybe he should join them for breakfast slipped through his mind, but he knew it was nothing more than a temptation, a distraction from his task, which in the end would be far more rewarding than the consumption of a few pastries.

He walked around the corner and found them sitting at a round table in a sunny breakfast nook. The windows stood in four tall panels with trim that formed square panes in each. Valances topped the glass, a pattern with seed packages, among them corn, sunflowers and tomatoes, all in all a colourful, cheerful design. The tablecloth was red and white chequered – God's country-farmer décor. Freshly frosted cinnamon rolls rose in a stack between them. Coffee and orange juice, with bacon as well. To a lesser man, a true temptation indeed.

All of this he'd observed in less time than it took the two women to face the cop in the mismatched uniform who'd walked in without knocking.

Quinton lifted his gun. 'Please don't make any noise or I will have to shoot your mother,' he said.

Nikki, the beautiful brunette who was to be the sixth favourite leading up to the seventh and most beautiful bride, wasn't buying his act. 'Excuse me?'

Rather than argue with her, Quinton walked towards them, over to the grey-haired mother, and knocked her out with a single blow to her head. She fell off the chair and landed with a thump.

Nikki had overcome her initial shock and jumped to her feet. She screamed, 'What are you doing?'

Quinton pointed the pistol at her. 'I don't want to hurt you. It's important that you realize that. I really don't want to hurt you, but there's been a change of plan and if you try to resist me I will subdue you and then fix you up later.' He took a breath. 'So please sit down, Nikki.'

Her face was white. She stared at him with terrified eyes, like a rabbit, he thought. Except a rabbit appeared to be looking out of the sides of its head, whereas Nikki was staring directly at him with large, round, glassy eyes. The way you killed a rabbit was to club it over the head, but he didn't want to hurt Nikki.

Her fingers were shaking, but she seemed to grasp the situation then, because she closed her mouth, swallowed and stood a little taller. When she spoke, her voice was low and breathy.

'The Bride Collector.'

'The Bride Collector. Yes, that's what you call me. My name is Quinton. Will you turn and face the wall to make this easier?'

Nikki stared at him, neither sitting nor facing the wall as he'd suggested. He prayed that she wouldn't force him to hurt her or do anything stupid like the last one had, running into her dresser.

'Please, it won't hurt. Let's make this easy.'

'Quinton.' She was still coming to grips with his name, but she'd calmed. The psychiatrist in her was rising to the surface. He knew her type. He'd spent countless hours opposite psychiatrists who'd tried to dig through his mind. He hadn't considered this aspect of his choosing Nikki.

Could God choose a psychiatrist as his favourite? At first blush Quinton would think not, but the fact of the matter was that God had chosen Nikki. In his great wisdom, he had put his finger on this woman in front of Quinton and said, *I choose this one because she is my favourite. Send her up to me.*

Still, filled with the deep and unshakable knowledge that nearly all psychiatrists were profoundly deluded and interested mostly in money, like the drug companies they served, Quinton was momentarily confronted by the irony of God's choice. He had selected one of the six lesser brides from the sewer.

Perhaps Quinton's role was to help Nikki see the light, and then deliver her. Remove from her this one thorn in her flesh to perfect her in God's sight. After all, every human carried their sin with them. In Nikki's case, the sin was a little more obvious than most.

'You won't hurt me,' Nikki said.

'Please face the wall so—'

'You don't even want to hurt me,' she said. 'You're ill, Quinton. May I call you Quinton?'

She was trying to psychoanalyse him. He had a gun on her and she had the strength to attempt this trick. The mother moaned; time was running out. The psychos were probably hard at work on the 'jack in the whole'. They probably had some savant decoding the pattern in his last note.

'If you don't turn to the wall, then I'm going to have to kill your mother,' he said. 'I'd rather not, because I've already killed two people today and I'm not a killer at heart.'

'Listen to yourself. You're not making sense.' She edged to her left, and he thought she might be working up the courage to make a run for it.

'If you run, I will kill your mother. If you don't turn around and face the wall, I will kill your mother. We can talk later, but right now I need you to use your head so that I won't have to hit it. Can you manage that?'

'You won't do that. I can help you. You think you're doing this for God, but God hates people who take innocent lives. You don't have to do this.'

Buzz, buzz. He lost some of his composure then, infuriated by her willingness to thumb her nose at God. But the mother was stirring, so he was confronted by a choice: which first?

Bride. He needed the mother alive in the event he would require more leverage.

Quinton headed for her using long strides. Nikki darted to her left and he tore after her, cursing her recklessness. This wasn't what he wanted. Now he would have to stop her and return to the mother before she had a chance to crawl to a phone and alert the authorities. This was undoubtedly Nikki's hope. But Quinton would help her put her hope in a higher power.

Adrenaline flooded his veins. He was in good shape, but with God's help he was perfect. Nikki sprinted down the hall, black sundress flying behind her thighs like a bat's wings.

He closed the gap just before she reached the entrance, hit her head from behind with the pistol, and snatched a handful of her dress so that, when she fell forwards, she wouldn't hit the wall.

Unfortunately, her momentum carried her into the door. Her forehead slammed into the wood panels before she collapsed, though she came up short from hitting the floor, held up by his grasp on her dress.

Quinton swore again. Her face had undoubtedly been damaged. Shaking with a rage that he fought to control, he turned and dragged her back down the hall.

The mother was on her feet by the phone, already stabbing at the numbers when he rounded the corner into the kitchen. He released the sixth's dress, lifted the gun and shot the older woman through the head. She hit the wall and slid to her seat.

Sorry, Mother, but you saw me. I know, I know it's not fair.

The nine-millimetre now had six bullets, but the gun would no longer be useful to him. The FBI forensics team would find three bullets – one in each of the cops and one in the mother – that matched this weapon. The pistol itself could not be traced, he'd made sure of that, but any bullets fired from its barrel could be matched to this particular gun. He would put it in a paper bag and throw it in a dumpster when he retrieved his M 300.

Returning to Nikki's unconscious form, he applied some chloroform from the bottle in his pocket to a rag and pressed it against her face. She would remain still long enough.

With a broom from her pantry, he quickly swept the floorboards where he'd walked in the kitchen and the hall. Stray hairs could fall from one's head easily enough, and he hadn't been wearing his shower cap. He placed the dust and the broom head in a garbage bag, hoisted Nikki over his shoulder and looked about the room, running through his checklist. No fingerprints, none of his blood, urine, sweat or spittle. No food, no clothing, no hair. Clean.

Using Nikki's key, he opened the door to her Range Rover and dumped her in the back. He hog-tied her with some string from his case, taped her mouth closed with duct tape and shut her inside.

Using a small battery-operated vacuum, which he'd bought in the event that their blood didn't drain as intended, he sucked up any traces of himself that might have floated to the cruiser's carpet. He changed back into his own shirt and rolled the cop's shirt into the black garbage bags from his seat. Clean.

Ten minutes after Nikki's blue SUV had rolled up the driveway, it drove back down, this time with Quinton in command, seated on three more plastic garbage bags.

The ride back to the rest stop was uneventful. The sixth lay quietly in the back, dreaming perhaps of her true destiny. Quinton scanned the radio waves, listened to a political talk show for ten minutes, but then had to turn it off. Thinking of what was to come elevated his excitement to the point that he found it difficult to remain focused on avoiding detection, and he'd hoped the talk radio would distract him. But the political nonsense only replaced his excitement with agitation. He'd long ago concluded that nearly all humans who went to such lengths to achieve political success had to be both extremely egotistical and at least somewhat mentally ill.

The exchange from the blue Range Rover to his M 300 took twenty minutes, only because he had to wait for perfect timing, which required three aborted attempts. But he finally managed the switch cleanly, vacuumed out Nikki's floorboards and settled behind his vehicle's more familiar controls for the last leg of his trip.

It was twelve minutes after noon. Quinton felt positively giddy.

CHAPTER EIGHTEEN

Three hours passed, and to Paradise it felt like thirty minutes. Both Roudy and Andrea had thrown themselves into sifting through the data, though Paradise was certain that, while Andrea was applying strict method to her search, Roudy was only playing the role of sleuth. He was intelligent, to be sure, and he could connect dots, but he wasn't able to see patterns in numbers the way Andrea could.

Neither could she nor Brad. They were relegated to the cheerleading section, filling in ideas when questions arose, no matter how irregular those ideas might be. There was electricity in the room, a fascination with the investigation, as if it were an epic game of charades. The answer was there, just there, hidden in the mounds of evidence and data, waiting to be identified by the jack in the whole.

Allison came in twice to check on them, eyeing Brad and Paradise with particular interest, Paradise thought. Allison was up to something. She wanted Paradise to connect with Brad, clearly. It was the psychologist in her trying to help Paradise climb out of her hole, and although Paradise had no intention of climbing anywhere, she was surprised at how eager she was to play along.

In fact, she was playing him, not the other way around.

'How many words in the first sentence?' Roudy was asking.

'Eleven. Times eleven, times two. Two forty-four, but the last sentence only has eight. Eight words.'

'And what, pray tell, is that?'

Andrea's eyes darted. 'Don't know. Just there. Like two holes, snake in the hole. Jack in the whole.'

'This is too random!'

Paradise walked around the couch where she'd been watching them. Brad was in the adjacent room, connected by an open door, talking quietly on his phone.

'Random to you, Roudy. You know that's not the way Andrea's mind works.'

'Eight, thirteen, five,' Andrea said. 'But that's not it, not it at all. Does the number of pictures count?'

'No, the photos were taken by the FBI, not the killer. And don't assume the key he left is mathematical. It could be any pattern.'

Andrea scratched her scalp and started to whimper, then glanced at the corner. She listened and looked back at Paradise. 'That's not what *Betty's* saying. It's a number. Like the number of raindrops. A showerhead, cleaning the world. Maybe it's about water.'

Paradise ignored the reference to Betty; Andrea's mind had to run through its own secret labyrinth to find the centre. Brad's voice carried softly through the open doorway. Her skin tingled at the sound. She had no business allowing a man's voice to make her feel like this; she had a job to do. She had to play him.

'Let's go, Andrea!' Roudy said, snapping his fingers. 'Work to do, work, work. We're running out of time!'

'What time?'

'Time, time, it's always about time. They never come to me unless they're at their rope's end and the ticker is seconds from blowing. You think the FBI would have brought us all this' – he motioned at the piles of data – 'unless they were beyond the limits of their own wits and needed me? I don't think so. Focus!'

She whimpered again and hurried to a large white wallboard, where she'd written out the last note, then marked and remarked it a dozen ways that could only make sense to her. Next to it, the original photocopy of the Bride Collector's writing:

They're trying to kill me, everyone is trying to kill me. But the advantage of being God is that I get to change my mind. Why did you move my bride? My time. Have you killed Jack lately? The snake waits in the garden, seeking a new bride to join him in the hole. Perfect twice. Me.

Paradise lost. It takes one to know one. To know the insane. When the jack is in the whole. Does jack want me to hide from you? No, I'm not sick, I'm just better than you.

I'm the sunshine and you're the Rain Man.

Paradise read the note, but her mind wasn't on the killer's writing or Andrea or Roudy or the mounds of evidence. Her mind was lost on Brad.

I'm a twenty-four-year-old woman and I have not yet had a single romantic relationship. I am unlovable and I would make a lousy lover. I am the dirt on the bottom of society's shoes.

For three hours she'd paced around the room, pretending to help them work, but half her mind was running circles around her feelings, justifying, criticizing, accepting, rejecting, a non-stop mess of emotions and reasoning that should have left her exhausted.

Truth be told, she couldn't wait for Brad to finish his phone call and rejoin them. She had good reason for this. She had to play him for everyone's sake; this was her contribution. Even knowing that she was, in part, fooling herself, she was eager to continue. She was pathetic.

The emotions came suddenly, as if she'd been swept away in a flash flood. Any other time she would have fled to her room and buried herself in her novel in the making.

But it was okay; it really was okay, because nothing was happening. There was no flood. She was simply imagining more than what was there. Brad would look at her and she would see soft, imploring eyes, yearning to know her more intimately. *Puke.*

Brad would speak and she would hear a voice calling to her gently from the darkness, asking if he could stand beside her, telling her that he liked being close to her. *Sick.*

And that was only the half of it. Her highly imaginative mind, cursed from birth, had already spun off a dozen fully fleshed scenarios, including everything from she and Brad as co-pilots on a deep-space probe to their attending an extravagant royal ball.

Puke, puke, sick, gag.

It was all a sad joke. In reality, Brad was only doing his job. He was showing kindness to all three of them because he was a kind man who found each of them fascinating and their gifts helpful. That was perfectly reasonable.

What are you looking for, Paradise? A lover?

'Pathetic!' She growled more than said the word, and the others looked at her.

'We are?' Andrea asked.

'No, not you. Keep going, I'll be right back.'

She had to put an end to this or risk flipping out, because, if she did that, Andrea would snap and it would be over.

Paradise marched up to the open doorway and stepped in. Brad was seated on one of three couches that formed a U for group therapy. He saw her and sat up.

'Okay, Frank. Anything else, let me know. I'll call you when I leave.'

She walked up to the couch and stopped five feet from him as he ended the call.

'Any luck?' he asked, lifting his eyes.

Looking at him now, she was certain that she'd made a complete fool of herself with him, prancing around the room like a filly in heat while the big stallion here strutted back and forth. His face, square and tanned, with neatly combed blond hair. Those eyes searching hers, seeing her stringy hair, her short frame, her stubby fingers with chewed-off nails, her white face, which had not once seen a jar or tube of makeup.

Apes did not marry men, birds did not cohabitate with whales, and men did not like Paradise. Which was okay, because she did not much like men in that way either.

'I'm sorry, we can't do this any more,' she said.

Brad stood up. 'They're giving up?'

'No. I'm not talking about them.'

'So . . .' His eyes twitched, one of those slight movements that signalled he had just caught on to something.

She spoke quickly, before he could embarrass her. 'I know what you're doing, Mr Raines. I know you're toying with me. And I need to confess that I've been playing you as well. But now we have to stop.'

His face drew a blank.

'Please don't tell me you don't know what I'm talking about.' She stepped over to the adjacent couch and sat, facing him. 'You're trying to earn my trust so that I can help you. Allison has gone along with the idea because she thinks I need to break out of this shell that has me trapped. She thinks you might be able to win my trust, and, if so, you would be the first man from the outside to do so.'

He swallowed, looking guilty, and sat back down. 'No, not entirely. Yes, in part, Allison did say that, but that's not—'

'But you need to know, Mr Raines, that I've been playing you as well.'

He didn't laugh. He didn't cross his legs or sigh or condescend to her. In fact, he looked genuinely embarrassed.

'You should feel shame for what you're doing, I suppose,' she said, 'but I'm guilty too, so I guess we're both in the same boat.'

'I don't understand – you've been playing me?'

'Normally, I would panic if a man showed interest in me the way you have. All those looks and winks . . . I would normally take off running. Didn't Allison tell you? Men and I don't mix too well.'

'She did say that, yes. But—'

'Normally, I would flip out. But today a woman's life is at risk and, as a group, we've decided to do our best, no matter what the cost, to save her life. So, rather than flip out, which would cause Andrea to quit, you can be sure, I decided to let you play your games with me. And the only way to do that was to let you think you were being successful in accomplishing your goal.'

After a pause, 'My goal?'

'To win my . . . my affection. My trust.' She was moving her knees back and forth like a girl who had to use the restroom, and she stopped them.

For a long drawn-out moment, he just looked at her, face shy and red like a kid caught with his hand in the jar. 'I don't know what to say,' he finally said.

'Me neither. I'm ashamed to have led you on like that. Honestly, I don't know what came over me. I've never done anything like it.'

She looked out of the window and was struck by the realization that it would all come to an end. The idea of climbing back into her dark hole of loneliness, no matter how safe, terrified her. It wasn't supposed to go this way! He should be stopping her, saying, *'No, no. I do love you, I don't know what has come over me, but you've bewitched me. I look into your eyes and am swept away and I don't know what to do about it!'*

But that wasn't what he was doing. And why should he? She was right. It really *had* just been a game. A dream. A story. A nightmare.

She was not the princess. She was the toad.

'So, what do we do?' he asked.

Paradise turned back to him, struggling not to betray her deep disappointment. 'Well, for one, I can't afford to freak out. Andrea will quit if I do.'

He looked as if he was still at a complete loss. 'It's amazing that you see it that way. I mean, you're being very gracious. And I'm very grateful. I really . . . I'm sorry, I didn't mean to put you through so much. I just . . . I don't know what I was thinking.'

'It's okay.' She blew out some air, fighting to control a black cloud of sorrow settling over her. 'I just have to figure out how to go back in there and pretend that everything's okay.'

'I don't want you to pretend,' he said.

'Well, I have to do something. I suppose we could continue the charade. I think I might be able to do that until this is all over.' A foolish notion, but she'd said it already.

Brad thought for a moment. 'No, I don't think we should do that. I really didn't mean to give you the wrong impression.'

He moved to the edge of his couch and rested his elbows on his knees, leaning forwards, very close to her. Then he reached out his hands, palms up, as if inviting her to put her hand in his. Paradise felt her chest tighten with the first sign of panic.

'Listen to me, Paradise. It doesn't have to be like this. I know you're afraid and I would be too. But I'm not here to hurt you. I'm not sure I could live with myself if I intentionally hurt someone like you. You. Hurt *you.*'

She was hearing him, but her eyes were on his open hands and she was wondering if he really did expect her to put her small ugly hand into his large powerful hand. The idea was making her feel nauseated.

'I don't think we have to pretend,' he said. 'I think that we're just two adults who both have deep feelings when it comes to other people. I lost someone very close to me a long time ago, and I still can't get over it. You lost part of yourself a long time ago, and you still can't get over it. We're both deeply wounded.'

Tears filled her eyes, though she tried to stop them.

'It's okay,' he said softly. 'We don't need to be like that. Neither of us is ready for the pressure anyway. Let's just try to help this girl.'

He was right. He was so right and she loved him for those words. This was just ordinary. She was just an adult. They were two adults trying to save a life and help each other out. What had gotten into her?

Her tears slipped from her eyes and ran down her cheeks.

'Give me your hands,' he said, reaching out, supported by his knees. 'Please.'

She hesitated, then did what she had never done. She reached out and placed her palms on a man's palms. They were larger than hers by half. And warm. His fingers closed around hers.

'You want to know the truth, Paradise? The truth is I think you're an incredible woman.' His voice was low and heavy. 'I envy you in more ways than you could possibly know. I don't want you to feel pressured to do anything. Seriously, I'm beginning to have my doubts whether Sherlock and Brains can break this down anyway.'

'Oh, they will. Just give them time, they will. They'll at least figure out what the killer's jack is.'

'And what about you? Can you do this?'

Actually . . . She could, couldn't she? The fear she'd felt earlier had somehow dissipated. She felt a bit blue and quite foolish, but otherwise comfortable. Maybe Brad had done exactly what he'd set out to do without intending to do it? Maybe he'd just won her trust in a way no man ever had?

She looked into his gentle brown eyes, then at his hands, and allowed him to hold onto her. 'I'm okay. I can do this. It takes one to know one. Right?'

Brad smiled. A bright, genuine, loving smile that frightened Paradise with the emotions it evoked. But she immediately set the foolish feelings aside and stood.

'So let's try to save her.'

CHAPTER NINETEEN

The apartment was nice enough on its own, but now Quinton had transformed the back bedroom into something majestic. A temple of sorts. The inner courts, complete with his own altar.

Due to his change in plans, he'd decided not to use the barn east of Parker, which might still come in useful for the seventh, most beautiful bride. Instead, he had set up in the apartment, hoping that the Rain Man's idiots would soon crack his jack and find the hole.

He'd brought the sedated sixth here and injected her with a half dose of benzodiazepine, a psychoactive sedative that would help her accept the truth with less fuss. Then, working efficiently yet quickly, he'd prepared the room, covering the brown carpet with thick clear plastic that could easily be rolled up when he was finished. A gurney with a white mattress sat in the middle of the room. He would take the gurney with him, dressed in the same white smock he'd worn when wheeling the bride in. No one had seen, but the precaution was necessary.

His case and the tool he would need rested atop a folding table along the right-hand wall. Two posts that he'd secured with drywall anchors protruded from the adjacent wall, precisely five feet from the ground. The body had to be positioned evenly, not cockeyed, so he always measured the height of each peg.

Once the bride hung in place and was glued to the wall, Quinton would arrange each and every appendage for optimal beauty. Like adjusting the bride's dress just right before she walked down the aisle. He removed all of her outer clothing, leaving her only in her underwear, facing the ceiling. Using a gauze pad, he cleaned the blood from the wound on her cheek where she'd crashed into the door. He used superglue to seal the gash, a trick that worked surprisingly well.

The makeup took him another half an hour, beginning with a foundation that matched the colour of the soles of her feet. With meticulous care, he applied eyeliner and mascara. Then a hint of blush. When he was finished, her faced looked lighter than the rest of her body, but that would soon change.

Quinton stood back and looked at her, awed at God's handiwork in creating such an exquisite being. If he could be reincarnated, he would certainly wish to come back as a woman. As a bride. And he would grow up dreaming of one day being chosen in this exact manner.

Normally he had no need for electricity, preferring battery-operated devices that were just as functional, but since he had power, he plugged in a fluorescent strip lamp with yellow plastic over the bulb and set it on the table. It filled the room with an atmospheric golden hue that she might appreciate when she awoke.

Quinton's final preparation was to prepare himself. Having already bathed earlier in the day, he now stripped off his clothes except for his black leather shoes, his socks, and his black Armani Exchange underwear.

He already wore black gloves, but changed out of the leather ones for rubber dishwashing gloves. Ordinarily he would wear a shower cap, but because he'd covered the entire floor with plastic, he opted for fashion over function this time.

Satisfied that all was in order, he pulled up the folding chair, sat down, and waited for the bride to awaken. It shouldn't be long now. She was stirring already, and he'd only given her a half dose of the sedative.

It was all business from here on in. He was only the messenger, come with good tidings for the lucky chosen one. A steady buzzing rode the bottom of his brain, and he knew that was because his mind was being stretched to its human limits. The doctors might call it a symptom of a psychotic break, but they were dim-witted and knew little about the true nature of things.

Ninety-eight percent of the world's six or so billion inhabitants could apply common sense to the most fundamental, obvious observations of human existence and conclude that a higher power existed. Yet few of the self-proclaimed experts called psychiatrists could see the same thing. So, then, were the six billion mentally ill, or were the few psychiatrists mentally ill?

Both, for the most part, but that was another story.

The story today was Nikki, the sixth favourite, chosen for her inner beauty, her outer splendour and her relationship to Rain Man, the devil who was trying to blot out the sunshine.

And now Nikki opened her eyes. Quinton stood and waited for her to orient herself. He tied her wrists and ankles to the gurney's aluminium frame using cloth strips. Slowly her eyes widened as awareness dawned.

'Hello, Nikki.'

She turned her head in his direction, took one look at his nearly naked body and tried to scream through the duct tape covering her mouth. Her legs and arms jerked, but the cloth strips held her securely.

'Sh, sh, sh. Don't get yourself all flustered. I'll just have to give you more drugs and do this without your participation.'

She quieted, eyes frantic.

'I would like to talk to you. We should have a dialogue, because I think I can help you see some things more clearly. But we can only do that if you promise not to start hollering. It's unbecoming for a person of your stature.'

She didn't react.

'Do you know who you are?'

Her eyes searched the room, then returned to him. She shook her head.

'No, so few people know who they really are. I want you to listen to me carefully. Then we can talk, okay? You can nod your head.'

She did.

'Okay, good. Do you believe in God?'

She nodded.

'Really? It's no wonder he chose you. Do you believe he is infinite?'

Another nod.

'And that he is a God of love?'

Yes.

This was a surprise. Perhaps too good to be true. He wouldn't have pegged her, being a shrink, as someone capable of faith, much less understanding love.

'You're sure? It's one thing to believe in God, but an infinite God of love is quite another thing. You really believe this?'

Yet another nod.

He was still having difficulty believing her, so he pressed it further.

'Do you go to church?'

This time she tried to respond through the tape but only muffled nonsense came out. She shook her head. No. So, then, she was telling the truth.

'You don't bow your knees with the mentally ill hypocrites who throw the humble to the wolves. Instead you believe in a loving, infinite God. Is that right?'

A muffled yes. Quinton believed her.

'Well. That's very good. Then it will be pretty easy for you to understand that the love an infinite God of love has for each person is also infinite, right? That there's no limit to how much he loves you. You can't say that he loves this one only *this* much and that other one *that* much, because in God's economy his love is unending. Yes?'

A dip of her chin. He felt quite good about her predisposition to understand, considering her comprehension of the basic facts.

Quinton paced in his black underwear, using his gloved hands to make each point as he spoke. 'This is common knowledge, shared by even dumb priests and pastors. But most clergy do not have the mental capacity to understand what necessarily follows. There is no greater love than infinite love, which is God's love. When you love someone infinitely, there is no one that you love more. You, Nikki. There is no one that God loves more than he loves you. Do you follow?'

She stared with plate-round eyes, but he was sure she did follow. Even an imbecile could follow this if they stopped to think a moment. Which didn't say much for clergy.

Nikki, on the other hand, was undoubtedly soaking in his wisdom, preparing her heart, letting it not be troubled.

'You see, everyone is God's favourite, even the mentally ill, which is most people, but don't let me digress. They are God's favourite too, all of them. This is possible only because God is infinite and can therefore have more than one favourite without violating the meaning of the term. He can have multiple favourites and each one is truly a favourite, receiving the greatest God has to offer, which is infinite. Follow?'

He paused briefly but pressed the final point, so eager was he to tell her.

'The point is that you, Nikki, are God's favourite.'

It was a stunning revelation. Every time Quinton wrapped his mind around the notion, his brain buzzed, and now was no exception. He wanted to kiss Nikki, God's favourite, but he couldn't risk leaving any of his bodily fluids behind. He would leave the kissing to God.

'Imagine it. You are God's favourite. Out of all his creatures,' and he spread his hands like a preacher making a grand point, 'you are his absolute favourite. Do you know what that means?'

She was soaking it in, speechless.

'It means every power in heaven and on earth is perched on the edge of their seats, watching to see what the favourite one, Nikki Holden, will do. Will she respond to her lover's call? Will she love God in return? Will she be with him for eternity? Or will she spit in his face and turn her back and find another lover? They all want to know, have to know, because you are the one. The favourite. All of eternity past has been waiting for the one God did it all for. Did it all for you!'

He'd said it masterfully. No one could possibly resist the raw reason behind such a delivery of truth.

'And, tonight, you can finally join him, as his bride, to live forever. Imagine that, Nikki. Tonight is your wedding night.'

The thought made him shiver. He stepped up, worked his gloved finger under the edge of her tape and – 'Not a word, not a sound or I'll put it back on' – ripped it off.

She gasped for air and coughed.

'Are you okay? Would you like some water?'

She looked as if she might cry, but she held herself together and turned her head slightly to face him. Tears were running down her temples. He would have to reapply the makeup when she was gone.

'Quinton . . .' Her face was all twisted up, making it hard for her to speak.

'You should be crying for joy, Nikki. Tears of joy. Unless a seed fall to the ground and die, it cannot grow into the beautiful flower it was meant to be.'

She finally found her voice. 'Listen to me, Quinton. Please, listen to me. I want to ask you a question. Can I do that? Will you let me ask you one question? I mean really ask you?'

It was the first time he'd faced this kind of reaction. 'Of course.'

'What if you have one thing wrong. I'm not saying that you do, but what if you just have one small thing wrong?'

But he didn't. What was her point?

'What if it's all true? Everything you said about God, including his favourites. That makes sense to me. It's perfect logic. It's true, all of that is true. But what if it's *my* choice when and how to go to him, not yours? Not even his. What if, because I am his favourite, he gave me that choice? Because he loves me.'

She didn't quite get it. 'I'm his messenger,' he said.

'What if you've made a mistake and are hurting his favourite. That would make you an enemy of God. Like Lucifer. That would make you—'

Quinton wasn't really conscious of what happened next; he was only aware that he was leaping forwards, swinging his arm, slamming his fist into her face.

He stood over her form, breathing hard, mind buzzing like a hornet's nest someone had taken a bat to. He'd never lost his temper, not during a ceremony like this. What did it mean? He felt dirty and used, but she'd pulled this reaction out of him.

'Forgive me, Father. Forgive me.'

Now he would have to use even more makeup. Maybe he should just give her more drugs and drill her heels now. Like he'd slapped sense into Joshie in the bathroom at Elway's eatery, he'd now beat this lie out of the bride.

Quinton took a deep breath and calmed himself. No, he wouldn't drain her yet – he still needed her. He needed Nikki because she was wrong, he wasn't the devil.

Rain Man was the devil.

CHAPTER TWENTY

Brad Raines paced with his hands on his hips, allowing Andrea and Roudy to run through their antics while he tossed in comments as he saw fit. Three hours had passed since his encounter with Paradise. From what he could see, little progress had been made in their efforts to find the jack in the whole, this key they insisted was hidden in the evidence. Depending on how he judged the day, it could be counted as a complete waste of time.

On the other hand, these last six or seven hours had been strangely rewarding. The nature of investigative work often demanded a kind of role playing, a cat-and-mouse game of wits, endless rounds of twenty questions without any obvious answer emerging, connected dots that formed senseless pictures.

But Brad was used to searching for the hidden clues with 'ordinary' people who worked according to unspoken rules.

Working with Paradise, Roudy and Andrea involved no such rules. They were more like three children playing house or, in this case, detective. Instead of guiding them, he'd quickly become the fourth playmate in their world of make believe.

There was a freedom here, without expectations, other than those that Roudy placed on them to *hurry, hurry, hurry* because his report was due.

'Everyone knows this kind of snake lives in the trees,' Roudy said. 'You think the snake that came up to Eve in the garden slid along the ground? Too obvious! Much too obvious. The snake in the hole came to her from the trees, if he was a worthy devil. From the sky, like the apple, which he offered her, not from a hole in the ground.'

Andrea was in her own little world. 'Holes are like zeros. One zero, but anything divided by zero is zero. So he had to add the woman. Now it's one plus one, which is two. Twice. Perfect, see? *Perfect twice* and then *Paradise lost*.' She underlined the corresponding words on the note to underscore her point. ₁

'What's your point, Roudy?' Paradise was the most lucid of the three, the ace in the hole here. The glue that held them together. And although her constant apologetic glances at Brad indicated that she knew this, she rarely tried to set them straight except through a gentle nudge.

Roudy rolled his eyes as if his point should be painfully obvious. 'He gives them apples, not worms. He tempts them. They like what he says. Apples, apples, Paradise!' He snapped his fingers twice. 'Focus!'

'I am, Roudy, and I'm seeing the snake plucking the apple with his skilful tail and hurling it at the girl with so much force that it knocks her out. Then he wraps himself around her throat and drags her into his hole.' It was undoubtedly only a fraction of the fully fleshed story that had mushroomed in her mind. Her mind was a fertile, exotic jungle teeming with life.

'Men are like snakes,' Andrea said, without turning from the white board. 'Only one thing on the mind. You tell them, Paradise.'

'Men are like snakes, Roudy,' Paradise agreed. Then added with another glance at Brad, 'Most men.'

'Most men,' Andrea agreed. 'Twice perfect. Twice perfect.' She whimpered.

Roudy looked at her. 'Seven is perfect.'

Brad had trouble containing his amusement. Unrestrained as they were, their thoughts jumped from track to track like a train with a mind of its own. Still, there was method to the madness in their world without rules.

He couldn't help feeling as if they were on the cusp of discovering the solution to the perfect mud pie. It was every child's playtime fantasy. There was a perfect mud pie here, they just had to keep kneading the dirt until they formed it. And in the process they would throw a few globs of mud at each other and laugh and stomp off angry, because that's what children did when they played with mud.

'Are you okay?' Paradise asked, walking up to him at the back of the room.

'Couldn't be better.'

'I doubt that's entirely true.'

'Well . . . we *are* running out of daylight.'

'I told you it might all be pointless. But you're okay, right? I mean . . . you're not bored?'

'Impossible.' And it was the bone-dry truth.

She grinned. 'Nothing like a trip to the zoo, right?'

'If this is the zoo, then I'm the monkey,' he said.

She stared into his eyes for a moment, then blushed. Which concerned him a little, because he wasn't sure his earlier exchange with her had quite dismissed the awkward connection between them.

They had re-entered the room and thrown themselves into the puzzle-solving like best friends. Relieved of any pretence, Paradise had opened up and bounced around with a bright smile. But the old, unspoken awkwardness had started to creep back in as the hours ticked by.

Brad was no stranger to relationships with women, as long as they didn't demand commitment. If he could take any lesson away from his thirty-two years, it might be that any bond with Paradise would be a disaster in the making, for her and for him.

Not that he could afford to be even remotely interested in that way.

At first his thinking was that he had to protect her. He couldn't give her hope while earning her trust, just to drop her later. Then again, Allison had made a good point: even a short relationship that ended in disappointment might be beneficial to Paradise.

Either way, it didn't matter. His fear wasn't for Paradise, was it? He was more disturbed by his own reaction to her, however shameful that was to admit. And that thought gave birth to another, even more disturbing: could he truly love someone like

Paradise? The notion struck him as absurd. He had to end it completely, so he had.

But now she was blushing, as she had several times over the last half hour.

Her white cheeks were flushed with just a hint of red to match her ruby lips. She smiled, with perfect white teeth. It made him wonder if she'd ever been kissed. She was frail and fair, as innocent as a broken dove. She had no fashion sense, choosing now to wear button-fly Levis that were wrinkled and an inch too short, and a sleeveless yellow collared shirt that was tucked in. Also wrinkled. The outfit was accessorized with a pink vinyl belt.

She'd dressed up for him, he thought, and ninety-nine out of a hundred people would think of her as a fool for doing so.

He couldn't do this.

'H and O,' Andrea said. 'Ho.'

'Who's the ho?' Roudy came back. 'He isn't killing whores.'

'No, "h" and "o" then "perfect twice". Fourteen.' She spoke quickly, drawing a shaky finger along the line. '. . . join him in the hole. Perfect twice. Me. Paradise lost. That's fourteen letters, perfect twice.'

Andrea's mind was lost in numbers, but her voice carried an urgency that made Paradise turn and face the board. 'What's fourteen letters, Andrea?'

Brad's cell phone buzzed in his pocket and he slipped it out. The screen read *Nikki Holden*. She was checking in as agreed. He thumbed the green talk button.

Andrea was clearly excited now. 'Ho, then fourteen letters. Then me. It happens twice, here and here.'

Brad lifted his phone to his ear. 'Hello, Nikki. How goes it?'

The small speaker on his cell phone hissed. Then another sound popped softly. The sound of someone trying to speak and unable to get words past raw emotion.

There are times in life when that dreaded phone call comes, making real the stuff of nightmares . . . a car accident, a broken back, a death . . . and Brad knew immediately that this was one of those dreaded calls. His heart thumped hard once, then seemed to seize up. But his mind was racing, desperate to know that he was wrong.

'Nikki?'

She was trying to speak. Brad shivered.

'What's wrong?' He couldn't move. 'Nikki?'

She found her voice, but it came out tight and stretched to the breaking point. 'Brad . . .'

'What is it? What's going on?'

She was crying. 'Brad, he . . .'

That was all he got. He. There was only one 'he' that came to mind.

And then 'he' spoke. 'Hello, Rain Man. Did you find my jack in the whole? It wasn't supposed to be her, you know? Come and get me, Rain Man. Time's running out.'

The connection ended.

'Nikki! Nikki!'

His world compressed around him. Andrea was talking about perfection and Paradise was asking something, but all Brad could hear was the dead silence on the phone.

He had Nikki. The Bride Collector had Nikki.

That couldn't be right. There was a mistake. Nikki was at her mother's! She wasn't even on the case today. But . . .

. Brad couldn't breathe. The phone was still pressed against his cheek, silent. Everything seemed to have stalled and he couldn't remember what he was supposed to do.

Then training and instinct dropped into his mind and resumed a semblance of control.

He jerked the phone from his ear. 'It's Nikki,' he said.

They stared at him, unsure what was expected of them.

'The Bride Collector has Nikki.'

'We're too late?' Roudy asked. 'What did I say? What was I saying? Hurry, hurry, and now look at this!'

'Nikki,' Paradise said, unbelieving. 'He's taken Nikki?'

'Yes.' Brad was punching in James Temple's number, hand shaking like a leaf in the wind. *Get control, calm down. Take a deep breath, just calm down.*

The special agent in charge answered on the third ring. 'Temple.'

'He's got Nikki. I just got a call from her cell phone. The killer's got her . . .'

'Slow down. She had a protective—'

'Call the unit. Get a car from Castle Rock PD out to her mother's house immediately. I'm going to call her back.'

'You're sure—'

'Get out to her mother's house!' Brad snapped. 'Now!' He disconnected, brought up recent calls and selected Nikki's number. Hit send.

The phone rang him right into her voice mail.

Think. Think!

Andrea was speaking again, sweet and soft. 'Home,' she said. "Ho" followed by fourteen letters then "me." That sequence occurs twice. That's perfect seven times two, perfect twice, and that happens twice. Perfect, twice. H . . . O . . . M . . . E . . . Home.' She had the pattern underlined in red.

The snake waits in the garden, seeking a new bride to join him in the hole. Perfect twice. Me. Paradise lost. It takes one to know one. To know the insane. When the jack is in the whole. Does jack want me to hide from you?

'That's it,' Roudy said. 'The jack in the whole! Home. He wrote this note after he planned on taking her. He has her at home.'

Silence gripped the room.

Paradise looked up at him and blinked. 'Where does Nikki live?'

The pattern filled Brad's mind like fireflies, almost impossible to see now that Andrea had illuminated the darkness.

Home.

'How do we know it's *her* home?' he asked aloud.

'He wouldn't hide a key in his message unless it unlocked

meaning,' Paradise said. 'His home would have no meaning to us unless you knew where it was. Nikki's home would. The killer has Nikki in her home.' She paused. 'And if you were just on the phone with her, she's still alive.'

Brad was already running for the door. Roudy was demanding to be taken along, but Brad didn't have the presence of mind to respond. He entered the hall at a full sprint, mind spinning with one question: What was the fastest way?

He tore past a dozen bewildered residents in the great room and raced across the yard.

Or was it *his* home? Or her mother's home?

Nikki lived in a two-bedroom apartment on Simms Street, west of Denver. He'd taken her home after the Christmas party last year rather than allow her to drive after one too many drinks. A cruiser might be closer – he'd put out a call. But he was less than fifteen minutes away himself, assuming traffic didn't hold him up.

Brad hit seventy by the end of the driveway, honking for the guard to open the gate, which he did, but only after Brad slid to a stop with two inches to spare.

If the killer had reduced Nikki to the woman he'd heard on the phone, he had to assume that the Bride Collector now knew everything Nikki knew, including the fact that Brad was at the Center for Wellness and Intelligence, only fifteen minutes away without traffic.

But the killer said he believed Brad hadn't found the jack in the whole tipping them off to his location. He might not feel any urgency.

Nikki was alive. If the Bride Collector intended to kill her the same way he'd killed the others, the operation would take some doing. Even after the drilling, he would have to get her up on the wall and unplug the wounds before her blood would drain. Kim had said it would take up to ten minutes for the heart to pump out five litres through the anterior tibial artery.

With any luck, Brad still had time to reach her. *Dear God, help me.*

He got Temple back on the line as he hit Hwy 170, doing ninety. 'No time to explain now, but he's got her at home. Either my condo, her mother's house or her apartment on Simms. Get Frank down to my condo now, send backup to Nikki's apartment. I'll be there in fifteen minutes.'

'There's no answer from the squad car that followed her. ETA two minutes.'

'Just send the cavalry out to Simms. Now, Temple. Now!'

CHAPTER TWENTY-ONE

She wasn't cooperating the way Quinton had hoped. Her spirit was too strong and she had a rebellious nature, making him second guess his choice to take her. The psycho-sedative was starting to kick in now, but he always preferred to get at least a nod of appreciation for God's plan before he gave the brides the rest of the drugs. Unfortunately, she hadn't been easily convinced of her opportunity.

The reason for her stubbornness was quite plain. Unlike the others, she was a psychologist, and therefore her mind was badly bent in the wrong direction. To complicate matters, she was full of antagonism towards him for taking the other favourites and she didn't seem to be able to grasp that this was all in her best interest.

Which presented a problem for Quinton. As God's messenger sent to find the bride, much like Isaac's servant had been sent off to find Rebecca, Quinton had to convince the bride. She had to become a willing participant, like the other five favourites. But Nikki wasn't submitting to her destiny as she should, perhaps because she was mentally ill.

'Now, listen to me, Nikki,' he reasoned, standing over her restrained form on the gurney. 'You're not listening very well. I'm going to give you one more chance, but then I'm going to have to become more persuasive, and you won't like that.'

The makeup he'd applied had smeared. He would have to touch it up. Time was running out. He couldn't risk lingering with her forever just because she wasn't right in the head. God would take one flawed bride for the sake of all those in the world who were equally flawed. And there were a lot of them. Perhaps that was why he'd chosen this one?

'Why is it so difficult to understand God's love for you?' he asked. 'Why don't you want to be his bride?'

She'd finally settled down after the phone call to Rain Man and now seemed stoic. Perhaps she was ready to accept her fortune?

'You don't want to be his bride?'

'It's my choice, not yours,' she said quietly. Her face was flat and emotionless.

'It is. But, in saying that, you're only highlighting the fact that you're *choosing* to turn your back on him. I could understand your rejection of him if you didn't understand how much he's taken with you. You do understand that you are his favourite? Is that where your confusion comes in?'

'God loves me, so he wouldn't force me. I am his favourite. We all are. Which is why he doesn't force us.'

'I'm not forcing you. The choice is yours. Do you want to be with him?'

She refused to answer this question. There was no hope for her twisted mind.

'You need me to agree, don't you?' she asked.

'It would be nice, yes.'

'And you think I would do something because you think it's nice? After what you've done to me?'

'Your incompetence is outrageous,' Quinton said. And again he wondered if he'd made a mistake by plucking such a dim-witted goof from the sea of women who would be grateful to be chosen. 'You're trying to stall. I understand. You think that, because Rain Man now knows the sun has come out and is shining on his precious little lamb, he'll come running. Even now, he might be on his way. But I doubt Rain Man and those retards he's working with are as smart as all that. Although, I will say, the women there put you to shame.'

She didn't get it, of course. She truly was a mental case.

'I get that I am his favourite,' she said, in an obvious attempt to keep the discussion going. 'But I don't want to die.'

'So, all of heaven and earth is waiting with baited breath to see what the favourite one will do, and you're willing to put it all on hold because all you can think about is yourself? Nikki wants to live longer. To milk small pleasures from another hour, another day, week, month, year. Well, excuse me while we all sit and wait for the selfish little brat to suck down as much ice cream and strawberries as she can before taking the trip down the aisle for a much better life. He loves no one more than you. Why so greedy?'

Fresh tears slipped from her eyes and ran back towards her ears. 'Going down that aisle doesn't feel right to me, Quinton,' she whispered. 'I'm scared.'

'Of course you're scared. You're so busy, busy, busy in your tiny mind, obsessed with this puny life. But once you know the truth, Nikki, it will set you free.'

Her lips quivered, and for a moment he thought she might start to sob again, which would effectively end the discussion, this time forever.

Instead she said something else that required him to end the discussion.

'Even the demons know the truth and they tremble. It doesn't make them any less evil. God loves me, and he wouldn't do this to me.'

And then she followed it up with an even more outlandish claim.

'You're jealous, aren't you? You are afraid that God hates you, and you will do anything to be his favourite, like us, like the women you're killing. No matter what you keep telling yourself, you really think God hates you. You're jealous. You want to be God's favourite too.'

Quinton stared at her, stunned by her audacity. Was she really so dense?

The buzzing in his mind grew so loud that he had to press back a growing panic. There was something truthful about what she was saying, he thought, but then he dismissed that thought as a plant from the evil one.

It occurred to Quinton that the seventh bride, the most

beautiful woman in the world, whom he'd already selected and who put this woman to shame in every conceivable way, might be strong in spirit as well. What if she too resisted her invitation?

The thought made him feel ill. It wouldn't happen, of course. Rain Man would see to that. He was sure of it. But the thought still made him nauseated.

Quinton picked up the syringe, pressed the needle into the vein in Nikki's right arm, and pressed the plunger to the hilt. The large dose of sedative would make this easier for all of them. She had at least recognized God's great love for her. That would have to do.

'Please, Quinton,' she whispered. Her eyelids looked heavy. 'Please don't kill me.'

She really was beautiful, Quinton thought. And then he taped her mouth shut and went to fetch the drill.

The dashboard clock read 4:02 when Brad cut across two lanes, ran the red light, despite the blare of horns, and entered Simms Street off of 8th Avenue. Nikki's apartment was on the right over the railroad tracks, just after 72nd Avenue.

His palms were wet and his shirt drenched with sweat no amount of air conditioning could stem. Backup was on the way.

Two thoughts drummed through his mind, driving him faster. The first was that Nikki was alive. She had to be alive. The killer could not know they'd found his jack. The woman who'd fallen into his clutches because of Brad's involvement with her, however thin that connection, was still alive. She simply had to be, because he couldn't go through this again.

The second thought drumming through his head was that the killer wouldn't kill her. He couldn't kill her, not for the sake of killing, because his psychosis demanded he follow a ritual that couldn't be satisfied with a bullet. He might try to kill Brad when he broke in on the act, but he wouldn't turn his gun on Nikki.

She was meant to bleed and remain angelic.

It was as much a hope as a conclusion, but Brad depended

on it now as he weaved in and out of traffic on Simms, headed for the Golden Hills Luxury Apartment complex just now visible two blocks ahead.

An eighteen-wheeler pulled into Brad's lane and braked. The same one he'd cut off at the intersection, now that he thought about it. Cars on both sides limited his options.

Brad laid on his horn and was immediately repaid by a loud honk from the truck in front of him. The eighteen-wheeler came to a stop at the red light at 72nd Avenue.

Panic lapped at his mind. He slammed his steering wheel with both palms. 'Come on, come on, come on!'

Nikki lay perfectly still, fighting off the effects of the drug. He'd hovered over her or sat in the chair watching her nearly every waking moment. Twice he'd retreated to the corner and urinated into a large plastic bottle. Once he'd left her alone in the room while searching out the rest of the apartment, and once he'd tinkered with his tools on the table across the room for an extended period, maybe half an hour. Preparing.

Each time she'd fought through the haze and gone to work on the strips of cloth that fastened her arms and ankles to the gurney.

Her first sliver of hope had come when the killer left the fingernail clippers on the edge of the mattress after he mani- cured her nails and painted them with a ruby-red polish. She'd managed to snake her fingers over them and tuck them under her back.

She'd spent desperate minutes unsure if the clippers would prove any use at all. Then he'd turned his attention to his tools, and she'd cut away at the cloth that tied her right wrist to the aluminium frame. She'd nearly cut through the strip before stopping and considering her intentions. She couldn't sit up and cut her legs free without being found out.

Armed with the knowledge that she had the capacity to cut herself free, she bided her time.

Then he'd left the room. She'd sat up and frantically gone to work on her ankles, sure he would walk back in at any second. And she couldn't cut all the way through. Not yet, he would see it! Not until she knew she had a path out, when he least expected it.

He had to be in the room, unprepared, when she made her break. And now that moment had come.

For the first time in half an hour, Quinton turned his back to her and walked back to the table of tools. To get the drill, she thought. He was going to get the drill and go to work. This was it. She had to get out now.

The only problem was the lock. He'd fixed a padlock to the door, and the key was in his right pocket, she'd watched him use it twice now. Unless she disabled him and broke out with force or using the key, she didn't stand a chance.

But it was now. She had to go now, before the drugs wiped her out completely.

Nikki turned her head and saw that he was plugging an orange extension cord into the wall while humming softly. She jerked both feet up towards herself, tearing them free with a soft ripping sound. The haunting violins in the music he'd played over and over helped to mask the tear, but she quickly straightened her legs so he couldn't see what she'd done.

Quinton glanced back. 'You're a strong one,' he said. 'I'm going to have to numb your legs. I don't want you to feel any pain. It's all going to be okay.' He bent over a black case for the Novocain and a syringe.

Head swimming in a whirlpool of fear and drugs, Nikki took a deep breath, rolled off the gurney, took two steps to the table, snatched up the hammer that lay there and, with her final reserves of strength, she threw herself at him.

The light turned green but the truck was taking its time and Brad was starting to lose perspective.

The car on his right was a Lincoln Continental, and its driver apparently felt no need to teach him the same lesson the truck driver had. The moment the Lincoln surged forwards, Brad lay on his horn and whipped the BMW into the right lane, before the Honda behind the Continental could close the gap.

He squeezed into the vacant spot without being hit, shoved the accelerator to the floor and shot past a cursing truck driver on his left.

He clamped his mouth shut, letting the heat of frustration wash over his face. None of this mattered at the moment. What did matter was that he was able to veer back to his left in front of the stalled eighteen-wheeler, accelerate the BMW to full speed without a single car to slow his progress, and whip into the apartment complex's gated entrance without being held up again.

He flashed his badge at the guard. 'FBI, you got the call?'

'Yes, sir.'

The gate was opening already. *Thank you, Temple.*

He gunned through, heard his tyres squeal and immediately backed down. The killer might hear beyond her walls. Brad had made it clear that the police should not use sirens. His greatest advantage, maybe his only advantage, was coming in unexpected. The Bride Collector wasn't ready for him, not this soon after the call.

He took the BMW down the side street fast, ignoring the speed bumps. Two police cruisers sped past, headed north on Simms – backup was here.

Hold on . . . Hold on, Nikki.

The blow came from behind, glancing off the side of his head with such force that Quinton wondered if he might be dying. He'd heard her grunt and started to turn when it landed, otherwise he might have taken the blow full on his skull.

Surprised, he leaped to one side as the favourite's almost-naked form flew by him and slammed into the wall. Other than her underwear, she wore only four strips of cloth, one tied to each wrist and one to each ankle.

Quinton knew immediately what had happened. She'd pulled herself off the gurney and come at him like a plucked goose. And she'd hit him on the head with his own hammer, the one with a fibreglass head that he never used but brought in the interests of being prepared for every eventuality.

She spun around, hammer still in hand, eyes fired like stars.

She'd smeared more of her makeup! 'What are you doing?' he demanded.

The favourite swung again, but Quinton blocked her arm with his own. The hammer hit her own leg and she cried into her tape.

'What are you doing?' he demanded, angry now. 'I had you nearly perfect and you're messing this all up! Stop this!' He snatched the hammer from her hands and tossed it into the corner. 'You're acting like a child.'

She sagged against the wall, sobbing under the influence of drugs and hopelessness. A glance back at the gurney and he saw the fingernail clippers on the mattress. He'd been careless. He deserved the extra work she was forcing upon him.

Nikki slipped down to the floor, pulling the extension cord free, then she became quiet. It was amazing that she'd managed an escape attempt despite being drugged. None of the others had tried to resist like this. Perhaps that was why she was so luckily chosen. She was a strong one, physically and mentally, even if she was a bit of an idiot. The tough, stubborn type of woman, blessed also with true beauty.

This was the kind of woman who did well on Wall Street, he thought. The executives of the world. Beautiful and strong. He understood why God loved them so much.

Quinton hauled her up, carried her to the gurney and flopped her face down. He would drill her now, apply the glue to her back and place her on the wall. Then he would redo her makeup as she gave up her ghost and became his bride.

Forgive me, Father, for I have sinned. I have caused a real mess.

Quinton had decided to use the new Black and Decker electric drill he'd bought for this occasion. He wanted to see how it compared to his previous choices.

He plugged the orange extension cord back into the wall, picked up the drill and approached Nikki, God's favourite.

Brad left his BMW parked two buildings south of Nikki's second-floor apartment and ran under the causeway. A car squealing up to the front door would alert anyone keeping an eye out.

He took the outdoor stairs two at a time, checked to see the police cars pulling in behind his, and swung onto the landing. Brass numbers above the door: *7289*. A stained-panel door with a one-foot square bevelled glass panel at eye level. The tenants had their own locks, he'd checked already. Management didn't have access. The only way in was to break down the door.

Shoot out the dead bolt.

He slipped out his FBI-issued Glock, chambered a round and approached the door on the balls of his feet. Shoes padded up the stairs behind him.

Brad swung around, gun in both hands, trained on the dead bolt, fighting the urge to go in on his own now because every second felt like an hour and Nikki might have seconds or minutes but not hours. Now. Now!

He waited. The two uniformed police were by his side in seven seconds, sidearms ready. They'd been briefed, and if they hadn't, he didn't have time to do it now.

He nodded once, pressed the Glock's muzzle close to the wood, directly in line with the dead bolt, and pulled the trigger.

Boom! The gun bucked hard and he threw his full weight into the door. But the door was stronger than one dead bolt and he didn't break through on the first attempt.

The Bride Collector would now be aware that someone was trying to shoot their way in. He was setting up for a shot in the hall or climbing out of the back window, where the two other cops would pick him up. Or he had something else up his sleeve.

The thoughts only pushed Brad's sense of urgency. He pulled back and pulled the trigger four more times, obliterating the lock, the bolt. This time a single kick swung the door in silently on well-oiled hinges.

Brad went in with his weapon extended. Chips from the back of the door lay scattered on the floor. On the wall, a painting of Vail shattered by a bullet hung askew. Dust filled the air from the splintered wood.

Nothing else was out of place. The tan couch, the large-screen

Samsung television, the ornate table lamps, the walls with the rest of the paintings – all undisturbed, unmarked.

No sign of the killer.

Brad ran to the hall on his left, hesitated one second against the wall, then jabbed his head around the corner. Nothing but hall. It was a two-bedroom apartment, she'd told him once. Both rooms down this hall.

Not a sound. No sign of any disturbance at all. What if he was wrong? What if Andrea's jack in the whole was just a big mistake and Paradise had sent him on a wild-goose chase?

He stepped around the corner and ran down the hall. The doors to both bedrooms were open. He knew then . . . He knew, but he could not say it or even think it. Something was wrong.

The first room on his left looked like a bedroom. Empty. He ran past, down the hall, into the room at the end. The shades were pulled up and bright light illuminated a queen-size bed with a brown comforter and matching lamps on the nightstands. Paintings of castles in rich English meadows.

Nikki was not in her home.

The blow was so unexpected that Brad didn't react. They had been wrong. They had come to the wrong place. Nikki . . .

Nikki would pay the price.

'Sir!'

He spun at the sound in the officer's voice, calling from back down the hall.

'Sir, I think you want to see this.'

He pushed past one officer who'd followed him down the hall and saw that his partner had turned the light on in the first room.

'What is it?'

The room was decorated in rich purples and greens, larger than the one at the end. At its centre was a king-size bed neatly dressed in a silk comforter with six or seven decorative pillows and two beautiful chiffon lamps. This was the master. Nikki's room.

The officer was looking at an eight-and-a-half by eleven sheet of paper, folded in half and set atop one of the silk pillows. It was addressed with red ink and it read, *Rain Man.*

The killer. He'd been here. Which meant that Andrea was right: this was the jack in the whole. A note from the killer addressed to Rain Man. To *him*.

'Call Temple at my office. Get a forensics team out here immediately.'

'Yes, sir.'

He grabbed a tissue from the box on the nightstand and used it to pick up the note, then opened it gingerly to the Bride Collector's familiar handwriting:

The jack is in the whole, but today the jack is the joker and he's got a smile. So sorry, Rain Man, but the sun has come and things are looking bright. I have taken God's favouritefavorite back to him. He waits for his bride. You'll have to find your own.
P.S. We are at 2435 4ᵗʰ Street. Boulder. #203.

He stared at the words, trying to think past the voices screaming in his mind. The killer had outwitted them, played them in a fixed game. Nikki was gone. GONE!

But that wasn't true . . . No, the man couldn't know that they'd broken his code so quickly. He was sure to think he had some time. Brad had heard Nikki's voice only twenty-five minutes ago.

He pulled out his phone as he ran. Temple picked up on the first ring. 'I have a team on the way, Brad. I . . . I . . .'

'He's got her in an apartment in Boulder,' Brad cut in. 'I'm half an hour away – more, it's rush hour! Get the Boulder PD out there now! And tell them to go in silent. He doesn't know we're on the way, he can't, not . . .' Brad ran out of breath as he took the stairs at a run.

'You're saying she's alive?'

'I don't know. 2435 4ᵗʰ in Boulder. Number 203.' He shoved the note in his pocket. 'Hurry, Temple. Please hurry.'

Temple would make the call, but local response time would be five, seven, ten minutes. Depending on where the closest cruiser happened to be. Depending on how fast the dispatcher got the interagency message. Depending on everything but him.

No longer concerned about stealth, Brad took out of the apartment complex on screaming wheels. He headed east on 72nd and took the Foothills Highway north. The cards were now dealt, the bets made. They would either reach Nikki in time or they would find her dead.

Brad had faced death. Victims. Ruby. He'd grown accustomed to the stench of it. But that stench never faded, not for him, and particularly not if it arose off someone like Nikki.

But something had happened deep in his psyche these past ten minutes. Something he recognized. He'd rushed into her room and assumed that he was too late. That Nikki was dead.

He was horrified, yes. But she wasn't Ruby. No one had been Ruby. No pain had come close to shutting him down the way he'd shut down following her death ten years earlier. And this, he thought, was because he had given himself to Ruby, heart and soul. When someone you love dies, something inside of you dies. You die. She is you. You are her.

He shook the thought from his mind and called Allison at the CWI.

'Well, young man, you've certainly left the place buzzing.'

'Hello, Allison. Sorry about—'

'Don't apologize. You've put all three on top of the world. Did you find her?'

'Not yet. But they were right. Tell Paradise we found another note from him. I want you to write it down and ask them to study it for . . . anything. Can you do that?'

'Tell me.'

He read the note to her.

'God's favourite,' she said softly, repeating to herself. 'Interesting.'

'Does it mean something to you?'

'Well . . . In general, yes. Basic theology. So, besides this note, you found nothing?'

'No. Boulder PD is on their way now. I have to go, Allison.' He hesitated. 'You used to be a nun?'

'Yes.'

'You still believe in God.'

'Of course. I'm not terribly religious, I'm afraid, but I do what I do because of that belief. And, yes, I will pray.'

'Thank you.'

'Don't count her out, Brad. She still has that image locked in her head somewhere.'

Paradise. He never would have guessed that Allison, of all people, would push for him to exploit her own patient.

Then again, Allison saw the exploitation as her patient's salvation.

A tone in his ear indicated an incoming call. He glanced at the phone screen. Temple.

'Nikki's seen him too,' Brad said to Allison. 'We're going to get to her in time. Gotta go.'

He switched over to Temple. Nearly fifteen minutes had passed since he'd made the call to dispatch Boulder PD. This had to be it. His heart pounded in his rib cage like a fist.

He brought the phone back to his ear. 'Yeah, hello . . .'

'Brad . . .'

And he knew immediately by Temple's tone that it wasn't good.

'What is it?' he demanded, flushing with anger.

'I'm sorry, Brad. They found her.'

His vision blurred. 'Found her? How?'

When Temple answered, his voice was all too matter-of-fact. 'On the wall.'

Images of Melissa and Caroline, white on the wall like angels, flashed through his mind. He couldn't form an image of Nikki like that.

'Brad, I'm sorry, I know you two were close . . .'

He switched the phone off and set it in the cup holder. There was something wrong. They'd come too close to lose now. Andrea had figured it out! Roudy had paced all day and exposed the jack. Paradise had told him that Nikki was home. And they had been right, he'd found the note . . .

They'd cracked it wide open, it couldn't end like this! Not after what they'd accomplished.

Brad pushed the BMW to its limits, ignoring the repeated horns from all sides, weaving in and out of traffic as he raced towards the crime scene. His head was in a drum, knocking around in the darkness. He wasn't thinking straight.

At least half a dozen cruisers had beat him to 2435 4th Street. Lights were flashing on four of them. Yellow tape already formed a barrier around the entrance to the courtyard inside. Spectators hung back on the street and under two large trees, watching. A low-rent district. The rental information would take them nowhere; the Bride Collector was too careful, too smart.

Brad stepped over the yellow tape and flashed his badge at an officer. He might have said 'FBI', but he wasn't sure. His eyes were on the open door across the courtyard, up on the second floor, where several more police stood talking quietly.

He ran. Through the entrance, up steel stairs, down the walkway, past two uniforms at the door, into an unfurnished apartment. Someone was saying, 'Hey, hey!' behind him, telling him to slow down. But he couldn't get to the room quickly enough.

And then he was there, in the room down the hall marked as the crime scene. The room was empty except for a plain-clothes detective, a uniformed officer. And Nikki.

She was on the wall and she was wearing a white lace veil.

'FBI, out!' He flashed his credentials. 'Both of you, out now.'

'Now hold on just—'

Brad grabbed the detective by his shirt and shoved him towards the door. 'This is my partner, this is my case, now get out!'

They stumbled out and he slammed the door behind them, breathing as heavily from what was on the wall as from the run. He turned slowly and faced her.

Nikki's skin was like ivory, drained of life. Naked except for her underwear. Her arms were spread wide and her head tilted to her right so that her dark hair draped over her shoulder. Eyes closed, lips ruby with lipstick, fingernails manicured and polished.

She'd been positioned exactly as the others. But she was in an apartment. And there was a small pool of her blood on the carpet beneath her feet. The Bride Collector had left without plugging her wounds. He'd taken the bucket of blood and left her dead.

Brad slid down the door, gripped his face with both hands and cried.

CHAPTER TWENTY-TWO

The buzz at the bottom of Quinton Gauld's brain had come and gone repeatedly since the last favourite, Nikki Holden, had turned it on. Her absurd accusation that everything he was doing was a pathetic attempt to become God's favourite was outrageous. He was no hunchbacked freak willing to serve his master in any capacity to win favour. She hadn't said quite as much, but he knew that she was thinking precisely this.

He'd delivered her to God two days ago, and he was now sure that she had indeed been chosen because of her mental illness, as God's way of reaching out to all the world. Because God loved them all, even the densest of the dense. And especially him.

He dismissed Nikki's claim.

Quinton walked to his kitchen and opened the refrigerator, hungry for a snack. Maybe some peanut butter on a slice of orange. Organic peanut butter. Nature's Choice brand.

He pulled out the jar, chose a particularly large orange from the fruit bowl, washed it thoroughly and sliced it up while thinking ahead. Back on track.

He'd done his part and now he could focus on the prize at the end of his race. On the true bride. The most beautiful woman in the world, without exception. He'd watched her for years, waiting, knowing that, in the fullness of time, he would take her and present her, blameless, to her suitor, a perfect bride.

Quinton knew just how perfect she was because he had known her. Not in the biblical sense, although not for a lack of trying. But she hadn't appreciated his advances, and now he understood that she'd been right to save herself for God. She was a virgin, he was sure of it.

What was particularly tricky about the final bride was that she must come willingly. Not just die willingly, but join him of her own accord.

He'd considered a thousand scenarios over the years leading up to this date. Stepping out on the sidewalk with a bright smile. 'Hello, Angel. Remember me?' She'd likely slap him and scream rape.

He might send her boxes of chocolates with sweet notes, pretending to be a handsome man with a heart of gold inviting her to dinner. But she wasn't the kind who met strangers for dinner.

He even considered getting plastic surgery and attempting to win her as a suitor, but he wasn't confident in his ability to pretend long enough to earn her trust. She undoubtedly had many potential suitors, and the only reason she wasn't yet married was because she could afford to be picky. Any man with more than half a brain would fall for her; not that there was an abundance of those.

He'd eventually narrowed his options down to a couple that might work if he was very clever, one involving her family. And now Rain Man had inserted himself into the picture, like a gift from God, allowing Quinton to settle on a plan so perfect that it gave him chills.

The only problem was this buzzing in his brain. This *buzz, buzz, buzz.* The onset of a particularly harsh psychotic break, the doctors would say. Truth was, he was the poster child for psychosis. But so few really understood psychosis.

Quinton sat at his table and wiped a small portion of peanut butter on a slice of orange, then placed the whole circle in his mouth, peel and all. So many nutrients in the orange peel.

See (and he waved a finger in the air as he thought this), people didn't understand the nature of psychosis. It was defined as being out of touch with reality. Psychosis was a thought disorder, like schizophrenia, which disconnected one from reality, unlike multiple-personality disorder, which caused the afflicted to split. The former was very common, the latter was extremely rare.

Over time, the world had attempted to correct psychosis with a myriad of inhuman treatments, ranging from electric shock to carving out parts of the brain with a knife. In the same way that the world now cringed at the memory of such treatments, it would one day cringe at having drugged up the afflicted and locked them in prisons as if they were witches.

There was a growing suggestion among scientists that psychosis was a sign of evolutionary progress, the brain's way of growing brighter, at least in some cases. Like Quinton's.

In truth, being 'out of touch with reality' could only occur when one understood reality itself. Quinton's superior mind was indeed out of touch with the world's understanding of reality, yet supremely in touch with a higher reality, largely misunderstood by the world.

Namely, the spiritual reality, which gave him purpose and destiny.

The smooth texture of peanut butter combined with sweet popping orange – such a perfect snack, it should be called a food group all by itself. Some probably would think peanut butter with oranges strange. What they failed to see was that, from another perspective, *they* were strange.

The world had once been determined to be flat, and the belief that it was round was considered to be out of touch with that reality. But which was true reality?

In the same way, many believed that God did not exist. One day they would all know the truth. There was a terrible battle raging between good and evil, and few were as aware of this battle as Quinton.

He took his last bite of orange smothered in peanut butter, wiped his fingers on a napkin and threw the napkin in his self-sealing waste can under the sink. The perfect snack indeed. His only regret was that he himself, a human, was not perfect, as much as he tried to be perfect. Instead he had the buzzing at the base of his brain to mar his perfection.

Forgive me, Father, for I have sinned. And I will sin again.

Now, to the matter of Rain Man. The agent couldn't possibly

know that he was already on a course to bring him the beautiful sister. The seventh and most perfect bride.

It was fantastically ironic that Angie Founder's real name was Angel. That sicko father who'd killed his family and taken his own life had named his two daughters Paradise and Angel. A religious nutcase.

Either way, the father had played his role by bringing into the world a beautiful daughter who would now present herself as a spotless bride. God indeed worked in mysterious ways.

Quinton left his house at noon, slid behind the wheel of his black M 300, and headed out to complete a few errands before he drove into downtown Denver, where he would drop the hatchet. So to speak.

God willing.

The sound of bagpipes playing 'Amazing Grace' at Nikki and her mother's funerals earlier in the day haunted Brad. The last two days had drifted by like a vessel lost in a white fog. Nothing could have been worse for the FBI, for the case, for him.

And Nikki . . .

Brad still had trouble accepting the fact that she was gone, much less that he had played a central role in her fate. She was dead. She was dead because of him. She wasn't Ruby, no, but she was a beautiful woman with a spirit that had touched thousands of people. The sudden end to her life left him as shocked as he'd been since Ruby's death.

The Denver office had slipped into a terrible morass, rage and grief all rolled into one. The assistant director in charge had flown in for the funeral and spent two hours in the office, reinforcing the sense of failure they all shared.

Temple had been the first SAC to lose an agent to a ritualistic killing in the history of the FBI. He wasn't taking it well.

Details of the case were finally beginning to leak to the press – far too many people knew and loved both Nikki and Michelle Holden to be satisfied with anything but the truth surrounding their deaths. Most of the truth, anyway. To date, they knew that a crazed killer had broken into the house, killed Michelle, then taken Nikki to his apartment and killed her there in a ritualistic fashion. It would only be a matter of time, a day at most, before the fact that Nikki had been the Bride Collector's sixth ritualistic killing made the news.

The fact that the Bride Collector was not only out there but homing in on his seventh victim deepened the desperation that had pulled the investigation into its jaws. They couldn't take time to mourn. Brad had hurled himself back into the dark murky waters like a man who'd jumped overboard, knowing that the killer was in the deepest part of the ocean.

But there was nothing new out there, and in the end the waves had washed him back up here. At the Center for Wellness and Intelligence.

Allison sat at her small wooden desk in front of a wide book-case filled with psychiatry and psychology books. She leaned back in her chair, studying him like a mother who knew more than she let on. 'It's not your fault, Brad.'

'I could have stopped it. It feels like my fault.'

'Of course it does. And now you're terrified to take the next step because you're afraid that you'll be at fault again.'

She was speaking about Paradise. Her insistence that Paradise might hold the key had whispered through his mind, drawn him back. Without Allison's encouragement, he wouldn't be here. And even now he was torn.

'Help me out here, Brad. You have a lead in a case—'

'We have a girl . . .'

'A woman.'

'. . . a woman who forgot what she saw when she made contact with one of the killer's victims. Is that a lead?'

'Isn't your obligation to fully explore every lead in a case like this?'

'She can't remember.'

Allison nodded, then winked at him. 'Not yet.'

In Brad's world what she suggested made no sense whatsoever.

Then again, neither had her suggestion to turn the evidence over to the 'team' and that had yielded the 'jack in the whole', hadn't it?

Allison leaned forwards and put her elbows on her desk. 'Do you know what I think?'

'No.'

'I think you're afraid. Not of violating any protocol. You're afraid of Paradise herself.'

'No, that's not—'

'I think you feel for her and you're afraid of hurting her. It's the same reason you probably have difficulty committing to any relationship. You're wounded by a monster called guilt and you just can't go there again because of the pain.'

She'd hinted at this already, but hearing it so clearly put Brad back in his seat. He didn't know how to respond.

'I think you're falling in love with her,' Allison said.

'What? No . . .' He crossed his legs and folded his hands, uneasy. 'Listen, I know you think all of this is good for her, but you can't just push an absurd relationship like this . . . This is crazy.'

'No, she's crazy, and that's the real problem, isn't it? Any other witness and you wouldn't be sitting here like a small boy, feeling sorry for yourself. Well, let me tell you something, FBI: the last thing you need to worry about is whether Paradise will or won't get hurt. Stop treating her like she's subhuman.'

'So now I'm wrong for not leading her on?'

'I'm not suggesting you lead her on. I'm only saying that she deserves to be treated like any other human being her age. With complete honesty.'

'She's *not* any other human being!'

'She is!' Allison cried. 'Do you think God loves her any less because of her condition?'

'Don't put words in my mouth.'

She sighed and leaned back again. 'Fine, FBI. I'll be straight, then. I hope you find this killer and put an end to what he's doing before he hurts another woman. He's clearly psychotic, and it's the few like this maniac who give my children a bad name. Despite the vast majority of wonderful people learning to cope with their psychosis, there's always the one Michael Laudor who'll graduate from Yale, then snap and kill his wife. On account of those few, the world treats them all as if they have leprosy, and that makes me sick. You have six dead women on your hands, and that's a terrible thing. But I have dozens living in my care who face a kind of death every day because they are made to feel like the dirt on the bottom of your feet. Less than human. Dead already.'

Point taken.

'You cannot hurt Paradise more than she's already been hurt. You can only help her. Don't let your fears and insecurities stop you from treating her like any other woman.'

'Okay.' Brad stood and walked to the window. 'Fine, I won't. But you're wrong about one thing.' He turned and walked to the back of his chair. 'I'm not falling in love with her. Maybe I am wounded and maybe I'm afraid to let a woman love me, all that psychobabble. I like Paradise very much. She's . . . precious. But, please, I'm not falling in love with her.'

The idea of it . . .

Allison's eyes twinkled. 'Fine. Then you'll treat her like a human being. Like a woman.'

'I said I would.'

'Because, if you do, she'll trust you. She might let her guard down and tell you what's hidden inside her. And she'll probably fall in love with you, if she hasn't already.'

He couldn't believe she was saying this.

'And I'm telling you that's okay,' Allison said, standing. 'Let her fall in love with you. It will do her wonders.'

'I refuse to lead her on—'

'I didn't say lead her on. I said treat her like any woman. Just don't penalize her. There's a difference.'

Allison walked around her desk and headed towards the door. 'And this bit about God's favourite, from the killer's note.'

'"I've taken God's favourite back to him",' Brad quoted.

She gripped the doorknob and turned back. 'You realize that's theologically sound. In God's infinite love, he loves no one more than another. We are all, therefore, God's favourite. Each soul is immeasurably valuable, no less than the value of a single bride loved by her suitor. Few humans understand their relative value to God.'

'And you're saying the Bride Collector does,' Brad said.

'Whoever this man is, he thinks he's doing God a favour, finding the bride of Christ for him. What he doesn't realize is that he's actually killing God's favourites. He's got it backwards, you see? He's not an angel, he's the devil. Someone needs to correct his thinking.'

'Yes, well, he's delusional.'

'Yes. But he's not the only one who's got it backwards.' She opened the door and stepped out. 'Now, we should go. Paradise is waiting.'

'She is?'

'She's been waiting for an hour.'

CHAPTER TWENTY-THREE

They're coming!' Andrea cried. She whipped back from the window overlooking the park, eyes wide. 'Quick, they're coming!'

Paradise was hanging back, pacing by the couch, determined not to give in to all of their antics, but, hearing the announcement, she rushed forwards with Casanova and Roudy for a look.

'Who's coming?' a voice shouted from behind. 'Zeus?'

They spun and faced a goggle-eyed Flower in a pink dress. 'Out,' Roudy snapped.

'But my sculpture isn't ready for Zeus! It's going to be majestic.'

'This room is reserved for a meeting with Allison. You have to leave.'

'But . . .' Then Flower turned and fled, uttering something about the gods.

Paradise was already homed in on Allison and Brad crossing the lawn towards her. She was suddenly unsure she could go through with this. Worse, she wasn't entirely sure what *this* was.

'Now, remember what I told you,' Cass said, straightening his shirt. He was feeling better, full of vim and vigour, he said. 'I know I tend to be straightforward, but it doesn't always work so well. Trust me. Try not to stampede. Try to be subtle.'

'Subtle?' Andrea queried. 'Is that what *you* are?'

'I said it depends. You have to know how women think!' He held up a finger authoritatively.

'I still think we should accompany you,' Roudy said. 'Why on earth would he want to meet with you alone?'

'Don't be a fool, man,' Cass quipped. 'Three's a crowd.'

'Thus speaks the man who was sleeping when we found the jack.'

'This is about Jill, not Jack,' Cass said.

Paradise couldn't bear their nonsense a moment longer. 'Stop being ridiculous! All of you! We don't know who he wants to meet with, or why. This has nothing to do with anything you're talking about!' Her voice rang through the atrium in the women's housing. 'Andrea, tell them, for heaven's sake.'

'It's true. Paradise wants me to flirt with him.'

'I didn't say that.'

'That's the spirit,' Cass said. 'But go slow, Andrea.'

'You didn't?' Andrea asked with a look of confusion. 'Sorry, sorry. I thought . . .'

'I said you *could*, for all I care,' Paradise snapped. 'That doesn't mean I *want* you to.'

The door burst open and Bartholomew, a skinny resident who suffered from delusions, pulled up sharply. 'They're coming, Paradise! And he looks good today. Handsome devil.'

Paradise faced Casanova. 'You told the whole Center?'

He shrugged. 'Just a few.'

Bartholomew spun back. 'Sorry. My lips are sealed.' He set off towards the hub, where he would likely tell every living soul, assuming they weren't lined up at the window already.

'Out,' Paradise said, seething now. 'I want all of you out!'

'We can't, Paradise,' Roudy protested. 'Like you said, he might want to talk to all of us.'

'I doubt it.'

'So you see, he *is* coming for you,' Cass said. 'I can see that look in his eyes from here. He's got one thing on the brain, that one. Not to worry, it's all I think about as well. Just remember what I told you.'

Before Paradise could respond, the door opened and Allison walked in, followed by Brad Raines. Two thoughts collided in Paradise's mind. The first was that they'd been caught staring out the window.

The second was that she'd forgotten how beautiful Brad Raines was. He was wearing jeans today. She'd never seen him in jeans.

They made him look more like her, in some ways. She felt silly for comparing herself to him.

'Hello, friends,' Allison said, smiling. 'I see you've been expecting us.'

'No,' Paradise said. 'Yes, they have been. Talk, talk, talk, talk, you know. Can't shut Casanova up.' She wished she could meld with the wall.

'Hello,' Brad said, dipping his head at them all. His gaze settled on Paradise. 'I guess you all heard.'

'What's this all about?' Roudy demanded. 'More evidence? He left another note, I suspect.' He flipped out his hand. 'Give it to me and I'll have my assistant prepare it for my analysis immediately.'

'You look handsome today,' Andrea said.

Paradise glanced at her friend and saw that she was staring at Brad with those eyes. How could Andrea be so forward now, after everything?

'Yes, you do,' Paradise agreed, then felt silly for saying it. But she wasn't going to let Andrea walk all over her either.

'Thank you.' His eyes were on her. 'If you all don't mind, I need to speak to Paradise. She may be able to provide us with information—'

'What, the ghost thing again?'

'Roudy, please.' Allison *tsked*. 'Don't be like that. There are a lot of desperate people out there right now. Now, please, give us a few moments. Hmm?'

'How long?' Roudy persisted.

'An hour, Roudy. Maybe two. Please. Paradise will be along.'

'I need a shower,' Andrea said. 'Sorry, sorry.' She walked quickly towards the hall door.

Roudy set his jaw and headed towards the exit behind them, pouting.

Casanova walked up to Brad and took his hand and kissed it. 'I'm so sorry for your loss, young man. She was indeed a stunning beauty. Just remember, there are more where she came from.' Then he too left.

'The room's all yours,' Allison said. 'But I wouldn't linger here long. You're bound to be interrupted.'

'You're leaving?'

'I am, Paradise.' Allison walked up to her and touched her cheek with a warm hand. Her words were as soft as her smile. 'It's okay, young woman. Not that you need it, but you have my permission to tell him whatever you want. He's a good man. I think you can trust him, I really do.'

Paradise nodded slowly. 'I do trust him.'

'Yes, but I think you can really trust him. And I think you can trust yourself. Don't be afraid, child.'

Then she turned and walked towards the door. 'I'll be in the reception area if you need me. Oh, and I think the south lawn is the most private place on the grounds. At the pond behind the aspen grove. Paradise, you know the place.'

The pond. Why so far? It was near the fence and Paradise avoided going so close to the fence at all costs.

'Paradise?'

'Yes. The pond, yes.'

'Good.'

And Allison was gone.

'Well.' Brad was smiling, a little red in the face himself. 'That was a bit ridiculous.'

The comment eased her a bit. But she had to stay on point here. From the moment Allison had told her that Brad Raines was visiting CWI again, she'd been a complete mess. Within fifteen minutes she'd broken down and told Andrea, and the rest was history.

You would think that Romeo and Juliet had come back to life and were reuniting on these very grounds! The very fact that she'd allowed herself to entertain the most fleeting fantasies over these past few days was horribly embarrassing.

The fact that the mere sight of Brad now made her palms wet was downright shameful. She had to maintain control.

Brad cleared his throat. 'Do you know why I'm here?'

'Because Nikki's dead,' she said. Then added, thinking her delivery too crude, 'I'm so sorry.'

'So am I. But you were right about the jack in the whole.'

'Allison showed us the last note. Roudy and Andrea spent a whole day on it, but they couldn't come up with anything.'

'I think it was a note for me.'

'That's what I told them.' She paused. 'Did you love her?'

He blinked. 'Nikki?'

What was she doing?

'Not like that, no,' he said. 'But we were very close.'

Paradise almost asked him what he thought about *her*, but she caught the words in her throat before she made a fool of herself. The room was feeling stuffy and she was sweating, so when he said that maybe they should take Allison up on her suggestion to find some privacy near the pond, she jumped at it, fence or no fence.

She caught sight of Bartholomew's afro behind some bushes as they exited the women's wing. Fortunately, they were headed away from him. They walked in silence, and her awkwardness grew. She became aware of every step she took. Her sandals, which she'd never worn until today, looked like something out of a bad Cleopatra movie. His leather shoes, on the other hand, looked as if they might have cost her full monthly allowance.

They were both wearing jeans, but hers were too short. Why were all her jeans too short? She'd never realized that until just these last few days.

Andrea had told her yesterday that her hair stank, so she'd washed it. Andrea always thought everyone's hair stank. But now Paradise was thankful, because she was walking just in front of him and he was probably looking down on the top of her head at this very moment.

She couldn't bear it any longer. So she stopped and let him pass her.

'What is it?'

'Nothing. I need to fix my shoe; just keep going.'

She made a show of fixing the strap on her sandal and then followed when he continued down the sidewalk. If she stood on her tiptoes, the top of her head might reach his underarms. He was built like a god, Andrea had said. She had to agree.

Her mind spun with an image of Cleopatra inviting the newest servant, the strong, bare-chested specimen from the south who'd only just joined her court, to demonstrate how he shot his bow. She wanted lessons in the garden. Just the two of them. She must know precisely how he held the bow, and she walked up behind him as he flexed, bowstring drawn back tight. She traced his back and his arms with her delicate fingers as she studied his posture. His muscles were like vines beneath his skin. Suddenly, from behind a tree on their right, came his lover, a witch from the north who had cast a spell on . . .

'Okay, stop.' Brad halted, holding up his hand.

She ploughed into his back, then scrambled back. 'Sorry. Excuse me, I didn't realize you were going to stop. If you had told me, I would have gone around. I didn't mean to run you over.'

He didn't seem to care. 'I can't do this,' he said.

Dread spread down her face. 'Me neither.'

'I just don't feel right about it.'

'Exactly. I never did feel right. And they're not really Cleopatra sandals.'

That stalled him. 'I'm sorry?'

'Nothing. What were you talking about?'

'Allison said I should just be honest.'

When he didn't elaborate, she agreed. 'As opposed to lying, yes, she would say that, she used to be a nun. I mean, I would too, of course. Honesty is always best, particularly around someone like me who despises a fake.'

'Really?'

'You like fakes?'

'Then you know why I'm here?'

'Because Nikki is . . . you know . . .' She made a motion with her hand but quickly gave up, realizing she didn't know how to say *dead* without saying it. 'Dead.'

'I mean . . . Why I'm here with you,' he said.

She had no clue, because she was purposefully controlling her own mind and forbidding it to wander. Well, yes, she did have a clue. They were here to try to shake loose the memory of what she'd seen in the kitchen. The ghost. 'To get me to remember . . .'

'And the only way to do that is to get you to trust me,' he said. 'You realize that?'

'I do. And I already do trust you.'

'Yes, but . . . I mean . . .' His eyes shifted and he used his large, strong hands absently. The ones with trimmed nails. Her nails were trimmed as well, but with her teeth, which Andrea said was a nasty habit. Had she bitten her nails while he was watching? She couldn't remember!

'More than just trust,' he was saying.

'Like what?'

'Like become comfortable with me. Release your fears. Whatever's blocking your memory.'

'Okay.'

'Okay?'

'I think so. You want me to let go of my inhibitions so that my mind lets go, so to speak, and recalls what I saw.'

'Something like that. Yes.'

'But you're afraid that we might get too emotionally involved,' she said.

His eyes widened slightly. She'd spoken too frankly; she knew that the moment the words had left her mouth, but seeing his reaction, she felt strengthened. She had some power over him. It was the first time she'd exercised this kind of power over a man like Brad, and she found it amazingly satisfying.

'You're afraid I might fall in love with you,' she pressed. And now he blinked. Then blushed. Not much, but just enough to encourage her even more.

'Or that, however unlikely, you might fall in love with me.'

'No.'

'No?'

'Well . . .' Now his face was bright red.

Then Paradise thought about everything she'd just said, and she felt her own face turn hot.

'Don't worry, Mr Raines. I have no intention of falling in love with you.' She walked past him. 'Now come on, let's go to the pond and see if we can't figure this out.'

'Brad,' he said. 'Please call me Brad.'

And, for a moment, she felt like his queen.

They spent an hour at the large fountain that Allison called a pond, doing nothing but talking and walking about the stained concrete patio and sitting at one of the four benches, twirling aspen leaves and flicking small stones into the pool, yet it felt to Paradise like five minutes.

She kept looking back to see if any spies were peeking around the building, and when none appeared she decided that Allison must have set things in order. To think of it, here she was, Paradise Founder of all people, meeting with a man alone by the pond, and the whole Center knew about it. It made her feel quite special.

She'd never spent time with a man before, even if it was to talk about a killer. But they didn't talk about the killer. They talked about the Center a lot. He wanted to know about her daily routine. *Everything* about it. How one person could be so interested in the details of what she did every boring day was a surprise in itself.

How she got up at seven most mornings. Had two eggs for breakfast, sunny side up on wheat toast, with hot cocoa and a small glass of orange juice. Usually with Andrea.

How Andrea then followed her back to her room and insisted that she brush her teeth. She showed Brad her teeth and asked him what he thought. He laughed and told her they were surprisingly white and straight, then stumbled all over himself to explain that by *surprisingly* he didn't mean he would have expected anything less from her. But straight teeth, especially without braces, were actually quite rare.

He wanted to know more, so she went on through the day, describing her card games with Roudy, who equated everything with codes and espionage and clues and such. She was friends with most of the residents who'd been around for more than a year, but not like she was with Cass, Roudy and especially Andrea, whom she'd taken under her wing at Allison's request.

They talked about her connection to the outside world. Yes, they had phones in their rooms and could receive or make calls any time. And of course they had access to high-speed internet.

He seemed surprised when she told him about the pictures of naked women that a resident named Carl kept taping to other residents' doors before Allison removed his privileges. It hadn't really bothered Paradise. After all, a naked body was a naked body. But some of the residents were far too upset, like Andrea, or far too interested, like Cass. She didn't quite get the way people reacted to nakedness, and Allison said this opinion was part of Paradise's makeup, as was her general disregard for appearances in general.

She shrugged and he laughed. She had to admit, she liked him. She really did like Brad.

They talked about her family, or what she could remember of it, meaning she only talked about Angie, her half sister, whose real name was Angel. He seemed surprised by that.

She pulled out the old photograph she always kept in her back pocket. 'See?'

He took the picture. Then looked at her and the photograph. 'I can see the resemblance between you two.' He eyed them both again. 'She's beautiful.'

Paradise didn't know what to do with that. Had he just called her beautiful? No, that wasn't right. But he had said they were similar, and everyone said that Angie was beautiful.

His questions weren't the general kind she got from most. He wanted to know, really know, the details. What does your room look like? Where do you buy your socks? You buy *everything* online? Which sites are your favourites? So she told him.

His visit had nothing to do with the killer and everything to do with her. Sure, he was doing it all to win her trust, but, even knowing that, she still sensed genuine interest from him. He didn't have the cold eyes of an investigator trying to trick her into answering, or the dead eyes of a psychiatrist listening because it was his job.

His eyes were filled with fascination and focus. They reached deep into her own, wanting to know more, what she was really like. On a few occasions she could have sworn he looked as if he wanted to consume her with those eyes. And twice he touched her shoulder while he was talking.

'No, I didn't mean it that way!' he said, reaching his hand out and touching her lightly on her shoulder. 'I love *Hell's Kitchen*, trust me. We all love watching a taskmaster whip a bunch of losers into shape. I just . . .' His eyes searched hers. She could think of little besides his hand on her shoulder and, when he removed it, she missed it.

'You what, can't imagine me in a kitchen?' she asked.

He grinned wide. 'I can, actually.'

They talked and laughed and he touched her one more time. Then he wanted to know about her writing. Her stories.

'Really? They're just stories. I don't tell them to anyone.'

'You're kidding. They're you! Now you have to tell me. And I want to know everything, not just the basic plot.'

'Really?'

'Yes, really.'

'We don't have time.'

'We have all day. Trust me, they know how to find us if they need either one of us. Tell me about your first novel. Who knows, maybe one of these days it will be published and I'll have been the first person on earth to know the story. I insist!'

Paradise hopped to her feet. 'Okay.' Her heart was pumping in her chest. 'Okay, but you have to promise not to laugh.'

'I can't help but laugh with you.'

'Okay, but not at the way my story goes or because you think it's silly.'

'I promise,' he said, standing. 'What's it called?'

They started walking, and he stayed right by her side. '*Horacus*,' she said. 'It's about a world two thousand years from now called Horacus.' She told him the plot and he demanded to know more.

What the people on Horacus did at night, what they wore, what their wedding ceremonies were like. What did their bedrooms look like, what kind of internet did they use, what brand toothpaste did they use?

Delighted beyond her wildest expectations, Paradise told him. Everything. She told him more than she'd ever told anyone about her stories.

By the time she'd finished with Horacus, another hour had passed and she felt embarrassed for hogging so much of the time. So she impulsively grabbed his hand, led him to the closest bench, and sat him down.

'Now,' she said, facing him on the bench. 'Tell me about *you*.'

'Me?'

'Yes, you. If you're going to earn my trust completely, you have to share your secrets with me.'

He chuckled and shook his head.

'What?' But she was smiling wide too.

'I can't trick your mind into coughing up the goods, huh?'

'Well, yes you could try to trick it. It would have to believe, without doubt, that you trust me implicitly so that I, in turn, can trust you implicitly. For that I need secrets. Your deepest, darkest secrets. Maybe not darkest, but, yes . . . Something like that.'

He laughed and covered his face. 'Boy, oh boy . . .'

'What?'

He just shook his head, still shaking with laughter. So she reached out and pulled his hands away from his face. 'What?'

What she saw struck wonder in her mind. His face was red, grinning like a schoolboy's, and his eyes were bright like the sun. She couldn't help but chuckle with him. He was delighted.

Brad wasn't laughing due to humour. He was actually delighted by her. And his face was red because he felt embarrassed by just how much she delighted him.

Could that be right?

They finally gathered themselves, and he leaned back and clasped his hands behind his head. 'My, oh my, I haven't laughed like that for a while.'

'It doesn't get you off the hook, my stud.' Dear, what had she said? She began to blush. 'I say that only as a means to perpetuate our attempt to trick my brain. You know. Make it think we're close enough to use silly words like that.'

He just grinned like a kid and shook his head as if he couldn't quite believe this was all happening.

'Tell me about yourself.'

Brad took a deep breath, settled into the bench, and told her.

He spoke about growing up in Austin, Texas, in a family with two sisters, no brothers. His father worked as a criminal defence attorney, which explained why he'd chosen to join the FBI, though on the other side of the case. He spoke about UT football, watching as a child, going to the games, then as a student with a tennis scholarship. Drinking on 6th Street and making a fool of himself that first year.

He eventually moved to Miami, where he took his first job with the FBI. It was a strange story in so many ways; strange because Paradise knew it was absolutely normal.

Compared to her own childhood, something he hadn't asked about, his younger years had been a vacation. The cars, the parties, the friends, Sunday Mass, confession. He and some friends had once locked a priest in the back room, and he'd taken the stage in the priest's robes. For half the service, the congregation had assumed he was a visiting priest. He'd been an absolute rascal once. Oddly enough, the stunt endeared him to her. He wasn't quite the clean-cut man he projected.

But Paradise couldn't shake the stark difference between them, and it reminded her that she was the freak here. Inside the protective walls here, she was the sanest of the bunch, but one step past the gates and she was nothing but a basket case. How could she ever meet and love and marry someone, unless he lived here, at CWI?

'Are you okay?' he asked, when she fell silent after a long string of questions.

An image of her and Brad walking down the aisle of the chapel on the other side of the campus hung in her mind. At the last minute he spun and faced the congregation. *Just kidding! Ha, ha, ha!*

Then to her, seeing her shock. *What? Come on, Paradise, you didn't really think I was serious, did you? I can't live here – you know that.*

Brad would never do that, of course. In fact, he would take any man who would do that and flush him down the toilet. Which was the real problem here: Brad was a beautiful, gorgeous, sensitive man and he was, forever, completely out of the reach of a piece of trash like her.

She should be running from this place for the sake of her sanity. Instead she was sitting here falling in love with him. Oh no, it was true, she thought with some alarm. She didn't know what falling in love felt like because she'd never done it before. But the warm, thrilling, frightening emotions now bubbling up through her must be it.

She probably already *had* fallen for him!

'. . . me what you're thinking?' he was asking.

She shook the thoughts free, realizing she must be staring, white-faced. 'Sorry.' She swallowed. 'Can you tell me about Ruby?'

He grew quiet and looked at the fountain. But she wasn't ready for him to be silent on this topic. So she pressed him.

'You loved her . . .'

'Yes.' His voice was tight and he lowered his voice to hardly more than a whisper. 'More than you can imagine.'

'I'm pretty good at that,' she said. 'Was she beautiful?'

'Really, Paradise, I'm not sure we should—'

'Was she prettier than me?'

She knew of at least four or five responses that could ensue. The back-pedalling, or the denial, or the out and out lie, or the clam up.

He faced her, eyes searching her face, her body. 'No,' he said. 'Only in the way she dressed and the way she made herself up, but that's the easy part. Inside, she was as messed up as you.' He looked at the trees. 'And as me.'

What a beautiful answer, she thought. He meant it as a

compliment. He was saying that she was on the same level as him, rather than throwing lies at her.

Everything about him was beautiful.

'She killed herself because she didn't think she was beautiful,' he said.

A sudden and heavy silence settled over them. His eyes were locked on nothing, misted with emotion, and Paradise knew where he was going. But she didn't want to stop him. A terrible empathy tugged at her heart.

'It wasn't your fault, Brad.'

He sucked air in through his nose, closed his eyes. A tear leaked from the corner and she felt even worse for him. Tears flooded her own eyes. She knew nothing about love and tenderness, and even less about how to be a woman with a man, but he was here and he was crying and she had to help him.

'You've never loved another woman since?' she asked.

The words broke a dam in his soul. He set his elbows on his knees, lowered his face into his hands and started to sob. What had she said?

What was she to do? She could only say what came to her mind. That was her gift, Allison said. She could look at a single leaf and see the whole tree. So she said what she saw now.

'You're afraid that you can't love another woman because in your mind no woman can measure up to Ruby. But that's not why you haven't been able to love another woman. It's because you're a kind man and you can't bear the thought of hurting another woman by making her feel like she isn't beautiful. Because that's why Ruby took her life.'

Her words didn't encourage him.

'But that was her choice, not yours. Life is worth living because of the risks, Allison always says, and I think she must be right. And I think it's the same with love.'

Now he was sobbing quietly into his hands, elbows on his knees. He suddenly leaned closer to her, put one hand down and rested it on her knee, the other hand still covering his face.

The contact might as well have been a current of electricity through her bones. She sat perfectly still, head swimming through a thick sea of sorrow and elation and fear and wonder.

He was letting his pain go. Here. With her.

She wanted to throw her arms around his head and hold him close and tell him not to cry, not to feel sad, because she would love him. She would hold him and protect him and never let the monsters in the dark come up behind him and pull him back.

But Paradise couldn't do that. Not yet. She had to control herself. But she could and she must touch him. And so she did. She slowly lowered her hand onto his head and gently smoothed his short, wavy blond hair.

Then she hushed him, but her hushing was interrupted by her own sobs, not of sorrow, but of relief. Her control began to slip and, rather than fight it, she leaned over him, rested her head on his, and together they wept.

They sat like that for what must have been a long time, although Paradise lost track of time in this small envelope of hope and safety. Of love. Gradually they both quieted and Paradise thought she should sit up, because she was holding him down. But she didn't want to.

She was here because Allison wanted her to risk falling in love, and she was doing that. She was here because Brad thought she was beautiful, even though she needed help with her face and hair and clothes. She was here because she'd touched a dead body and seen the man with the dark hair who looked a little like Clark Kent without the glasses and who was leaning over Melissa telling her how beautiful . . .

Paradise gasped and jerked upright.

Brad sat up and stared at her. 'Are you okay?'

She faced him. 'I remember.'

He sniffed and then wiped his eyes. 'You remember what?'

'I remember what I saw. The man who killed Melissa!'

'You do?' It seemed to be the furthest thing from his mind.

'Yes!' Paradise jumped to her feet, ecstatic. 'I do, I do. I can see him now, as clear as day.'

Brad stood up, stunned. 'That's . . . Are you sure? We have to

get you down to the office immediately. We'll need to recon-
struct—'

'No, I can't go. Of course I can't go. But I can draw him. I
told you, I'm a good artist. Or they can come here.'

'Of course. Yes, here. Do you know who it is?'

'No. Nobody that I can remember.'

She'd broken out! Allison would be thrilled. Paradise started
to walk back towards the centre. 'I need to draw now, before I
forget!'

CHAPTER TWENTY-FOUR

Cars came and went from the underground parking garage next to Rain Man's condo, and Quinton watched them all from the protected darkness of his M 300, which he parked in a corner space that was reserved. He'd picked the spot two days earlier after noting that it remained empty into the early morning hours. From his vantage through his window, he could see the yawning ramp that headed up to the street.

He'd placed a sun blocker on the inside of his front windshield to keep prying eyes from seeing his form behind the wheel. A single security camera recorded all cars that came and went from the garage, but he'd parked his car on the street at four p.m., manually snipped the camera cable, then taken up his position in the garage, knowing that it was too late in the day for a repairman to be dispatched. By the time they fixed it in the morning, his work here would be finished.

Watching Rain Man's domicile over this last week, Quinton had confirmed his assumption that Brad Raines was the kind of man who would work late into the night in his misguided effort to find the Bride Collector.

He'd seen the agent's BMW parked at CWI earlier in the afternoon, then watched for a few minutes as Rain Man walked to the pond with Angel's sister. His heart had crashed about his chest like a hard rubber ball.

The seventh favourite had to come of her own free will, without compromise, and though he'd fretted and fussed over the detail for weeks, God had surely provided the way.

The lengths that people would go to for the sake of a loved one was both disturbing to him and uplifting at once. Being created in God's image, humans shared a seed of his unconditional, infinite love, though most had done their best to stomp that seed underfoot with greed and self-preservation.

Yet when the final test came, most would go all out to save their child or husband or wife or brother or sister. Now Quinton's errand depended on that seed blossoming to life. He'd been sent to collect her, and she would come.

He tapped the steering wheel with his gloved hand. His gun rested on the passenger seat, ready for when the time came. He prayed that no one else would be in the garage when it did – he had no desire to kill or even see anyone else tonight. His focus was pure and fixed. He was about God's work and God's work only.

It was now past eleven and the underground garage was quiet, like the inside of a casket. What if Rain Man didn't come home tonight? He stopped tapping the leather-wrapped wheel. What if the infidel had uncovered . . .

Lights brightened the ramp and the beautiful, snarling grille of a BMW nosed down into the darkness.

Rain Man was home.

A jolt of nervous energy ripped through Quinton's bones, then was gone, replaced by relief. God was good. All the time. And his love was inexhaustible.

The BMW drove by, turning right towards its customary spot just around the corner. As soon as its red tail lights vanished from his view, Quinton started the M 300, pulled out, turned the car around, then nosed the car back into the same spot so that the trunk faced the driveway. Lights off.

Without killing the engine, he grabbed the tranquillizer pistol, popped the trunk and stepped out of the vehicle.

A car door thumped shut around the corner. Rain Man was out – Quinton prayed he hadn't made a mistake in taking the time to turn the car around, but he had wanted to face out for easy viewing while he waited, and he now needed the trunk to face out for easy access.

The garage was still quiet. He ran around the corner on his

rubber soles, silently, just as Rain Man was crossing the driveway towards the elevators. Twenty yards. He had to be closer – the man was trained to use his weapon and wouldn't hesitate if he had the chance. Quinton's first shot had to put him down.

Throwing caution to the wind, he sprinted forwards and closed the gap to ten yards before Rain Man heard him and spun.

But the mouse was in the trap and the spring was sprung. Quinton lifted the tranquillizer gun and shot the man in his chest. The two-inch, red-feathered dart made a soft slapping sound when it struck. Rain Man cried out and jumped back, stunned.

His eyes widened as he, being trained in these sorts of things, recognized the instrument hanging from his chest. He grabbed the dart and tugged it out, then clawed for the weapon holstered beneath his jacket. 'You sick son of . . .' His voice slurred and he staggered. But the powerful sedative would take up to fifteen seconds. Less if the man's heart was pumping very hard.

Quinton ducked behind a car and crouched, counting the seconds . . . six, seven, eight . . .

Thump.

He stood up and saw that Rain Man had fallen in a heap, still clutching his pistol. Tucking his own behind his belt, Quinton rushed forwards.

Rain Man was heavy. Dead weight was always heavy. He'd mounted each of the women on the wall without their help, but this . . . It felt as if the man weighed five hundred pounds.

Quinton heaved him up over his shoulder and ran back around the corner. Now his decision to turn the car around rewarded him. He shouldered the man into the trunk and, working quickly before another car drove into the garage, he fastened handcuffs to Rain Man's wrists. The drug would keep him down for half an hour, but he could take no chances.

Having secured his man in the trunk, Quinton slid into the front seat, pulled the car out and roared up the ramp into the dark night.

Five minutes later he was on I 25 north. No flashing lights in his rear-view mirror. No helicopters overhead. No sign of pursuit at all. With any luck, no one would even know their star was missing until the morning, when he failed to show up for work.

One of the distinct disadvantages that came with a career in God's service, like his own career, was all the bad press. No one cut the clergy enough slack; they got far too much negative attention.

But there were some distinct advantages as well. Having God on your side, for instance; the smoothness of Rain Man's abduction being a case in point. It was enough to reaffirm Quinton's calling, not that he had any doubts.

Still, having Rain Man in the trunk gave him a very good feeling.

He turned right onto Interstate 70. From here the Kansas border waited, 171 miles distant. The small town called St Francis slept through the night, ten miles past the border. The barn Quinton had prepared was nine miles south of St Francis.

Ordinarily, the trip would take at least three hours. In the dead of night, he could make it in just over two, thanks to a powerful Chrysler engine and a state-of-the-art radar detector-slash-laser diffuser.

The search for him had primarily been confined to Colorado. But, to avoid all the attention, Quinton would unite the seventh and most beautiful favourite with God in Kansas.

The thought made Quinton shiver.

CHAPTER TWENTY-FIVE

Frank Closkey pushed open the door to the SAC's office. 'Nothing.'

Temple spun from the window where he stood overlooking the street below, hands on hips. His tie was gaped and the top two buttons on his shirt were undone. 'His condo, his phone, his emergency pager? Nothing?'

'Nothing since he left the office last night just before ten. We checked with his favourite restaurants, no luck.'

'But he arrived at his condo . . .'

'His car's in the garage, yes. No indication that he actually entered the building. And get this, the cord to the garage camera was cut.'

The SAC stared. 'And no one was notified? When?'

'Late yesterday afternoon. They put in a repair order, but the security company didn't get out there till this morning.'

Temple walked to his desk, lowered his hands for a moment, then put them back on his hips. 'So, it's the Bride Collector.'

'We don't know that.'

'As of this moment, we assume we do. First Nikki, now Brad. What on earth happened to the detail?'

'Brad called it off after we found Nikki. There was no reason to think the killer hadn't satisfied his threat when he took her. He's never taken a man.'

Temple's jaw flexed. 'The assistant director's going to . . .' He yanked out his chair and sat. 'Okay, I want his photograph in every government car in this state. Check every known location he frequents. Get his cell records from the company and work through each call. I want to know every step he took in the last twenty-four hours. What about the sketch he brought in?'

Frank still didn't understand exactly how Brad could be sure the sketch he'd delivered late in the afternoon was of the killer. It was, after all, based on a ghost. He'd put the highest priority on linking it with any known offenders in the photo identification system. The sketch was rough and would require manual comparisons, but it was the first hard lead they'd had since Nikki's murder, and the team had dropped everything else.

'Nothing yet. We sent it out to the other agencies and every hospital in the state. We also have a forensic artist headed out to CWI this morning for another sketch.'

'What do we know about this girl? Besides the hogwash about her ability to see ghosts?'

'Not much. Brad was a little evasive.'

'So you're telling me Brad's fate now rests in the hands of some mental case?'

'He seemed to think she was pretty smart.'

'This can't be the best we've got.' Temple shook his head. 'This really can't.'

It was a beautiful day. The trees looked somehow greener, the birds chirped and darted, as if they'd found a pot of coffee beans and eaten every one, and the sun even seemed brighter. The eggs she was eating at this very minute tasted richer, sweeter, maybe the best food she'd ever tasted.

But Paradise knew that neither the trees nor the birds nor the eggs nor the sun had changed. She, on the other hand, had.

For starters, she'd become a bit of an overnight sensation. She might have imagined some of it, but nearly every eye seemed to be on her when she walked into the dining room half an hour ago. There was no denying that many, if not most, of the residents knew she had become a very important person in the eyes of some very important people.

Roudy went out of his way to take credit whenever he could. It was he, after all, who'd demanded they bring the evidence to his team. And, in the end, they would still need him to connect all the clues.

'Can't you just be happy for her?' Andrea demanded.

'Of course I can. But there's a killer on the loose! Have you no heart for all those poor girls?'

Hopeless.

Either way, Paradise had changed. She had seen. And she had been seen. A cloud had been lifted from her heart. The wool had been pulled from her eyes. Every cliché in the book had happened to her, all at once. In her dark world, the sun had come out as if for the very first time.

But only she and Allison knew why. It wasn't because she'd become a sleuthing hero. It was because of Brad Raines. Or, more precisely, because of what she and Brad had shared. Did share.

Because Brad had shattered the fear that had kept her mind in the shadows. Because she trusted Brad more than she trusted any other living soul, except maybe Angel and Allison, but Angel was her sister and Allison was like her mother.

Brad was a man.

There was something special between them. She wouldn't go as far as to say that he loved her; it was far too early for that. And she knew that nothing could become of whatever it was he felt. After all, she was here at CWI and he was out there, in the world with all of its demons.

But she'd decided last night that she would do nothing to temper the way her heart felt in the wake of his departure. She'd gone to bed tossing and turning, with butterflies flying circles in her belly. And she'd woken with images of Brad whispering through her mind.

She wasn't in love with him. That would be going way too far. But if this was what being in love felt like, it was no wonder so many people risked so much for it.

Andrea was staring at her, wearing a shy grin.

'What?'

Her friend nibbled at her toast. 'I don't know. Did you kiss him?'

'Andrea!' Paradise set her fork down and blushed. 'Just because you lift your skirt for the first thing that comes along doesn't mean everyone does.'

'I said kiss. You've never kissed a man, you said.'

'And I still haven't.' How embarrassing was this? But her mouth was fighting a smile.

'You will, though.'

'Don't be ridiculous! It's not like that. Please, Andrea, you're going to ruin everything.'

'You're smiling!'

Someone tapped her on the shoulder. Jonathan leaned over and spoke softly. 'There's someone on the phone for you, Paradise. I thought you might want to take it.'

Normally they would take a message. Then she saw his smile and caught her breath. 'A man?'

'It is.'

She jumped up. 'I'll . . . Send it to my room.'

Paradise took off, then whirled back and pointed at Andrea. 'Stay.'

She sprinted down the hall, into the women's wing, then up the stairs to her room just as the phone started to ring. She slammed the door and engaged the lock, and approached the phone, heart pounding. Her hand was shaking when she lifted the receiver.

'Hello.'

A soft chuckle. 'Hello, Paradise.'

She was so tuned into Brad's voice that it took her a moment to wonder if this was someone else.

'Brad?'

'No, not Brad. Brad's all tied up. I have him here with me.'

Was this someone that Brad worked with? Something seemed odd about . . .

'I'm the one who killed Nikki,' the voice said. 'And now I have your lover all tied up. I'm going to make him squeal like a pig and then I'm going to gut him, if you don't do exactly as I say.'

The phone was silent. She stood frozen in place, unable to breathe.

'Are you there, dear?'

She tried to say something, but nothing was working.

'Don't be afraid, Paradise. I need you to think clearly. I need you to save Brad. Can you do that?'

Her voice shook. 'Yes.'

'Good. The first thing you're going to do is keep your mouth shut. I can see you, your every move. I can hear everything that happens in that prison of yours. If you tell anyone, including that old nun, that you spoke to me, I will kill Mr Raines. Do you understand?'

Her mind whirled with the worst possible scenarios. She was in the dark fog again and behind her came the monster, scrambling for her legs as she crawled. The bodies were on the ground, and she was crawling over them.

'Do you understand?'

It was real. She was on the phone talking to the man she'd seen. This was his voice; she recognized it now from when she'd touched the girl.

'Yes.'

'Are you listening? It's important that you don't panic. If you panic you'll do something stupid and I'll have to kill him. Okay?'

His voice wasn't angry or sinister. Just calm and direct. But that only made it more frightening.

'Okay?'

'Yes,' she managed.

'In thirty minutes the gardener will climb into his red pick-up truck and leave for an extended coffee break, like he does every day. You will climb into the back of his truck, under the green tarp he uses to keep the rain off—'

'I can't leave!'

The man paused patiently. '. . . off his tools,' he finished. 'You don't have to leave in the red truck, Paradise. But if you don't, then Mr Raines will be found dead, and it will be because you allowed him to die.'

'I . . .' Paradise began to panic. The room spun and she managed to steady herself by putting her left hand on the wall. Her voice came in a hoarse whisper. 'I can't leave.'

The man ignored her. 'The red truck will drive into the city and stop at a Starbucks. When it does, you will get out without drawing attention and you will walk due east one block until you see a shopping strip with a beauty salon. At the end there is a large green garbage bin. Under that bin you will find an envelope with money and a cell phone. Are you getting all of this?'

'I can't . . . I can't leave . . .'

'Repeat it back to me.'

She hesitated, then stumbled through the instructions, but her mind was mostly on the fact that, if she didn't leave, the man on the phone would kill Brad.

'But I can't . . .'

'Listen, Paradise.' She heard his voice away from the phone, speaking to another man, demanding he speak.

Then Brad's familiar voice. 'Tell Allison, Paradi . . .'

Crack!

The phone went silent and the killer came back on. 'So you see, I do have him, and I will kill him. Are you listening?'

It was Brad, she was sure of it. His voice had sounded scratchy and breathy, but it was him!

'Are you listening, Paradise?'

'Yes . . . I'm listening.'

'Take the money in the envelope, go into the beauty salon, and ask them to make you pretty. Like your sister Angel. Can you do that for me?'

What was he asking? She had to go into a beauty salon? What did this have to do with Brad?

'Pay them all the money. There's five hundred dollars there. Tell them to cancel their appointments if they don't have space. When you're done, take a picture of yourself and send it to me so that I know you've done exactly as I've asked. Then go across the road to the park and wait for me. I'll call you and tell you what I want you to do next. Now, repeat that back to me.'

She did, haltingly.

'Good. Don't tell them, Paradise. Do not say a word. Once you're gone they'll start looking for you. Stay out of sight. If they pick you up, it's all over. Okay?'

Her mind seemed to have shut down. She had to figure this out, but she didn't know where to begin. It was a nightmare. How could she get out of a nightmare?

'Okay?'

'Okay.'

He hesitated. 'Thank you, Paradise. I've waited so long for this.'

The line clicked dead.

CHAPTER TWENTY-SIX

Light peeked through a dozen cracks in the barn's high roof, but there was no other indication of what time it might be. Morning, Brad guessed, but it could be afternoon. A sack had been over his head when he'd climbed out of unconsciousness, and he'd been sedated at least twice since then.

The picture, now clear, was one only his worst fears could have conjured up. He'd been taken, drugged, stuffed in a trunk. Now he faced his end as Nikki had faced hers. After spending so many hundreds of hours putting himself in the place of killers and their victims, he found himself actually in that position. In and of itself, it was more surreal than terrifying.

But the killer had called Paradise, and the claws of dread were encasing him. He felt nauseated.

They were in an old barn with greying planks for walls and dirty hay for a floor. The stale scent of grain and old horse manure hung in the air. Sagging eight-by-eight timbers spanned the sloping roof overhead, begging for an excuse to fold under the weight they supported. An old dilapidated relic.

His wrists were tied together behind a splintering four-by-four post. He sat on the damp ground, facing the killer's stage. Several large wool blankets with wide red and black stripes, the kind for sale at roadside stands that advertised Native American souvenirs, had been spread out and bordered by railroad ties. On one end the killer had constructed a makeshift planked wall against a large pile of hay bales.

Two pegs stuck out of the boards three quarters of the way up. On either side of his wall, the Bride Collector had placed candles on two wooden barrels. It took little imagination to understand that he'd prepared the wall to drain his seventh victim.

The details had filtered through as he woke. But the one piece of information that dominated his mind sat on an old folding chair ten feet from him, legs crossed and arms too, studying him in silence.

This was the Bride Collector, and he looked somewhat similar to the drawing Paradise had laboured over as she'd excitedly pulled at her memory. But there were some key differences that might throw the team off, he thought. Small details that forensic artists would focus on, knowing how important they were.

In person, the killer's mouth was full, but looked flatter on the sketch. Paradise had drawn the distance between his eyebrows and hairline too narrow, giving him a more sinister appearance than he had in the flesh and blood. And his eyes were wider as well. But a forensic artist would be rendering a more accurate drawing today, maybe already had.

He was a large-boned man who, at first glance, would inspire confidence. Nothing about him looked suspect. His dark hair was short and well groomed. His hands were manicured. His eyes were dark, but not deep-set or threatening. He was handsome, like so many serial killers.

He wore grey slacks and a light blue short-sleeved button-down shirt, the kind that might pass for an auto mechanic's shirt with a *Midas* or *Good Year* logo on the pocket.

Apart from the phone call to Paradise, the man hadn't uttered a single word. But his intentions loomed in Brad's mind like a shadow in a darkened doorway.

'You should be feeling better now,' the man said. His voice was soft and low. Matter of fact. 'You call me the Bride Collector, which is appropriate, all things considered. But you can call me Quinton now. My last name is Gauld.'

Quinton Gauld. Brad cleared his parched throat. 'You don't care if I know your real name.'

'Not now, no. My task on earth is nearly finished.'

'You're going to kill me.' A simple statement of fact.

'I don't know yet. Only if he tells me to.'

It was a lie, Brad thought. Only a fool would leave him alive after this, and the killer had proven that he was anything but a fool. The real issue now was his final victim. God's favourite.

Then again, if the man was as psychotic as his notes suggested, gripped in the fist of an uncompromising delusion, he might not be lying.

The phone call Quinton had made played through Brad's mind again. The thought of this man even looking at Paradise knotted his gut with deep offence, and he had to swallow to hide it.

The killer was luring her out. It was almost as if he'd orchestrated all the events of these past two weeks to this end. To lure Paradise out of the Center for Wellness and Intelligence. But why?

He could still see the picture of the beautiful girl Paradise had shown him yesterday. Angel Founder. Angie, Paradise's sister. They'd had the identity of the seventh victim in their sights the whole time. But it still made no sense to him.

'You're luring Angie. Angel. She's your seventh victim.'

Quinton just looked at him.

'But why? Why not just take her? Why all this extra trouble with me and with—'

'The seventh favourite has to come willingly. It has to be her choice.'

'So you *coerce* her?'

Quinton uncrossed his legs and lowered his arms. He stared at Brad, as if he were charged with the task of educating a stupid child. He finally stood, then walked to the pile of straw and grasped a fistful. Smelled it.

'I don't want to coerce her. But she doesn't know who she is yet. Humans are afraid of the unknown.' He turned back, tight jawed and agitated. 'I did try once before. I tried to consummate our relationship. She slapped me. I haven't been able to have normal relations since. Sometimes life has to deal all of us a little motivation to keep truth in perspective.'

'So, all along this has been about Angel. The rest of us are just pawns? That's all we are to you?'

'It's not about me, Brad,' he said, regaining his confidence. 'It's him. I'm only the messenger. Have you ever wondered why most people who say they believe in God and heaven don't actually want to leave this life to be with him? Not until life has slapped them around enough for them to beg for it. And for the record, a few do fall by the wayside when God calls his bride home. Or haven't you read the book of Revelation?'

It struck Brad then that, if anything, intelligence was Quinton's Achilles' heel. If there was anything he might respond to besides force, which Brad wasn't in any position to leverage, it would be reason. Quinton's variety of reason.

But, at the moment, Brad's own mind wasn't able to engage the man on such a level. He couldn't shake the image of Paradise back at the Center at this very moment, shaking in her room. That this beast would take such a pure, innocent woman, only just discovering herself in a dark world, and subject her to horror after all she'd been through . . .

Nausea rolled through his stomach. He swallowed again and tried to focus. He had to keep Quinton talking. He had to move him down a path, any path, that might lead to distraction.

'I don't want you to hurt Paradise,' he said. 'She's just a pawn to you. Why take another innocent life?'

'None of them are innocent. And he's still chosen them, despite that. Get your theology straight, Mr Raines.'

'Okay, I'll give you that. But was Nikki's mother chosen? Were the two police officers you killed? Am I? Is Paradise? You don't have to kill others.'

Quinton looked at him with fascination. 'That's what Nikki said. She was begging for her own life. But you're begging for Paradise, aren't you? For her life.'

'She's . . .' His chest swelled with emotion, choking off his words. 'Please, she's done nothing to deserve this. For the love of God, she's . . .'

'For the love of God, Brad? Not for your love? Do you love her?'

Looking into the man's eyes, Brad saw a darkness that made him want to turn his head away, a deep evil that had fooled itself into thinking it knew what it could not know. Yet here from behind this dark stare came the question that had battered his own mind.

'Love?' Brad asked. 'What's love?'

'You don't know what love is?' Quinton said. 'Then you don't have the right to speak to me about it.'

'Of course I know what love is . . .'

'Then tell me, do you love her? Or are you embarrassed by her? She's an idiot in your small world. You throw people like her in the garbage.'

The accusation bared a strip of raw emotion that surprised Brad. 'No, don't say that.'

'Then why aren't you in love with her?'

Because he couldn't be! How could he love someone who . . .

Brad closed his eyes and bore down on the conflicting emotions. The man had turned the tables on him in a matter of minutes, throwing him into a defensive posture that gave Quinton the power. He had to turn this back around.

He looked back up at Quinton. 'You win. The truth is I think I do love her.'

'You love Paradise.' His tone was mocking, unconvinced.

It was odd, sitting here, tied to a post, debating with himself about his love for a woman. But at that moment there was nothing more important.

'I think so, yes.'

Quinton stared at him for several beats, then walked up, pulled him roughly to his feet, and, holding his collar with his left hand, slapped him hard across his jaw with his right hand.

Brad's head snapped back. Pain flashed up his jaw.

Sweat covered the man's face and it twitched. 'God loves her. You don't. Get that straight.' Quinton released him.

He left Brad standing and walked to a table on which lay a single suitcase. He opened the case and pulled out a yellow drill with a battery pack. He squeezed the trigger once, ran it up to full speed, then let go of the trigger and set it down. He pulled out a plastic housing that held silver drill bits and carefully set it beside the drill.

A tin bucket sat at the end of the table.

Brad knew he had to keep the man talking. Distract him. The post behind him was only four inches thick and moved with his weight – how would it respond if he threw his weight back against it? How long had it stood here, rotting?

'So, you're using me as bait,' Brad said, 'to lure in your bait for Angel.'

The man spoke without turning. 'If only it was that simple. These are complicated matters, Mr Raines. God, the devil, all that fighting going on in the sky. But this is a love story. Love stories are never without their complications. The fights, the betrayal, the crying . . . It's all part of the plan. Including you, the twisted man who doesn't know how to love a woman. It's a good thing God doesn't have that problem.'

Brad wanted to say something. He knew he had to engage the man and talk him down, plant a seed of doubt, earn the upper hand, throw him off. The problem was, he was thrown off himself.

The killer had been the one to plant a seed of doubt, this gnawing question about love. Why hadn't he been able to love, really love, since Ruby had taken her life?

Because he was fearful, not for himself, but for the woman he might love. When Paradise had said as much yesterday, he'd fallen apart right there on the bench. But not because she was right.

Because she was wrong! He wasn't that noble. If they knew what he was really like . . . The FBI, his co-workers, the waitresses at the bars he favoured, the women he dated. If they only knew how focused he was on protecting not them but himself, how bothered he was by the failings of others because his standards were so high, how unlikable he was, stripped of all his charms and his quick mind and his face.

If they only knew . . .

He couldn't love Paradise because she would learn just how unlovable he was. And because she couldn't possibly live up to his standards, which was what made him so unlovable.

The realization had crushed him, because he knew that, as much as he couldn't love Paradise for these reasons, deep inside he *wanted* to love her. He wanted to burn all of his standards. To stamp on them, together with Paradise, as they smouldered. To take her in his arms, far away from everything that had moulded him into this monster who required a woman to look and speak and think in a way that met his lofty expectations.

Standing here now, tied to the post, his feelings of shame and desire returned. But with them a very simple thought came to him.

What he'd just said was true. He did love her.

Brad blinked. Why not? Why didn't he love her?

He was only pretending that he couldn't love her in order to protect himself. In reality, under all the foolishness that made him so pathetic, he did love her. And maybe, just maybe, he could win her love as well.

His pulse surged, beating now like a pump, desperate for more blood so that it could stay alive. Quinton was laying out his tools, preparing to ruin a life because he thought it was the right thing to do, and Brad stood behind him, thinking he had to save this one life, Paradise, who had inadvertently wandered into the killer's crossfire, a pawn to draw in his seventh victim.

Saving Paradise was suddenly the only thing that mattered to him.

Allison's words whispered through his mind. *What he doesn't realize is that he's actually killing God's favourites. He's got it back-wards, you see? He's not an angel, he's the devil. Someone needs to correct his thinking.*

'They say you're delusional,' he said, 'that you are mentally ill and suffer from delusions of grandeur. That you think God speaks to you because you're psychotic. But they're wrong, aren't they?'

Quinton set a bottle of fingernail polish next to three others he'd lined up. Everything in perfect order.

'You don't need to worry, Mr Raines. I've decided not to kill you.' He turned around. 'And don't try to patronize me or use your intelligence to talk me down. I've been over this before and I know exactly who I am.'

'You do, I can see that now. But you don't know who I am.'

'You're Special Agent Brad Raines. You've been trying to find and stop me for a long time.'

'Have I? What if I had an entirely different purpose in this' – he looked about the room, then settled back on Quinton – 'this mad shambles of a world? More specifically, a different purpose for being here today, with you, before you deliver God's bride to him for eternal bliss?'

Quinton's face twitched again, but he wasn't buying it. An unbelieving smile twisted his mouth.

'What if I could prove it to you?' Brad asked.

'Prove what?'

'That I'm not who you think I am.'

The man looked slightly amused.

'Would you listen to me?' Brad asked.

Quinton hesitated, then pulled out his cell phone and checked the time.

'Okay. So what's your point?'

CHAPTER TWENTY-SEVEN

Paradise stood in the middle of her room for long minutes, trembling. The cold sweats had started immediately after she'd hung up the phone. Her fear made no sense to her. How could a person fear something that clearly didn't bother most people? Like a fear of the ground – whoever heard of such a thing? Or a fear of air.

Agoraphobia was like that, and she knew she should be able to stop it. But she couldn't.

The panic attack came so fast and so hard that she couldn't think, much less get to the medicine cabinet for a Xanax. The anti-anxiety medication was supposed to work quickly, but in her case it did nothing but take the edge off. Still, Allison allowed her to keep a small supply, in exception to house rules.

She stood here while the world spun around her, and she was sure that this time her heart would finally tear loose and get stuck in her throat, and then she would suffocate.

She was so disoriented that she forgot how she got here. But then it all came back, like a flood. The phone call. The killer wanted her to climb into the red truck and go to the beauty salon. If she didn't, he was going to kill Brad.

An image she'd never seen before, of her father pounding on the door of the closet she'd locked herself in, crashed through her mind and she gasped. Then it was gone. Now the panic was back, stronger, and she knew that she was going to at least fall down.

She staggered to the bathroom, desperate for a pill, water, anything that might keep her from dying. She'd just had a new memory. But she couldn't think about that now.

He has Brad and you have to get into the red truck.

She shook a couple of Xanax from the bottle; all five came out. She picked two out of the sink, pressed them into her mouth with trembling fingers and gulped some water, spilling it down her flannel top.

She knew she had to do what the killer wanted. As far as she was concerned, she didn't have a choice. Because no matter how much she told herself that she didn't love Brad, she did.

She loved him more than she loved anything. Much more. Because Brad undid everything her father had done.

In thirty minutes the gardener will climb into his red pick-up truck . . .

Paradise looked at the clock on the bathroom wall. How much time had passed? But she had to get to the truck before Smitty did, and without anyone noticing.

She spun from the bathroom and ran to the door, grabbed the knob. Then stopped. Her breathing whooshed around her like a jet engine. She wasn't dressed to go out.

She was still in the flannel pants she'd slept in!

What does it matter, Paradise?

It mattered a lot. She didn't fit out there. To her, stepping past the gate was like stepping out onto a platform in a huge stadium with the world's worst case of stage fright. They would all be watching, and she would be standing in her pyjamas!

But she had to get to the red truck. If she could somehow get under the tarp, then she might be safe.

Tears flooded her eyes again. No, no, she wouldn't be safe out there!

But neither was Brad. And she loved Brad more than she loved herself. What would Brad think about her looking like this? How could she say she loved him and go to him looking like a skank? The thoughts flew around her mind, one on top of the other.

She tore over to her dresser and yanked out the first pair of jeans she could get her hands on. Quick, quick, she had to get into the red truck.

Paradise pulled the jeans on and ran halfway back to the door before realizing she'd forgotten a shirt. She hurried back, clawed into a yellow T-shirt, then rushed back to the door. *The first thing you're going to do is keep your mouth shut.* She had to go quietly. No one could know.

So she slipped into the hall and snuck towards the stairs as quickly and quietly as she could in her flip-flops. Her panic attack was back, thumping, spinning, gasping, but she kept her mouth shut and went before anyone could see her.

Smitty usually parked his red truck by the tool shed beyond the men's wing. Paradise made it to the back door and ran out into the hot sun. She turned left, running on the gravel back there without stopping to see if anyone was watching. She should, she knew. This wasn't the way not to get noticed, but she was too terrified to stop.

She saw the red truck next to the shed when she tore around the corner. A green tarp was stretched over a mound of something in the back, she didn't know what. The idea of climbing underneath . . .

She couldn't do that. They would see the lump and know someone was hiding, intending to sneak out, which was strictly prohibited.

But there was a lump of something under there already. Another dead body. A pile of dead fish. A dead cow. Manure for the garden. So they might not notice another lump.

Paradise bent down and hurried up to the truck. Without waiting for her nerves to fail her completely, she slung her leg up over the opened truck bed and threw herself in, expecting a yell from someone who'd seen her.

But no yell came.

She scrambled to the edge, yanked back the tarp, making a terrible ruckus, and rolled under it as if it were a blanket. Then she pulled it back down over her head and lay still, panting into the green plastic.

The acidic stench of manure filled her nostrils. She was right. The fertilizer felt soft and mushy against her back. Breathing hard, she thought the smell might poison her.

They would plant her in the ground, dead from asphyxiation.

Bringing all her will power to bear, she lay as still as she could, praying that no one would notice the green tarp moving as she panted.

With each passing minute she was tempted again to throw the tarp off because she knew she couldn't do this. She could not go beyond the gate!

The sound of footsteps prevented her from fleeing. A door opened and slammed. The truck growled to life and, with a grinding of gears, it rolled forwards.

Please, God, please save me. Please, please . . .

She was suddenly in a closet, and a fist was pounding on the door. 'If you don't come out here right now, I'm going to blow your mother's head off.'

The new black memory slammed into her mind and she started to scream. But she clamped her hand over her mouth. She'd been here before, seven years ago.

'If you don't come out of there, I swear I will kill her!'

Everything went dark and quiet.

Pop.

It was the first time she remembered hearing the gunshot that killed her mother, and she knew now that it was because she hadn't come out of the closet she'd barricaded herself in.

Her father was swearing.

Pop. Silence.

That was him? He'd shot her and himself. She could barely breathe, barely cry, barely whisper. 'Sorry, Mommy. I'm so . . .'

Then darkness lovingly took her away.

When Paradise opened her eyes, she was surprised to see that the sky had turned green. Or she was lying on her back, staring up at green leaves. She'd been dreaming of a prince on a white stallion, sweeping in from the desert with the heroine hanging on for dear life behind him. They plunged into the trees and then into a meadow, where the white bats had joined with a thousand warriors in eager . . .

She gasped. No! She was in the back of the red truck under

the green tarp. The guards had stopped them at the gate. They'd caught her!

Her first thought was one of immense relief. She couldn't leave. They would take her back and she would cry on Allison's shoulder and somehow everything would be alright.

Her next thought was of Brad.

She bolted up and swept the green tarp off her head. A bright sun blinded her and she squinted, and in the brief second before she instinctively squeezed off the light, she saw that something was terribly wrong.

She was facing a street and cars were driving by. This wasn't the gate that led into CWI.

Paradise twisted around. The large green sign above the glass windows read *Starbucks. The red truck will drive into the city and stop at a Starbucks . . .*

She was . . . She was out? Out!

Paradise dropped back down and whipped the tarp back over her head, trembling from head to foot. This was not good, this was not good, this was not good . . . *Dear God, help me, dear God, dear God, dear God . . .*

Nothing happened. She could hear the hum of traffic and the sound of voices far off. Then the voices were gone. She had to get a hold of herself. Or she could lie here and wait till Smitty drove the truck back to the Center. Where was she? How far did Smitty go for his break?

Her memory of her father came back. 'If you don't come out here right now . . .'

Pop.

She couldn't do it again. She had to come out, or this time . . . She had to come out and stay out. This time, if she didn't, Brad would die.

Head swimming with resolve, Paradise eased the tarp away from her face, held her breath as she listened for voices and, hearing none, peeked over the truck bed. Some people huddled together way down the street.

You will get out without drawing attention and you will walk due east one block until you see a shopping strip with a beauty salon.

She clambered over the wall of the bed, dropped to the asphalt and ran away from the Starbucks, crouched over to make herself smaller. She got all the way to the end and onto the sidewalk before two things became clear to her.

One, she looked and smelled like a dog who'd rolled in a pile of manure. And running hunched over wasn't the way to avoid attention.

Two, she didn't know if this was due east.

But she couldn't stop now. She'd never get her legs moving again. She glanced over her shoulder and saw that the road headed in the opposite direction ran past a wide open field. No strip mall. So she must have guessed right.

Paradise stood as straight as she dared and hurried forwards, refusing to look to her right or her left, afraid of what she might see. Cars, people, the killer, monsters, ghosts, demons . . . Any or all of them were hiding in wait, she was sure of it. She just had to keep her legs moving until she could find that garbage bin. Maybe she could hide inside until she figured out what to do?

She was hyperventilating, so she closed her mouth and forced herself to breathe through her nose, counting as taught. One, two. One, two. What had to be half a block passed. Maybe more. Buildings loomed ahead to her right. That had to be it. If she could just make it . . .

A car honked, and she let out a startled cry, but she didn't look up. Then she thought it might run her over, so she glanced to her right, just to be sure. It was on the other side of the road, trying to get past another car.

The sidewalk ended in a parking lot and she stopped. *At the end there is a large green garbage bin.*

'What's your problem?'

She spun towards the voice on her right. Two young women sat on the hood of a car, facing the direction she'd come from. She knew the type from her outings on the internet. The narrow jeans like tubes, the black fingernail polish, the cigarettes, the silver-studded belts.

'You lost, you freak?'

'You think I'm a freak?' Paradise heard herself saying. 'Have you looked in the mirror lately?'

She had no idea why she would say such a thing, not now, not ever, especially not here. She'd lost her grip on reality and was suffering a psychotic break.

The girl who'd spoken looked as if she'd been slapped. 'Tramp. You look like you just crawled out of a garbage bin. I bet the men just love you, don't they?'

The words settled into Paradise's mind, then burned down to her soul, the utter truth of them. Her wit, so quick behind protected walls, failed her completely. She was a skank. Dirt. Now she both looked and smelled the part.

Paradise turned and fled towards the green garbage bin, which she could now see. At the back of the bin, a cement enclosure hid her.

She crouched down on her heels and threw her hands to her ears to stop the ringing and, although she felt a little safer holding herself, the tone went on, like a signal, warning that she was about to break apart.

Slowly, she sank down and let herself cry.

Under that bin you will find an envelope with money and a cell phone.

A cell phone. Angie. She caught her breath. She could call Angie! She would know what to do, right? The man had demanded she keep her mouth shut, but she could call her sister and no one would know. Angie would know what to do.

Paradise dropped down and peered under the garbage bin, saw the manila envelope and pulled it out. Frantic now, she ripped it open. Some hundred-dollar bills spilled out. A cell phone clattered to the stained concrete.

She snatched it up and quickly entered her sister's cell number.

The phone rang. Again. Then again, and her sister's voice come on asking the caller to leave a message. But she shouldn't leave a message!

The whole idea of calling her sister suddenly struck her as terribly dangerous. What if the killer found out and felt he had to tie up loose ends? She ended the call and tried to think.

Take the money in the envelope, go into the beauty salon, and ask them to make you pretty. Like your sister Angel. Pay them all the money. There's five hundred dollars there.

Everything had happened so fast, and she'd been so terrified that she hadn't asked the most obvious question: What exactly did the killer have in mind? Why did he want her to come out?

But she knew there was no value in asking a question that had no immediate answer. It would only make her task more difficult.

The answer to what would happen if she *didn't* come out, on the other hand, did have an immediate answer. He would kill Brad.

Brad, the man whom she thought she loved. But she was a fool, wasn't she? Floating around her room like a bird, imagining that she loved a real man and that maybe, just maybe, a real man loved her. The thought of it now made her ill. It was all absurd!

You look like you just crawled out of a garbage bin. I bet the men just love you.

Paradise picked up the bills one by one and stood to her feet. The sign over the beauty salon read *First Impressions – Health and Beauty Spa.*

She'd sometimes wondered what it would be like to be beautiful like her sister, but she'd never found the need to chase after impossible dreams. Actually, it had never even been a dream. She didn't spend much time thinking about how she looked.

But she couldn't save Brad's life looking like a skank – even the killer knew that. She was on the outside now, and out here people noticed ugly people. Even Brad would notice her ugliness.

Paradise slid the money into her pocket with the phone, noticing then for the first time that her jeans were two inches too short. She'd mistakenly grabbed the pair that Andrea had told her never to wear again unless she wanted to look like a dork.

The walk across the parking lot to the beauty salon was a long one, but she made it without being stopped. A barely audible chime sounded when she pushed her way past the glass door. *Hang on, Paradise. Be brave.*

She'd never been in a beauty salon before, and what she saw sent a bolt of terror right down to her heels. The room was large. Around the perimeter a dozen chairs faced mirrored walls. Seven or eight women looked up as she walked in, all strangers.

Monsters. Demons. More women were under helmets. Aliens.

She'd seen pictures, but actually standing here in a salon triggered a fresh panic attack. Her heart began to pound like a piston and the air was suddenly too thin to breathe. She had to grab the counter to keep from falling.

Stringy hair, high-water jeans, chewed down fingernails, hairy armpits – she didn't belong here . . . She smelled like she'd rolled out of a compost heap, because she had. Now she was playing the part of the mentally ill, and she was pulling it off so well that she had them all fooled. Even her name made a mockery of who she really was.

'Can I help you?' She jumped back. She hadn't noticed the girl in the chair behind the counter.

'Um . . .' Paradise dug out the money, all of it, and placed it carefully on the countertop. 'Can someone make me look beautiful?'

'You're sure?'

'Yes!' Allison nearly shouted. 'Of course I'm sure. There's no sign of her. We've searched every inch of the grounds. She's gone and there's no reason for it.'

'Is the artist there?'

'He's been waiting in the lobby for half an hour. That's what triggered the search. We went looking for her, but she's not here. And I can't seem to get Brad Raines on the phone. I figured he might know something, but I can't imagine that he'd take her out. Or, for that matter, that she'd agree to go out.'

The scenario was truly impossible, Allison thought. Paradise would never leave, no matter how much she thought she loved someone, not without talking it through with her.

'Why would Brad know anything?' the special agent in charge asked.

She gave her best answer. 'They shared something special. She trusts him, which is saying more than you can probably realize. He might have asked her to leave, but not without speaking to me about it.'

James Temple hesitated. 'We have another problem. Agent Raines has been missing since sometime last night.'

Allison sat down, phone plastered to her ear. 'Dear God. Dear God, he's going to kill her.'

CHAPTER TWENTY-EIGHT

The buzz was back with a ferocity that unnerved Quinton, truly bothered him, for the first time since he'd been sent by God to find the bride. For half an hour he'd let Rain Man talk, methodically weaving his tale of alternative theories. What if, what if, what if, what if . . . Like a demon trying to seed doubt.

It was all madness. Quinton had learned a long time ago that one man's madness was another man's sanity. What most in the world saw as twisted might not be twisted at all, but profound truth. Or vice versa.

Wasn't that the tale of every great prophet? Wasn't that why the world had killed the Messiah? Wasn't that why the assassin had pulled the trigger on Gandhi? Wasn't that Martin Luther King's downfall? In each case, someone believed each man to be dangerously mad. Yet the so-called madness proved to be an alternative sanity of the highest order, a better way of looking at the world, a way that went against the grain but was, in fact, the truth.

Likewise, the beautiful truth that Quinton bore was the product of a profound enlightenment.

Buzz, buzz, buzz . . .

A drop of sweat leaked down Quinton's temple. 'The problem with your theory, Rain Man, is it presupposes that I'm the mad one. Rather presumptuous, don't you think?'

'Who said anything about mental illness?' Brad asked with an involuntary tinge of smugness. He'd slid back down to the floor and now looked up at his captor with steady eyes, which also bothered Quinton. If he didn't still need the man alive, Quinton would be tempted to blow a hole in his head right now, at this very moment. Thankfully, he had more self-control than most.

'I don't know why I'm bothering to listen to you.' He glanced at his phone again, begging it to vibrate in his hand with the call from Paradise.

Buzz, buzz, buzz . . .

'I'm only saying that a small part of your thinking may be flawed,' Rain Man said. 'That there might be an alternative.'

'You finished?' He couldn't ignore the buzzing, and he couldn't ignore the man's logic, and he was aware of the sweat gathering on his brow. It all bothered him, and now he was agitated by the fact that he was bothered. He'd dismissed Nikki's pathetic attempt at reason. Why would Rain Man's words – and he must remember that they were mere words – bother him?

'No, Quinton, I'm not finished.'

'I don't have to listen to this.'

'No, but you're not like the rest. Shutting your ears to an argument isn't your way. Only fools do that.'

The man was using Quinton's own arguments against him.

He sat down in the chair and crossed one leg over the other, willing the phone in his hand to buzz before the buzzing in his head turned him senseless. He had the time and he had a brain. Buzzards were flying low and dive-bombing the world with demonic spirits. The boy was on the pier. Fishing. Eating ice cream. While angels plotted the death of all politicians.

His mind was jumping.

Too active. Too manic. And it was hurting.

Take your medication like a good boy, Quinton. There you go, you worthless piece of buzzard meat.

'Are you okay?'

Quinton blinked. Who was this man to ask him such an absurd question? *He* was the one tied to the pole. For the buzzards.

'What's your point?' Quinton asked.

'My point is that you're right. An infinite God can have multiple favourites. His love for every human is . . . how did you put it?'

Quinton frowned. 'Inexhaustible,' he said.

'Yes. Infinite love, which is by definition the greatest kind. If he has the greatest love for every single human, he can't have a lesser love for one of them. They are all his favourites, so to speak. Some would say that *favourite* means to favour one over the other, but used loosely it helps us understand that his full and utter devotion is fixed completely on each one, in the same way one would think of a favourite. That's quite insightful.'

'Very good, Rain Man. So you think the fact that you've seen what is obvious should earn you some favour, is that it?'

'No. Not for me.'

'Oh, that's right. This is about Paradise. You haven't proven that you aren't who I think you are. You've been shooting your mouth off making points that are as plain as the dirt. You're trying to stall to give your friends more time to find us. And now I'm getting bored with it.'

Rain Man drilled him with that smug stare, and Quinton suppressed a ferocious urge to hit him in the head with something.

'I'm getting to that, Quinton—'

'Stop calling me that!'

'What would you like me to call you?'

'Anything closer to how you really feel about me. How about Devil? Or Demon. I'm not your personal little Quinton. As you speak, the buzzards are being dropped by demons.'

Buzz, buzz, buzz.

He knew his thinking was fracturing and, for the first time in many years, he'd betrayed that fragmentation in front of someone. Maybe he would have to kill this man after all?

Rain Man didn't seem put off. 'My point is that I share your logic. That I'm on the right side. Your side. I've been looking for you for months, and I knew that when I finally found you I would need to persuade you that I was one of the good guys.'

The man wasn't making sense. Quinton's head was throbbing. Dive-bombing.

'I'm one of the good guys,' he said. 'And you're trying to stop me.'

Rain Man seemed prepared for the comment. 'That's what they told me you would say.'

To calm down, Quinton turned his mind to the seventh favourite. The one who'd rejected him seven years ago this very month. She had come in looking like a wounded dove and he'd fallen madly in love with her during those first few months. He'd treated her like a queen, keeping his loving eyes ever on her, as if he were God himself and she the broken angel.

And when he had finally decided that consummation was in order, he went to her room and dropped his gown to show her his entire magnificent body. But instead of recognizing how precious their union would be, she'd scratched him and hit him, screaming. He'd tied a rag around her mouth as he tried to explain. But the more persuasive he became, the more she resisted, until finally he'd lost his senses and hit her hard enough to knock her unconscious.

It was only then that he'd realized the truth. She was reserved for God, not for him. She was the most beautiful woman alive, created only for God himself. And now he would deliver her to him.

Rain Man had concluded that she was Angel. But he was wrong. If he was one of the good guys, he would know her true identity, wouldn't he?

'You're full of yourself, Rain Man.'

'Yes, I know that's what you think. And you should. But I've found you now, and I can say what I was sent to say.'

The audacity of the man. 'If you knew who I was, you would know who she is. I'm finished with this ploy.'

But he was now sweating profusely, and his skin was starting to itch.

'You have everything right,' Rain Man said, 'except one thing. You're not delivering the brides to God. You're killing them.'

'There's a difference?'

'I'm here to tell you that there is. That you've made a mistake.' Now Rain Man's voice was trembling. 'That you are killing God's favourites, like Hitler killed them, like Nero killed them. Like

Lucifer is trying to kill them. That's the alternative conclusion to your logic, and it's the truth. You've made one mistake, and it's the deepest offence possible.'

An electric current spread through Quinton's body. What if what the man said was true?

The buzzards are dive-bombing. The ice cream is melting. Forgive me, Father, for I have sinned.

The buzzing in Quinton's mind grew and he began to shake. 'You don't know what you're talking about.'

But what if he did?

'I'm here to tell you that you're serving the wrong master, Quinton.'

Quinton was on his feet before he could process the statement. He bounded across the blankets and slammed his fist into the man's head.

'I told you not to call me that!'

Rain Man sagged, lips bleeding. He looked back up, eyes pleading. 'That's what God calls you, and he's begging you not to kill her.' Tears flooded the man's eyes. 'Please . . . Don't kill Paradise.'

And with that one word, seven years of Quinton's life collapsed in on itself. He *knew*? Rain Man knew that Paradise was the seventh?

He staggered back, stunned. Was it then possible that he was right about the rest?

You're a buzzard, boy. You're a buzzard and you've been flying with the demons all along.

'What are you saying?' he stammered.

'I'm saying that you're right – she's the most beautiful woman in the world. I see what God has always seen. And you . . . You're on a mission from hell.'

Quinton's mind was snapping. The barn was spinning. The buzzards were screaming, *What does that make you? What does that make you, you pathetic, mindless boy?*

He said it aloud. 'I'm a demon?'

'No, you're . . .'

But he didn't hear the rest. His ears were filled with rushing blood and screaming buzzards. This is the way it had been all along! Paradise was the most beautiful; he'd seen that when she'd first walked into the Center for Wellness and Intelligence. A precious, innocent lamb who walked around the grounds like an angel from heaven. The world saw a wasted life, abused, discarded, but he'd seen her true beauty and he'd tried to make her his own.

She'd rejected him, not because he was an angel of mercy, but because she'd seen him for what he was, a demon out to kill the most beautiful. And he was back to make things right.

But he was wrong.

He was back to kill her because she'd rejected him.

What Quinton found most confusing in that moment was how this truth had remained hidden from him for so long. And yet, he knew why. He'd embraced his delusion. Like a deluded politician, or a tyrant who'd convinced himself that rape was justifiable.

'. . . if you want, Quinton,' Rain Man was saying.

'I . . . Please don't call me that,' he heard himself say.

'You can still change this.'

I've killed a million people and I want to kill a million more, because I'm a demon and that's who I am.

'I'm . . . I'm a demon.'

Rain Man didn't respond.

Quinton felt himself falling, sinking to the ground. His knees landed on the earth, jolting his mouth shut with a clack of teeth. He began to cry, then sob, then he stretched his jaw wide and he began to wail.

Rain Man was saying something, but his words were swallowed by Quinton's rage. He thought his head might explode. Panic beat him in the face and chest and he gripped his temples to contain it. But it grew.

There was only one way to stop it.

Brad Raines watched the breakdown with a mixture of dread and relief. He'd gotten through to the Bride Collector, and anything was better than the course they were on before.

But he'd also guessed the bitter truth: Quinton wasn't using Paradise to lure her sister. He was luring *Paradise*. All along it had always been about Paradise.

Now the man was screaming and his face was white as he trembled on his knees like a man possessed.

'You can stop it,' Brad said. 'You can end all of this.'

The man suddenly stopped screaming and lowered his head, panting.

'Quinton . . .'

Slowly he came to himself, breathed deep and unsteadily pushed himself to his feet. He stood there, limp. His jaw muscles bunched, relaxed, then bunched again. He finally looked up, face fixed.

'You're right.'

He turned around, walked to the table, picked up his pistol, returned and shot Brad from a distance of ten feet.

Boom!

The bullet punched into his chest, knocking the wind from him. He gasped and tried to jerk his arms around, but they were held tight by the restraints.

'God!'

'I'm sorry, I can't help you there.' Quinton walked back to the table, picked up a small bag, and headed for his Chrysler M 300.

The bullet had missed his heart or he wouldn't still be breathing. It had passed to the right of his chest, most likely through the lungs and out his back. Pain spread down his side in throbbing waves.

'Please . . . Where are you going?'

Quinton stopped. Then faced him, eyes deadpan.

'I'm going to finish what I should have finished a long time ago. And when I'm finished with her, I'm going to find another one. And I'm not going to stop until they're all dead, because that's what I do. I kill God's favourites.'

He turned back around and walked on.

'Enjoy the last few minutes of your life, Mr Raines.'

CHAPTER TWENTY-NINE

Paradise didn't know how long she'd been in the beauty salon. Two hours, she guessed. At least.

Jessie, the youngest of six hairdressers working today, had taken her by the hand, led her to one of the chairs at the back and sat her before the mirror. 'So, what do you think we should do?'

Paradise was at a complete loss. The smell of chemicals made her dizzy. They were going to gas her with something and turn her into a monster, but of course that was absurd. They would do no such thing. She might be a bit naïve, but she wasn't stupid. Psychotic maybe, just a tiny bit, but not stupid. Still, she couldn't stop the thoughts ramming the inside of her skull, trying to get out.

Monsters, they're all monsters and aliens and they're going to poison you.

Jessie took Paradise's hair and pulled it back. She was a young woman with a head swimming in blonde curls. One of those magazine faces painted with makeup that reminded Paradise of Andrea, except with blue eyes to match the sky, where aliens came from.

Stop with the alien stuff!

'Why don't we cut it off?' the alien said.

'No.'

'You don't think? Oh, I think your hair would be adorable short.'

Just the thought of those scissors snipping around her neck was too much. 'I'd rather not.'

'Okay . . . Well, I can do whatever you want. It's your hair, not mine. What do you think, Cassandra? She doesn't want her hair short.'

Cassandra, the mother hen here, walked over in her floor-length dress, smiling warmly. 'Well, let's just take a look at you, Samantha.'

It was the name she'd given them, afraid to be caught. She slipped out of the chair and stood, keeping her eyes on the scissors in Cassandra's hand. At the Center, the sight of a woman with shears wouldn't bother her, but it was different here.

Out here, aliens were on the loose.

Cassandra must have seen her eying the scissors, because she set them on a shelf next to neatly stacked white jars of hair product. 'You want a complete makeover, right?'

'I need to look beautiful.'

'Well, honey, that pretty much means a complete makeover. The hair, the face, a manicure, pedicure . . . What about your clothes?'

She looked down at her jeans. 'I want to cut my jeans off. Short.' She drew a line across her thigh.

The two beauticians exchanged smiles. 'Okay, I think we can do that. But you're going to need some new clothes. What's this for? You have a date, honey?'

The question brought the killer to mind, and it took some concentration to keep from unravelling in front of them. 'Yes. I have a date.'

'Okay, okay.' Cassandra walked around her, nodding. Both women were probably doing everything in their power to keep from bursting out in laughter. But as far as aliens went, they seemed nice enough. Not that they were really aliens.

'Okay, flip-flops, shorts. But the T-shirt has to go,' Cassandra said.

'I don't have another shirt.'

'We'll worry about that later. But you have to put on something that doesn't smell like you rolled in it, honey.' She played with Paradise's stringy hair. 'Let's give her a sexy sporty look, Jessie. Highlights, bangs, a little texture. Not too much makeup, just a healthy glow and some lipstick. What do you say we keep you looking natural, honey? Bring out your natural beauty.'

She nodded, lost.

'French manicure, not too long, Jessie. Red toenail polish.' She stooped over and lifted her left jean leg. 'You need a wax, honey. You okay with that?'

Did Angie wax? Paradise wasn't particularly hairy, but she knew that most girls shaved their legs and their underarms. Brad would approve.

So she nodded.

'Perfect. Get her into a robe, Jessie.' She touched Paradise on her cheek and smiled. 'Don't worry, Samantha, you're in good hands. Just sit back and let us pamper you. Okay?'

Paradise blinked, frightened but certain that she had little choice.

She stripped out of her smelly T-shirt and jeans and put on the long white robe they gave her. First the shower. She'd never heard of taking a shower in a beauty salon, but then she didn't know much about these kinds of places. Jessie insisted she wash off the smell, so she did, using what they called an exfoliating scrub. It smelled like flowers and made her whole body tingle. Under any other circumstances she might have found the hot shower relaxing.

But she couldn't get rid of the killer's voice in her head. Or the hollow pit in her gut, the gnawing sense that she was somehow prostituting herself, cleaning herself on the outside but still being dirty on the inside. But what choice did she have?

Then they went to work on her. Washing, scrubbing, painting, polishing, waxing . . . Though they decided they didn't have to wax, thank goodness. Instead they shaved her legs and underarms. She kept thinking that the aliens had captured her and she was in their experimental room, where they were prodding and poking her to better understand the human specimen they'd taken.

A white facial mask. Hair colour, cut and style. Makeup.

All the while Jessie and Barbara, who did both nails and makeup, kept commenting on how she was really beautiful. Her strong nails, her healthy hair, her porcelain skin . . .

Paradise sat back and accepted the torture, mind lost on the haunting voice that had spoken to her on the phone. The killer. Who had Brad.

Really, she was doing this for him. For both the killer and Brad, however ashamed she was to admit this to herself. For the killer, because he would hurt Brad if she didn't follow his directions to the letter. For Brad . . . No, not for Brad. Brad wouldn't want her to go through this just to look more beautiful.

But he wouldn't mind, would he?

Her mind couldn't process the whys of what was happening to her. The aliens, the demons, the killer. And worst of all, her father's voice, back from the dead, demanding she come out of her hiding place or he would kill her mother. As he had.

She looked down at her new white-tipped nails, which looked more like claws. Barbara put her file down and took her hand.

'Are you okay, Samantha?'

'Yes,' she answered, startled.

'Your hands are trembling. It's okay . . . Is it a problem with drugs?'

She was talking about substance abuse, but Paradise immediately thought of the anti-psychotics in her medicine cabinet. Because her mind was bouncing around like a rubber ball. The chemicals, the uniform-like robes, the scissors, the painting of nails and faces – all frightening snippets from a horror movie.

She almost stood and fled then.

'No. I'm just a bit scared.'

The woman glanced around. 'Are you in danger?'

'No,' Paradise answered, too quickly.

Barbara patted her hand. 'Okay. It's okay.'

But it wasn't okay, and Paradise continued to fight against an almost insurmountable urge to run out, bathrobe and all. She refused to look in the mirror, terrified of the monster she would find in her place.

Cassandra returned from her lunch with a shopping bag just as Barbara finished painting her face. 'I hope you don't mind, Samantha. I took some of your money and bought you a few things.'

Money? 'I don't have any money,' she said.

'You overpaid us. Now we're even.' She pulled out a pair of frayed jean shorts, a red blouse, and a pair of white sandals with silver buttons on the straps. 'What do you think? I hope a size 4 fits you. Aren't they adorable?'

She had no clue what to think.

'Well, go on,' Jessie said. 'You know where the dressing room is. Show us your new sexy self, honey.'

'Put them on?'

'That's why I bought them.'

'Now?'

'You wanted shorts, I got you shorts, but I can't put them on for you.'

Jessie, Barbara and Cassandra were all looking at her expectantly. So she took the bag, beating back stray thoughts of how foolish she was, and put them on in the dressing room.

When you're done, take a picture of yourself and send it to me so that I know you've done exactly as I've asked. Then go across the road to the park and wait for me. I'll call you and tell you what I want you to do next.

The voices echoed in her head. What if she was too late? What if he was waiting in the park now?

Despite their pampering, or perhaps because of it, she was more nervous now than when she'd first walked in. Keeping her fingers from trembling was now impossible.

Paradise grabbed her dirty jeans and dug out the cell phone. No calls. She stuffed it into the right pocket of the shorts and hurried out into the main room.

Seven or eight heads turned to look at her, freezing her with their stares. She looked at the mirrored wall directly in front of her. The girl facing her was an alien.

Same height, same face, but that was it. Her dark hair hung around her face to her shoulders like a picture-perfect wig, with bangs that swept across her forehead. Dark eyelashes curved up into light pink eye shadow, and dark brows had been thinned to half their former thickness. Blush coloured her cheeks, just enough to change the stark white face she was accustomed to.

And the lipstick. Red lipstick, like apples for lips!

Her first instinct was to rub it all off before her transformation into this alien whore was complete. 'What . . . what did you do?' she stammered.

'My, my, look at you!' Cassandra was all smiles. 'Now that's what I call sexy.'

A chorus of *oohs* and *ahhs* agreed, and Jessie went on about how unfair it was that she could look so pretty in no time at all.

The red shirt hung to the top of her jean shorts, which weren't long enough. She knew they were right, though; that she looked way too much like people Andrea would point out as pretty or cute or sexy.

But all Paradise could think was that this woman staring back at her wasn't actually her. She was an imposter! And even as the thoughts pummelled her mind, she knew they weren't the right thoughts.

She was on the verge of a psychotic break. No, because she wasn't psychotic. She had her phobias and had her visions, but they were real. This . . . She didn't know what to think about this!

Her head spun and she was suddenly convinced that, if she didn't get the monster off her, it would take over. She rushed over to the nearest station, grabbed a white towel, and had almost taken a swipe at her face when she remembered his words again. *When you're done, take a picture of yourself and send it to me so that I know you've done exactly as I've asked.*

'Samantha?'

Now they were all watching her as if she had lost her lid. She was in a box. She had to get out before she made a complete fool of herself and ruined everything.

Get out here or I'll shoot your mother . . .

She fled. Past Jessie and Cassandra, past three customers now seated for their turn. Through the door and outside into the bright sun, where a new reality greeted her.

Parked cars. A road. And, across the road, a large park.

She was shaking so badly now that she couldn't seem to get

her legs started again. This was what she had to do, right? She had to get over there and take a picture of herself and then . . .

The door swung out. 'Samantha, are you sure you're okay, honey?'

'Yes.'

Cassandra eyed her sceptically. 'Maybe you should come back inside?'

She got her legs going then, tearing away from the salon, past the parked car on her right. *I have to get out, I have to escape!* She got halfway across the lot and ran behind the green garbage bin.

Immediately, she realized that Cassandra had seen her, and that she was trapped like an alien back there.

She ran around the bin and headed across the road in a full sprint.

The cars started honking halfway across and she pumped her legs faster, right into the green park. Straight towards some trees fifty yards away.

Paradise reached the first large tree and threw her back up against the far side for safety. Breathing like a hurricane. Her mind was shouting at her, scolding, instructing, splitting, crying, begging it all to go away so she could stay in the closet.

But nothing went away, because there was no closet and no aliens and no father.

She got her wind back and snuck a peek around the tree. No one had chased her. So she'd made it. She was okay.

Now what? Now she had to take a picture of herself to prove she'd made herself beautiful.

Paradise pulled out the cell phone and fiddled with the controls, searching for the camera button. Both Andrea and Roudy had cell phones and she'd messed with them some. She dropped the phone in the dust once, grabbed it back up and rubbed it on her red shirt, hoping she hadn't damaged it.

By the time she finally figured out which button operated the camera, her heart was racing again. She was going to establish communication with the killer. Where would this all lead? What if he wanted something else from her? Why had he wanted her to look pretty for him? What if he actually wanted *her*? The thought was terrifying.

Pushing past the fear, she managed to hold the camera out and take a picture of herself. Figuring out how to send it was much easier than she would have guessed – there was only one number stored in the phone.

Now what?

She sank down to the ground, trembling. *Then go across the road to the park and wait for me. I'll call you and tell you what I want you to do next.* Her mind was twirling like a ballerina in outer space.

'Brad.' She whispered his name, feeling both foolish for thinking that she mattered to him and desperate for him to notice her. All of this was for him . . . She'd thrown herself into the land of demons and aliens for Brad, because she had been so certain that she mattered to him.

What if she was wrong?

He'd awoken a part of her that she didn't know existed. Even if she didn't matter to him the way he now did to her, she had to save him. She would do anything to save him, because she loved him.

Sitting here trembling at the base of the tree, all alone, dressed like a whore, she loved and needed him more than she needed air. A knot filled her throat; an ache so terrible that she cursed herself for allowing it to live inside her. But she couldn't deny it. Not now that she realized how lonely she'd been before Brad had—

'Excuse me.'

She gasped and jerked her head up. A man in uniform stood ten feet away, looking down at her. A policeman. She scrambled to her feet, tipped dizzily to her right and stumbled to her knees before pushing herself back up.

'Whoa, easy there. Are you Samantha?'

She gasped. The killer? He was the killer here in disguise. 'What do you want?'

'Take it easy, I'm not going to hurt you. We received a call.'

The policeman, if that's what he was, eyed her with scepticism, hand on his stick. 'Can you tell me your full name and where you live?'

'I . . .' At any moment the phone in her pocket was going to vibrate; she had to be here! 'Samantha,' she said.

He nodded, understanding, though he understood nothing. 'And where do you live, Samantha?'

'I . . . Nowhere.'

He stepped closer. 'Do you mind if I look at your arms?'

So then he probably wasn't the killer. 'Why?'

'It's okay, I just want to see the inside of your arms. Do you use?'

Drugs? 'No. Please, you have to leave me.' She glanced around, half expecting the killer to walk into sight at any moment.

The cop spoke into his radio. 'Yeah, I think we need to take her down to the station. Pupils're dilated slightly, she's obviously on something. She's refusing to show me her arms. I'm going to bring her in, copy?'

'No!' Paradise showed him the insides of both arms. 'I don't use drugs!'

'Copy that,' his radio squawked. 'Bring her in.'

'No, that's not it!' She frantically scanned the park for any sign of the killer, that demon. 'He's after me!' she blurted. 'I have to meet him here, you can't take me.'

The man followed her eyes. 'I don't see anyone. *Who's* after you?'

'*He* is. The killer.' Panic crowded her thinking and she tried to stop it, but the voices were stampeding now.

'You can either come the easy way or we can make this difficult. But you have to come with me, young lady.' The cop stepped forwards, hand extended. 'Look, this is as much for your safety as anyone else's. You almost got yourself killed crossing the road, they said. Please, don't make this diff—'

'I can't!' she cried, now fully fearful that she was abandoning Brad. 'No, you don't understand! I can't, I can't!'

His hand closed around her arm and she spun and was running

before having time to think through her decision. Straight into the bush behind her. It tugged at her shirt and scratched her legs.

A hand grabbed her collar from behind and hauled her down. She cried out. She was flipped onto her back, then roughly over onto her belly.

'Stop!'

He pulled her arms behind her and slapped handcuffs over her wrists. She was yelling hysterically now and all she could think of was Brad. *They're going to kill Brad. The aliens, the killer, the demons are going to kill Brad.* And the more she tried to explain, the louder and more incoherent her explanation became.

The cop was telling her to calm down, it would all be alright. He pushed her around the trees to a side street, where his partner waited in the police car. Together they muscled her into the back, slammed the door shut and rode off.

It was the end, she thought, staring back at the park. They were all going to die. This was it. Once again her father was going to kill them all because she didn't do what he said she had to do.

Aliens, demons, the killer, her father. It was all happening again.

The memory suffocated her. She slumped over on her side and began to moan. 'I can't, I can't, I can't.'

'You can't what, Samantha?' a voice asked. 'You can't take your medication?'

'You can't make me take medication. I can't let him kill him!' A small inner voice suggested she tell them everything, but then the voice on the phone was in her ear demanding she tell no one, or he would kill Brad.

Paradise lay on her side and let her moan grow into a wail. She was a whore angel in a demon's world and the aliens had finally captured her and were taking her to the hospital, where her father waited with his gun to finish the job.

'Not the hospital!' she moaned. 'Please, not the hospital.' They'd tied her to a bed and tried to kill her after her father had failed.

'We got a nut, not a druggie. She's psychotic. Let's take her to the mental health ward – let them make the determination.'

A fear deeper and more terrifying than the fear of facing the killer swept over her mind. *You're only as sick as your secrets.*

In her tangled mind, going to the mental ward was like going to hell. And Paradise wasn't ready to go to hell yet.

CHAPTER THIRTY

Allison rummaged through the drawer with Andrea. Paradise had shed the flannel pyjamas, which now lay in a heap on the floor, and put on something else before vanishing. If they could figure out what she was now wearing, the police stood a much better chance of finding her. Several major media sources had already agreed to broadcast her picture in the next newsbreak; Temple was going live with the case.

They'd found the bottle of Xanax, a drug Paradise hated and rarely used – the only reason Allison allowed her to keep a few on hand. So what had frightened her into taking two of the five pills?

Of greater concern to Allison was the other medication Paradise would miss, a small dose of a psychotropic drug they had been calling a vitamin and slipping to Paradise for years now. Without it, Paradise would undoubtedly betray her own psychosis. Slowly, over the course of twenty-four months, they'd begun a process of trying to wean her off the medication, but without much success. Allison and the staff had operated under the agreement that no one would ever make mention of the medication – there could be no opportunity for Paradise to learn that she was on chemicals to control the symptoms of her schizophrenia.

If anyone could beat the illness, Allison thought, Paradise could, and she wanted the girl to be given every opportunity, including assumption, to do so. She was convinced that Paradise's symptoms didn't include hallucinations, and that her so-called ghosts were precisely that.

But trauma would likely force other psychotic symptoms to

the surface, particularly given the extent to which she was *un*medicated. If she was out there now, there was no telling what symptoms she might be experiencing.

'What's missing?' she demanded.

Andrea was as nervous as a manic mouse. 'I don't know, I don't know! Sorry. It's my fault, it's all my fault, Allison. She's my friend and I let her go with that man. I tried to warn her, I tried to tell her that the only thing he wanted was to get—'

'Focus, Andrea!'

Normally she would never snap at the girl. But she'd lost her child, Paradise. Nothing about today was normal. Allison was taken aback by her own reaction to what had happened, her sense of utter loss, as if her whole world was about to crumble in on itself.

'Her yellow shirt isn't here,' Andrea said, searching again.

Yellow shirt. Yes, of course, the pale yellow T-shirt, one of only four or five that Paradise favoured!

Allison hurried over to the phone and called the laundry. 'A yellow shirt, José. If there's one down there, call me back. Hurry.'

She hung up and ran to the wicker laundry basket in the corner. Opened it. Nothing. Good. Good, they might have narrowed this down.

'Ma'am.'

She spun to the door now filled with Roudy's bow-tied frame. 'What is it?'

'I would like to make an announcement.'

'What is it?' She didn't have time for this.

'I have broken the case.'

'What do you mean? You've *found* her?'

'No. I know who the killer is.'

She let her hope fade. They really didn't have time for this! 'Please, Roudy, this isn't the time to be . . .' She stopped herself. How many times had she encouraged them not to reject their gifts outright? 'Never mind. Who is the killer?'

Roudy held up the drawing that Paradise had made late yesterday. Allison had given the drawing to him an hour ago when he demanded they turn the critical elements of the case over to him immediately, more to keep him occupied than with any hope he'd actually do something with it.

'It took me a while, seeing past the drawing itself to her intention. I'm quite familiar with the way police sketches are made, and once I was able to compare the—'

'Please, Roudy, get to the point.'

He looked at the drawing in his hand. 'It's none other than Quinton Gauld.'

Allison blinked. 'Quinton? You mean *our* Quinton Gauld?'

'Yes, ma'am.'

'Quinton who?' Andrea asked. 'Who's Quinton?'

Roudy strutted into the room and pinned the drawing to the wall with the dramatic flare of one who'd solved world hunger. He pivoted on his heels. 'One of our very own therapists, seven years ago. He left for greener pastures, as I recall.'

Allison stared at the picture. Could this be Quinton Gauld? 'But Paradise was here then. She would have recognized him the moment she remembered.'

'Unless Paradise saw Quinton Gauld in her vision, but no longer remembers who he is.'

'You're . . .' The thought was horrifying. 'You're suggesting she shut him out of her mind because of a bad memory connected to him.'

'It is the most natural conclusion for those with strong deductive skills.' He pointed at the picture as if this were a lecture and he the professor. 'Quinton did something that terrified Paradise. Then he fled under false pretences. Paradise has wiped the event from her mind, but now our villain is back to take his revenge and kill her once and for all.'

Andrea whimpered and scratched her head. She fled the room, crying.

Allison stood in stunned disbelief. Could this have happened right under her nose? They'd hired Quinton Gauld because he understood schizophrenia like so few therapists, having suffered and recovered from a bout of the illness in his twenties himself.

He'd gone on to acquire a master's degree in psychology. But after only six months at CWI, he'd confessed that being in close proximity with so many mentally ill people didn't sit as comfortably as he'd hoped. They'd mutually agreed that he should move on.

But he'd shown no signs of a psychotic break on his part.

She saw it now, staring at the drawing: the slope of his cheeks, the nose, the hair. It was him, wasn't it?

'Are you sure, Roudy? Are you absolutely certain that this drawing is Quinton Gauld?'

'Of course I am. Show the FBI a photograph from his employment file and I think they will agree. Our killer is, without doubt, Quinton Gauld.'

So then, she was right about Paradise. She did see ghosts!

Allison started to run.

'Where are you going?'

'We need to get his picture on the air. We have to get both of their pictures on the air as soon as possible!'

'I will not take a press conference yet!' he cried down the hall. 'Not until we have this villain behind lock and key where he belongs!'

By the time the officers arrived at the hospital, Paradise had managed to accomplish three things in her favour, and therefore in Brad's favour.

First, she'd managed to stop her moaning and wailing, which she knew only reinforced their perception of her as a nutcase.

Second, she'd climbed into a place of relative security in her mind. A closet, like the one in which she'd hidden from her father. Or, as she knew it better, a fog of comfort that hid all the demons trying to grab her ankles. In this place she could find some peace.

And third, she'd managed to develop a plan of sorts. The only way she had any hope of saving Brad was to survive herself. The hospital wasn't hell – she knew that – and the doctors weren't demons, although she was quite certain that demons, however or wherever they manifested, were after her. She had to stay in the closet – the fog – so that she wouldn't start thinking the hospital was hell. And she had to get at least one person on her side, believing in her. Someone besides Brad.

This meant she could not act like a loon. Even though she was going through something that probably appeared to be a psychotic break, she would not, could not, must not, give any indication that she was anything but completely sound. The only way to do that was to focus.

As a result, she ignored her surroundings until she was in the emergency ward itself. She stood perfectly still, arms still hand-cuffed behind her back, for her own safety, they said, and focused on appearing completely casual as the officer spoke to a pleasant-looking man in a pale blue smock. The man nodded and called over another man, bald and tall, strong enough to deal with three of her.

The next thing she knew, her hands were free and the attend-ant was leading her past the stations to one of a dozen spaces separated only by grey drapes.

'Have a seat on the bed. The nurse will be along soon. And please don't try anything stupid. The police are still outside for now.'

Don't try anything stupid? Like jump on your back, you big gorilla, and beat the demon out of you? But he looked kind and his nose was like a huge green pear on his face. A green Ronald McDonald without the afro.

Focus, Paradise. Focus.

'I won't,' she said, in a small voice that made her sound like a mouse. She sat on the edge of the hospital bed and put her hands in her lap. She felt nearly naked in these jean shorts. The three hours she'd spent being made to look beautiful seemed like a life-time away.

But maybe looking like a whore would be a good thing just now. Who was she kidding? She looked nothing like a whore! That was just her – pathetic little Paradise – talking. She looked more normal now than she ever had in her entire life.

Her mind swirled. She was an angel dancing on the tip of a needle, and if she didn't dance just right, they were going to impale her and the demon would get Brad. She had to save him!

'Do you want to dance?' she asked, looking up at the attendant.

He smiled. 'I'm afraid I have to pass. Don't worry, we'll get you back on your medication as soon as the doctor gets a look at you.'

His mention of medication brought back her urgency. She could not, under any circumstances, let them force any antipsychotic drugs down her throat. Under their influence she would become a drowned rat and lose all her capacity to imagine her way out of this.

'Do you think I'm beautiful?' she asked, standing. 'Like a ballerina on the head of a needle?'

Sit down, Paradise.

'Please sit down.'

She stared at him.

'Look, you're very pretty. You are, trust me. But this is a hospital, not the beach, and you're ill. I'm going to have to ask you to sit down. Now. As soon as you take your medicine, you'll feel better.'

'No, you can't let them do that.'

'Sit . . . down!'

'Okay.' She lifted both hands in resignation and sat back down. She realized that she had to make him understand.

'I'll sit down, but that won't stop him.'

'It won't stop who?'

'The man who's trying to kill me.'

The curtain parted and a grey-haired female nurse with a round face and beady eyes walked in with a clipboard. A demon?

'Okay, what do we have here?'

The bald demon smiled. 'She thinks someone's trying to kill her.'

'Don't they all? Okay, honey, what's your full name? Samantha who?'

'I'm not like everyone else!' Paradise snapped, standing once again. 'He's trying to kill me and my boyfriend, and that's why he made me do this! You have to listen to me!'

'No, honey, you're safe here.'

Paradise felt her pulse pound. Her thoughts fought through the thick fog now suffocating her. It took all of her self-control to stand still.

'Do you know what kind of medication you're on now?' the grey-haired demon asked.

'I told you, I'm not schizophrenic. I'm not any kind of psychotic. I have to get back to the park, and, if I don't get there, he's going to kill him. Aren't you listening?'

The nurse sighed and plopped the clipboard on the counter. She filled a small paper cup with water from a cooler and dug into her pocket. 'Okay, Samantha, have it your way.' She pulled out a bottle of pills.

This was what had happened last time. The memories came at her like guided missiles, pounding home. Something terrible had happened at home when she was locked in the closet, and now the demons were trying to finish the job.

The phone in her pocket vibrated and she gasped. She'd forgotten his instructions to wait for his phone call. It buzzed again, and Paradise didn't know what to do. The demons were buzzing through, trying to make contact.

It had all gone wrong! She couldn't help Brad in here. She had to escape these demons.

'Take these,' the nurse instructed, shaking out two pills. 'It will help you calm down.'

'No.' Her head felt as if it was going to explode. She backed up. 'I can't.'

The nurse glanced at the bald attendant, who moved closer, boxing her in. 'Don't make this difficult. Either you take it or we give it to you. Do you want to go back with the police? They'll throw you in jail. Is that what you want?'

'I can't,' Paradise whimpered. 'I can't.'

The attendant reached for her and Paradise bolted for the gap between them. The bald demon's thick arm shot out, caught her around the waist, lifted her up and slammed her back onto the hospital bed. She grunted and kicked her legs, gasping for breath.

'Get the restraints!'

The word triggered a scream that ripped through the air over her head. *Her* scream. And she knew then that it was all over. They had her, and now the only thing she could do was protest for Brad's sake. Paradise flailed and beat at the air and kicked like a cat caught on her back. And all the while her mind was seeing Brad.

They strapped her down. From there things got foggy. Voices yelling, her own cries of outrage, hands squeezing her arms and legs, the bite of a needle on her arm. She couldn't think straight, but she understood that they were killing Brad, and for that she hated them more than she hated her own father, who had tried to kill her.

She was screaming for Brad's sake. 'He's going to kill him, he's going to kill him!' She was his lone saviour and now these demons were trying to kill her.

'Please don't kill me, please don't kill me!'

The world started to fade and her voice got lost in it. She heard and felt and saw snippets, like bits of an old memory, and maybe this was just that, a memory from the past. From hell.

'. . . to General until we can get her to West Pines . . .'

She was rolling under long lights.

'. . . stronger than she looks.'

Chuckling.

'Who woulda thought? Just Samantha?'

'For now, just Samantha . . .'

Darkness.

Silence.

Brad? Brad, are you in here?

Silence.

I'm sorry . . . I'm sorry, I just . . . I lost it.

'It's okay, Paradise. I love you, Paradise. You're beautiful, Paradise.'

You don't think I look like a whore?

'I think you're the most beautiful woman in the world.' A breath. 'Be careful, Paradise. He's coming for you. His name is Quinton Gauld and he's coming for you tonight.'

CHAPTER THIRTY-ONE

That Brad had survived this long was a clear indication that the bullet hadn't punctured his lung. It had struck his right side and been deflected around and out his back. He was pinning his hopes on it.

But this hope was quickly being diminished by the fact that the wound was still bleeding. Ironic, that he would bleed to death at this killer's hand. He had to stop the bleeding and get to the black medical bag Quinton had left on the table, intended for use on his victims. Plugging their heels, fixing their wounds . . . At the moment, Quinton's sickness was Brad's greatest hope.

Then again, all of these hopes were dashed if he couldn't break the round support post he'd been tied to.

He pushed himself back to his feet, alarmed by the dizziness spinning his world. He couldn't pass out. The whole case had changed shape in these last twenty-four hours, and the stakes were now both personal and terrifying.

Paradise. Everything had always been about Paradise.

The thought made him sick with rage.

He leaned forwards, stretching his restraints and arms as far as he could, took a deep breath, then threw himself backwards into the post.

The beam shook with a dull thud. Debilitating pain ran down his side and he shuddered. Dust and debris from the ceiling rained down on him.

Thirty-two.

With any luck at all, age had rotted the wood. Brad clenched his jaw against the pain, straightened, leaned forwards again, and threw himself back. Another deep slice of pain. Another rain of debris. Another groan.

Thirty-three.

He repeated the procedure twice more before sagging back to the floor to rest.

The killer's name was Quinton Gauld and he had become the demon. Brad was responsible for the transformation.

His success was now his greatest problem. With no more need for the bleeding ritual designed to deliver the most beautiful to God without blemish, Quinton was now playing the part of killer. Rather than bring Paradise here, he might kill Paradise where he found her.

In any other situation, Brad might have reacted with a renewed urgency to find the killer before he could strike again. Instead, he reacted with raw outrage. He couldn't seem to stop the desperation. Not desperation for his own life.

For her life. For Paradise.

He didn't know what to call the feelings he had for her, but staring his own death in the face had made the emotions razor sharp. He knew they were the most powerful he'd felt since he first learned that Ruby had taken her life.

Brad grunted, fought off nausea and struggled back to his feet. The pole didn't seem to be weakening, but he had to keep trying. Still, even if he did manage to break it, the whole roof might cave in and end his life.

For some reason, that possibility meant nothing to him.

He held his breath and threw himself back into the pole.

Thirty-four.

Quinton pulled the M 300 off of I 70 and headed into the Texaco station. The trip back to Denver had taken him just over two and a half hours at top speed and consumed ninety percent of his fuel. He had too much to do now and so would need plenty of gas.

Gas 'em, gas 'em all, the sky is raining gas.

The game had changed once again, but as he slowly worked

his mind around that change, he came to realize that there was no change at all. Seven years of planning and growing and learning had delivered him to the final and greatest understanding. No longer satisfied with the milk that made babes fat and kept the devout stupid, he'd finally moved on to the meat of the matter.

Rain Man had rained the truth upon him and then died, having satisfied the purpose of his life. Quinton was not an angel of mercy sent by God to find and deliver his favourites to him, bloodless and pure. Rather he was an angel of death, sent to kill those very same brides.

The realization had disturbed him at first, naturally. As Nikki had said, with insight he had not appreciated at the time, even demons know the truth and tremble. So, yes, he'd spent half of the last two hours trembling.

Once he'd taken firm hold of this new realization, he'd quickly brought his superior intelligence to bear. He was who he was, and he must do what he was meant to do. Really, it changed very little.

Humans were still mostly stupid, particularly the ones who thought they were not.

Despite this fact, God did indeed love them with an unfathomable love. They were all his favourites.

And Quinton, in service of the other master, hated them with more steel and fire than he'd ever loved them. In hindsight, he'd always hated the females. They were sick and weak and deserved a far more brutal slaying than he'd ever administered. The fact that he'd been led by his master to think he was in the service of the Almighty was a useful deception that he couldn't help but respect.

He had evolved, however, and rather than fume with bitterness, he embraced his new knowledge and committed to carrying out his mission with ruthless haste and purpose.

Who was this female, Paradise, but a worm that deserved to be trampled underfoot and pissed upon. Thinking clearly now, he realized that he'd never before met a woman as sick and infuriating as her.

He'd received the picture she'd taken of herself. He was surprised at how transformed she looked. The sight of her looking frightened but undeniably beautiful had frozen him for a moment. His loins had become a beehive.

And then his hatred for her had reared so large and so terrible that he'd broken from his usual calm and ended up on the shoulder of I 70, weeping with bitter fury. And gratitude. Today he was finally mature enough to put an end to her life.

He'd called her then. But she hadn't answered his call.

So he'd placed his phone under the tyres of the M 300 and squished it flat, in the event her phone had been compromised.

Quinton finished filling up the gas tank with premium petrol and decided to leave his urine in the bathroom here. He strode towards the sign of the stick figures that indicated outdoor bathrooms.

He would go to the park. If she wasn't there, he would pay the beauty salon a visit. Then he would find her, haul her out by her hair and, rather than kill her with a bullet to her face as he'd fantasized, he would drill her full of holes and let her bleed all over the ground.

He stepped onto the sidewalk in front of the store and glanced up at the television over the counter inside. What he saw made him stop.

A news anchor was speaking silently over words that read: MISSING PERSON. And there, next to the words, was a large photograph of a skinny, twenty-something girl with dark, stringy hair.

Paradise.

In the space of a single breath, Quinton knew what this meant: the Center had reported her missing, which meant that the authorities didn't know her whereabouts, unless this was a ploy to draw him back to the park. That was unlikely – they wouldn't go to such lengths to draw him to a location they already expected him at.

Paradise was likely still at the park, cowering beneath a tree. This was very good news.

The picture changed. The words now read, ARMED AND DANGEROUS. Beside the words was a photograph of a man named Quinton Gauld. An old picture of him from his employment file at the CWI. He remembered having the picture taken when he was first hired.

This was alarming news. He'd worn a moustache and beard back then, and his hair was long. Black plastic-framed glasses were perched over his nose. He'd forgotten how homely he'd looked seven years ago. Once he'd learned about his important role in attracting the world's most beautiful women, he'd changed his habits to reveal the true beauty in himself. The result had been a smashing success. He now looked nothing like the ugly toad in the photograph.

But the authorities knew his identity. How? His mind flipped through a dozen possibilities and settled on the M 300, which was indeed registered to him. It had always been his weakest link. Some camera somewhere had likely snapped a picture of his vehicle coming out of the garage at Rain Man's residence. Together with other bits and pieces, they'd deduced his identity.

This made his mission even more critical. He would have to swap the M 300 for the Green Chevy pick-up truck parked at his apartment. He'd rented the apartment and registered the vehicle under an alias – neither could be tracked to the man who had once been Quinton Gauld, now Ghost Gauld. But an astute observer might connect his face to the one on the screen.

To be sure he wasn't overestimating his improved appearance, he walked into the mini-market and approached the cashier, who was counting the change in her drawer.

'Another freak,' he said, nodding at the television.

She followed his eyes. 'Yeah, he's been on for the last half hour. Can I help you?'

He caught her eye, then smiled. 'What's the world coming to, huh? Pack of Marlboro.'

'Reds?'

'Yes, Reds. Gotta die sometime, right?'

She grinned sheepishly at his joke about the perils of smoking. 'I guess.'

Quinton paid for the cigarettes, threw them in the trash on his way back to the car and climbed behind the wheel.

His need to urinate had passed. Instead he felt a terrible urge to find the deceptively named Paradise before some other lucky soul found her.

Allison pushed the door to Roudy's office open and sighed a silent prayer of relief. Roudy was pacing in front of his desk, lecturing Casanova and Andrea about the finer points of police sketching, which he'd demonstrated in rather horrible fashion on the white board behind him. Seeing Allison, he pushed his point with a burst of intensity.

'It's in the details, I'm telling you, much finer than even most trained eyes can see. This is why they come to me.' He pointed to his eyes. 'I have that sight. I can tell if a single hair is out of place.' He nodded at Allison. 'Greetings.'

Andrea jumped up from her position on the couch next to Casanova. 'Did you find her?'

Allison stared at Roudy. 'I need your help, Sherlock.'

'I'll have to check my schedule.'

'I need all of you again. Andrea and Cass, I need you to stay here and keep an eye on things for me in case Paradise returns on her own. She knows and trusts you, and I need you to be here when she comes back.'

'What about Roudy?'

'Roudy, I need you to come with me. I need those eyes of yours.'

'My eyes.'

'Yes, your eyes. We're going out to look for Paradise. And for Quinton.'

The announcement caught them off guard. Roudy was still dressed in his pyjamas and slippers. It would have to do.

'Out?' Roudy said.

'Out. Now.'

'I don't drive.'

'I do,' she said.

'And you need me because the FBI is looking for the wrong person.'

'What do you mean?'

'This serial killer has demonstrated superior intelligence at every turn,' Roudy explained. 'And no wonder, with his background. After all, you hired him, Allison. But anyone with those kinds of smarts isn't going to walk around looking like his old self. The photograph of Quinton Gauld won't help them. I assume you've informed them of this?'

Bingo. This was on his mind already?

'That's right, Roudy. And that's why I need your eyes. You better than anyone may be able to recognize him. Or her, for that matter.'

'Where?'

'Hospitals.'

'You do realize that we won't find them. He's smarter than that — he's got her stashed somewhere already.'

Andrea dropped to the couch and began to bawl.

'Sorry, but it's true,' Roudy said.

'That was uncalled for,' Allison snapped.

He looked away, fiddling with his hands.

'Will you help me?'

He caught her eye, then made a show of looking in his appointment book. 'I'll clear my calendar,' he announced.

'Let's go, Roudy.'

'It's a waste of—'

'Stop it!' Allison cried. Andrea's sniffing swelled to a wail. 'I don't care if it is a waste of time! This is Paradise we're talking about here, and I'm not sitting around a moment longer. She's my *child.*'

They all understood her meaning.

'Now, are you going to help me or not?'

'I would do anything for Paradise!' His jowls shook as he emphasized his commitment. 'Where to?'

'The Lutheran Medical Center. Quinton Gauld took his internship there. It's also the closest major medical centre with a psychiatric ward.'

Roudy nodded, then marched up and past her. 'Follow me.'

CHAPTER THIRTY-TWO

It took Quinton an hour to switch his M 300 for the truck and reach the park. With each passing minute his ire rose, resulting in a condition of constant buzzing and, far worse, some twitching. Any physical reaction to the stakes at hand would have been beneath him twelve hours ago. He would have refused to give in to any such cliché, but the discovery of his true identity had sent him over a cliff and he had no choice but to accept the truth: that he had hated Paradise all along.

He loathed her with every synaptic firing in his brain. He would rather cut and crush her than take even one more breath. He would rather vomit down her throat than make her beautiful for God.

But then, forcing her to make herself beautiful *was* his way of vomiting down her throat. He could have made her beautiful himself. He'd perfected the skill of applying makeup and manicures and all of the pampering most women paid dearly for. So then why had he really demanded she take herself into the salon?

Because even then, deep inside, he'd known how humiliating the experience would be. His true desire had been to mock her because he hated her.

He let the image from his crushed cell phone linger in his mind – the red blouse, the sexy jean shorts, the flowing dark hair, the long lashes – as he studied the park for a glimpse of her.

He drove the Chevy around the perimeter twice before concluding that she had been disobedient. This realization made him furious.

He drove the truck into the high street, aimed for the beauty salon and parked directly in front. Shoved his silenced pistol between his belt and back. Exited the vehicle and entered the establishment, uncaring now that he might not be hiding his emotions as well as he would have liked.

The door chimed softly. He walked past a receptionist and gazed at a large room that reeked of perm solutions and scented shampoo. Three hairdressers worked over women who'd paid to be more beautiful. Another leaned against a counter, drinking a Diet Coke. Skanks, every one of them. Favourites who neither knew they were loved nor deserved to be.

'Where is she?' he demanded, in a clear voice.

A maternal woman who looked as if she might be in a position of leadership lowered her scissors and faced him with a curious, undisturbed stare.

'I'm sorry, who are you looking for, honey?'

Honey? She looked like a woman with some spine, which could be a problem. So he pulled out his semiautomatic pistol, chambered a round and shot at her forehead.

The gun bucked. *Pffft.*

Her head snapped back.

His hand twitched.

She fell.

'Paradise,' he said. 'Where is Paradise?'

They jumped and screamed like a batch of terrified monkeys; the receptionist reached for the phone.

Quinton shot her before she could lift the receiver. 'Be quiet!' he shouted over them all. 'I'm going to kill all of you. That's what I do. But first I need you to tell me where the girl who paid you five hundred dollars for your services is. My patience is fragile. Some would even say that I'm psychotic.'

A younger, blonde beautician was staring at the fallen body near her as if it were a bloodied deer that had slammed through her windshield. She lifted her head and tears sprang from her eyes.

'Samantha?'

Samantha. Paradise had changed her name. Smart.

'Where is she?'

'We called the police, they came and got her. Please, mister, please don't hurt us, we—'

'Shut up. What did you tell the police?'

'We . . .' She looked back down at the body, trembling from shock now.

'You what?'

'She was acting strange. Cassandra has a brother who's . . .'

'You called the police and told them you thought this Samantha might be mentally ill; is that what you're trying to say?'

'She called them.' The woman glanced at the fallen leader.

'And it never occurred to any of you that you, not Samantha, might be the ones who are mentally ill? That she was far more beautiful the way she was than after you got finished painting her body and dressing her up like a doll? She is a favourite, you thick-headed, harebrained slut!'

He was shouting. It was unbecoming.

So he shot the woman in her face.

The rest were screaming again and Quinton didn't need witnesses. He walked up and shot their cowering forms in the head, one by one, *pffft, pffft, pffft, pffft*.

One was still alive.

Pffft.

It was a bloody massacre and he hated unnecessary violence.

But then he remembered that was wrong. He no longer hated unnecessary, brutal violence. It was who he was now. His only regret was that some or all of these dead favourites now bleeding on the floor might live eternally in bliss. Wouldn't that be a cruel twist?

Quinton grunted, shoved the gun back under his belt and left the salon. A strong wind was blowing. His visit to the salon had been fruitful. He now knew that the dead Good Samaritan called Cassandra had called the police. They'd collected Paradise. The fact that Paradise's picture was on the tube meant that no one had connected Samantha to Paradise yet.

Following protocol, the officers had likely determined her to be mentally ill and taken her to the closest hospital with a psychiatric ward. This was territory familiar to Quinton, who found all news regarding such matters interesting. The closest psych ward would be West Pines at the Lutheran Medical Center, on 38th Street in Wheat Ridge. She was likely there now, under the name Samantha. If not there, then in another hospital, perhaps Denver Health Medical Center, which had thirty-eight beds in its psychiatric ward but was much further off.

Quinton backed the truck out and rolled down the parking lot, happy to see no commotion behind him.

But he wasn't happy. His face was still twitching and his mind was still buzzing and now he was sweating. His mind was full of images – violent images of Paradise being made to look disturbingly ugly. Before he drilled her with holes and bled her dry, he would make sure she understood just how ugly she was. Just how unfair it was that God had let her be born. She was, in fact, so ugly that God had sent him, the angel of death, to rid the earth of her. Put the garbage out, so to speak.

He would crush her spirit the way she'd crushed his when she'd rejected him seven years ago.

'Careful! Please, you're going to kill us before we arrive.' Roudy wasn't coping well with traffic. He lived comfortably in his delusions of grandeur, but out here, the mundane rendered him nearly incompetent. He flung his arms out and lifted his slippered right foot towards the windshield. 'Watch it, watch it!'

'Roudy, please... I know this is a stretch for you, but I would like you to trust me.'

The poor fellow was white. 'Okay, okay, if you could just slow down a little.'

'We're only going half the speed limit.'

She'd done her best to distract him with the case, but Roudy's belief that Quinton was already a step ahead of him didn't help. His opinion bothered Allison immensely. Roudy might not be too good with traffic, but he had navigated the case well enough. She could only pray that he was wrong.

'Careful!' he warned again. 'Get us there in one piece. Please!'

'You might be right,' she said.

'We're going too fast?'

'No, it might be too late. James Temple from the FBI says they've already called all the hospitals. No one by the name of Paradise has been admitted.'

'Assuming she was admitted under that name.'

'No one with a yellow T-shirt and jeans or anyone who fits that description.'

'Careful, please. Perhaps we should go back home and have them bring the files to me?'

'You told me yourself that ninety percent of good detective work is about sifting through leads. So, this is a lead. It's the nearest psych ward. Quinton worked here. If you're wrong and he doesn't have her, assuming he's going after her—'

'But he is,' Roudy said, facing her. 'Of course he is.'

'Because something happened between them,' Allison said.

'That's not why. He's going after her because she is the seventh and most beautiful, whom he must deliver to God.'

'You're sure it's Paradise? Just because she's missing—'

'I believe he loved her and tried to rape her,' Roudy said. 'Now he's back and he's going to finish the job by killing her. It all fits; it's all in the details. Watch it, watch it!'

Allison was taken back by his frankness.

'Dear God, help her. I hope you're wrong, Roudy. I really hope you are wrong.'

CHAPTER THIRTY-THREE

The blue scrubs fit a little tight, but Quinton didn't have time to delay his mission any longer. He could fit into any hospital for a few hours without raising anyone's eyebrows, but here he could pass as a doctor for a day and probably kill a dozen people before being found out. He knew the place inside and out from his employment here a decade ago, and from what he'd seen so far, nothing had changed except for their computer system. And he'd solved that challenge already.

He would only require ten minutes to find and take the little skank, and he doubted he'd need to kill more than the one doctor who'd been so kind as to give him the scrubs.

Quinton pushed the man's head into the large clothes hamper and looked in the mirror above the sink. From a distance he might pass as Dr Robert Hampton. Up close they would see the difference. It didn't matter – he had no intention of speaking to anyone up close.

He'd never had to use tremendous force to execute his role before, but now that he was freed up to be himself, he found the skill natural. And at a time like this, while the world scoured the streets for poor little Paradise, brute force was his friend.

The nice thing about technology was that it gave immediate information to anyone with access. He could have run from room to room in search of a psychiatric patient named Samantha, but there was no telling where or if they even had her, and he didn't have time for a full-fledged adventure.

He could have forced the doctor to do the research on any one of many rolling, portable terminals in the halls, but there were no terminals in the laundry closet, and he couldn't risk the man making a scene.

Thanks to technology, he needed neither a manual search nor Dr Hampton to find out where they'd put Paradise, if they had her. The good doctor's magnetized ID card would do the trick.

Quinton turned his head with a long slow twist to the right and then the left, relieving the tension in his neck and upper back. The chrome shelves next to the sink were stacked with supplies: folded smocks, white towels, ace bandages, green plastic bedpans, rolls of gauze, thermometers, blood pressure cuffs and cloth sacks imprinted with the hospital logo. Three wheelchairs were folded and stored next to the shelves.

He took one of the bags from the shelf and transferred his clothes and the gun into it. Then he unfolded one of the wheel-chairs, wheeled it from the closet, carrying the bag with his personal possessions in his right hand, and walked down the hall, before activating the first rolling computer terminal he came to. When the system asked for authorization, he simply slid the card through the reader, magnetic strip down. The machine beeped and he was in. Dr Robert Hampton.

Forgive me, Father, for I have sinned.

He recited it out of habit, but he now knew why this had been his prayer. He *had* been sinning. He was perhaps the chief of all sinners. And his job was not done. There was more sinning left to do in this one day than most folks would enjoy their entire lives.

Within thirty seconds he learned what he'd come to learn. *First name: Samantha, Last name: Unknown* had been admitted two hours ago and was now housed in room 303.

Walking with the purposefulness of a doctor, he headed directly to the elevator, took it to the third floor and made his way to the rooms, careful not to make eye contact with anyone. He set the wheelchair against the wall next to room 303 and continued on, checking the other rooms across the hall.

Room 316 suited his purpose. Inside slept an older gentleman connected to a heart monitor. He flipped the monitor off, exited the room and pretended to be examining the patient's chart outside of room 303. It took the nurse on duty fifteen seconds to abandon her station to investigate the disrupted heart monitor.

The moment she passed him, Quinton took the wheelchair from the hall and wheeled it into room 303.

There she slept. God's favourite.

Oddly enough, she was strapped to the stripped bed, still dressed in her street clothes, though her feet were bare. The blue cell phone he'd left for her lay on the bed table.

The sight of her sleeping so peacefully on the hospital bed took him off guard. She was more beautiful in person than in the photograph she'd sent him, and, for a moment, he wasn't sure if he wanted to kill her or take her as his own.

But the moment passed and bitterness flooded his mouth. He could make no mistake; he did indeed hate this little wretch whom he'd been sent to savage.

He walked up to Paradise and slugged her in the head. Her head jerked and lay still. The girl hadn't even known what had hit her.

Quinton set his plastic bag on the table next to the cell phone, hooked his hands under her armpits, dragged her out of the hospital bed and plopped her into the wheelchair. He arranged her feet in the footrests, placed a blanket over her body and sat her straight. Her head lolled to one side, but he kept her upright by grasping the back of her shirt as he wheeled her forwards. She would look like any sedated patient, rolling down the hall.

Quinton stuffed Dr Robert Hampton's ID along with the blue cell phone into his pocket and set his bag of personal items on her lap. Then he wheeled her from room 303 and headed towards the elevator that would take them down to the emergency exit.

Less than a minute had passed since he'd turned off the monitor in room 316. And in less than another minute, Quinton was beside his green Chevy truck, loading Paradise into the passenger's seat, like a caring father taking his daughter home after a visit to the emergency room.

He strapped her into the seat, closed the door, set the wheelchair into the truck bed and slid behind the wheel. The Chevy fired after a quick twist of the key.

Not until he was pulling out of the parking lot did the immensity of his accomplishment settle over him. She was his. Paradise was finally his.

To hate and to kill as he saw fit.

'He's brilliant, I'm telling you.'

Roudy floated around room 303 in his pyjamas and slippers like a butterfly – to the bed, to the bathroom, to the door, to the window – unsure of where he wanted to alight in this, the first actual crime scene he'd visited in his entire life. He was himself again, having left the perils of traffic behind.

The nurse on duty and the administrator, a salt-and-pepper-haired thin doctor whose chin dipped below his Adam's apple, stood by, still in shock that their patient had been abducted.

It had taken only ten minutes after arriving to track down the admission of *First name: Samantha, Last name: Unknown,* who'd been admitted two hours earlier after being picked up by police in a park not too far from the CWI.

'Brilliant,' Roudy said. 'Always a step ahead.'

'We can't know for sure it was her,' Allison protested, without a shred of confidence. She snapped open her cell phone and called the number Temple had given her.

'Of course it was,' Roudy cried. 'All the details fit. A girl just over five foot. Clearly psychotic. Dark brown hair. Found near the centre. I can smell Paradise in the air.'

He answered after the first ring. 'Agent Temple.'

'You heard?'

'I heard. And I just received confirmation. Seven bodies were just discovered dead in a beauty salon opposite the park. Best guess is the killer tracked her location to the hospital. We don't know how yet.'

Her legs felt weak and she sat on the edge of the bed. 'A beauty salon?'

'Does it mean anything to you?'

'He's . . . He's trying to break her spirit.'

'Frankly, that's the least of our concerns now. What matters most is that Quinton Gauld now has both Brad and Paradise, and we don't have a clue where.'

'He's going to kill them.' She said it to herself as much as to him.

'We have every law-enforcement agency in the state searching the most likely locations: barns, abandoned buildings, anything. A Chrysler M 300 is registered to his name; we've included the car to the profile. Rental records, banking – we're digging up everything we can tie to his identity, but this guy ran a pretty tight life. Not much coming up. False address.'

She forced herself to her feet, past her weakness. 'You have to find him!'

'We're trying, ma'am. Trust me, this affects us all.'

'How could he just escape? He just walked in here and took her without being seen?'

'Slow down. He may very well have been seen. I'll have a team there in three minutes. In the meantime, security is asking around. We still don't know how he managed to get in, much less get her out, but we will. These things take time, Miss Johnson.'

'We don't have time!' she cried.

His end was silent.

'I'm coming down,' she said.

'I'm not sure what good that will . . . Hold on.' She could hear his muffled voice off the phone, swearing.

'What is it?' she demanded into the empty phone.

'. . . down there, Frank. Now!' He swore again and came back on. 'Sorry. We have another body.'

'They found her?'

'No. Sorry, no. At the hospital.'

'Okay, I'm coming down to your offices. I'm not going to just sit around as long as he's out there with Paradise, you hear me?'

'This is an FBI investigation, ma'am. I know you're upset, but there's no way you can help us down here.'

'*I* may not be able to, but Roudy may.'

He paused. 'Roudy. This is . . . one of your patients . . .'

'This is the man who identified Quinton Gauld. This is the man who helped Agent Raines put this case together while the rest of your team stumbled around in the dark. And I'm bringing him down.'

He remained quiet for a moment.

'If you insist, ma'am, but I really don't think—'

'I agree.' She looked up at Roudy, who was staring at her with wide eyes. 'Yes, he's invaluable.'

She hung up. Grabbed her purse.

'Let's go. The FBI is waiting.'

'They're asking for me at headquarters?' Roudy stammered.

She spun back. 'They are begging,' she said, then walked out with Roudy at her heels.

CHAPTER THIRTY-FOUR

Brad had lost track of time. Two oil lamps on the table cast yellow light inside, but it was dark outside. He knew this because the winks of white sky in the room had gone black. Twice he'd passed out upon collapsing to the ground after his regiment of slams against the wood pole to his back.

Slam . . .

Deep breath. Lean forwards. Another deep breath . . .

Slam . . .

Deep breath. Lean forwards. Another deep breath . . .

Slam . . .

Deep breath. Lean forwards. Another deep breath . . .

Slam . . .

Deep breath. Lean forwards. Another deep breath . . .

Slam . . .

Five slams each time, like a football drill in reverse, ignoring the pain before sliding back to the ground for a rest.

Hours had passed, he knew that much. But he'd stopped trying to keep track of his progress or gauge his hope. He had no hope. The reasoning that had gotten him into this futile escape attempt had long left him.

The exercise had become a simple one. As long as he still had enough strength to stand and throw himself backwards, he would. Thinking about whether the strategy was working only weakened his focused resolve. He had no destination now, just the will to place one foot in front of the other. He kept only one thing on his mind.

Paradise.

With each thrust of his body backwards, an image of her filled his mind. He didn't harbour any illusion about saving her, because, back when he was thinking things through, he concluded that he'd long ago run out of time.

His exercise became as much a perverse form of penance as an attempt to escape. Even if he did manage to break the post, he had no clue where he was or how far from help. And even if he did get to help, he knew he was too late.

There was always the possibility that Quinton would grab Paradise and bring her back here, but that thought terrified Brad more than any other. The killer would find him alive and awake and would take twisted pleasure in forcing him to watch while he tortured Paradise in new, unthinkable ways fuelled by the audience. Her death would be worse because of him.

Brad slammed into the post in bitter protest at his own weakness. For every woman who had ever been told she wasn't normal or that she was ugly. For every girl who'd been abused by a father. For every man blinded to the true beauty of every Paradise.

What he wouldn't give now to sweep her off her feet and rush her to the highest mountain refuge, far away from all the cruelty the world threw at those it judged to be less than ordinary. Because Quinton Gauld was right about one thing, even Allison would say so.

They were all God's favourites.

They were all beautiful, exquisite creatures in their own way. Men as well, yes, but this was about women. Every one was a treasure of the highest order, and with the pain of each crash into the post, this truth, no matter how melodramatic it might seem in less pointed circumstances, was driven deep into Brad's mind.

Crash . . . crash . . . crash . . . crash . . . crash . . .

If only he had protected her. How, he didn't know, but that hardly mattered now. A week ago she was nothing more than a curiosity to him; a monkey in the zoo, as she put it. It didn't matter that he had only known her a short time; it didn't matter that there was no obligation on his part to love her over any other woman.

Had he ever met a woman as desirable as Paradise? Had he ever connected with such a deep soul, seen such soft eyes light up when he walked into the room?

Forgive me, Paradise . . . Please, I beg you . . . Forgive me. I was a fool for not knowing. I wouldn't do it again. I swear I would sweep you off your feet. I would smother you with kisses and promise to never allow a man to lay a hand of harm on you again.

In Brad's tortured mind, now stripped of the pretence that distorted the world's view of beauty, he understood clearly: Paradise was the favourite. The one bride every man would kill for.

And now Quinton Gauld, this demon from hell who strutted about the world in a man's body and called himself human, would rob Brad of all second chances.

Tears had long ago dried on his dirty cheeks, but now his eyes flooded with them again. He pushed himself to his feet, sliding up the pole, which creaked angrily against his body weight. He leaned forwards, body quaking. It was all pointless, but he couldn't think like that.

He threw himself back, crashing into the post. The loud impact took his breath this time, and he had to wait for it to return. If the pole broke and the timber it supported collapsed and crushed Brad, his death would not be wasted.

Brad hurled his weight backwards. *Crack.* This time the collision did not take his breath, because he was falling.

His impact with the earth behind him, however, pounded the air from his lungs. He tried to breathe and blinked up at the splintered end of the post over his head, still hanging from the beam above.

It took him a moment to fully realize that he'd just broken the pole and that the bottom half was lying on the dirt floor beside him.

His breath and his mind returned to him at the same time. Adrenaline flooded his veins, jacking his heart rate up to a steady hammer.

He rolled to his right, desperate to be on his feet, but his hands were still secured behind him, and for an awful second he wondered if Quinton had tied him to a stake in the ground in case he managed to break the post.

He frantically rolled away from the post. In the process, his hands came free – the knot having apparently loosened as he fought to free himself. Brad scrambled to his feet, ignoring the pain on his right side. If he'd survived this long, he wasn't in danger of dying from the wound now.

He stood tensed, hands clawed, beside the blanketed stage, at a momentary loss. His freedom had come so unexpectedly that he forgot what it was he'd had in mind.

Escape.

A phone, he had to find a phone. Or a car. He had to make contact with Temple.

No, first the medical kit.

He leaped over the blanket and threw the black medical kit open. Scissors, gauze and a scalpel lay in a neatly arranged tray. A thick bunch of first-aid antiseptic bandages was bound together with a yellow tube of antibiotic ointment. Besides these items, he saw a large assortment of medications and some putty, a small chisel and hammer.

Brad ripped open his shirt and stared at the angry, bloody wound in his side. He picked up a small brown bottle of hydrogen peroxide, spun the cap off with unsteady fingers and splashed the disinfectant on his side. The liquid foamed as it made contact with the wound, which was not as deep as it looked. He deduced that his weakness was more from dehydration and blood loss than injury.

It occurred to him that he might not want to leave evidence of his pilfering out for Quinton to see. He stopped. Then again, the broken pole was evidence enough. His mind wasn't working right.

Think!

Without taking any more time to cleanse the wound thoroughly, he applied a finger of antibiotic cream directly onto the entry point, slapped on an adhesive bandage, then wrapped his lower body with an ace bandage. Then he quickly drained a bottle of water that sat on the counter.

He closed the bag.

On second thoughts . . . He reached back in, took out the scalpel, and closed it up again. Then he took a clawed hammer from the table, and strode towards the open barn door, moving fast.

Dark outside, pitch dark. A gravel driveway snaked into the night. Without any knowledge of where he was, he had little choice but to follow the road to wherever it led him.

For the first time in several hours, Brad began to hope. For what, he wasn't sure, but he could hope now and so he did.

Please, God. Please let her be alive.

CHAPTER THIRTY-FIVE

She remembered the lights over her head as they rolled her down the hall, and she remembered hearing the attendants' voices talking about the way she looked, but whatever they'd shot into her veins had pushed out the light, and so Paradise had retreated into her fog of safety, away from the demons snapping at her heels.

The last conscious thought she could remember was that she'd finally gone crazy. For real crazy. Psychotic. But that was okay, because Roudy and Andrea and Enrique were also psychotic now and then, and she loved them just the way they were.

They must have placed her in a hospital bed and pulled a blanket over her head. Either that or she was dead and they'd taken her to the morgue. But she'd opened her eyes and could feel the blanket over her face. It was pitch black under here.

Her arms didn't want to move.

No sound. She wasn't lying flat on her back. She was slouching against the elevated mattress behind her. She'd been in this situation before, seven years ago. The only way to avoid more medication was to act totally normal, which was a problem for a person who was *not* normal. But she was normal, right?

Her first impulse – to throw the blanket off in a panic – was tempered by her slow-moving muscles and by her clearing reason.

Depending on what drug they had given her, she might soon be clear of the fog they'd induced. Most anti-psychotic medications took days to work their way out of a person's system, but maybe they'd only given her a sedative.

Or they'd given her an anti-psychotic and her mind would clear *because* of it. She wasn't psychotic, but she had no other explanation for the behaviour that had led to her being brought here.

At the moment this was the least of her concerns.

The phone call from the killer suddenly blasted into her mind, explaining why she was lying here, incapacitated in the hospital while . . .

Dear God! He had Brad!

Her pulse raced. She had to get out into the hall, find a phone and call Allison. The killer had prohibited it, but that didn't matter any more. She had to tell Allison everything!

She forced her hand off her belly, where it rested, and clawed at the cover. Her muscles nearly didn't obey. The blanket slipped off her head, freeing her eyes to see the darkened hospital room.

But it wasn't a room. She blinked, fearful that she was hallucinating. Her drugged mind was telling her that she was inside a pick-up truck parked at a gas station, but she knew better. She was in the hospital, where she'd been drugged and admitted.

Unless that was the hallucination and this the reality.

Or unless she *had* been in the hospital but was now in a pick-up truck, staring out of a dirty side window at a row of Chevron pumps. She blinked again, but the image remained.

Paradise sat up and pulled the blue blanket down to her waist. She *was* in a pick-up truck, one with a centre console that divided her seat from the driver's. A can of Dr Pepper sat in one cup holder, a phone in the other. The phone the killer had left for her.

So then . . .

She snapped straight as a springboard, face throbbing with heat. This was his truck, she was in his truck. He'd somehow managed to get her, she didn't know how, but she was here at a gas station and she was in the killer's truck.

For a full ten seconds Paradise tried to think clearly enough to make a decision. She tried to move, to run, to scream, to hide, to do anything but sit here like a lump waiting for him to come back, because he was gone and she didn't know where and she had to do something, anything.

But she couldn't move.

Her muscles broke free of terror's grip all at once and she was clambering. She grabbed at the door handle, yanked it. Her hand slipped off and it banged loudly.

Locked.

She searched for the locking mechanism, but couldn't find one. She wasn't familiar with cars, but it didn't matter, because he wasn't stupid enough to leave her in an unlocked truck. But she had to get out!

A strange whimpering sound, like a kitten in trouble, broke the silence. She shut her mouth to still her cry and breathed through her nose in shallow, panicked draws of air as she twisted left and right, searching for something.

Anything!

Pale light washed over the interior, revealing clean, uncluttered surfaces. The dash was empty. The seats looked new. She jerked the glove compartment latch and the drawer flapped down. Inside she found a map, still folded neatly, a black comb and a packet of tissue paper. That was all.

It occurred to her then that she should kick at the window and break it out.

She slammed the glove compartment shut, pulled her legs up, leaned back against the centre console and kicked her bare feet into the window with all of her strength. They bounced off with a thud, and she did it again . . . and again.

Screaming this time.

She pressed her face against the window and was about to pound on it as hard as she could to draw attention from someone, anyone, when she saw him.

The man she'd seen upon touching the dead body, the same one she'd drawn for Brad, was at the corner of the convenience store, walking towards the front door in even strides, unconcerned. He was tall, dressed in grey slacks, dark hair. In his right hand he held a piece of wood with a key attached to it.

He was the only one in sight and theirs was the only vehicle as far as she could see.

Paradise pulled back and ducked, trembling. The only person's attention she would draw here would be his.

She waited a moment in her slouch, but he would return soon. She had to move now, get out now.

She peeked over the doorframe and saw that he was inside. On the window a sign read *Welcome to St Francis Gas and Go* in large red letters trimmed in black.

She was peering over the doorframe at the outside world, and it was as threatening as her worst fears had taught her.

She was crouched in a closet peeking through the cracks, and her father was out there, pointing a gun at his head, pacing around her dead mother.

She was hiding in her bathroom with the lights off at CWI, after clawing at the beast who had tried to rip her clothes off while holding her mouth with his large hand.

That psychologist who'd befriended her. Then tried to rape her. That man with a beard and large glasses whose breath smelled like mothballs. The memory presented itself to her like a déjà vu, fresh for the first time, yet she'd been there. It was a memory set free. She could remember it as if it had happened only . . .

Familiarity flashed, as if two live wires in her brain had brushed up against each other, and she gasped. Without the beard, without the glasses, this man was Quinton Gauld!

She threw herself into a crouch and whimpered. No, no, she couldn't do this! But she couldn't not do something! She couldn't let the memories incapacitate her as they always had, because this time her fear alone would result in her death, and in Brad's death.

But the memories flogged her. Darkness, closets, mothball breath, grunts, and big strong hands. And in this closet that smelled like mothballs was his phone that had only one number in it.

Paradise straightened and stared at the blue phone. She didn't know any phone numbers except her sister's, and the last time she'd called her sister she hadn't been home. But she had to try something, so she grabbed it. Turned it on. Pressed the illuminated numbers with a rattled finger.

Send.

It rang once. Twice.

'Come on, Angie, pick up, pick up, pick up!'

She spun to the side window. Quinton Gauld had finished his business inside and was walking towards the door.

A voice came over the phone's small speaker. Her sister's, asking the caller to leave a message.

Paradise began to hyperventilate. *411*, she thought. *I have to call 411.*

'The files,' Roudy announced, swishing into Temple's office in his pyjamas and slippers. 'I need to see them all.'

'Excuse me?'

They'd been in the office for half an hour, and Allison insisted they give Roudy his nose, let him sniff around. He'd been in and out of every office asking obtuse questions, giving strange advice. The staff watched him with lost and often amused expressions. All but Temple, who had no clue how to deal with a man of Roudy's temperament.

'You have your unsolved cases in the basement under lock and key, I presume?' Roudy asked, pacing.

'Yes, that's—'

'Then bring them to the conference room, lay them out in order, beginning with the oldest case and working up to the newest and I will make an attempt to solve all of them for you. You really should have brought these to my offices much sooner. It's hardly excusable.'

Temple glanced at Allison, who allowed herself a small grin despite the cloud of fear that had settled over her. The minutes had ticked by without any word on either Paradise or Brad.

Law enforcement was out in full force, and four other FBI field offices were helping sift through leads that had poured in since they'd gone public. It went on and on, but not one concrete lead led them closer to finding her Paradise.

This was her fault. She should have known that something was wrong with Quinton Gauld when he left. If only she'd been more sensitive, more in tune, listened more closely. He'd come and gone like any employee who came and went without any incident that might raise a brow. But shouldn't she have been able to look at a man who would do the things Quinton Gauld had done these past few weeks and know, just know, that there was something wrong with him?

Apparently not.

If that monster put one finger on Paradise, she personally would pull the trigger and send him to be with his god.

'We don't have all day,' Roudy was saying.

'I'm afraid you wouldn't have enough hours in your lifetime to work through all those files. Either way, you don't have the credentials—'

'Nonsense. Talk to your superiors. Have them shipped to my office.'

Temple's phone rang and he picked it up, saved from his own awkwardness.

'Temple.'

Roudy turned to Allison and spoke in a soft if urgent tone. 'You must speak to these people. Don't you just love this place? It's fantastic. Makes me consider moving my own office.'

Temple tensed and, with him, Allison. He grabbed a pencil. 'Put it through.'

Silence. Even Roudy remained frozen. Temple pressed the speakerphone button and the sound of fast breathing crackled over the speaker.

'This is special agent—'

'Hello?'

Allison's veins turned cold. It was a whisper, but she was certain . . .

'Hello?'

'Yes, ma'am, we're here, please identify—'

'Paradise?' Allison stepped forwards. 'Is that—'

She was interrupted by Paradise's terrified rambling. 'He's coming, he's coming now, walking towards the truck! You have to help me, Allison! He's got me.'

She was alive!

Temple sat and snatched up a pencil. 'Try to calm down. Can you tell us where you are? What kind of truck? What do you see outside?'

'Green . . .' came the panicked voice. 'He's coming, he's . . .' Her voice softened to a bare whisper. 'He's coming . . .'

Paradise was crouched, peering just over the doorframe as he approached. Her mind spun with a hundred options but none was much different from the other and they all ended badly.

The side windows were tinted, so he couldn't see in yet. But the front window was much clearer and he would cross the front of the truck to get in on the driver's side.

'Green,' she whispered into the phone. 'He's coming, he's . . .' She lowered her voice, swimming in fear. 'He's coming.'

'Tell us what you see, Paradise. We have to know where you are. Look outside.'

'St Francis Gas and Go,' she whispered. 'In a green pick-up truck that's clean inside. A gas station.' She didn't know what else to say. 'It's Quinton, Allison. It's him. He's here to kill me.'

Allison spoke with a tone that demanded calm and strength. 'Stay strong, Paradise. I'm not going to let him kill you. You hear me? I'm going to save you, Paradise. Just stay calm and do what you need to do.'

The killer was ten feet away. She couldn't let him know she had used the phone.

'Paradise? Paradise, are you there?'

She didn't have time to say more. She didn't dare. She had to do what she had to do.

She clicked the phone off, set it in the cup holder, pulled the blanket over her head, slouched back in the same position she'd woken in, and tried her very best not to tremble or breathe too hard.

Back in her closet. Back to safety. Back into the fog.

The driver's door opened. Then shut.

Quinton coughed. He pulled the blanket down off her head

and, evidently satisfied by her sleeping form, replaced it with a soft grunt.

'I'm sorry about this, Paradise,' he said, in a very normal voice. 'I really am.' The engine rumbled to life. 'And for the record, although you won't ever hear me admit this, I really did love you. I think I was a little mixed up back then. My father hurt me too.' A pause. 'Maybe I still am mixed up.' Another pause. 'You're every bit as beautiful as I remember. I can see why God loves you. I should probably just kill you now.'

And then he didn't say anything for a while.

CHAPTER THIRTY-SIX

The dirt road ran straight south, that much Brad Raines could tell by the position of the stars in the night sky. What he couldn't know was how far south the road went before meeting up with any sign of civilization.

He walked beside wheat fields as flat as a golden sea in eastern Colorado, or possibly as far east as Kansas. Twin ribbons of worn earth ran parallel under the moonlight, overgrown in patches. Tufts of grass grew calf-high down the centre. No sign of telephone or electric poles. The road offered private access to the fields and was likely used only by farm equipment and trucks. If he could find a driveway, he might follow it to a house, but in the hour he'd been walking, he'd seen only fields, access paths and the occasional wide sloping ditch.

His previous penance of slamming against the support beam became a desperate walk for hope, because he'd allowed himself that. It was a thin hope built on a weak trail of new leads that could now be followed; he'd rehearsed each over and over as he walked and sometimes jogged south.

What did he now know? The killer's name was Quinton Gauld. He had lured Paradise out of the CWI because she was his seventh victim. He drove a Chrysler M 300 as well as the truck that matched the tyre treads they'd found at other crime scenes. He was roughly six foot and wore grey slacks with a blue shirt. More importantly, he had once been a psychologist who'd worked with the CWI and, as such, would have left a rich history in the public records.

The killer had left a treasure trove of leads in the barn and was sure to retrieve them, either with Paradise or after he killed her.

Brad's task was plain. He had to make contact and bring the cavalry back to the barn without tipping off Quinton Gauld. And he had to hope that he could do so while Paradise was still alive.

His right side ached; the pain flared when the inside of his elbow brushed up against the angry wound on his ribcage. He'd tossed the heavy hammer long ago, now thinking it useless. The moon lit the road and the ditches fell away on either side towards the wheat fields, but nothing else. No mountains, no cars, no houses. Only the road, the fields and his feet slogging into the night as he marched south.

Regardless of her fate, he would live. With or without Paradise, he would live, and this single thought dominated his mind.

In the end it was all going to be pointless, wasn't it? All his slamming and this desperate march would amount to nothing. Quinton Gauld was too far ahead of them. They would eventually catch up with him, but by then she would be gone. Paradise would be dead.

Her suffering would be made complete. She would pay a price no human should have to pay. Brad would leave the FBI. This time . . .

He pulled up and squinted. The road ended in a T roughly fifty yards ahead. He caught his breath. He ran up to the intersection, searching for a sign of a house, electric lines, irrigation ditches, anything.

He stopped at the intersection and faced west, then east. As far as he could see by moonlight, the road continued in both directions exactly as it had behind him. He had to pick one, and there was no indication which would take him closer to civilization and which would take him further from it.

For a second he had to fight to push back a swelling fear. Rather than offer him any new hope, the intersection only threatened to smash the weak framework he'd been clinging to.

He faced west. At some point the plains would yield to the mountains west of here. Closer to home, closer to Quinton Gauld's familiar stomping grounds. But how far? Ten miles, a hundred miles? It was pointless!

He began to walk west, broke into a jog, and had covered no more than twenty feet when he saw light approaching from the horizon like a silent UFO breaking the natural plane.

He couldn't be sure the light was actually coming from a car or truck. It was a star on the horizon, a trick played by the eyes. But then the light parted and became two perfect spheres and Brad knew he was staring directly at the headlights of a fast-approaching vehicle. A truck.

His first instinct was to run, forwards, screaming for them to stop. But what if this was Quinton Gauld, returning?

With Paradise.

The thought hit him broadside like a boot to his head, and he dropped to a crouch. His throat was parched, his side flared with pain, his head throbbed, but now all he could think was, 'What do I do? What do I do?'

The sound of the vehicle's purring engine reached him; within seconds the truck's lights would reach out and reveal him in the middle of the road.

But, if this was Quinton and he did have Paradise . . .

Brad was out of time. Mindless of his wound, he lunged towards the ditch on his right, tripped over a tuft of grass and somehow managed to throw his arm out to break his headlong fall. He hit the slope and rolled onto his shoulder to protect his side, but the resulting stab of pain took his breath away.

Facing the stars at the bottom of the ditch, he struggled to get his lungs moving again. The truck's purr was accompanied by the soft roar of tyres rushing over the ground. The vehicle was almost on top of him. It could be a farmer, it could be the FBI, it could be a teenager and his girlfriend out for late-night fun, or it could be Quinton Gauld, with or without Paradise. Whatever the case, Brad decided upon the only course of action that made any sense to him at all.

He found his breath just as the truck slowed for the intersection. Its headlights reached into the night above him. Then it was beside him, gearing down, breaking. Which meant it was turning left.

North, back in the direction of the barn.

Wait, wait . . .

The lights grew bright above. He had to see who was in that truck, but if he rose too soon they might see him.

Wait . . . Not yet, not yet . . .

Brad rolled to his left and pressed his belly onto the slope with his arms cocked beside his chest so that he could push himself up quickly.

Wait . . .

He waited until the roar was nearly on top of him, pried his head up, saw that the truck was now ten feet away, and was prepared to leap to his feet when he caught a snapshot of the driver through the front window. No one in the passenger seat. Just that, one driver.

But that driver was unmistakably Quinton Gauld.

Brad dropped his head. Breathed hard into the dirt. Quinton was his only link to Paradise. Quinton was in the truck. Quinton was on the way to the barn. Paradise could be on the floorboards or in the truck bed.

He pushed himself to his feet the second the truck passed, scrambled up the slope into the road and ran towards the vehicle's red tail lights as it braked for the sharp turn.

He had to get into that truck bed. And he had to do it without being heard or seen.

Brad sprinted up to the rear bumper, crouching low so that his head would not show over the gate.

Quinton Gauld had spent the last two hours contemplating his success. His achievement was so lofty, so advanced, so perfectly executed, so angelic, that he wondered if Rain Man had been mistaken. Perhaps he really was an angel sent by the Most High to bring home the most beautiful bride humanity had produced after millions of years of evolution.

Paradise was unmatched in beauty and perfection, so wonderfully made, that he had never planned to leave her body for the authorities to discover, glued to the wall. He intended to take her dead body to Robert Earls, a taxidermist who lived like a hermit outside of Manitou Springs. Robert would be plied into preparing and stuffing her body before Quinton killed him. Quinton had wanted to mount her body on the wall above his mantel with one of two inscriptions. Either, *Here rests God's favourite Bride, Paradise,* or *Creation groaned for a million years and gave us her, God's Perfect Bride.*

Quinton slowed for the corner, turned the wheel to his left, and pulled out of the turn. The truck bumped over lumps of grass growing in the middle of the uneven road. Something thumped behind him and he glanced in the rear-view mirror, saw nothing. He would have to ditch the truck and the M 300 later tonight. He would then have to pack and move before sunrise.

Mounting Paradise above his mantel was no longer an option.

But it didn't matter. As much as he was tempted to think he was in the Most High's angelic service, he knew that Rain Man had been right. His head was buzzing and the buzzards were dropping demons and he was one of them. And now he resolved to accept himself without giving any further space to Rain Man and his demented thinking.

CHAPTER THIRTY-SEVEN

Brad lay perfectly still in the empty, ribbed truck bed, facing the sky, ready to throw himself over the edge the moment it stopped.

He'd managed to slip over the tailgate and duck low as the truck bounced over the corner. For ten minutes he'd thought through his options, wondering whether Paradise was with Quinton. But the back window was tinted and he couldn't see inside the cab.

So he lay still, dogged by insecurity and questions and pain from the wound.

He methodically rehearsed his course of action at the end of this road. His chances of incapacitating the killer were nearly nonexistent. But he would have an opportunity to slip out while the man was distracted by the scene in the barn.

And if Paradise was in the cab? Dear God, he hoped she was and that she was alive. As long as she was still alive and he was in the same vicinity, there was hope for her. How he could save her, he didn't know. He would have to deal with events as they played out.

A thousand thoughts strung through his mind as the truck rumbled north, back to the barn. Thinking more clearly, Brad estimated that Quinton had left him in the barn seven or eight hours earlier, give or take an hour. He would have needed time to take Paradise and switch vehicles. The round trip had likely taken him five or six hours.

He was in a green Chevy pick-up roughly three hours east of Denver. Not west, in the mountains, not south, in the dry country, but east. Near the Kansas border. How many large abandoned barns were there in this vicinity?

Quinton likely had the cell phone he'd used earlier. If Brad could get his hands on that phone, place a call to Temple and tell him to get every law-enforcement agency in the region to canvas farmers, cops, residents – anyone who knew the area – to identify all large barns in wheat fields two to three hours east of Denver, they might be able to find him.

No. Even then, it would be too late. His first order of business must be to ascertain if Paradise was alive and in the cab. His second, if she was, would be to get her out. If she wasn't, he would assume she was dead and kill the demon in his own barn.

It took fifteen minutes at a steady clip to reach the barn. Brad knew they were close when the truck made a turn into the driveway, and he would have rolled out then if not for the possibility that Paradise was in the cab. He was unwilling to squander a chance to act quickly for her sake.

So he lay still, against every impulse that demanded he roll out now, while he was still shrouded in darkness.

He'd left the barn door open, and Quinton drove the truck straight in. Yellow light flickered off the rafters from the still-flaming oil lamps. This was it. Quinton Gauld now knew that Brad had escaped. He was surely staring at the broken post already, even as he brought the truck to a stop.

Brad felt naked in the back of the truck, exposed and hopeless. The end would come now. He would rise with cramps, fall out of the bed and Quinton Gauld would shoot him before he could stand. He should have gotten out as they rolled down the driveway, made a run for it, returned in stealth.

But, no, he'd reasoned this through. Paradise was his first priority.

The truck lurched to a stop. For a count of ten, nothing.

The driver's door opened. The killer stepped out.

Rain Man had survived. The man had taken up superhuman power, survived the gunshot and snapped the post like a twig before fleeing. Quinton cursed himself for not having taken more certain measures.

He took the keys from the ignition but left the lights on to illuminate the scene. He stared at the broken post for a few seconds, flooded with respect and some concern. This was the first time he'd ever been bested by any adversary, and he wondered if it was because Rain Man's God was stronger than the devil.

A thousand crickets screamed in his head.

He silenced them and stepped out of the truck, bringing a calm reason to bear upon the situation. He surveyed the barn quickly. No sign of the man. No, of course not. Rain Man wouldn't just stand out in the open like an idiot.

But perhaps he was not superhuman, either. In all likelihood he had only recently escaped and then only after repeated bashing back into the post. He would be too exhausted from the effort to travel far, too smart to stumble out into fields to die. He was likely nearby, passed out in a ditch or crouching in fear.

Yes, Quinton preferred that scenario. The truth was, Quinton hadn't been bested by Agent Raines because the game was not yet finished. This was only one more test, an opportunity for him to demonstrate to all those looking on that their selection of him as their servant was a wise one indeed. He'd switched sides and now they wanted to know if he was up to the task.

He stepped in front of the truck's powerful beams and scanned the scene from right to left, methodically surveying everything, making calculations and decisions as his senses absorbed details.

The amount of blood on the ground told him Rain Man was seriously weakened. The post was also smeared with blood. A lesser man would be dead, he was sure of it. Unless he'd misjudged, and the dark stains on the dirt were from other bodily fluids as well as from blood. He could smell no urine, though, nothing but blood and sweat.

The medical bag had been moved, meaning Rain Man had taken what he needed to staunch his wound. He might be armed with either a knife, a scalpel or the hammer, all of which were missing from the table.

So then, Rain Man was a worthy adversary after all. This, the final hour, came down to the beast's attempts to consume the bride and the man on the white horse's attempt to rescue her.

But whose shadow was larger now? Cast by the truck's light, his loomed monstrous and dark on the far wall. His veins were full of blood, and he was at full strength. Furthermore, he had guns. He had his buzzing mind.

And he had Paradise.

Quinton knew then that Rain Man would be back.

Brad slipped out on the passenger side like an escapee going over a fence. He lowered himself silently to the ground, thankful that the barn had a dirt floor. The killer stood in front of the truck's large hood, obscured from view. He'd left the truck's lights on – if he turned back his eyesight would be blinded.

Brad crawled to the passenger's door, reached up and tried the handle. Locked. Okay. Okay, maybe that was better anyway.

He quickly backed away, remained crouched, rounded the back of the truck, then snuck up on the driver's side, blocked by the open door. The killer could not have suspected that Brad had come back in on the truck and was already moving.

Wasting no time, he hurried to the driver's door on the balls of his feet. Looked inside. There, with a light blue blanket covering all but the top of her head, and round eyes staring over the dash at the scene before her, slouched Paradise.

Alive.

Alive, awake and, by all appearances, unhurt. Relief and panic jolted Brad's heart. At any moment the killer could turn back.

And what if she yelped in surprise at seeing Brad?

He looked at the ignition. Quinton had removed the keys. Brad tapped on the seat. She spun her head, blinked and jerked with recognition. He frantically motioned silence. Reaching in, he slid a Dr Pepper can out of the cup holder and set it on the floor. The other cup holder was empty.

He eased the centre console up, turning the two divided seats into a bench seat for her to slide across, then motioned her to stay low.

Needing no further encouragement, eyes as round as the moon, she put her elbows on the seat and pulled herself towards him like an inch worm. The sound of her rapid breathing was loud, and all the while Brad could only think that at any moment they would be found out.

The killer still stood in front of the truck, surveying the scene like a good investigator. Rushing out to hunt for his escaped victim before fully reconstructing the scenario would be imprudent, and Quinton Gauld wasn't an imprudent man. But, if he looked back past the glare of headlights, he might see Brad's feet below the door.

Brad reached for Paradise when she was only halfway across the seat, hooked his hands in her armpits and dragged her slight frame out of the cab as if she were a doll. But her breath in his neck, and the warmth of her flesh against his arms – these weren't the makings of any doll.

He pulled her into himself gingerly, careful not to disturb the truck and even more careful not to hurt Paradise. He slid his right arm under her legs, cradled her against his chest, turned from the door and walked away as quickly and as quietly as he could.

She was shaking in his arms and he was afraid she might release a sob. So he cupped the back of her head and pushed it gently into his neck as he fled the barn.

He didn't allow himself to breathe until he was ten feet past the door. Then he could hold his lungs no longer and he veered to his left and sucked at the night air.

Paradise began to cry into his shoulder.

'Sh, sh, sh, not yet, not yet,' he whispered. 'Hold on . . .'

Upon discovering that they'd escaped, Quinton would likely assume they had run away from the barn and headed south to safety. Brad rounded the barn and ran in the opposite direction, north along its side, thinking he should set Paradise down and let her run beside him so they could move faster.

But he couldn't let go of her. Not now, not after he'd lost her once, not following the suffering he'd put her through, not out here where she was exposed and terrified. So he held her close and he ran.

He considered heading directly into a corn field thirty yards behind the back of the barn, but they couldn't do so without leaving tracks through the drying corn and, in this moon, their passage would be seen. Instead, he ran for a grove of large trees at the edge of the clearing. Reaching them, he spun behind the furthest tree, dropped heavily to his knees and set Paradise down like an invalid.

Her arms clung stubbornly to his neck. And now she sobbed in earnest.

'Shhhh . . . It's okay. We can't make any noise. Sh, sh, it's okay.'

'Thank you,' she whispered softly. She pressed her wet face against his cheek and kissed him. 'Thank you, thank you, thank you.'

The emotions of the night swelled in his chest and spilled over. He held her as if he were holding onto the last whisper of his own life and let tears fall.

Quinton saw the movement through a crack at the back of the barn, a fleeting form rushing past like a ghost in the night, and his first thought was that Rain Man had come back sooner than expected. A holy ghost. Or a fox. He was outside the barn at this very moment, running like a fox in search of the perfect angle of attack. His judgment was compromised by his affection for the favourite, and he was scurrying in a panic, trying to gain the advantage. But armed with only a hammer, the man was outclassed.

Small-minded and foolish, but admirable in the way an animal was admirable.

Quinton turned and hurried back to the truck to retrieve his gun case from under the seat and to check on God's bride, whom he'd left alone for too long. It occurred to him as he rounded the open truck door that he should have closed it. The sight of the broken post had caused a slight lapse in judgment.

He cleared the door and stopped.

The seat was empty. The favourite was gone.

Buzzards screamed through his mind.

He knew immediately what had happened.

He considered the possibility that Paradise had flown the coop on her own, but the holy ghost he'd seen was too tall to have belonged to the bride.

This turn of events would have caused any normal man to panic. But this too was a test. Quinton aimed to pass it with a calm that would impress even the vilest and most demanding master.

He retrieved the gun case, slipped out the nine-millimetre, chambered a round, and turned off the headlamps. It took great effort to control his anger, this despite his advanced sensibilities. But emotion only impeded good judgment, a fact that he'd proven twice already tonight, first when he'd left Rain Man in a rage after thinking he'd mortally wounded the man, and then again when he'd left the door open upon seeing the broken post.

He would not make the same mistake again.

Thinking clearly now, he walked to the door that led out the back of the barn. Rain Man had headed north, not south along the obvious route, which meant he was thinking clearly enough to do what he thought was unexpected.

But Quinton knew these grounds, having surveyed them during his selection process. If Rain Man was thinking clearly, he would avoid the corn fields, because this variety grew on small stalks planted closely – they would leave unavoidable tracks of their passing. Instead, he would make for the clump of trees at the edge of the clearing. Unarmed and encumbered by bride and wound, Rain Man would be easily caught and killed.

He crossed the clearing towards the trees without fear, gun by his side. The buzzing in his head impeded his hearing slightly, something that had undoubtedly allowed Rain Man to sneak away with the bride. But now he listened carefully past the persistent buzzing. Any attempt on their part to flee the trees would force them to crash through the fields.

He approached the trees, gun extended. The moonlight made the earth look grey, revealing a bed of foot-high grass scattered at the base of the trunks. They would have gone to the back of the grove. Quinton rounded the trees, peering through the trunks for sight of the holy ghost and his little angel.

The ground behind the largest was bare. He considered this for a moment, knowing that he had not been wrong, not again. He was too evolved for that. They had come this way, they had stopped here. In their condition they would have had to, if only to collect themselves.

He lowered his weapon, studied the corn behind the trees, and saw the broken stalks immediately. So, they had gone further in after resting here.

Now a dilemma presented itself to Quinton. He could chase them down and surely catch up with them. Kill the fox. Take the bride. Or he could let them come to him.

His mind sifted through the possibilities and, as he put himself in the mind of his adversary, he knew the course Rain Man would take. The man was a hunter. His mind was on the bride's safety, but as soon as he felt he'd secured that much, his mind would return to the adversary he'd pursued for such a long time.

Thinking clearly, Rain Man would realize that by morning Quinton would be long gone. His evidence cleaned up, his truck nowhere to be found. Surely the man must know that anyone as extraordinary and superhuman as Quinton wouldn't be found by registration and rental records. Rain Man would know that Quinton, having been so exposed, would vanish into thin air. Another state, another country, another world, another universe.

And, indeed, by first light Quinton would be gone. As far as the east was from the west.

Furthermore, his adversary would conclude that there was

no way to reach either a phone or a travelled road before sunrise. It was now, man on man, ghost on ghost, angel on demon. This was it, this was the end game.

For these reasons and for his newfound love for the bride, Rain Man would come back tonight in an attempt to put a final end to the demon that had entered his world.

And when he did, Quinton would be waiting for him.

CHAPTER THIRTY-EIGHT

They had remained under the tree for less than a minute before Brad knew their raw emotions would only betray them here, so close to the barn. Paradise could not stop crying and he could not stop trying to comfort her. Quinton was already on the hunt and they couldn't stay here in such a state of ruin.

He'd taken her by the hand and together they'd run into the field, careless for a few minutes, then with calculation when they came to the ditch that ran perpendicular to their flight. In this light the killer would not know if they'd turned right or left.

Brad took them left, single file down the centre of the ditch. A hundred yards, no further. From where they crouched they could just see their original point of entry. If Quinton followed them, the moon would reveal him on the bank without betraying their crouched forms in the ditch.

They would rest here until he decided what to do next. The sun would be up in a few hours, and they had to put some distance in before the light made tracking them an easy task. It might take hours for them to reach safety. In the meantime, the more distance between them, the better.

There was another alternative. He could hide Paradise and go on the offensive. Not even Quinton Gauld would expect such a brash move. In a matter of hours the killer would be gone, and the more Brad considered it, the more he was sure that Quinton would be gone for good. But he would never be gone, because in one week or one month or one year he would return for the one he had lost. For the last favourite.

For Paradise.

But, for the time being, they were safe.

Paradise clung to his arm, still trembling, staring back down the ditch.

'Are you okay?' he asked, smoothing her hair back. She looked different. Even by moonlight he could see the change in her. Her hair was still messy, but wavy and cut to cup her delicate features. She wore a red shirt and jean shorts.

She faced him, lips trembling. 'I'm scared.'

'I know you are. It's okay, I swear we're going to make it out of this.'

'You came back for me?'

He hesitated, then nodded.

Her tears glistened in the moonlight. 'I love you, Brad.'

It was a simple declaration of understanding, stripped of any social posturing, etiquette or purpose. And Brad's heart flooded with this same understanding.

'And I love you, Paradise.'

But her face twisted with anguish. 'I'm scared, Brad.'

'No, you don't need to be scared any more. I have you and I won't let you go.'

'But . . .' She could barely speak past her emotion.

'But what?'

'Is that okay?'

He was reminded then of her own horrors extending beyond this night. Her fear of memory and the outside world. Any human would crumble if taken by the likes of Quinton Gauld to be drained of blood and glued to a wall. But Paradise faced a thousand demons more.

And didn't they all, he thought. The struggle with inner demons was fierce and private and universal.

Brad extended his hand to her and Paradise was hardly capable of taking it. She couldn't accept love from a man like him. Not yet. She might try, but she faced a history that darkened the waters of love like brine. Like himself, but worse, so much worse. The truth of this covered him with shame for his self-absorption. To think that he'd felt sorry for himself for so long . . .

'Yes,' he said. 'Yes, it's okay.'

Then he leaned forwards and kissed her on her forehead. He wanted to kiss her lips. He wanted to hold her gently and swear his undying love for her. He wanted to take her from this place and never let her out of his sight.

But she was too delicate for any of that. Too precious. Too beautiful and rare and beyond his clumsy ways. She, not he, would dictate what she needed and when she needed it.

So he just touched his lips to her forehead, let them linger for a moment, then pulled back and said, 'You are very special, Paradise. And I love you, the way a man loves a woman.'

Paradise heard the words and she believed them. For the first time in her life she really did believe that a man loved her, not the *idea* of her or the image of what she could be, but her, Paradise, the woman crying in the ditch and battling an inner demon that had made loving any man impossible.

I'm a woman, she thought. *I'm a woman and Brad loves me.*

It was such a startling revelation that for a moment she forgot to breathe.

His hand touched her cheek. Maybe he would kiss her the way a man kisses a woman? She was far too nervous for that, but secretly, so secret that she wouldn't admit it even to herself, she begged him to kiss her on the lips.

But no, a prince would wait to be invited by the princess. And Paradise didn't know how to be a princess.

'Are you okay?' he asked again, cocking his head to look in her eyes.

She didn't know what to say.

'You're safe, Paradise. I swear, as long as I live, I won't let anyone lay a hand on you ever again,' she heard him saying.

But you can't save me from myself, she thought. *My problem is me.*

She looked down the ditch again. No sign of Quinton. Her mind went back to the confession he'd made in the truck, thinking that she was passed out.

My father hurt me too.

The comment had run through her mind like a merry-go-round. Quinton, the man she now clearly remembered from her early days at the Center, was just like her, at least in some ways. They were cut from the same cloth. He'd been born into an abusive family.

Maybe I still am mixed up.

The longer they had driven, the more she fantasized about ending all of this by sitting up and giving Quinton a hug. Absurd, of course. A product of her own intense fear and a profound desire to survive him by making him her friend.

But the notion refused to leave her.

My father hurt me too.

She tried to imagine the ways in which a younger boy named Quinton might have been hurt. It was no wonder he'd studied to be a psychologist. Like it was no wonder Brad had joined the FBI because of his own pain.

If Quinton could see and confess that he was mixed up, couldn't he see the light?

'If he faces the truth, he might change,' she said aloud.

'What do you mean?'

Paradise faced him. 'In the truck, he told me his father had hurt him. That he was mixed up. I was thinking . . .' She looked back down the ditch. 'Has anyone ever shown him love?'

'I know the kind of love he needs,' Brad said. 'It's administered in a chair that's plugged into a very powerful generator.'

She hardly heard him. 'He's like me,' she said. Truth began to fall in place. Not just about Quinton, but about her. 'Sometimes we have to face our demons.'

'And sometimes we have to kill our demons.'

'He's psychotic,' she said. 'I think I might be psychotic too.'

'He's a psychopathic killer. He isn't Roudy or Casanova, and he isn't anything remotely like you.' An edge had entered his voice. He seemed deeply bothered by her logic.

But there was something else whispering through her mind. This crisis wasn't just about a psychopathic killer named Quinton Gauld or a schizophrenic girl named Paradise. This was about a man named Brad Raines and about the fact that he loved a woman who couldn't be a woman because she lived in fear of herself.

It was suddenly clear to her. Like a sunrise in her mind. She was able to remember details she'd never remembered because she was facing her past. She was even okay out here in the ditch with Brad, far from the safety of CWI.

But until she confronted the abuse that had crushed her head seven years ago, she could never be free to accept love or to love in return. And there was nothing in this world that Paradise wanted more than to love and be loved.

'I have to go back,' she said, dazed by her self-revelation.

'What?' He was appalled. 'Absolutely not.' Angry even.

Paradise eased her arm away from him. 'Don't you see? I have to go back for my own sake. I have to confront and forgive—'

'No!' He gripped his right side in a way that made her wonder if he'd been hurt. 'There's no way I'm going to allow you to go back there. You're wrong about this, he's a monster.'

But Brad didn't know how Paradise worked. She felt a strange resolve. This ditch was just another crack in the surface of her mind that would lead to another and another until the whole world was full of cracks. To reach the barn was to reach freedom.

'It's not your choice,' she said. 'If you . . .' She stopped, but then finished anyway. 'You should allow me to do what I know is best for me.' He started to open his mouth, but then shut it.

'I'm sorry. I didn't mean it like that. But I have to live with me,' she said, standing.

Brad grabbed her hand, on one knee, trying to hold her back. 'Please, Paradise. You're not thinking! He's a ruthless killer. He abducts women like you and drills holes in their feet and bleeds them dry! Please, get down.'

'You're right, he's all those things,' she said. 'And I know it makes no sense to you, but you're going to find that lots of things in my world won't make immediate sense to you. I've lived with the fear of this monster for seven years and it's debilitated me.

Now I'm out and I'm staring the monster in the face and I have to kill him.'

'Kill him? With what?'

'With what I do and say. With me.'

He looked over her shoulder at the point where Quinton would appear if he followed their tracks. 'Sit down. Please just sit down and listen to me for a second, Paradise.'

She squatted in the ditch.

'Okay, look, you've been through hell. Your mind isn't seeing the picture—'

'My mind has never seen the picture clearer,' she said. Her tone was stiff, but his concern for her was making her feel weak in the knees. So she said something about it. 'What you don't realize, Brad, is that the more heroic you are, the more I have to go. You're only making my case.'

What she said was true: Quinton was a monster. But so was *she*. And as she saw it now, clear-headed or not, the only way to defeat one monster was to defeat the other. She stood again, desperate and hopeless at once.

'That's it, isn't it?' Brad said. 'You feel you have to go in there to somehow prove your worth to me?'

Tears flooded her eyes and she looked away. He was only making things worse by being even more understanding. Didn't he see that?

'Stop it,' she said.

'Stop what? Saying the truth?'

'Trying to save me. You've saved me enough.' She took a deep breath and wiped the tears from under her eyes. 'I have to do this, Brad. It's for him, but it's for my sake. You understand?'

'No, I don't understand. I really don't understand. You don't have to overcome the monster in you for me to see your beauty.'

He couldn't really mean that. No man could really feel that way about her.

'Listen to us!' he whispered. 'We've both just escaped this freak and we're a few hundred yards from his barn arguing about whether you should go back. This is crazy.'

'Yes, I am.'

They remained silent. He was right, of course. Going back was crazy. But then so was she, and she knew somehow, some way, this would end in the barn tonight. A fresh batch of tears flooded her eyes. She couldn't even stand next to him without falling apart.

Where was she? What was she doing out here? A sudden darkness crept over her horizon and she felt the familiar tendrils of fog curling into her mind. She couldn't do this! She had to get back to the Center!

The world was closing in on her and it took all of her strength to stand still. Brad was right: everything she'd said was hogwash! Even now, she was only saying things that proved she wasn't sane, that she wasn't worth anything out here, that she could never, never be loved that way.

Brad's arm slowly settled on her shoulder. He pulled her close and she put her forehead against his chest, trying hard not to fall apart. But it was almost impossible.

He kissed the top of her head. 'I can't lose you, Paradise. You have to understand that. I just can't lose you again. We can find another way for you to face and defeat your fears tomorrow when this is all over, but I just can't bear the thought of letting you go back to that barn.'

She lost it.

She threw her arms around his stomach and she held him as tight as she dared and she wept long bitter tears into his shirt. She knew she didn't deserve this kind of love, but it felt like heaven to her. She would repeat everything that had happened to her over the past seven years for this feeling. To be loved, even for one minute, the way she imagined that Brad was loving her now.

The way she *knew* he was loving her now.

She couldn't tell him this because a knot had stopped her throat and she couldn't speak. She could only sob as he stroked her hair and kissed the top of her head.

If God was love, as they said, she never could have guessed

that she would find God in the bottom of a ditch three hundred yards from the man who'd tried to rape her seven years ago.

The night seemed to end, or at least to stall. She rested in his arms for a long time and she didn't ever want to let go.

But then it occurred to her that he had gone very still. And his breathing seemed heavier. She calmed herself.

'There is one thing, though,' Brad said. She looked up and saw his steeled stare back in the direction of the barn. 'This has to end tonight.'

Now it was her turn to ask. 'What do you mean?'

But there was no mistaking the look of rage and resolve on his face, the flexing of his jaw, his glare in the moonlight, his flat lips. They sent a shiver down her spine.

Brad kissed her forehead again, then gently took her face in his hands and looked into her eyes. 'Listen to me, Paradise. I know this isn't going to make a lot of sense to you, but I want you to do something for me.'

'What?'

'I need you to wait here for me. Wait fifteen minutes, and if I'm not back, I want you to run west, down this ditch, as fast and as far as you can. They'll see you from the air, he won't—'

'No!' she cried, pulling back in disbelief. The thought of his leaving her was like a mule kick to her head. 'No, I can't.'

'Shhhh, now listen. Yes you can. He won't catch you.'

'You can't leave me!'

He paused. 'I know I can't. And I won't. I won't because I'm going to go back and put an end to this tonight.'

'You can't leave me!' she said again. 'Not now. You've just found me, you've just said you love me, you've just . . .' The words came out in a rush, but all the while her mind was saying, *He must, he loves you, he has to go back and kill the monster, he has to because he loves you . . .*

'You can't leave me . . .'

And you have to let him go.

He stared at her. 'He's going to get away if I don't, Paradise. He'll disappear and then come back for you, and I can't allow that. He's obsessed with you. He won't stop until he kills you. You understand? I can't let you live with that threat over you. I have to end this tonight.'

You have to let him go because you love him and you have to trust him to be who he is for you . . .

She threw her arms around him to keep him from going and trembled with fear, knowing he must. How many times had she longed to be rescued, written about the man on the white horse sweeping in to save the maiden . . . But now she had found the man on the white horse and she dreaded the thought of losing him.

'Paradise . . .' He kissed her head again, then gently pried her arms away. 'Paradise, please.' He kissed her face, her lips, just lightly. 'Please, I love you. I'll be back. He isn't expecting me, right? No one in their right mind would go back, he knows that.'

She just looked up at him, letting his stumbled words fall away because, in truth, he was right: neither of them was in their right mind, not her for wanting to go earlier, not him for going now. They were thinking with their hearts, and she would trade nothing for it.

'I didn't mean it that way,' he said.

Paradise stretched up and kissed him on his lips. It was the first time she'd ever kissed a man. His lips were warm and soft. And she wanted to cling to him and cry and kiss him again.

Instead she put on her bravest face and looked up into his eyes. 'Come back quickly,' she said.

He nodded once.

'I will.'

CHAPTER THIRTY-NINE

Brad cut down the ditch, past the point they'd exited the field, pulled up twenty yards further, and listened. Crickets chirped in the grove of trees to the south. A light breeze rustled through the fields, like blowing sand on this endless shore of corn gilded by a round white moon.

He looked back up the ditch. If he used his imagination, he could make out the form of a woman huddled up against the ditch slope in the far distance. A precious woman named Paradise who deserved and now had his complete devotion.

But, without his imagination, he couldn't see her, and the thought of never again seeing her terrified him.

Leaving her there to suffer yet another abandonment had wrenched his heart. But he knew that he might never have another opportunity to save, really save, Paradise. As long as Quinton Gauld was at large, Paradise's life was in mortal danger.

He faced south, into the corn field. There was only one way to maintain the upper hand. He had to go in silently, quickly, and with a ruthlessness that once belonged only to those he'd hunted. For all he knew, Quinton Gauld had already fled. But assuming the man was either mounting an effort to sweep the fields or still cleaning up, Brad had to move and move now.

He stepped into the field and snaked between the stalks as carefully as he could. At this pace, the sound of his brushing against the closely planted stalks could be noticed, but not easily distinguished from the slight swaying caused by the breeze. Either way, he had little choice. The corn field had to be crossed.

His plan was a simple one. Without a weapon, he didn't stand a chance in any kind of confrontation. But there was another way. A way that would require him to gain entry to the barn without being seen. But if he could just get in, he could finish this tonight.

Heart pounding like a large rabbit's thumpers, he snaked forwards. Quickly, low, breathing as quietly as possible. He stopped ten feet from the end of the field and listened for any unusual sound.

None. What he would give for his gun now. Even the hammer. He could have grabbed something on his way out of the barn, a rake, a stick, a metal rod, a rope, a brick, anything, but he'd neither seen nor considered taking anything. And why should he have? Only a person who'd lost his mind would come back.

Brad slipped up to the edge of the field and peered out from the stalks. Orange light still flickered in twin upper windows and from a dozen vertical cracks along the wall. Quinton was still here.

The fissures between the old shrivelled boards were large enough to give an attentive person on the inside a view of someone on the outside. He would have to keep that in mind. Now that he thought about it, there was the possibility that Quinton had seen them as they made their escape, illuminated by the strong truck lights shining through the cracks. But he hadn't pursued them. Either way, it no longer mattered.

There were fewer cracks on the right side of the barn. Brad crouched low, stepped from the corn field and ran across the clearing towards the barn's far corner.

The barn was nicely lit by the moon, and from Quinton's exterior perspective fifty metres from the southwest corner, he had a perfect view of three quarters of the building rising like a tomb against the starry sky. He sat with his legs crossed in a yoga position, palms up, thumb and forefinger circular to help him concentrate.

He blended into the wheat field that rose behind him just above his head. Rain Man's flight into the field had taken them to the northwest; assuming he returned, he would probably come from the same direction. Even if he changed his angle of approach considerably, Quinton would see him coming.

Fully expecting Quinton to be inside the barn cleaning up like a madman, the fox would peer through one of the cracks and be unnerved by the fact that his prey was not in sight. The fox would then circle the barn stealthily, trying to pinpoint Quinton's whereabouts before he rushed in for the kill – assuming Rain Man was as smart as Quinton thought he was.

If Rain Man did not return, Quinton would clean up and leave in the next hour, long before the sun rose. And he would return later to finish what he'd started. He was a patient man. He'd waited seven years already; another few months would not be a problem.

All was in order. Quinton would not disappoint those peering eyes in the night again. Particularly not now that he finally understood his true purpose.

The only thing slightly off was the sound. The buzzing in his brain had become a grinding. It was so loud now that he could hardly distinguish it from the crickets. Not that his hearing mattered at this point. He would rely on his eyesight and superior intelligence, having set hearing and emotion aside for the moment.

His mind was bright enough to illuminate the world.

His hatred, on the other hand, was so dark that he had begun to relish the thought of killing Paradise for the smell and taste of the blood alone.

His advantage wasn't limited to these strengths. His buzzing intelligence had also shown him precisely how, armed with nothing but sticks and stones, the fox intended to kill him.

Rain Man would try to burn the barn down with him and his truck in it. And for that he would need only a well-thrown stick or rock. Like David slaying Goliath.

This was why Quinton waited where he did, safely on the outside, ready to move when the time came. Leaving the truck parked in the barn presented a risk, but he couldn't remove it without tipping his hand. Either way, sitting in the yoga position against the wheat field put Quinton in the perfect position.

The corn field on the opposite side of the clearing suddenly parted and Rain Man darted out, crouched low, offering a low profile to any bullet.

Quinton was on his feet already. The fox was there, scurrying.

But the Hound of Hell was ready and his fangs were already barred.

Brad came to a gliding halt against the corner of the barn and pressed his back against the boards, breathing through his nose. He'd stuffed five rocks into his pockets from the ditch, two in his right, three in his left, but he would use them only if he couldn't find something large with which to smash the lamps.

Once broken, the kerosene would spray over the hay-strewn ground and the bales nearby, and in a matter of two or three seconds, a blaze too large to contain would be raging.

Next would be the truck. He'd considered a dozen possible scenarios that might allow him to disable the vehicle, but they all required him to gain an advantage once the chaos ensued. It would take surprisingly few hay bales to stop the truck long enough to smash a second lamp over its hood or bludgeon its radiator with Quinton's small sledgehammer.

Brad didn't necessarily need to kill the man here. A burning barn would make a signal fire visible for miles, and the road out of this place took a considerable amount of time to navigate.

They were all long odds, but allowing a sociopathic monster of Quinton Gauld's intelligence to escape offered even longer odds for Paradise's survival.

The night was quiet. He eased to his right and peered through a half-inch crack. The truck's green paint looked dark by the flame's light. Both lamps sat on wooden barrels on either side of the makeshift wall, untouched. Hay bales rested everywhere. But Brad's view of the table was blocked by the bales.

No sign of the man. He had to determine the killer's location, track him, wait for the right opportunity, create his distraction at the back, then run around to the front and enter the barn with the truck between him and Quinton, who would have been drawn to the rear by the distraction.

Then and only then would he go after the nearest lamp, and then the truck.

But there was no sign of Quinton. From this angle he could only see part of the barn, the bed of the truck, the blankets, but little else. The man could be anywhere.

Thinking about it now, Brad feared something would go terribly wrong. Quinton Gauld wasn't the kind of man who made many mistakes, and having made one or two that allowed Brad and Paradise to escape, he would be prepared.

Breathing deep to calm himself, Brad slipped along the wall, keeping low. He had to get to the far side to get a clear view of the table. As soon as he could track the man, a simple bang on the wall would draw his attention while Brad hurried around to the main entrance.

The details drummed through his mind as he rehearsed the unknown, ears tingling with tension.

The rear door was cracked open. He stopped and considered this. But it made sense – Quinton would have searched at least the perimeter before retreating, perhaps through this door. That was fifteen or twenty minutes ago. So what had he been doing since? Why all so quiet?

Brad moved forwards on the balls of his feet. He had to make visual contact. He had to locate the man first.

A three-inch gap separated the door from the old rotting frame, filled now with orange light, like a monster's eye just barely open while it slept. Brad reached it, thought about looking inside, but decided that the door's slightest movement might betray him.

Just beyond the door, there was a gap between two boards, he would . . .

The blow on the back of his head came out of nowhere, like a giant cobra strike on his skull. Pain raged down his spine. He knew then, as he collapsed to the ground, why he hadn't seen Quinton on the inside of the barn.

The killer was out here with him.

CHAPTER FORTY

It was fascinating and immensely satisfying, and now Quinton knew why his subconscious had allowed him to make the small mistakes that had allowed Rain Man his short-lived freedom. Having faced defeat and overcome it by recapturing the fox, he was now able to relish the man's demise with unsurpassed satisfaction.

This is what Quinton Gauld told himself as he gazed at the scene he'd reconstructed. There sat Brad Raines, the man who would steal his bride, tied to the same post he'd escaped from, albeit only the stub.

Quinton had snuck up behind the man with supreme confidence, gun aimed at the back of his head, just in case he turned, in which case Quinton would have shot him before hauling him inside. As it turned out, the man's pounding heart had likely prevented him from hearing the footfall of Quinton's feather-light feet on the soft ground.

One blow to the back of his head had incapacitated the man, and Quinton had dragged him through the door and secured him to the post. Blood trailed down the man's neck from the fresh cut on his scalp. And he was now finally waking to play his role. The scene was intoxicating. Beautiful.

This is what Quinton told himself, but the buzzing in his brain kept him from truly relishing his victory in the way he was meant to.

He paced around Rain Man, absorbing his suffering, curious as to why this man would risk so much for a woman whom society had sequestered away in an institution.

He looked down at the slumped form laying on his side. 'Please sit up.' He nudged the man with his foot. 'Up, up, we don't have all night. It takes more time than you realize to drill and drain a human body.'

Rain Man groaned. Because his hands were tied behind his back, he struggled to get his legs under his body and sit. The man mumbled a curse.

'Please, we're beyond that, aren't we? Hmm? Cursing, shouting, spitting, pulling against the ropes – all behaviour that only under- mines people like you and I.'

Rain Man stared up at him with dark eyes, as if he was trying to explode Quinton's head with this bitter stare.

'And stop looking at me as if I'm some kind of monster. True, I am a monster, but then neither cursing, shouting, spitting, strug- gling against the ropes, nor harsh stares will help you any more than they helped Nikki. So let's be civilized for a moment, shall we?'

The man's glare did not soften. 'What kind of men are we, Quinton?'

'Real men. Stripped of the façade social conditioning paints on the masses. We see the truth, you and I. I am the hound from hell and you are the crafty fox out to steal my prize. We both recognize beauty and we are both in love with Paradise.'

'But that's wrong, isn't it? I love Paradise. You hate her. Remember?'

'Well then, I love to hate her. Either way, we both know how to love.' He frowned at his begging carcass of an adversary. 'This is the part where you begin to utter bitter protests, attempting to set me straight. One or two would be okay – get them out of your system.'

The man didn't comply, but then Quinton didn't expect that he would. Rain Man's resolve began to melt from his face, replaced by a sagging look of defeat. It was a bit pathetic, really. Watching such a worthy mind reduced to this defeated slab of flesh . . . Quinton had to hold back a sudden urge to kick him in the jaw. *Wake up, wake up, you holy ghost! Don't let me walk all over you like this!*

'You look pathetic,' he said.

A tear broke from Rain Man's right eye. His weakness was intolerable! Quinton considered changing his plan on the spot. He should put this shallow shell of a ghost out of his misery with a single blow to his head. Seeing a weak man beg for his life was expected and therefore acceptable. Seeing a frail woman cry for mercy was satisfying, because she was only playing a role that reflected the greater weakness of the world.

But watching this fox of a ghost crumble was beyond the pale. Like the boy whom he'd slapped in Elway's eating establishment, Brad Raines needed a good blow to his head.

'Disgusting,' Quinton said.

'You'll never catch her,' Rain Man said. His tone was strong and laced with conviction.

It occurred to Quinton then that the fox wasn't crying for himself. His tears were for Paradise. This wasn't a picture of a shrivelling mouse accepting his defeat. It was, in fact, the very opposite.

Rain Man was, uncaring of his own life, crushed by the prospect of harm to the one he loved. His tears were for Paradise, not for himself. This was not cowardice but nobility.

Quinton was so upset by the realization that for a few moments he couldn't speak. But even in such a frayed state he had to ask himself why. And even as he asked himself why, his buzzing intelligence gave him the answer.

He was jealous of Rain Man.

Insanely jealous. He was, in fact, as jealous of Rain Man's love and nobility as he was of the beauty in Paradise, God's favourite.

It occurred to him that his hands were shaking badly. He looked down at them, mesmerized. This, then, was his greatest test. Not abducting seven brides, not draining their blood to present them unblemished, not realizing his true purpose, not manipulating Rain Man for his purpose, not even luring Paradise in with Rain Man's screams of pain.

His greatest challenge was to be who he was. To be what society wanted but didn't have the guts to be. To resist the respect and honour that tempted him at this very moment and to embrace the evil that haunted him.

'I find you disgusting,' he said, and he walked to the table, picked up the yellow battery-operated drill, and squeezed the trigger.

The strong Black and Decker electric motor whirred smoothly, filling him with calm. He'd adjust the tension on the clutch so that it would cut cleanly through bone without binding.

There was something about bones, something most people found deeply disturbing about the prospect of reaching through the skin of the human body and tinkering with the inner, hidden self. No one wanted their veneer penetrated. By drilling, Quinton accomplished two important tasks at once.

First, he made a small opening through the heel that allowed gravity to efficiently drain the body's blood supply. But second, drilling penetrated the façade and exposed the true bone of the bride. Or, in this case, the man.

Satisfied that the drill was fully operational, he lowered it to his side and walked over to Rain Man, who watched him with a surprisingly neutral stare. Was there no end to the man's valour? He could see that it might take more than one or two holes to make the man scream.

'Now listen to me,' Quinton said. 'This isn't necessarily personal . . .'

'Yes it is.'

A beat. 'Okay, so it is somewhat personal. The point is, I need you to scream. Your life doesn't mean much to me. But I need the little bride to come, you understand? I think she might be stupid enough to have fallen for you now that you've rescued her. So I need you to scream and scream like a little boy who's having his teeth drilled without a drop of Novocain.'

Rain Man seemed unruffled. 'You can't catch her. She's gone. I can scream till you beg me to stop. But you won't draw Paradise in.'

'Really?' Quinton pressed the trigger briefly and the drill whined. 'You seem to think you know her quite well.'

Rain Man was still unimpressed. 'Even if she were close enough to hear my screams, she knows there's no way she can stop you. She can't burn the barn down, she can't shoot you, she can't jump in the truck and drive off – she's powerless. She knew that before agreeing to run. You can kill me, but you will never touch Paradise.'

'Is that so? And what's to stop me from tracking her down next week?'

'I'm not that stupid. You'll never find her where she's going. As far as you're concerned, Paradise no longer exists. She'll be in a vault so far from you that no attempt on your part will turn up a single lead.'

The sincerity in his tone unnerved Quinton.

'You know, for a while there I was bothered by your character. But now you've turned into a bad liar, and it's making me feel better about my decision to kill you. I hate pretenders.'

'Shut up and drill me, Quinton. I'll scream my head off and it won't help you.'

Could the holy fox have out-foxed him yet again? Why was he inviting pain? Perhaps he really had lost his mind? Quinton's nerves were uncharacteristically taut. He was deeply bothered.

So he leaned over, squeezed the drill's trigger and pressed the quarter-inch diamond-tipped bit against the flat of the man's shin. The motor screamed high, then ground slower as it caught.

He straightened and examined his work. The man was looking up at him, face white, lips trembling, leg bleeding. But he did not scream or even moan.

'No scream?'

He had to be careful or Rain Man would pass out.

'Scream, Rain Man. Scream until you make me want to plug my ears.'

Nothing.

'No? Because you lied to me, Rain Man. You won't scream because she can hear, and you're afraid that, if she hears you scream, she'll come. Because that's what beautiful people do, Rain

Man – we both know that. They come running to save the poor saps in trouble.'

Nothing from him. With each passing moment Quinton respected, hated, loved and loathed the man more.

'I'm going to drill you full of holes and, if you don't scream, then I'm going to scream, and she'll come running, and, when she does, I'm going to drill her too.'

The man's eyes darted over his shoulder, then widened.

'Hello, Quinton.'

Except for over the phone, it was the first time he'd heard her voice in seven years, and the sound of those sweet, tender vocal cords pierced him in a way no sound this side of heaven or hell ever could.

He turned slowly towards the main door. There, dressed in her red blouse and cut-off jean shorts, stood Paradise. Her arms hung by her sides and her unblinking gaze held him.

This was also the first time Quinton had looked into her eyes since that night so long ago. Those devastatingly beautiful eyes.

'Hello, Paradise,' he said.

CHAPTER FORTY-ONE

Brad sat in defeat, begging God for one last mercy. *Please, please don't let her come. Send her far away. Don't let her hear.*

He watched the Bride Collector hovering over him with his drill, heard his threats, but his mind was on his prayer of desperation to God in heaven, if he was indeed listening – and Brad had to believe now that he was.

Protect her, I beg you. She's innocent, she's naïve, she will run here for love, but don't let my love draw her. Not now, please, not now.

Then Quinton bent over and pressed the drill into his shin and the pain was so vicious that Brad's whole leg began to shake violently. His stomach rolled and his vision blurred, but he could not allow the scream tearing at his throat a moment's breath.

Quinton stood. He was talking, but Brad didn't hear him. His mind was begging all the more earnestly. *Please, please save her. Save her, please. She's your child. Save her . . .*

Movement from the corner of his left eye stopped him, and he looked and he saw what he had begged not to see. She stood in the wide barn doorway, like an angel of mercy.

Brad could not breathe.

'Hello, Quinton.'

Quinton started. Then slowly turned. For a moment they stared at each other and Brad could only imagine what vile thoughts were running through the mind of this psychopath.

'Hello, Paradise.'

Brad wanted to scream out to her. *Run, Paradise! Run away! He's a monster and he's going to hurt you. You're too naïve! Run!*

A moan broke from his mouth, nothing more. He struggled

to keep from passing out. It couldn't end this way! She had to run.

Paradise just stood there, staring at the killer. And Quinton stared back.

Brad found his voice, breathy and stretched with fear. 'Run . . .' Then again, in a cry. 'Run, Paradise, run!'

'No, Brad. Not this time.'

Her voice was so light, so sweet, so innocent. And it sent a shaft of searing anguish through his chest. She was going to die on account of him! And she was too stubborn to see it.

Quinton walked over to the table, set down the drill and picked up his pistol.

Paradise looked at Brad, cheeks wet with trails of tears. But she didn't flinch.

He leaned against his ropes, frantic for her to run. 'Please, Paradise, you can't do this . . .' But she wasn't listening. 'Please . . .'

Her head turned back to Quinton, who stood in the middle of the quilted stage in front of the wall on which he intended to drain Paradise.

Brad started to speak again, but couldn't. His words were only noise in his mind. A great lament rolled through him.

Forgive me, Paradise! I'm sorry that I let you love me. I'm sorry that your tormented life has led you here to me, to the first man who showed you any love. You don't have to give your life for me! It doesn't work that way! Those are foolish ideas in stories. I'm not worth it, I'm a wretch. I'm sorry. I'm so sorry, Paradise!

Twenty feet down the middle of the barn separated them now. Quinton seemed caught in some kind of trance, as if, in facing the culmination of his plans, he could not find the words to express the import of the moment. He stood with his gun at his side, watching her. No wise words, no gloating, no expression of hatred, no cursing, not even a twitch on his face or a tremble in his hand.

He just stared at her, dumb.

Perhaps he couldn't believe that she really was stupid enough to come back, knowing what faced her. Yes. Yes, that had to be it. Both he and Quinton saw the same thing. Only someone so raw, so idealistic could have stepped willingly into harm's way with no hope for survival.

'You're wondering why I would come back,' she said.

She stepped forwards cautiously and stopped ten feet from him. Her face showed no expression, but new tears broke from her eyes.

'It makes no sense to you,' she said. 'Does it?'

He answered after a moment. 'You're innocent and foolish,' he said. 'That's what makes you so beautiful. That is why I have to kill you.'

'Then you'll be killing the one thing you want.'

They watched each other.

'I've been thinking about it, Quinton. That's why you came to me that night seven years ago. You wanted the innocence and beauty that you saw in me.'

'You can't manipulate me with your words. You're the most beautiful woman in the world, and I have been sent to kill you.'

'Because you can't possess me?' Her voice quivered.

'Because you're God's favourite and no one can have you.'

'The truth is, you're afraid of me, Quinton. I terrify you.'

'I can break you like any doll.'

But she was undeterred. 'I terrify you because you're afraid that you can never be beautiful like me. You're like a jealous boy, and now you're throwing a fit.'

Brad stared, caught off guard by the exchange between them. This was the Paradise who had first drawn him with her simple insight and logic, seeing and speaking about what only she could see outside the window. The naïve girl who could see ghosts when others could not.

'You were mixed up then and you're still mixed up now,' she said. 'You are a lost, lonely boy who was hurt by his father. Just like I was.'

Her words came to him and, in an instant, the buzzing stopped. The world went silent, as if someone had pulled the plug.

She knew this? It was a guess, of course – anyone could guess that someone had been abused as a boy, hadn't half the world? But her tone didn't hold even a hint of question. Her eyes were reaching past him, into the place of secrets. This was hallowed ground, a place so deep and holy that he himself was only rarely allowed to step into it.

And yet she was walking in, trampling his soul underfoot. Quinton felt suddenly and forcefully violated.

The silence between them stretched, and he searched for the buzzing, the voices, the calm, the intelligence that had made him so powerful and such a worthy servant. He hated her for stripping them away.

And then the buzzing was back, screaming in his mind like a swarm of angry hornets. His whole body tensed and his fingers clamped down on the gun by his side.

He'd removed the silencer when he'd replaced the weapon in the case. The discharge thundered through the barn as the gun bucked in his hand and sent a bullet into the ground by his feet.

Paradise did not flinch.

'Your father hurt you just like my father hurt me. That's what first drew you to me,' she said.

'No.'

'I didn't have a father to tell me that I was one of God's favourites,' she said.

He saw something so unnerving that he would have lifted the gun and shot her in her forehead if not for the fact that he had planned for so long to drill her. There was empathy in her eyes.

'But that's one thing you're right about, Quinton. I am one of God's favourites.'

'Please, be quiet.'

'My father never told me who I was, just like your father never told you who you were.'

Why didn't he move? Why didn't he just shoot her? Why didn't he grab her and tie her down and drill her full of holes? Why did he feel as if the glue that held him together was melting?

'Because you are one of God's favourites too, Quinton.'

★   ★   ★

Brad dared not utter a word, not now, not while Paradise was speaking and Quinton was listening. The slightest shift in tension might set him off, as it had discharged his gun moments ago.

Quinton had gone stiff. Sweat beaded his forehead. His hands were balled into fists and his blood vessels ran like cords down his forearms. At any moment it would all end. Brad knew what Paradise was trying to do, but it wouldn't work!

The rage in the killer would overtake him and he would crush her. She was naïve enough to believe that, if she just reached out to him, he would understand and change.

But men like Quinton Gauld did not change, not this side of a cosmic shift in their souls far beyond human words or any kind of psychiatric soothing. He might play along. He might even give in to the pain that her words clearly evoked. But, in the end, the monster would rise up and rip into her.

Even so, Brad dared not utter a single word.

He hopelessly worked to free the ropes that bound his wrists, but there wasn't a millimetre of play in them. He pulled at the post, but it was anchored deep.

And then, in the long silence, something changed. Paradise began to cry. Her small shoulders began to shake in a sob.

She drew a deep breath. 'I don't want to do this any more.'

What was she saying?

'I've lived with this pain so long. I can't do it any more.' She sobbed and sucked at the air, lips trembling. 'I don't want to hide in the closet any more. I can't take the darkness. I can't take the fear!'

Her words sounded obscenely loud in the barn. She stood shaking, gasping for air, looking now at Brad with pleading eyes, then back at Quinton.

'I can't do it . . . I can't live like this . . .'

She was crying for herself, he realized. She'd said it in the field and now she was saying it here. Paradise was here as much for her own rescue as for his. She needed to free herself from the claws piercing her heart.

This wasn't about manipulating the man who'd violated her

seven years ago in the hope of destroying him; this was about casting off her own fear so that she could be free.

'I can't fear you any more, Quinton. I can't fear my father. I can't take the hate and fear that's trying to kill me.'

Quinton stood on the quilts, eyes wide. His fists were shaking.

'I forgive you, Quinton.' She spoke the confession in a sob and then walked forwards, stood in front of him and reached out her hand slowly.

Pressed her palm against his chest.

The moment her fingers made contact with him, she sucked in a short gasp. But then, she could see ghosts, couldn't she? She was seeing something now, or was she only shocked at her own audacity?

Quinton was so appalled, so stunned by her actions, that he seemed to forget his options. He looked frightened. Lost.

Now, in a soft voice, Paradise pleaded with him through her tears. 'He's trying to kill you. The same monster that's trying to kill me because I'm God's favourite is trying to kill you too.' Then, very quietly, so that Brad could barely hear her: 'You're like me. He's trying to kill us both.'

A slight quiver had swept over Quinton's whole body. Brad didn't know what to say. He wanted to tell her to run, to claw at Quinton's eyes and sprint, to dart around him and throw the lamp to the ground and then run for the back door.

Instead she spoke softly, now without tears, like an angel sent here for his sake. 'I'm sorry you were hurt by your father, Quinton. But you're still a favourite. You don't need to prove yourself to God, or be jealous of his favourites.'

What happened next drained Brad's blood from his face. The quiver that had reached Quinton's extremities intensified. Tears pooled in his eyes, ran down his face. His lips twisted with despair and right there with the seventh favourite's hand on his chest, Quinton began to cry.

And Paradise cried with him.

But Brad could see no reason for gratitude or relief. He could only see this monster's guilt being exposed by his own innocent victim, and it made him sick with fear.

'Paradise . . .' He still didn't know what to say, because to say the wrong thing could as easily bring about her end as save her. And she wasn't paying Brad any attention.

'If I'm his favourite, then so are you,' she said. 'And he loves them all. Even me. Even you.'

Now the man towering over Paradise came unglued. He broke apart from the inside out. Shaking with his sobs, he began to sag. His hands went limp, spread wide. The gun fell from loosed fingers and he sank slowly to his knees.

Brad could not shout down the warning bells that clanged in his head.

Run, Paradise! Run!

Run because you are right and he knows that you are right and he can't live with that knowledge. He's going to snap, he's going to cut you, he's going to kill you, Paradise! Run!

Brad's mouth was parted, but he couldn't risk undoing what she was doing. He could only beg God for mercy.

Paradise did not run. To Brad's continued horror, she placed her hand on Quinton Gauld's shoulder, and he settled back on his haunches, a sobbing, slobbering mess of a man.

It was true, Paradise was the most beautiful woman in the world. She, who stood just a hair off five feet tall and wasn't too experienced in the fine arts of hygiene, makeup and fashion, was the most stunning creature God had created.

And Brad knew that the Bride Collector was going to kill her.

Quinton didn't know what had happened except that he'd been thoroughly violated. The very woman he had violated had returned and, with a few simple words, peeled back the layers he'd so lovingly wrapped around himself over the years.

He was a man who could not deny the truth, but neither could he accept that truth, not now.

He could only feel its effects and mourn his own pathetic nature, while before him stood the one whom God had granted such a lofty status.

He had been right. She was the most, most, most beautiful! It was no wonder he'd fallen madly in love with her. And he would again, because the man who could not or did not love Paradise needed to be summarily shot and buried in a deep bed of wet concrete.

And when she said that he too, Quinton Gauld, the man who had violated her, was as loved . . . The earth had crumbled beneath his feet and hell itself had sucked him deep. It could not be true. To compare him to Paradise was to compare a slug with a peacock, a dove, a bird of paradise.

Yet it *was* true. He knew it the moment the words came from her mouth.

Then she told him that evil was working in him to make a mockery of them both, and he knew that this too was not only true, but that he was powerless to change it.

So then he would have to kill her. She was crying with him and her hand was on his shoulder, and now he had to kill her.

Paradise touched the man the way she imagined a mother might touch another mother's hateful son who was having a change of heart. She felt no intimacy. He was still a monster.

It had occurred to her as she waited in the ditch that perhaps the killer was dead. Not physically dead, but spiritually and mentally. That, like her, he had died a long time ago when his father had taken his life as a boy.

And when her hand made contact with his chest, she had seen that, in many ways, she was right – he was dead. Because, in that moment, her mind had filled with the image of a small boy weeping on his knees as a bearded man twice his height stood over him with a piece of pipe.

Before this night she'd seen only images that the dead had seen, and then only a few times. Although Quinton was not buried, he was indeed dead, because she wasn't imagining this, was she?

If she ever saw Allison again, Paradise would beg her to explain how this worked; why God allowed her to see these things. What was his power and what was hers?

But for now she only knew that she had to love this man because, although he was pathetic, he was also the mirror image of the ugliness inside of her. The fear and hate that had haunted her for so many years were all wrapped up in this man.

How many times had Allison talked to her about God's forgiving power? More than she could count. *Judge not lest you be judged,* she used to say. *Love your enemies, mostly the ones who throw you away because they don't know what they're doing. Let the light of our Saviour shine mercy and forgiveness into your heart.* These impossible sayings had only come to full meaning as Paradise waited in the ditch.

If it was true and she was God's favourite, then so was he. And the only thing that would rescue either of them was to return that favour.

So she'd done what Allison had said God would do. She forgave him. And she let him cry on her shoulder as she embraced the light that freed her from him.

It was like walking down a path of coals into the gaping mouth of hell, and she still didn't know if she really had, in her heart of hearts, forgiven Quinton.

Then she remembered Brad. Brad was there, on her right.

She blinked, and turned and saw him. And for the first time she saw that he was bleeding.

He was going to snap, he was going to break, he was going to explode.

But he didn't snap. He didn't break, he didn't explode.

Paradise let him lay his head against her shoulder and she comforted him as a sister might comfort a weeping brother.

After several long minutes of tension, cut by the dreadful sound of sorrow and guilt, Brad first began to consider the possibility that he'd been wrong. Some power greater than any he'd seen had affected them both and was doing what no FBI agent could ever do. Maybe Quinton Gauld, the angel of death, had been undone by the forgiving words of an innocent young woman.

The man looked wretched, sobbing now with head bowed. His hands occasionally clawed at her back, but his fingers were too limp to grasp her shirt or back. His eyes were closed, and flecks of white spittle had settled in the corners of his mouth. White mucous ran from the broken man's nose. He was a mess, a shrivelled-up carcass that used to be a man.

Paradise seemed to accept the same conclusion. She calmed and looked at the miserable man before her, then turned her eyes to Brad, as if remembering him again. Her eyes shifted down to his shin, the one that Quinton had drilled a hole into.

Blood had run from the wound and pooled on the dirt under his calf. He'd forgotten the pain, but it throbbed now to remind him.

When Brad looked back up at Paradise, her eyes were still on his shin and they were wide with horror.

Her mouth parted and she took a step towards him, leaving Quinton. The moment she turned her back on him, something changed.

It was subtle at first, the catching of his breath, the stilling of his sob, as if the cue had been called and then someone yelled 'cut'. Brad saw it all, but now he refused to believe it, because, if Paradise had failed, then they were both dead.

Paradise started to walk towards him. 'Brad . . .' Her voice swam in empathy. 'I came, Brad.'

This was the young, naïve Paradise, and he cherished her for it.

The man behind her, however, was not nearly so innocent and, when his eyes opened, he turned to look at the back of the woman who'd left him on his knees and crossed to the man she loved. Brad knew he was going to kill her.

'Paradise!'

Quinton's face twisted with rage and he calmly reached for the fallen gun near his right knee.

Paradise rushed like a nurse on a battlefield to the man she loved. 'I'm sorry, Brad. I couldn't leave—'

'Get down!' Brad shouted. 'Run, Paradise!' If she ran she might make it. She might!

'Run!'

Paradise stopped halfway to him, confused. 'What?'

Brad watched the scene as if it were playing out on a huge screen in slow motion. His scream came out in a long groan, slowed to half speed.

'Run!'

'What?'

Quinton had his gun in his palm.

He swung it around to bear on her back.

Paradise saw Brad's horrified expression and slowly turned back to follow his eyes, blocking his view of the killer. And of the gunshot that bellowed like a cannon announcing the end of an era.

Boom!

Brad's heart stopped.

She started to fall. His eyes were searching for the exit wound because that's what his mind was trained to do, but in his heart he was dying with her.

Paradise sank to her knees, shaking as if even now she was refusing to die, because even now she was innocent enough to cling to hope when none existed.

'Are you okay, sir?'

The voice came from his left, but it hardly registered. What was registering was the fact that Paradise hadn't fallen.

Then, only when Paradise leaned over and sobbed, did Brad see Quinton Gauld's fallen form beyond her. He had been shot through the head.

Brad blinked.

A voice crackled over a radio. '. . . an ambulance here. One dead, believed to be the subject in question. Let the FBI know we have their crime scene secure.' A Kansas state police officer in a brown uniform holstered his weapon and nodded at Brad.

'Special Agent Brad Raines?'

'Yes,' he croaked.

'Sergeant Robby Bitterman, sir.' He glanced at the man he'd shot. 'I'd say that was a close one.'

Then Paradise was rushing towards Brad. Falling to her knees. Throwing her arms around his neck.

She said nothing; she only wept.

CHAPTER FORTY-TWO

'What about a trip to the beach?' Casanova asked, pacing the park lawn in his long robe and slippers. 'I would really love to take a trip to the beach. No offence, Allison dear. This park is lovely, the setting is beautiful, the mountains, the sky, the birds – all perfect to set the mood. But I would rather do a different kind of bird watching, if you catch my drift.'

Allison's eyes twinkled. She looked at her four children, as she had come to feel about this bunch. Roudy, the persistent sleuth, had dressed as always in plaids (which he mistook for tweeds), a bow tie and today even carried a pipe (albeit smokeless) that Allison had given him a week earlier when they'd found Paradise.

Andrea, the young one, let her blonde hair flow with a breeze that rustled up the park's summer greens. Her eyes were on the skate-board park two hundred yards down the hill. 'I see some birds flying down there,' she said.

'The more naturally clothed variety is what I had in mind,' Cass said.

Andrea faced the self-appointed love guru. 'You have a dirty old mind, Cass. Just because a girl has a bikini on doesn't make her natural. Not at all.'

Casanova didn't miss a beat. 'You could watch the hunks, Dre. Sweat dripping off the corded muscles of body builders pressing massive weights on the beach. While I give them pointers on bird watching.'

'Sounds disgusting,' she said.

Paradise giggled.

Allison looked at the girl she now thought of simply as her favourite, though she would never call her that aloud, particularly not in front of the others. Paradise sat on the grass with her legs folded back to her right, leaning with one arm hooked over Brad Raines' knee. There were two things about this picture that filled Allison with more joy than an ex-nun should be allowed.

One, Paradise was in a park, forty miles from CWI. The agoraphobia that had once cauterized the flow of her life was now gone.

Two, Paradise was in the arms of a man, and such a man as Brad Raines, whom they all thought might be God incarnate by the way they jumped at his every comment. They were all heroes in their own minds, but Brad was the one true hero. Even in Allison's mind.

After all, he loved Paradise. And Paradise loved him. That alone made them both heroes.

He had also brought in the Bride Collector, though Roudy took plenty of credit for cracking the case. To Allison's understanding, Paradise had apprehended the killer as much as Roudy or Brad.

Paradise had made the call that narrowed the authorities' search to a strip along the Kansas-Colorado border near the town of St Francis. Within fifteen minutes they had identified nineteen potential locations that fit the Bride Collector's MO – abandoned barns, shacks, silos, a couple of old farmhouses. In all, thirty-two state troopers, state police and local police had been pulled into duty and dispatched to those nineteen locations with strict orders to approach with extreme caution.

Fifty-four minutes after Temple had made the call to the chief of police in St Francis, Sergeant Robby Bitterman rolled to a stop seventy-five yards from Sam Warner's old abandoned equipment barn on the north side of his wheat fields, surprised to see it lighted. He had called for backup, then gone in on foot and, for the first time in his fifteen-year career, used his sidearm to kill a man. A single shot through the head from twenty feet.

The officer had shot Quinton, but Paradise had taken his power already, his power over her, over them all. God had reached down and saved his favourite. Why her and not the others, Allison didn't know.

Whether or not Paradise really had seen something in Quinton's spirit – his ghost or his past – neither she nor Paradise knew for certain. These things were mysteries to them all.

To see Paradise now, only a week after that harrowing night, shining like all young women in love should, Allison wasn't sure she could have wished a different scenario upon them all. Paradise had approached her and asked if, now that she was learning so much about love, she should become a nun. Allison freed her from the obligation immediately, and Paradise had run off with a light step and relieved smile.

'Have you talked to him yet?' Roudy asked, sidling up to Brad. 'The man upstairs, I mean.'

'To Temple, you mean?'

'That's the one. I really do think I've earned it. I'm sure you would agree.'

Allison stepped in. 'We've all earned a lot these last two weeks, Roudy. But sometimes it takes a while to get comfortable in our new skin.'

He looked at her and cocked an eyebrow. 'Please, Allison, I was born comfortable. Don't mistake any eccentricities on my part as being less than perfectly capable or smooth as silk in the halls of justice.'

'Never. But their world is still a new skin. It may take time before they fully understand your . . . talents. No?'

That made him pause.

'Well, I see your talents,' Brad said. 'And so does Temple. Frankly, you might have some challenges accepting their talents. They don't see the world the same way you do.'

'True,' Roudy said, lifting a finger. 'I see your point.'

'I'm not sure you want the office you asked for. It would require a lot of travel.'

'True. Good point.'

'I think it would be much easier to bring copies of the unsolved cases to you, to sift through at your own pace, unencumbered by the clumsy efforts of less insightful men and women. Don't you?'

'Now that you put it that way, I do. A very good point indeed.' He marched back towards Allison. 'So then, we should be getting back. No time to waste.'

Paradise was looking up at Brad. She winked at him. 'Not so fast, Roudy. You may not need to adjust to your new skin, but some of us might like the adjustment.'

'I vote for the beach,' Cass said.

'Does this mean you'll be moving out, Paradise?' Andrea asked, nibbling on her fingernail.

'We all move out sometime.'

'No, I can't.' Andrea paced on the grass, suddenly very nervous. 'It's too dangerous out here! I don't think I can ever live out here again.'

'But why would you, my dear?' Roudy asked. 'I need you. You don't expect me to handle the caseload my reputation will now heap upon me all alone, do you? We have cases to solve, lives to save!'

'Did you ever think Paradise would be out here?' Allison asked, ignoring Roudy.

'No.'

'There you go, then. Anything and everything can change in the space of one day. Not that you'd want to change.'

Andrea's eyes darted over to Paradise. 'Do I want to, Paradise?'

The girl didn't reply immediately. The hillside grew quiet.

'I don't know.' She looked at the horizon and her features softened. She was still the same Paradise Allison had always loved. She'd taken up a new interest in grooming, however, and she decided that she liked her jeans long, to the ground, and her blouses colourful – a yellow tank top today, layered with a white one.

But she was the same girl who'd always possessed extraordinary wisdom and beauty.

'If you find someone to love, maybe then you'll want to be with them.'

It was a tender expression of her love for Brad. They all seemed to understand and appreciate the breakthrough Paradise had made, but they were still courting their own delusions.

Unwilling to let an opening go to waste, Cass broke the silence. 'And you know that I can help you with that, Andrea. If you want to be in love or make a man fall madly in love with you, I need only a day or two. They'll be crawling all over you.'

'See, now there you go, spoiling a perfectly good moment,' Andrea cried.

'I can't help it. I'm mentally ill.' But Casanova was smiling.

'Aren't we all?' Brad said.

And that did silence them all, this time with a kind of finality that none of them wanted to upset. They were the same, he was saying. And there was nothing kinder he could have said to them.

Brad kissed Paradise on the top of her head. He caught Allison's eyes, smiled gently, and winked.

She returned the wink.

And that, she thought, said it all.

Sixty queens there may be,
and eighty concubines,
and virgins beyond number;
but my dove, my perfect one, is unique.
The *favourite* of the one who bore her.
The maidens saw her and called her blessed;
the queens and concubines praised her.

Song of Solomon
Six